BACALAO

BACALAO

J.T. McDaniel

Riverdale Electronic Books
Riverdale, Georgia

Bacalao

This book is a work of fiction. Names, characters, places and incidents
are either the product of the author's imagination or are used ficti-
tiously. Any resemblance to actual events, locales, or persons, living or
dead, is entirely coincidental.

ISBN: 0-9712207-5-1

Library of Congress Control Number: 2004093020

Printed in the United States of America

This one is for Mom

Contents

I
Changes

Vice Admiral Lawrence Miller, USN (Ret), pulled his car into the parking space, being careful to get the vehicle exactly centered. For a moment he looked at himself in the rear view mirror. He decided that he didn't look at all bad for a man who had recently turned 85. Still a good driver, too, he thought.

He was dressed casually, wearing canvas deck shoes, khaki slacks and a short-sleeved khaki shirt. The slacks had pleats, and the shirt was obviously a civilian style, with only a single, flapless pocket instead of the pair of flapped pockets on a Navy uniform shirt. Miller was willing to admit to himself that the choice of khaki for this day hadn't been random. He'd be seeing a lot of old friends, and the color was a link to their shared past.

He picked up the navy blue ball cap from the middle of the front seat and settled it on his head. The front of the cap sported embroidered gold submariner's dolphins and the name of his old boat. Back in his day, officers didn't wear baseball caps. Times were changing, though, and now you rarely saw the proper peaked cap aboard ship.

Miller got out of the car and walked around to open the door for his wife. As he held the door he found himself looking through the chain link fence to the lakefront seawall and the old submarine tied up there.

So much like the old girl, he thought. There were differences, to be sure. This boat had a more modern deck gun, and her conning tower fairwater was painted up with the old fleet boat's citations, victory flags and hull number. His old boat had sported none of those except the number, and that had been painted out on the day the war began.

But the fairwater and bridge were the same. Both periscopes were fully extended. Just abaft the number two periscope he could see the SJ radar antenna. That had been forward of the periscope shears in his old boat. The SD dipole on its free standing mast was the same, though. The fairwater had the same "covered wagon" cutdown, and the same 40-millimeter guns were mounted fore and aft.

He held out his hand to help his wife from the car. She was still lovely after all these years. Not like him. He was an old codger now, and his brief self-appraisal in the rear view mirror had been more than a little optimistic. Sometimes he had to be honest with himself. With all those old crew members getting together for this mid-July reunion, he decided, a little honesty was called for.

"Looks like some of them are here already," his wife said, gesturing toward the submarine.

True enough, he thought. There were several elderly men gathered in a group near the brow. Miller recognized several of them. Others would be coming over the next hour or so. The plan was for all of them to tour the sub, a slightly newer sister of their own, and then eat a picnic lunch.

There was a lot of gray and white hair sticking out from under their more or less identical ball caps—the former enlisted men had silver dolphins instead of gold—and many of those caps would now be covering bare scalps. We're all so old now, Miller thought. Even the youngest of his former shipmates was in his mid-70s by now. Most, like himself, were in their mid-80s and at least one, sitting in a wheelchair in the middle of the group, was over 90.

"We've become a pack of redundant old geezers," Miller said.

"Not to me." His wife still seemed to see him as the handsome young submariner he had once been. Maybe she had better eyes than he.

"The boat looks good," he said. "A little high in the water, but otherwise looking really good. She'll be light by a few hundred tons without the battery cells." He smiled. "Paint the fairwater gray and put an old 4"/50 on the forward deck and you could have the old girl back with us."

Miller noticed a hand go up in the crowd, and then a heavy figure was moving toward him down the walkway. "There's Bill," he said.

Yes, he thought. A lot of old men. But they hadn't always been old. Once, long ago, they were young and another boat like this one represented their future and not their past.

•   •   •

Lieutenant Lawrence Miller's first view of *Bacalao* was far from impressive. On the day he arrived at the Electric Boat Company yard in Groton, Connecticut, he had been out of the Naval Academy for six years, with the last three in submarines. If it had been up to him, he would have spent the whole six years under water, but in those days an officer had to put in three years in the surface fleet before he was allowed to report to Submarine School.

He had never wanted to be anything other than a submariner, even as far back as his first year at Annapolis, when one of his instructors had beguiled the class with stories of service in the old L-boats during the war. If he could have arranged to go directly to New London, he would have done so and felt himself fortunate. But rules are rules, so he spent his first three years of active duty aboard a destroyer, based in San Diego.

It wasn't that he considered those years wasted. He had learned a lot about hunting submarines. Knowing the way the enemy thinks is always a valuable tool, so even as he was studying how to sink subs he was thinking about the best way to counter the techniques. By the time he finally walked into the classroom at the Submarine School, New London, he figured he knew it all.

By the time he graduated, finishing fourth in his class, he was sure of it. The next three years taught him otherwise. But he had somehow managed to go from an ignorant young JG, knowing about 98% less than he thought, to a competent full lieutenant and executive officer of *S-35*.

In those prewar days, it took about a year for the average officer or enlisted man to qualify in submarines and earn the right to wear the proud dolphin insignia on his uniform. It took Miller eight months, but he liked to think he had a natural aptitude. He had been *S-35*'s XO for eight months when he was offered the job of electrical officer in the still under construction *Bacalao*.

Promotion was slow in peacetime. Miller knew he was probably within a year or so of getting a command if he stayed in S-boats, where the crews were small and the CO was normally a lieutenant. So taking the position in *Bacalao* was going to slow him down. He was going from second in command to fourth.

And fleet boat commands went to lieutenant commanders and commanders, not lowly lieutenants. Not even brilliant ones.

But he figured it was worth it. He would now be serving in a thoroughly modern vessel. *Bacalao* would be air conditioned—they didn't call the old S-boat "pig boats" for nothing—ten torpedo tubes instead of four, an advanced fire control system, and all the comforts a young officer could hope for. He would be able to take a shower every couple of days when they were at sea, and would share a stateroom with only two other officers.

A civilian might look at a fleet boat's officers' staterooms and pronounce them to be medium-sized closets with three narrow shelves holding mattresses, but when compared to the cramped and uncomfortable wardroom in an S-boat the little rooms were like palaces.

So Miller accepted the posting to the new *Bacalao*, which was now taking shape on the ways at Electric Boat. She was a new *Gato* class boat, one of the most modern submarines in the world.

His first sight of her, though, was of a long steel beam, resting on wooden blocks on the building ways. The beam would become the boat's keel. At the moment, he thought, it didn't look very much like a submarine—or like anything else that would ever be able to float, for that matter.

During the next few months the boat slowly took shape. Curved sheets of 11/16" steel plate were welded to the keel and frames, and before too long the basic shape of the pressure hull, a long cylinder with tapered ends terminating in rounded caps, became clearly defined. Over the pressure hull, which was the *real* submarine, the part where people could live under water, the yard added the external ballast tanks in the double hull section at the center, as well as the framing for the superstructure that would define the familiar shipshape of the completed boat.

After a time, those external frames were covered by steel plates, perforated at the top to let air and water flow freely in and out when the boat submerged. This superstructure concealed the piping and ductwork, as well as providing a deck where the crew could work when the boat was on the surface. Before the superstructure was added, most of the hatches had been sticking up in the air at the top of their trunks. Now they were all at deck level.

After the deck was in place, the conning tower was hoisted into position by a big crane and secured to the frames. This was a long steel cylinder, resembling nothing more than one of the big steel tanks that were buried under filling stations, though the ends of the conning tower were dished in, rather than out. One trunk, on the port side, connected the conning tower to the pressure hull below, while another stuck up at the forward end, on the starboard side. That would eventually lead up to the bridge.

Then the conning tower, and the thick, mushroom-shaped stump of the main induction valve just abaft it, were covered over by the fairwater. This was the part that civilians usually thought of as the conning tower, but really wasn't. The actual conning tower was inside.

The open bridge was located well back and high up, just forward of the streamlined periscope shears. The fairwater was massive and fairly well protected, with a covered bridge forward, and the small, open upper bridge above and behind it.

As the boat took shape on the ways, Miller found himself falling into the odd routine of an officer serving in an under construction submarine. It was a strange combination of an easy life ashore combined with the stringent need to keep an eye on the workers, for it was their skill that would ultimately determine if Miller, and the other 70 or so officers and men who would serve in the boat, would live or die.

While all this was happening, the crew began to appear. The officers were the first to show up. They were all there almost from the first day of construction.

Lieutenant Commander Karl Hammersmith, selected to become *Bacalao*'s first commanding officer, was the first to arrive. He arrived on the same day as Lieutenant Commander William Dunstan, who was to be executive officer. They had been present when the keel was laid.

Miller showed up three days later, one day ahead of Lieutenant William Morgan. Morgan was to be third officer and chief engineer. He had been a year ahead of Miller at Annapolis.

If there was ever an officer who was destined to be an engineer, Miller thought, it was Bill Morgan. In most other navies he would surely have become a specialist, spending his entire career working with engines and turbines. But the United States Navy had never seen a need for a specialist engineer branch. Anyone who wanted to command an American warship first had to be an engineer.

You also had to know something about what you would command. The captain of an aircraft carrier had to be a pilot, and the captain of a submarine had to be a submariner, with a good background in the complex engineering systems aboard.

While the boat was under construction, Miller was rooming with Morgan in the Bachelor Officers' Quarters at the Submarine Base, New London, a few miles up the Thames River from the yard. When the boat was completed the two of them would share a stateroom, along with Orville Hanson, the most senior JG.

Miller had known Morgan for a long time. They had become good friends at the Academy, where the relationship had begun when Morgan realized that, plebe or not, Miller could be useful to him. Miller had been sailing since he was a kid, growing up within walking distance of Lake Erie in Cleveland, while Morgan came from a farm in Iowa, where the extent of local maritime facilities consisted of a leaky rowboat on a small lake.

Being an obsessive kid, Miller had managed to learn celestial navigation by the time he was a teenager, and spent his last two high school summers as part of the deck crew on an ore boat running between Cleveland and Duluth.

Annapolis plebes didn't normally arrive at the Academy with practical experience in maneuvering a vessel the size of an aircraft carrier, and Morgan had quickly figured out that Miller would be happy to help him with his navigation and practical seamanship as long as he offered a little protection. So he helped Miller avoid the worst of the hazing and Miller helped him pass astronomy.

The other two officers in *Bacalao*'s crew were Lyle Winston and Tom Hartman, who were both JGs. Hartman was the junior by a year, and was also the only officer aboard who had yet to qualify. *Bacalao* was his first boat. By tradition, he was nicknamed "George," and given the job of assistant torpedo and gunnery officer. The logic behind this was that even a non-qual officer could still direct a gun crew.

As for the torpedoes, the boat naturally had a good chief torpedoman's mate attached, along with an experienced crew, so it was unlikely that even a completely inexperienced officer could manage to screw things up. His crew would take care of him, as would Winston, who was the actual torpedo and gunnery officer.

There was a lot of work involved getting a boat completed and ready for service. There was also a lot of reading. On one particular evening, Miller and Morgan were relaxing in their room in the BOQ. Miller was on his bunk, studying the manual for the General Electric main control unit that would be installed in *Bacalao*'s maneuvering room in a few days. Morgan was sitting at the desk, writing in a notebook, a thick engine manual open in front of him.

"These new engines," Morgan said, "are absolutely fascinating. Huge improvement over the older types."

Miller looked up from his own manual, perfectly willing to be distracted for a while. He knew that he needed to know as much as possible about the board from a theoretical viewpoint, but there was virtually no chance that he would ever have to actually *operate* the thing. They had electrician's mates for that. Would have, at least—they hadn't arrived yet.

"Just about anything will be better than those old M.A.N.s we had in *S-35*," Miller said.

"Larry, it's a great design. Nothing like them before."

"New isn't always better, you know. And I don't think these are really new."

"Well, I just think it's a great concept. A double-acting diesel fires on both the up and down stroke, so you have power being applied no matter which direction the piston is moving. It's a little like a reciprocating steam engine, when you think about it. You get twice the power in the same size package"

"Sure, but they already tried these things and they didn't work. I'm not sure why they picked our boat to experiment on. It would have been just as easy to give us a nice set of Wintons, like the rest of them."

"No, Larry, these are different. The original design was eight-cylinder and these are nine, which gives you the same power output as an 18-cylinder design. And after the first lot, the factory figured out they had to be a little more careful in their production methods. They screwed up the heat treatment on the timing gears the first time around—made them *too* hard, so they turned brittle and tended to break in use. That's all been fixed now."

"It's your department, Bill," Miller said. "But I think I'd be just as happy with something I can be sure is more reliable. And you can bet it's going to annoy the hell out of your engine room crew when they have to keep an extra set of tools around just so they can work on those engines."

Morgan just shrugged. "So, they're metric—so what? The last time I checked it was still a lot easier to count to ten than working with fractions."

"Sure, but everything else on the boat uses normal fittings. I just think it would be easier if the engines did, too."

Morgan laughed. "You just worry too much, Larry."

"Well, the way things are going, I expect us to be at war sometime soon. When that happens, reliability is going to be a lot more useful than modernity."

"Like I said, you worry too much. I'm sure the engines will be just fine, and we'll even have a little extra room to move around in the engine rooms. The design is more compact than any of the others."

Miller shook his head and went back to studying his manual. Morgan had been like that for as long as he'd known him. He was always looking for the latest thing, the newest innovation, and enthusiastically promoting it to anyone who would listen—at least until it blew up in his face, which it frequently did.

Miller was more cautious. He liked to take a good, hard look at things before he decided what he thought about them. It wasn't that he doubted the engines would really work. The Germans were using a larger version in a light cruiser, and he hadn't heard that they were having any particular problems. It was just that the first batch of the license built engines, installed in some earlier boats, had been clearly inferior to the more conventional designs, setting something of a record for unreliability.

True, the company thought they had the problem isolated and repaired. Bad heat treatment of the timing gears, they said. It was plausible, but just because they thought they'd fixed it didn't mean they'd actually done so. If it was up to Miller—which it obviously wasn't—he would have simply decided not to employ that engine again.

But the Navy had decided to install the new design engines in a *Gato* to see how they'd hold up in service and *Bacalao* was the lucky boat.

With any sort of luck, Miller decided, if there were any problems with the new engines they'd show up during the boat's initial trials, before she was handed over to the Navy. Electric boat had their own test crew for trials, headed by a retired captain, and composed mainly of retired chiefs with years of practical experience.

While there was something appealing about having the crew that would ultimately man the boat conduct the trials, Miller had to admit that EB's concept made a lot of sense. Except for the captain, who had been XO in *Gar*, all of the officers had got most of their experience in S-boats.

Miller knew all about those old boats—they all did—and they were nothing like a *Gato*. The Electric Boat trials crew were completely familiar with the newer boats, which made them a lot better equipped to deal with an emergency.

When something goes wrong on a submarine it happens in a hurry, and when it does, the natural tendency is to fall back on the carefully drilled behavior imparted by hundreds of exercises. That was the purpose behind the drills, to insure that each man did exactly what was necessary, without having to take time to think about it. Moving the wrong lever in an emergency could easily have exactly the opposite effect to what was desired.

That had been one theory after *Squalus* went down during a test dive, though the surviving crew members vehemently disagreed with that particular notion. The thought was that, in the rush to get under, the operator had moved the wrong lever and instead of opening the negative tank flood valve preparatory to blowing the tank, had accidentally opened the main induction. There was no question at all that the valve had opened somehow, flooding the after part of the boat and, in the process, killing everyone aft of the control room.

The vent operator had survived, and insisted that he had done exactly what he was supposed to. And, besides, the diving panel showed that the main induction was closed the whole time—even though the flooding made it obvious the indicator was wrong.

Despite the operator's protests, the Navy decided to take precautions. The vent and flood levers were rearranged, and the handles were given distinctive shapes. The idea was that now it would be impossible to confuse them, even in pitch darkness. If the lever had a T-shaped handle, it was the negative flood valve, and if it had a ball-shaped handle it was the main induction. A spring loaded locking pin was also added to the induction lever, so that it now required two hands to move it.

Changes were also made in the main induction itself, for another theory was that there was a flaw in the Portsmouth valve's design that could indicate the valve was closed while it was still open. At the same time, the inboard induction valves were redesigned so that they could be closed with far less effort, and the Navy imposed strict orders to do so.

Squalus's problems had been aggravated by the inboard valve design, which had made it impossible to close the valve in the engine room before the compartment was completely flooded.

Morgan closed his notebook with a thump and swiveled around in his chair. "What do you hear from Claudia these days?" he asked.

Years before, back in their Academy days, Miller and Morgan had been rivals for the same girl. Morgan had graduated a year earlier, which should have given him an edge—midshipmen weren't allowed to marry until after they graduated—but it hadn't helped and Miller got the girl. In retrospect, Miller figured that Morgan had won. While Miller had married Claudia in the Academy Chapel six weeks after graduation, he had long since realized it wasn't the smartest thing he'd ever done.

"I got a letter from her a couple days ago," Miller said. "She has four more weeks in Reno and then the divorce goes through. She says she met some cowboy called Ernie and is seriously thinking of marrying the guy once she's free."

"So, what do you think of that, Larry?"

"I think it's a great idea. If she marries the cowboy, I won't have to support her for the rest of her useless life. Who know? She may even like living on the guy's little ranch."

"You could always have let me have her way back when, you know."

Miller laughed. "Sure, and then I could sympathize with you as she took your life apart. No, Claudia just had no business marrying anyone who wouldn't be home every night. Anyway, the whole thing just makes me glad we've got so much going on here right now. It keeps me too busy to think about the whole mess."

•   •   •

With *Bacalao* still under construction, Electric Boat provided her crew with office space in a wooden building near the ways. Even an incomplete boat still had a crew assigned, and there was always plenty of paperwork to keep everyone busy. The assigned offices were small, but still provided more than five times the amount of space that would be available once they moved aboard. Miller's *desk* was nearly as large as the entire ship's office would be.

Naturally, the crew didn't arrive all at once. The officers were there almost from the beginning, but the others dribbled in as building progressed. There wasn't much sense in filling the enlisted quarters with torpedoman's mates if there were no torpedo tubes installed yet.

So the chief petty officers, who would really run the departments, came in early, but the rest of the crew remained in their old jobs, or in school, until they could be useful.

By this time, it was April 1941, and there wasn't much left to do before the boat was launched. That would soon be accomplished with all due ceremony, the traditional bottle of champagne smashed over the bow by the lady—in *Bacalao*'s case, an admiral's daughter—chosen to sponsor the boat, the usual speeches, popping flashbulbs, and the boat sliding down the greased ways into the Thames River with all flags flying and the crew swaying precariously on deck while trying to look properly military and not falling into the river at the same time.

But that was still in the future. At the moment, Miller was seated at a desk in his temporary office, working on a stack of requisition forms.

Looking out the window, he couldn't help thinking that it would be a nice day for a long walk in the country. It would certainly be better than being stuck behind a desk. The sun was shining, with just a few fluffy cumulus clouds scudding across an azure sky.

In the sunlight, *Bacalao* now looked like a proper submarine, with the superstructure in place and the conning tower fairwater completed. He could imagine himself up on that high bridge, the boat pulsing under his feet as she raced through a tropical sea.

While Miller was thinking about this, Chief Electrician's Mate Peter Harrigan entered the office, carrying another personnel folder. He placed it on Miller's desk.

"New man for our department, sir," Harrigan said.

Miller looked at the folder. It was labeled, "OHARA, KENNETH, EM1C."

"Good," Miller said. "We can use another first class." He looked at the first sheet in the folder and smiled. "Especially one who's already qualified in fleet boats."

"Want to meet him, sir?"

"Naturally. Send him in."

"I think you'll find the guy interesting, sir," the chief said, a mischievous smile on his face.

Miller was studying the file when the new man entered. Everything looked good. Ohara was that rare rating who had not only attended, but actually been graduated from college, earning a degree in Spanish Literature from the University of Georgia. He'd been born in Atlanta, his parents listed as Irving and Louise Ohara.

"Electrician's Mate 1st Class Kenneth Ohara reporting, sir," the new man said, in a voice that absolutely reeked of the gracious atmosphere of the Old South. Obviously not your usual New York or Boston Irishman. Miller couldn't help thinking of *Gone With the Wind*, the new man being an O'Hara from Atlanta.

Since he was looking at the file, at first all he could see of the new man was a blue uniform, with embroidered white dolphins sewn to the jumper sleeve to confirm the declaration in the file that he was a qualified submariner.

So when Miller finally looked up, it was about all he could do to keep his mouth from dropping open. He'd sure as hell been right that this guy wasn't a typical Irishman. And, despite the deep, resonant voice and rich Southern accent, he wouldn't have fit in very well with Gable and company at Tara, either.

The man standing in front of his desk, wearing a neatly pressed blue uniform, was 32-years-old, about an inch over six feet tall, and weighed in the area of 190 to 200 pounds. His jet black hair was cut a little shorter than regulations mandated. His voice was deep and well modulated and very obviously Southern.

He was also, equally obviously, Japanese.

"O'Hara?"

The man smiled. "Well, sir, that's the way *I* pronounce it. I suppose my great-grandfather said it differently, but no one in my family remembers how, and none of us understand any Japanese, so we just go along with the neighbors.

"Not recent arrivals, I take it?" The only other Japanese Miller knew in the Navy was the son of immigrants, a lieutenant assigned to Intelligence because of his language skills.

"No, sir. Great-grandpa arrived in California in 1864. My family has lived in Atlanta since the early '90s." He frowned slightly. "We got here a long time before the 'gentlemen's agreement,' you see."

That was an unwritten, but mutually enforced, agreement between the American and Japanese governments. It restricted Japanese immigration to the territories—mostly Hawaii—not allowing direct access to the mainland. One result was that many mainland Japanese, particularly those living in the midwest and east, were like Ohara, with little or no knowledge of Japanese language or culture after several generations of speaking only English.

"You have a degree in Spanish Lit?"

"Yes, sir."

"So how did you end up as an EM?"

"I took a minor in electrical engineering, sir. It seemed like the logical thing to do—my father and his partner make electronic parts—and he wanted me to join them in the business."

"Why didn't you?"

Ohara shrugged. "I wanted to get in a little adventure first, sir," he said. "The Navy seemed like a good way to do it. Turned out I liked it, so I decided to make a career of it." He smiled. "It could still work out, of course, sir. By the time I'm ready to retire after 30 years my father will certainly be ready to do the same thing, so I might still go into the business. Then again, I may retire after 20 years, go back to school for a graduate degree, and try teaching."

Miller looked at the file. Ohara had joined the Navy after finishing college in 1931, so he had been in the Navy for 10 years now. He made first class in four years, and there he had stayed for the last six.

"Just out of curiosity," Miller said, "why didn't you apply for a Reserve commission? You don't see many enlisted men with degrees."

Ohara shook his head. "The Navy didn't seem to be interested, sir. Now, if I'd been an EE *major,* maybe, or if I could actually speak Japanese. There was interest in Japanese linguists, because there aren't all that many of them, but probably half the officer corps took Spanish in high school. Anyway, I'm pretty happy with what I'm doing."

"Well, we can certainly use you here, Ohara. More than half our crew are non-quals, and we need all the experienced men we can find. And I see you even have fleet boat experience."

"Yes, sir. I was in *Tambor* until about a month ago."

"Good. Well, I'm Lieutenant Lawrence Miller, and electrical officer, among other things, which means you'll be in my department. Your primary assignment will be as a main control operator, which means you'll rate a bunk in the after torpedo room once we move aboard. It'll keep you close to the maneuvering room. For now, Chief Harrigan will show you where to bunk while we're living ashore."

Ohara smiled at that. The torpedo room berths were always the most coveted. Being at the ends of the boat, there was never any through traffic, which was a constant annoyance in the main berthing area in the after battery compartment. The after torpedo room was located immediately abaft the maneuvering room, which meant that Ohara would sleep only a few steps from his duty station.

As things stood now, Miller thought, Ohara would be the senior EM in the department, which would place him third in the departmental hierarchy, after Miller and Harrigan. Harrigan and Ohara would really do most of the work, though Miller figured he would be likely to get most of the credit.

•   •   •

Ohara decided he liked Miller right off. He could see that the young officer had been surprised when he first got a look at him, but he was used to that sort of thing. People would see his name and figure he was just an Irishman who couldn't spell until they got a look at his obviously Japanese mug.

Miller wasn't the first to wonder why he had never applied for a commission, either. His father had been after him about that ever since he resigned himself to the fact that his son planned to make a career of the Navy. There weren't a lot of Japanese officers in the Navy, but it wasn't like he was a negro and actually barred from a commission.

The truth was, he simply wasn't interested. Officers were paid a little better, and certainly had more prestige, but it had always seemed to Ohara that they didn't actually *do* all that much. If he wanted to spend most of his time sitting behind a desk signing paperwork he could have simply taken his father up on his offer and probably been a vice-president within a year.

His minor in electrical engineering had made it easy for him to get into the proper school after he enlisted. There were always stories about how the Navy liked to take men with extensive training in working with machine tools and make them cooks, but the truth was that, if they had a need for a man's existing skills, the chances were pretty good he'd end up doing what he'd been trained to do.

Ohara liked working with things. There was a lot more satisfaction in getting into the guts of a motor, maybe rewinding a burnt-out armature or carefully undercutting the mica in a worn commutator, than there could ever be in just telling someone else to do it.

And virtually everything in a submarine was electrically operated. The big diesel engines in a fleet boat had only a single function, to drive the generators. There was no physical connection between the engines and the propeller shafts. Everything in the boat was either run directly by electric power, or worked by hydraulic or air pressure, which was the product of electrically-driven pumps and compressors.

Ohara liked his job. He also thought it was going to be interesting doing it in a brand new boat.

•   •   •

After Ohara left, Miller spent a little more time looking through his service record. He seemed to be exactly what they needed. In his ten years in the Navy, he had spent eight years in submarines, starting in an S-boat. His background, including attendance at the proper Navy schools, suggested he'd have little trouble with anything in the electrical department. Besides his Navy schooling, there just weren't that many submarine qualified electrician's mates with degrees—even minors—in electrical engineering.

Come to that, Miller thought, there weren't very many with any kind of degree. Chief Harrigan was a high school graduate. A couple of the other chiefs, and quite a few of the enlisted men, hadn't even gone that far in school. A lot of them had dropped out when they turned 16 and gone to work.

That didn't mean that any of them were stupid, of course. Subs got the sharpest men in the Navy, and they were universally literate, which couldn't be said of sailors as a whole. The lowliest seaman or fireman had to make it through Submarine School before being allowed on board, and that meant he had to be able to read. Even the Negro stewards, who weren't allowed to attend Sub School, still had to qualify, and always managed to do so in about the same time as the others.

Ohara was unusually well educated, which Miller thought might present a different sort of problem before long. His ten years of service, and six years in rate, along with his fitness reports, meant that he was both eligible and qualified for promotion to chief. *Bacalao* already had her quota of those. And while officer promotions were still slow, qualified enlisted men were moving up a lot faster as the fleet was built up in preparation for what was probably an inevitable war with the Axis powers.

While Miller was pondering this, the captain came into the office. "Who was that?" he asked.

"Ohara—EM First, our latest addition."

Hammersmith shook his head. "Does the Navy know we're probably going to the Pacific after we commission? What's that guy going to think if we have to start fighting a war with his relatives?"

"Probably about the same thing *you* would think if we start fighting the Germans, sir," Miller laughed. "That they're the enemy."

He glanced at another sheet in Ohara's record. It was just about the only negative thing in there. "Besides, from the look of this, I think we need to worry more about our friends than our enemies. The only ding in his record is a fight with a Limey petty officer who made the mistake of referring to Ohara as a 'Yank.' Being from Georgia, Ohara evidently took exception to that. Hell, Captain, the guy sounds more like Rhett Butler than Mr. Moto."

Miller closed the service record and passed it over to the captain. "Anyway, my first impression is that just about the only thing Japanese about this guy is his face."

"Okay," Hammersmith said. "It's your department."

"Yes, sir."

The captain looked at his watch. "You'll be senior this weekend, Larry," he said. "I'm going to New York with Bill Dunstan, and Morgan is off on leave for the next week. Though I suppose you already knew that."

"He *has* mentioned it a few hundred times, sir, yes."

So now Miller would get a small test of his leadership abilities. With the three most senior officers gone over the weekend, he would be lord and master until they returned.

"I presume you've left enough to keep me busy, sir?"

Hammersmith smiled. "There are a few things you might care to handle, yes. Hill has a list."

Hill was Yeoman 2nd Class James Hill, *Bacalao*'s yeoman, or ship's clerk. Miller already knew there wouldn't be much on the list for Saturday or Sunday. The shipyard workers would be at home relaxing with their families, and most of the crew would have weekend liberty. He'd just have to supervise the few who remained.

Hammersmith spent a few minutes discussing the work that was scheduled for Monday, then went off to meet the XO, who would drive the both of them to New York for the weekend. The captain seemed to be looking forward to it, as his wife would be meeting him there. Dunstan was a bachelor, who would presumably be looking forward to a couple of days in the big city for other reasons.

As he was driving back to his quarters about an hour later, the main thing on Miller's mind was that he'd have a full week of privacy with Morgan on leave. It never crossed his mind that he had just had his last meeting with the captain.

•   •   •

Miller was back aboard *Bacalao* promptly at 0800 on Monday, keeping an eye on the technicians who were assembling the complicated General Electric main control board and cubicle in the maneuvering room. It was at this point that he started to get a clear idea of just how good Ohara was. He not only knew the design, but was even able to offer a few suggestions that made the installation easier.

It wasn't surprising. Going by his record, Ohara had more practical experience than most of the men aboard.

"You were aboard *Tambor* during the depth charge tests, weren't you, Ohara?" Miller asked.

"Yes, sir."

"What was it like?"

"Scary, sir. And no one was actually trying to sink us then, either. Not that it kept a lot of things from breaking, though." He pointed at the control cubicle. "That's why this thing is sitting on springs now, instead of being bolted solidly to the deck the way they used to do it."

"Shock protection, right?"

"That's right, sir. GE builds these units pretty strong, but when a depth charge goes off the shock wave the hitting the hull shakes the hell out of anything that happens to be solidly attached to it."

"How close did you actually get?"

"With the crew still aboard, sir, 100 yards. After that they took us off and moored the submerged boat at periscope depth. They set off the closest charge at 100 feet. It still didn't damage the hull, even when it was that close, but it broke so many things inside that they decided not to get any closer." He smile grimly. "We were still fixing things when I got my orders here."

Miller nodded. For the tests, the Navy had used a 300-pound depth charge. One result was that the size was being doubled for new marks. The tests had convinced the Navy that the old charges weren't heavy enough.

"Did those tests discover any other electrical problems?"

"Yes, sir. The cables are all strapped down a lot tighter, and the straps are a lot closer together. They discovered that the shock could make a cable snap against the hull like a whip and break. Other than a hole in the pressure hull, I can't think of a quicker way to sink one of these boats than to knock out all the electric power. Knock out the power and you've got no propulsion and without the electric pumps there's no hydraulic pressure. You've got what air is in the air banks, but no way to compress more.

"And, for the same reason, they also made some changes in the through-hull fitting to make them more secure."

"If it can move, it can break, right?"

"Exactly, sir. No one was really trying to sink *Tambor*, after all, but they did their best to find out what was likely to break and how to make sure it didn't." He laughed. "The captain wasn't very happy about it, either. He's got a brand-new boat and here's the Navy trying to blow her up almost as soon as he gets his hands on her."

Miller didn't think he'd have been very happy, either. Command of a ship was the ultimate goal for most officers, and new construction was particularly special, for it meant the Navy thought enough of you to entrust you with a brand-new boat. Warships were designed to fight, and there was an obvious risk involved in going into battle, but to have your ship deliberately damaged by your own side had to be even worse.

At about 1015, Miller went up on deck to smoke a cigarette. He had just stubbed out the butt when he noticed Captain Jones coming across the gangway, followed by a tall, gray-haired officer with the two and half gold rings of a lieutenant commander around the sleeves of his blue uniform jacket.

"Welcome aboard, sir," Miller said, addressing Jones.

Jones nodded ponderously. Some years back he had been a submariner, but he'd put on a lot of weight since then and now had trouble just getting through the hatches.

"Bad news, I'm afraid, Mr. Miller," he said.

"Sir?"

"Lieutenant Commander Hammersmith was killed in a car wreck on his way back here. Your XO survived, but he has two broken legs and the doctors say he'll probably be in the hospital for a couple months and unable to return to duty before early next year.

Miller wasn't sure how to respond to this news. After a moment, he decided that the best response was probably to just keep his mouth shut and let the captain finish.

"This is Lieutenant Commander Morley," Jones continued.

"Yes, sir. I know the commander." Morley was an instructor at the Submarine School. He remembered him as being pretty tough, but a damned good teacher.

"Lieutenant Commander Morley will be assuming command as of now. He'll supervise the boat's completion, then place *Bacalao* in commission once her trials are finished.

"Are the rest of the officers aboard?" Morley asked. "And the chiefs, too."

"Except for Lieutenant Morgan, yes, sir."

"Morgan is on leave," Jones explained.

The new captain looked at his watch. "I'll want to see all the officers and chiefs in the office in ten minutes."

"Aye, aye, sir."

"There's no easy way to do this, I'm afraid, Mr. Miller. You don't expect this sort of thing in peacetime. So just get everyone together and we'll try to get reorganized." Morley thought for a moment. "Who's the senior now, with the XO in the hospital?"

"That would be Lieutenant Morgan, sir," Miller said. "Then me."

Morley looked at Jones. "What about Morgan, sir?" he asked. Miller presumed Jones knew what he was talking about, since the question didn't make any sense to him.

"Maybe in another year or two, Andy," Jones said. "Not yet."

"Okay, then. We'll need to find an XO somewhere. I think I know someone who would be perfect, presuming we can get him."

Miller was naturally curious, but at the same time wasn't sure he should even be listening to these deliberations. The one thing that was now fully obvious was that Dunstan was out of a job as far as this boat was concerned. It was equally obvious that Morgan, the next senior officer, was still at least a year away from being considered for XO.

"Do you have anything else for me just now, sir?" Miller asked.

Morley shook his head. "No—just go collect everyone and bring them to the office."

"Aye, aye, sir."

As Miller went off to collect the other officers and chiefs, he decided that it wasn't his place to tell them just *why* they were being summoned. He figured he could leave that to Jones and the new captain.

• • •

Morley had wanted another command ever since he had to give up his last boat, but this wasn't the way he had imagined himself returning to the bridge. He'd known Karl Hammersmith for a good ten years, and considered him a good man and an excellent leader. He was the sort of officer who was always able to inspire great loyalty in his crew.

Standing there before this group of officers and chiefs, it was all too obvious on their faces. They were like children who had unexpectedly lost their father. This was, perhaps, most obvious in the demeanor of Chief Motor Machinist's Mate Albert Gordon, *Bacalao*'s COB.[*] He had served under Hammersmith for eight years, in three different boats.

Besides being the most senior chief, he was also, very possibly, the most thoroughly competent submariner Morley had ever known. He remembered Gordon from his first tour at the Submarine School, and had never been able to find even the most obscure detail that he could not speak to with authority. He was a good instructor, but had never cared for the formal environment of the Submarine School and seemed to prefer passing on his skill and knowledge to the few men at a time who made up his crew.

---

[*] COB: Chief of the Boat. Normally, the most senior chief petty officer in the submarine.

Bacalao was fortunate in her collection of chiefs. Besides Gordon, there was Peter Harrigan, the Chief Electrician's Mate. The crew roster indicated that Miller was in charge of the electrical department, but it would naturally be Harrigan who ran it on a day to day basis. Morley had served with Harrigan when he was a first class, and could wish for no better man in that slot.

Then there was Chief Torpedoman's Mate John Collins, who had charge of the boat's main weapons. He had come to the boat from Newport, where he presumably had something to do with developing new torpedo designs, though just what that entailed wasn't clearly set down in his service record. The demands of security, no doubt, Morley thought. Whatever Collins had done at Newport, it had earned him a Commendation Medal.

The rest of the goat locker consisted of Chief Quartermaster Elwin Hanrahan, Chief Motor Machinist's Mate Sam Jenkins and Chief Machinist's Mate Carl Morton. Morley already knew Morton from serving with him before. He was one of those men who could fix nearly anything and, as long as he could get the right piece of stock into the lathe in the maneuvering room, he could make just about any needed part.

Just now, everyone was in shock. In a war, you expected that people would be killed, and that others would quickly take their place. It wasn't something you expected in peacetime, where a commander normally served two or three years, then went on to other things with someone else taking his place in due course.

"This is going to be hard on all of us," Morley said. "We of the submarine service are like a family. You can't know every sailor in the Navy, but that's not true of our service. There aren't that many of us, and the nature of our duties requires that every man be able to depend completely on the skill and knowledge of every other. I've served with several of you, taught two of you who are here, and probably a good number of the enlisted men, and know others by reputation.

"Now it becomes my duty to lead you. Lieutenant Commander Hammersmith was a good friend of mine. I will miss him as, I'm sure, will you. He was a good man, a good officer and, of course, a good submariner. From what I have been told, and from what I have seen so far, he has left an efficient team and was well on his way to creating what would have inevitably been a top performing submarine.

"We still have lots of work to do, gentlemen. I'm sure we'll all remember Lieutenant Commander Hammersmith in our own way, and all of you will no doubt wish to convey your hope for a quick and complete recovery to Lieutenant Commander Dunstan. I regret to say that his injuries will keep him from returning to his duties here, so it seems I won't be the only new face joining *Bacalao.*

"Be that as it may, we have much to do and not that much time to do it. I'll be talking to each of you individually sometime today to get a feel for how everything is progressing. I know you're all good men. I'm sure we'll get along well and if, as seems likely, we are called upon to take this boat into battle, I know we will all do our best."

Some of them were nodding their heads. They were good men, just as he had said. They were all members of a very small service—most submariners knew each other, at least slightly. If you stayed in subs long enough you would almost certainly meet everyone else who wore dolphins pinned to his breast or sewn on his sleeve.

For now, they would return to their normal daily routine as quickly as possible. There was nothing go be gained by sitting around mourning their loss and these men all knew it. After the working day ended, then would be the time. Right now, Morley suspected that getting back to work would be the best thing for them.

So the officers and chiefs were dismissed to return to their duties. Morley had his own worries, too. The boat needed an executive officer, and he was hoping to get the right one. He knew who he would ask for, and could think of no one better suited. He just wasn't sure he was available.

•   •   •

Morley was right, Miller thought. There was a lot to do and they would all be better off if they got right to it and didn't spend too much time mourning their losses and wondering how different things might have been if Hammersmith had remained in command.

The big day came exactly one week after Morley took over. The expected admiral's daughter appeared, failed to charm anyone—she was a good 80 pounds overweight, and old enough that Miller thought her father had probably served with Farragut at Mobile Bay—but did manage to break the champagne bottle on the first swing. Down on the greased ways the shipyard workers swung their mauls, and *Bacalao* went sliding down the incline into the Thames River. On deck, the crew swayed uneasily, a couple of them nearly overbalancing and having to grab one of the wire guard rails as the boat gathered momentum, while up on the bridge the captain and other officers all did their best to look comfortable.

Inevitably, some were wondering if the boat would really float properly, or if she would suddenly decide to fall over on her side and throw everyone into the river. But Electric Boat had managed their usual fine job, and the boat floated quite nicely, if rather high in the water.

Before long *Bacalao* was taken in hand by a small tug and towed over to the fitting-out pier. Civilians often seemed to think that once a ship was launched she was ready for sea, but there was still a lot to do before that could happen.

Bacalao was floating high because she was light. Most of that was cured as the battery cells came aboard. These were lowered through soft patches in the wardroom and enlisted berthing area overhead. A soft patch was a hole cut in the pressure hull, which would be sealed by bolting down a steel plate the same thickness as the hull, with a duck canvas gasket, impregnated with red lead, as a sealer. Soft patches were used to allow access for items that were too big or awkward to hoist through the hatches, but that still had to replaced fairly regularly. Hard patches, which were welded in place, were generally much larger, and used for removing and replacing major components, such as engines.

Once inside the hull, the battery cells were lowered into the battery wells beneath the platform deck. A set of beams and cross tracks beneath the deck supported a special trolley that was used to position the huge cells, where they were secured in their individual acid-resistant tubs by paraffin-impregnated rock maple wedges. There were 126 cells in each battery, each cell four and half feet tall, 15 inches deep, and 21 inches wide. Each weighed about three-quarters of a ton when installed, and would become even heavier once the electrolyte—basically sulfuric acid and distilled water—was added.

Bacalao's battery cells were manufactured by the Gould Storage Battery Company. Other boats had Exide batteries. Down in the battery well, each cell was secured in its own acid-proof tank, just in case it might be damaged and start to leak. When all 252 cells were installed and filled with electrolyte the boat was some 208 tons heavier, and her waterline was much closer to where the designers had planned. The addition of the rest of her equipment, plus some lead ballast, would complete the job.

While all this was going on, other workers were busy aligning the motors and reduction gears with the propeller shafts. This was one of those jobs that couldn't be performed before launching, for until the boat was in the water there was no way to be sure of just how everything would line up. On the ways, the boat was supported at various points along her length by wooden keel blocks and support posts, which naturally caused her to sit differently than when she was supported evenly along her entire length by water.

After the batteries were installed, and while the shipyard workers were busy connecting the wiring and fitting the battery ventilation system, which was designed to remove the explosive hydrogen gas that was generated when the batteries were charged, the wardroom again became fully staffed as Lieutenant Commander Frederick Ames arrived from the Navy Department in Washington to take over as executive officer.

As Morley had informed the others, the doctor had decided that Dunstan wouldn't be returning to full duty until early in 1942, by which time *Bacalao* was expected to be in the Pacific. Everyone hoped that, once he recovered, Dunstan would get another shot at being XO, or even CO, in a different boat.

It turned out that Ames had been Morley's roommate at Annapolis, so the two of them instantly formed an imposing leadership team. Each always seemed to know what the other was thinking. Morley was in command because of their class standing at graduation, since both had the same date of rank as lieutenant commander. Morley had graduated as number 23 in the Class of 1928, while Ames was number 32, which made Morley senior.

In the way of the Navy, Ames could serve under Morley, but not the other way around.

Morley came from a naval family, and represented the third generation of Annapolis graduates, going back to the days just after the Civil War. He had grown up on a series of naval bases, though the bulk of his younger life had been centered around the Groton/New London area. His father had been a pioneer submariner, and ended his career as CO of the Submarine Base. He still lived with his wife in an old house in New London, overlooking the Thames River.

Rear Admiral John Morley had begun his submarine career in one of the original A-boats. He came aboard *Bacalao* on the day the periscopes were being installed. Tall and slender, like his son, his white hair was cut quite short, and he had dressed in a neat black suit, white shirt and black tie, which gave the impression of being a civilian substitute for the uniform he had worn for nearly 40 years.

He was an imposing looking man, made all the more so by the presence of a small rosette of star-spangled blue cloth in the buttonhole of his left lapel. Ironically, he had won his Medal of Honor while *hunting* submarines, for in those early days a sub was, at the very most, a senior lieutenant's command. A good officer was soon promoted out of them. By the time the United States entered the war in 1917, the elder Morley was commanding a destroyer.

He returned to submarines after the war as commander of a tender. When he retired in 1924, the same year his eldest son entered the Naval Academy, he was a captain. His Medal of Honor allowed him to take a "tombstone" promotion to rear admiral on retirement, which brought with it both the prestige of flag rank and a little extra money in his pension check.*

Miller heard most of this second hand. While the captain's father was telling sea stories in the wardroom after touring the boat, Miller was up in the conning tower watching the Electric Boat workmen run hoist cables and set the periscope shafts into the rugged bearings in the hoisting collars.

• • •

Morley wondered if anyone who had ever received the Medal of Honor really believed he deserved it.

"It really wasn't that much," his father related. "When we were hit a fire started in the forward fire room, so I went below and made sure that everyone got out. I was the captain—it was my job. Someone decided he wanted to hand out some medals and gave me this one.

To listen to him, Morley thought, a person might think the Old Man had done nothing out of the ordinary. That he had simply done what a captain was supposed to do. But Morley had read the full citation. His father hadn't simply gone below and helped a few men get out. He had gone back into that burning fire room eight times, each time carrying out an unconscious sailor and very nearly killing himself in the process.

All the while the fire was burning against the side of a fuel bunker, and the boiler was dangerously close to bursting, its relief valve held down by a collapsed frame. Either the bunker or the boiler could have let go at any moment while the rescue was going on. About five minutes after the last man was out, the boiler burst. The ship survived only be-

---

* The tombstone promotion system allowed an officer with a combat decoration to retire at the next higher grade. In 1949, Congress repealed the part of the law that gave retirement pay based on the higher rank, so that the only benefit then became the promotion. In 1959, the entire system was ended, and since that time officers retire in the rank they hold on their retirement date.

cause they were close enough to land to run her up on a beach before she could settle.

It was a curious fact, Morley thought. The nation's highest honor was almost exclusively a combat award, but it was rarely given for killing the enemy. Most often the award was for saving the lives of others at the risk of one's own. Even Sergeant York, who killed 25 German soldiers, prompting another 132 to surrender, did so mainly because he recognized that it was the only way to save his own men.

One thing Morley had noticed was that his father rarely told stories about his combat service, either in the Great War, or earlier, when as a young ensign he had been present aboard *Olympia* at Manila Bay. He much preferred to relate a vast collection of sea stories and tales from the early days of submarines, when the boats were tiny, and the old gasoline engines were as dangerous to their own crews as the boats might possibly be to an enemy. All in all, there was a lot more humor than heroism in his stories.

This seemed to be the way with those who had real war stories to tell. The most lurid tales of high adventure and grim combat always came from one of his father's friends who, it turned out, spent the entire war behind a desk at the Navy Department.

His father preferred to tell stories about the things his crew tried to get away with. Some of them, he thought, might even be true, though most seemed likely to belong to the "no shit" story category. The kind of story where the story teller began his tale with, "Now this is no shit," which, of course, it almost always was.

His father never started his stories that way. It would have offended his sense of decorum, which he expected in an officer. But Morley always knew, somehow, that they should.

The officers were certainly enjoying his visit. Miller was up in the conning tower, keeping an eye on the periscope installation, and Hartman was up at the Submarine Base running an errand, but all the others were there. Not one of them had seen any action—they all grew up after the war—but every one of them by now believed that war was coming. In those circumstances, the shared experiences of someone who had been in a real battle was useful.

Until it started, all they could do was train and speculate on how they would react. They trained constantly, so that their reactions in any emergency would be automatic. Then, in the end, they would still be no more or less brave than their own nature dictated.

The elder Morley summed it up nicely before he left. "Courage," he said, "is nothing more than your sense of duty overcoming your common sense."

•   •   •

Getting the two periscopes installed was a long, delicate process, requiring precise coordination between all members of the work crew, from the dockside crane operator who hoisted the 40-foot tubes from the dock and lowered them delicately into their shafts in the periscope shears, to the men in the conning tower who had to insure that the tubes were properly set into the hoisting collars.

Though designed for rugged service, a submarine's periscope was, in many ways, the most delicate device aboard. The 40-foot tube contained a complex collection of lenses and prisms, which allowed it to act as both a telescope and a range finder.

When the workmen had both tubes installed in their hoisting collars, a second group of civilian technicians, this time from the Kollmorgen Company, which manufactured all of the Navy's periscopes, spent several hours installing the lower sections. The optics had to be carefully aligned, the stadimeters calibrated, and all the air removed from inside the periscope and replaced with dry, pressurized nitrogen to prevent fogging.

Miller was an interested observer to this whole process. As Torpedo Data Computer operator, the approach officer's periscope observations would be a major component of the data he had to crank into the TDC. He was naturally interested in making sure that the periscopes were as perfect as they could be, despite the fact that their utility in a modern fleet boat was at that time essentially limited to clearing the area before surfacing.

The Navy had determined that showing a periscope during a daylight attack was too risky to attempt. An escort might spot it, or it might reveal the boat's position to an enemy plane. Any captain who let his periscope be spotted during an exercise could expect to be called on the carpet once it was over.

They would use the periscopes for targeting while they were working up, but when things got serious it was expected that targeting data would come from the sound gear.

While the Kollmorgen people were working with their pumps, nitrogen bottles and collimators, Miller just tried to stay out of the way. Most of the time he relaxed on the sonar operator's stool in front of the WCA stack, in the starboard aft corner of the conning tower, just across from the canvas-shrouded TDC. This device was so secret that it was kept covered whenever anyone other than a crew member, or a specially cleared worker, was in the conning tower.

The Mark 3 Torpedo Data Computer in *Bacalao*'s conning tower represented a huge advance over older targeting systems. While it served the same function as the Is-Was and Banjo Miller had used to aim S-35's torpedoes, the TDC automated the whole process. Inside the double cabinet a complex system of gears, motors, synchros and switches received their input from several sources and produced a continually updated stream of targeting data, which was automatically transmitted to the torpedoes in both nests.

The TDC was a logical companion to the advances in torpedo design. Originally, a torpedo could only travel in a straight line. Back then, it was necessary to literally aim the whole submarine at where the target was going to be by the time the torpedo reached it. Leading the target, which would be moving ahead at some rate of speed, was vital. If the torpedo was aimed directly at the target it would be gone by the time the fish arrived.

But modern torpedoes could be set to steer their own course, and could be aimed at any angle up to 130° from their original heading. It was no longer necessary to aim the boat at the target, but it also complicated the approach officer's job by requiring him to correctly calculate the gyro angle for firing.

Most navies had tackled the problem since the end of the war. A number of mechanical devices had been invented to do the math and the results were now installed in the conning towers and controls rooms of each nation's submarines. Most were fairly simple angle solvers. In some cases they were electrically linked to the gyro setting mechanisms in the torpedo rooms. In others, the approach officer had to relay the settings by voice.

All of these angle finders, including the British "fruit machine" and the German *Vorhaltsrechner*, suffered from a basic limitation. They could provide the gyro angles based on inputs, but it was up to the captain to keep track of where the target was at any given moment, and to decide the precise moment for firing. It was all a matter of matching angles and firing at the precise instant.

The TDC's designers had decided to go a step farther. The basic design was taken from the massive analog computers used by cruisers and battleships to keep their big guns on target. This was simplified considerably for submarines. A battleship's targeting computer had to be able to compensate for pitch, roll, the wind, calculate elevation and deflection, and so on. A submarine was mostly concerned with deflection, which allowed for a much smaller device.

The important difference from other countries' devices was that the American designers had found a way to include a position keeper. Now it was the TDC, and not the captain, who kept track of where the target was expected to be.

During the approach, the TDC would be programmed with the target's course, speed and bearing, while the computer would automatically add own-ship's course and speed, taking the readings from the gyro compass and Pitometer log. The TDC would then calculate the proper firing angle and, at the same time, keep track of where the target would be—presuming it didn't change course.

If every input was correct, it was theoretically impossible to miss. Miller didn't think that particular theory was necessarily the most reliable one. The TDC would make his job easier, but it certainly couldn't guarantee a hit every time. He might make a slight error cranking in the data, or a torpedo could run erratically, or an alert lookout on the target could spot the torpedo wake in time, letting the captain maneuver out of the way. There would always be too many variables to allow for absolute certainty.

While Miller was pondering his potential for screwing up an attack, the Kollmorgen technicians continued their work in a careful, unhurried manner. By the time they were finished, with both periscopes tested and pronounced ready for service, he was too late to get in on the discussion in the wardroom. The captain's father had already gone ashore.

II
Training

BENDING OVER THE TARGET BEARING TRANSMITTER on *Bacalao*'s tiny upper bridge, Lieutenant Lawrence Miller centered the crosshairs on the New London Harbor Light. Looking down at the scale he noted the reading, though it hardly seemed necessary, as it was an entirely predictable 090°. He didn't need a precision instrument to recognize a right angle.

He straightened up and looked across the bridge to where Morley was seated in the folding wooden chair built into the port bulwark. He had a book open in his lap and didn't seem to be paying much attention to his surroundings.

"Passing New London Harbor Light on the starboard beam, sir," Miller reported. He glanced at the gyro repeater. "Course is one-seven-zero."

"Thank you, Mr. Miller. Carry on."

They were still in the Thames River, with the helmsman following the buoys that marked the dredged channel. Miller could see the markers dotting the water ahead, setting out the course they would have to follow as they made their way out into Long Island Sound for a day of training.

This would be the first time *Bacalao* left the river with her full crew aboard. Until two days earlier she had been Electric Boat Company property, and had made her first dives with the company's trials crew operating everything. The captain and the other officers had been aboard, but only some key ratings had been able to come along. The petty officers spent most of their time looking over the shoulders of the retired chiefs who were doing what would soon be their own jobs.

Now it was mid-June, and everything was done. The last of the ship-yard workers had gone ashore for the final time a few days earlier, the boat had been turned over to the Navy, and *Bacalao* moved up the river to the Submarine Base, New London. In what often struck the casual observer as typical maritime illogic, the base was located on the north-ern edge of Groton, on the opposite side of the river from New London. It only seemed illogical, though, as the base was named for New London County, where it was located, and not for the city of New London, where it wasn't.

The last of the crew was now aboard. The officers had been there from the time the boat was little more than a stack of curved steel plates waiting to be lifted onto the ways and welded into place. The key en-listed men, chiefs and senior ratings, had arrived at just about the same time as the equipment they would use. The rest of the rated men had put in an appearance just before launching.

The last to come aboard had been the unrated men, fresh from Submarine School—a few of them rather horrified to discover that they would now be serving under one of their toughest former instructors. This last batch would fill the remaining slots while they completed their education in submarines and qualified for their dolphins.

As she headed down river, *Bacalao* had a full crew and, though she wasn't fully provisioned, had only exercise torpedoes in her tubes and carried no ammunition for her deck gun and light weapons, she was otherwise ready for action. That didn't mean the boat would be doing anything particularly energetic this day.

For the most part, they would be steaming around Long Island Sound, just getting a good feel for the boat. The schedule called for a short dive in two hours. This would also be the first time they submerged the boat with her regular crew manning all stations.

In the following days they would repeatedly dive the boat, putting her through her paces. Every officer would take his turn at handling the dives, so that each of them would become accustomed to her quirks. When the day came for *Bacalao* to go into battle—and no one seriously doubted that day would be coming within the next few months—there could be no hesitation, no sending for a designated dive officer, when it came time to get under water. The only thing that would matter then would be speed.

Fleet requirements called for the ability to dive within 60 seconds. It was said that the Germans could manage it in half that time, and Miller could see no reason why they shouldn't be able to get close. A *Gato* was a lot bigger than a German Type VIIc U-boat, to be sure. *Much* bigger, really, but Miller had no doubt they would be able to significantly increase diving speed with practice.

It was already standard practice in many boats to operate with the Kingston valves at the bottom of the ballast tanks open, so that only the air in the tanks kept the boat on the surface. This was what Intelligence said the Germans were doing, and it was logical to conclude that not having to take the time to open flood valves was going to speed up diving.

The Navy seemed to have had that very thing in mind when the *Gato* design was standardized. In the earlier fleet boats, the Kingston valves had been hydraulic. In the new boats they were all manual, which meant opening and closing them was now much slower than it had been. It seemed obvious to Miller that the new boats were intended to ride the vents most of the time, only closing the Kingston valves when there was little or no chance they would need to submerge.

All in all, he figured the dives would be the easy part. As electrical officer, it would be his department that kept the boat moving under water. A lot to think about. But he had a good chief and some very competent petty officers, so he expected they would take care of things most of the time. Even some of the unrated men seemed promising.

Miller would find out how good his own skills were during the practice torpedo shoots. If he was doing everything right with the TDC, then those attacks would be a success. It was quite a change for someone who had learned attack procedures in the elderly *S-42* and then practiced them amidst the islands of the western Pacific in *S-35*. For all practical purposes, he had to learn it all over again.

Target practice was still a few days off, so for now his only real responsibility was getting the boat into Long Island Sound without running aground or committing some other stupid error. He was a watch officer, just like every other officer aboard. Subs had grown considerably over the last few years, but the crews were still small enough that every officer but the captain would have to stand a watch at sea.

The captain had to be available on *every* watch, including those when he was trying to sleep.

Miller figured he could handle the boat. Even so, he didn't think Morley would be more than a few steps away. He'd keep a close eye on everything until he was sure they were all as good as they were supposed to be. You had to expect that sort of thing in a boat that had hardly left the dock before.

But not an obtrusive eye, Miller noticed. Lieutenant Commander James Andrew Morley—his family and friends called him "Andy," as he was named for his father's brother and one "Jim" was considered enough—was still sitting in his chair, his book open in his lap. Miller wondered if he was actually reading it, or if the book was just a prop, so that he would look a trifle less like he was waiting to leap to his feet and save the day the moment the OOD screwed up.

Either way, Miller appreciated it. He hadn't been sure what to expect when Morley first arrived on board, just after Hammersmith's sudden demise. In the time since, he had come to appreciate the new captain as a highly competent submariner, as well as an officer who had enough common sense to make the best use of his subordinates. He also knew when to stand back and let them do things for themselves.

Not every captain did.

Just then Ames' voice was heard shouting up through the circular hatch near Miller's feet.

"Permission to come up?" Ames asked. It was standard Navy protocol to ask, and even more important in a sub, where the bridge party had to be kept as small as practical in case they had to dive. The more men on the bridge, the longer it took to get them all below.

Miller glanced at the captain, who nodded. "Permission granted, sir," he said.

Ames climbed through the hatch, crossing the bridge to confer quietly with the captain. Miller wondered what they were talking about, but knew better than to eavesdrop. If it was anything he needed to know they would tell him.

Privacy was something everyone valued in the crowded hull of a submarine. There was very little to be found. Only the captain had a private stateroom. The other officers had to share a stateroom with one or two other officers—there were three bunks in each—or make do with one of the fold-down bunks in the wardroom. The chiefs had their own compartment, colloquially known as the "goat locker," located just across the passageway from the ship's office, just forward of the control room.

As for the enlisted men, even the most basic concept of privacy was hardly to be found. The lucky ones got to bunk in one of the torpedo rooms, which were relatively quiet and generally only dimly lit unless they were working on the torpedoes.

The rest of the men bunked in the after battery compartment, where 36 bunks were stacked three high. As there were fewer total bunks than men, some always had to share, a practice the Navy called hot bunking. Not as many as in some of the older boats, though.

Bacalao was approaching the final channel markers now, and Miller moved back to the TBT. Designed to transmit target bearings when the button on the left handgrip was pressed, the TBT was built around a pelorus, which made it very handy for taking navigational bearings.

Two quick bearings placed Goshen Point at 085° and the Seaflower Reef Light at 275°. In this case, the bearings were just a precaution, lest something had happened to the outer channel markers and the boat wasn't where they thought it was.

That was unlikely, as the entry markers were easy to recognize, but submariners had a strong tendency to be overcautious at times. When you served in a vessel where a seemingly minor lapse could kill everyone aboard extra caution was just common sense.

"We're clear of the channel, sir," Miller reported.

Morley stood up and walked to the front of the upper bridge. "Come right to new course two-three-zero," he ordered. "All ahead two thirds."

"New course is two-three-zero, all ahead two thirds," Miller repeated. When the captain didn't say anything, indicating he had repeated the order correctly, he called it down to Anderson at the surface steering position in the covered forebridge, who also repeated the orders before executing them.

Miller could feel the boat accelerating as more power was directed to *Bacalao*'s four big General Electric motors, which were connected to the propeller shafts through heavy reduction gears. It seemed odd not to hear the diesels speed up as the boat's speed increased. In *S-35*, surface power came directly from the diesels, coupled to the shafts by big clutches, so any increase or decrease in the boat's speed involved a corresponding change in engine speed.

In *Bacalao* there was no physical connection between the propeller shafts and the four huge engines. The nine-cylinder Hooven-Owens-Rentschler diesels drove DC generators. In the maneuvering room, a complex switching system sent the power from these generators to where it was needed. As the generators—like the motors and main control, built by General Electric—produced their optimum power at 750 rpm, the engine speed varied only slightly no matter how fast the boat was moving. There was an obvious difference in the sound under a heavy load, as the engines had to work harder, but the speed didn't change very much.

At the moment, engines number one and two were being used to charge the batteries. Number three and four were on propulsion. Speed control was managed by connecting or disconnecting the motor windings. To run at dead slow, all four motors were connected in series, quartering the available voltage, and power would be drawn from only one battery. For full speed, the motors were connected in parallel, as were the windings and the two massive batteries, which doubled available power.

In S-boats, they could connect the batteries in series for extra power, but each of a fleet boat's 126-cell batteries produced as much voltage as the motors could handle. A parallel connection doubled the available amperage, but didn't increase the voltage.

Below the elevated platform where they stood, Anderson was bringing the boat onto her new course. Miller had often thought that the relatively simple job of helmsman was the one task he would least like to have. It was easy enough now, with the helm at the surface steering position on the covered forebridge, but what happened once it was transferred to the main steering position in the conning tower. How did you steer when you couldn't see where you were going?

It was bad enough giving helm orders while submerged, mostly relying on the sound picture and dumb luck to keep from blundering into something. It had to be worse actually manning the wheel and carrying out those orders. In a submarine, the blind really did lead the blind.

Inside the conning tower, the helmsman had a gyro repeater, a rudder position indicator and a pair of motor telegraphs in front of him. His only view was of his instruments and of the smooth, painted cork insulation covering the curved forward bulkhead. He just had to take it on faith that his watch officer wouldn't steer him onto a sandbar—or into a pier.

Coming down river, their procedure had been about the same as in any surface ship. The helmsman followed the channel markers, rather than have the OOD give constant helm orders for every tiny course adjustment. Now that they were out of the marked channel it would be different, but the course adjustments would also be less frequent in open water.

Miller kept his eye on the gyro repeater as the boat swung smoothly to starboard and steadied on her new course. Just now, he noticed, they were following the Orient Point ferry route.

Miller saw that Ames had gone aft, and was now standing on the starboard side, looking over the bulwark plating and talking to one of the .30-caliber gunners. The guns were all manned, just as they would have been were *Bacalao* steaming on the surface in a war zone. As there was no ammunition aboard, they wouldn't be shooting at anything this day. The schedule called for the boat to move to the gunnery range the following week. They would take on ammunition then.

If a war started right now, and an enemy force suddenly appeared in Long Island Sound, about all they could do would be call in a sighting report and try to stay out of the way. The guns were manned because that was SOP. The gun crews also functioned as auxiliary lookouts, keeping an eye on sea and sky, just in case a plane managed to get past the regular lookouts and the radar watch, or a periscope suddenly popped up. Here and now, they would mostly be looking for any hazards in the water.

Just as well, really, Miller thought. A .30-caliber machine-gun was a fairly adequate antipersonnel weapon, but he didn't think it would be all that useful against modern aircraft. If they ever had to shoot it out with a plane he wanted something a bit more substantial.

Given the choice, he preferred not to engage aircraft at all. There had been much lively debate about the best antiaircraft armament for submarines, given the obvious problem of having to mount guns where they would be exposed to a corrosive salt water environment much of the time. Some thought the .30s should be replaced by .50-calibers, but most wanted heavier automatic weapons—20 or 40-millimeter wet-mount guns seemed like the obvious choice.

The majority, including Miller, favored a different approach. Few officers could fail to recognize just how vulnerable a submarine was. A heavy machine-gun might just be able to punch some holes in the pressure hull. It would be unlikely to sink them, but it would cause leaks and, depending on what else the slugs hit, could damage something that would keep them from diving.

Miller figured the best defense was to get under water as quickly as possible. A fighter couldn't sink them, but it might be able to keep them from submerging while it called up a destroyer. The light machine-guns they carried, and the little three-inch gun on the after deck, would be of little use against a warship.

At that very moment American destroyers were actively enforcing an Exclusion Zone in the Atlantic. The United States wasn't at war, but he doubted the German U-boat commanders those destroyers were hunting in the Zone would agree. It no doubt felt very much like a war to them.

Even worse for the Germans, Miller knew that the U-boats were under strict orders not to fire on American warships. It seemed Hitler didn't want to provoke the U.S. into actually declaring war. Roosevelt seemed less concerned with that, and was pushing things as far as an isolationist Congress and population would allow.

Miller figured war was inevitable. So did most of his friends. The only real question seemed to be just where it would start. Roosevelt seemed anxious to get into it with Germany, and the Japanese were running amuck in China. He had asked Ohara for his opinion on that once, but the man had pled ignorance. He couldn't understand the language, and had no useful knowledge of Japanese culture. He was, however, more than willing to explain why Southern culture was infinitely better than the Yankee sort.

One possibly significant factor was that *Bacalao* and her sisters were the direct result of the Japanese naval buildup in the Far East. The rumor mill had it that they would be joining the Pacific Fleet at Pearl Harbor once they finished working up.

Miller figured that would be confirmed as soon as the German phrase books and arctic clothing arrived.

• • •

Miller looked up from the TBT and closed the attached lens covers on the pressure-proof binoculars built into the device. "Position for diving, sir," he reported.

On the port quarter, *Falcon* was standing by. He wasn't sure if he found her presence reassuring or ominous. If something happened, they were in relatively shallow water, and the rescue vessel carried divers and a McCann rescue chamber.

On the other hand, the very presence of a rescue vessel suggested that the Navy *expected* something to happen. One of his friends had been in *Squalus*, and his description of the hours spent waiting for rescue made it clear that, even with a happy outcome, it wasn't an experience anyone would wish for.

Morley closed his book and walked to the front of the upper bridge. With the boat out of the channel and functioning as if she were at sea, the surface steering position had been secured and the helm shifted to the conning tower. There were now only nine men who weren't safely tucked away inside the hull.

Morley nodded decisively. "OOD, dive the boat. Make your depth six-four feet."

"Dive the boat. Aye, aye, sir." Miller keyed the microphone on the 1MC, the general announcing system, looking pointedly at Hartman, who as Junior Officer of the Deck would be the one in the control room taking the dive.

"Prepare to dive! Clear the bridge!"

The three lookouts scrambled down from their posts on the bridge overhead, while the two machine-gunners hurried forward from the cigarette deck, cradling the heavy machine-guns in their arms. The guns were passed down the hatch into the conning tower and the gunners quickly followed. Hartman was right behind them.

"Six," Miller said. He was now alone on the bridge with the captain and the Quartermaster of the Watch, who would be the last man down. "Everyone is below, sir."

The captain dropped through the hatch as Miller reached for the 'talk' switch.

"Dive! Dive!" he shouted into the microphone. From below, he could hear the raucous sound of the motor-driven diving klaxon. There were two sharp blasts, followed by a sudden silence, and he scrambled through the hatch and down the ladder.

The quartermaster of the watch—actually Seaman 1st Class Jacob Paul, still a striker and not yet rated—followed him down, pulling the lanyard to close the hatch and spinning the locking wheel, dogging it tight.

"Hatch is secure, sir," Paul reported.

•   •   •

Ensign Thomas Hartman was in the control room before the diving alarm had finished blasting its warning. Dropping down the ladder, he landed on a spot just abaft the planesmen, who until moments earlier had been on the bridge overhead serving as the forward lookouts.

"Main engines, all stop," he ordered.

He noticed that Chief Gordon was keeping an eye on things. On him, really, he thought. Leave it to the captain to make the most junior officer handle the first dive. The Old Man was still a teacher at heart, and no doubt equally confident that COB wouldn't let Hartman actually screw things up.

Back aft, the four big diesels rattled into silence with their usual clatter of protest. Diesels didn't shut down instantly, like a car engine, but were killed by shutting off the fuel supply.

Back in the maneuvering room, Ohara threw the big, chrome-plated levers on the main control board, switching the motors to battery power.

"All ahead two thirds," Hartman ordered. "Close main induction."

The big valve, located under the cigarette deck, closed with a loud 'thump' and the last light on the indicator panel turned green.

"Induction closed, sir. Green board."

That was Gordon, and Hartman found himself smiling. The truth was that he had never dived a fleet boat before, and the elderly training boats hardly seemed to count. The presence of the graying Chief Motor Machinist's Mate helped keep his confidence up. COB had probably done thousands of dives.

"Put pressure in the boat," Hartman ordered.

The manifold operator bled compressed air into the pressure hull, keeping his eye on the barometer. The needle rose slightly and, after the air was shut off, held.

"Pressure in the boat, sir. Pressure is holding."

Hartman nodded. That was the final test. If the additional air pressure couldn't escape it was a logical presumption that the water couldn't get in.

"Open all main vents. Flood negative. Rig out bow planes."

There was a roaring sound as the vents at the top of the ballast tanks opened, releasing the captive air and allowing water to rush into the tanks through the open flood valves at the bottom of the tanks.

"Full dive on the bow planes," he ordered.

"Bow planes, full dive, aye, sir."

"Make your depth six-four feet."

"Passing four-five feet, sir."

"Close all vents."

"Vents are closed, sir."

"Five-niner feet, sir."

"Blow negative to the mark." With the boat now 15 feet from her target depth the negative tank, which had been flooded to increase diving speed, was blown almost dry to restore neutral buoyancy. They would never blow the tank completely dry, always leaving a little water at the bottom of the tank. A complete blow would send a cloud of bubbles to the surface.

"Level off," Hartman ordered. "All ahead one-third."

"Six-four feet, sir."

"Cycle the vents."

Hartman stood between the planesmen. "How does she feel?" he asked.

"Holding steady, sir," the stern operator reported, "but I'm having to use about five degrees of down angle to keep her level."

Hartman looked at Gordon. "Let's pump 1,100 pounds from aft trim to forward trim," he said.

Gordon nodded. "Sounds about right, sir."

The trim pump set up a clatter as it began to move 125 gallons of seawater from the aft trim tank to the bow trim tank. Hartman idly wondered why no one had ever come up with a quieter pump. The standard design installed in *Bacalao* was copied from a wartime German model, so it had probably been quiet enough back in 1914. Sound gear had improved a lot since then, though, and he suspected a modern destroyer could hear that pump with very little effort.

"Noisy, isn't it?" he said.

Gordon nodded, watching the trim panel. "Belay pumping," he ordered.

Hartman looked at the planesman. "Better, Hendrick?" he asked.

"Yes, sir. She's holding fine now."

"Boat is steady at six-four feet," Hartman called, shouting up the ladder to the conning tower.

"Thank you, Mr. Hartman." It was Miller's voice, coming down from above.

Morgan came into the control room about then. "Looks like you're doing okay, Tom," he said. "I'll just watch for a while, I think." The control room was his normal action station, and he was also the 'official' dive officer. Not wanting to make Hartman any more nervous than he already was, Morgan had been hovering inside the radio shack, keeping his ears open, but staying out of sight. Now that they were safely at periscope depth and nothing had gone wrong he thought he could be there without bothering the young officer.

•   •   •

The captain had the number two periscope—the one movies call the 'attack' periscope—raised, his eye pressed into the buffer as he walked the 'scope around in a circle.

"Down 'scope," he ordered, snapping up the handles.

Paul worked the pickle and the periscope dropped into the well, the hoist sheaves squeaking as the heavy steel cable ran over them.

"Make a note of that," Morley said. "Have someone get those sheaves properly lubricated. I don't want to hear them squeaking like that any more."

"Aye, aye, sir," Paul said, writing in his notebook.

Morley leaned against the guard rail protecting the control room hatch, looking down at the top of Hartman's head. "Make your depth one-five-zero feet," he ordered.

"Make my depth one-five-zero feet, aye," Hartman repeated. A moment later he could be heard giving orders to the bow planesman and the boat started down to her new depth.

The captain moved over to the small chart table, located on the starboard side of the conning tower, just abaft the bridge ladder and protected from anything coming down the hatch by a stubby bulkhead. He took a quick look at the chart and then stepped across the conning tower to join Miller, who was standing near the helmsman.

"We'll run at 150 feet for five minutes," Morley said, "and then surface."

"Yes, sir."

"How was it, Larry?"

"Sir?"

"First dive in a fleet boat, right? Other than the EB tests, I mean, but the first time with our own crew."

Miller nodded. "True. It felt smooth enough, and I didn't hear Hartman give any wrong orders while I was eavesdropping at the hatch. He got the trim right on the first try, too."

"COB would have jumped in if he'd done anything wrong," the captain said. "In any case, it will do the young man good. In my experience, the only way to build confidence in a young officer is to let him do things for himself."

Miller nodded again. That was how he had learned, though he was now going to have to forget some of the old methods, like connecting the batteries in series at the beginning of a dive.

He looked at his watch. Five minutes already, he thought. "Time, sir."

Morley turned toward the after end of the conning tower. "Sound check?"

Jones 1—there were two Albert Joneses aboard, both of them rated radioman 1st class, and both assigned as sonar operators—was at the sonar stack. Jones 1 was the scrawny, always relaxed one. Jones 2 was the image of the stereotypical jolly fat man, except he wasn't jolly and was constantly getting involved in brawls every time he stepped ashore.

At the captain's order, Jones made a sweep of the area. "Vessel at one-niner-three, sir," he reported. "A little hard to hear over our own screw noises, but sounds like the *Falcon*, sir. Outboard motor noises at two-two-eight, range two-thousand, maybe more. Nothing close aboard, sir."

"Periscope depth, Mr. Miller."

"Aye, aye, sir." He leaned over the control room hatch, this time seeing the top of Morgan's head. Hartman would be close by. "Mr. Hartman, make your depth six-four feet," he called down.

"Make my depth six four feet, aye," Hartman responded.

Miller watched the conning tower depth gauge as *Bacalao* planed up to 64 feet. Hartman was still doing it right, and still with a minimum of comment from Gordon or Morgan. Their silence was the clearest indication that the young ensign was doing a good job.

"Six-four feet, sir," Hartman called up.

"Periscope depth, sir," Miller repeated.

Morley walked to the number two periscope and stood by the well. "Up 'scope."

Paul worked the pickle and the gleaming tube began to rise from the well. The captain met it as the eyepiece box emerged from the well, snapping down the knurled brass handles and pressing his eyes into the buffer before the head was clear of the water. He quickly made the standard three circuits of the horizon, starting with the optics on full elevation and clicking the prism down to the next lower detent setting with the left handle at the end of each circuit.

"Area is clear," he announced. "Prepare to surface."

The word was quickly passed through the boat, the men rushing to their stations with a speed that belied what should have been their relative unfamiliarity with a boat on its first time away from the pier under a Navy crew. Having mostly been present during construction, they knew where to go and what to do.

•   •   •

In the control room, Hartman ordered speed increased to two-thirds. "Surface! Surface! Surface!"

The klaxon sounded three times. Three meant surface, two meant dive. Even if a man somehow missed the order, what he had to do was always clear.

"Blow bow buoyancy and main ballast," Hartman ordered. "Three degree up bubble."

There was a roaring sound as 600-pound air was admitted to the main ballast tanks, restoring positive buoyancy. At the extreme forward end of the boat, the bow buoyancy tank was also blown, putting an upward angle on the boat as she surged toward the surface.

"Passing five-zero feet, sir," Gordon said, watching the gauge.

The boat continued on her controlled ascent. At 30 feet, Hartman ordered the air secured. There was enough air in the tanks now that the boat would inevitably rise to the surface. Once there, they would blow the rest of the water from the ballast tanks with low pressure air from the ten-pound blower located in the pump room under the control room platform deck, saving the air supply in the high pressure system.

The motion changed as the boat thrust herself to the surface. Above him, Hartman saw the lower conning tower hatch clank shut and the locking dogs engage. It was one step in the "proper" procedure, though one that was usually ignored.

A few seconds later, the indicator light for the bridge hatch turned red.

•   •   •

Salty water dripped down on his shoulders as Paul cracked the hatch, the slightly higher air pressure inside the boat making a whistling sound as it equalized. After a second the hissing stopped and he spun the locking wheel the rest of the way, retracting the dogs, before shoving up on the hatch, which swung open in its springs and clicked into the latch. Paul rushed up the ladder, followed by Morley and Miller.

Paul hurried to the after part of the bridge and began to check the area. Miller scanned the port sector, while Morley looked to starboard. The first priority on surfacing was always to take a good look around and make sure you weren't about to run into anything. And that nothing was about to run into you.

"*Falcon* fine on the port quarter," Paul reported. "Range about two-five-double-oh."

"Port sector clear, sir," Miller reported.

"Starboard clear," Morley said, for the record. "Routine."

The last word was not a comment, but an order. At that command the low pressure blower was started. The ten-pound air from the double impeller Roots-type compressor would bring the boat up to full surface trim.

Looking at sea conditions, Morley decided it would be safe to open the main induction before they were fully trimmed up. In a rougher sea, he would wait.

The lookouts now came to the bridge and climbed up to their stations on the bridge overhead. As the main induction opened with a thump, the engines were started, the exhaust boiling out of the submerged mufflers, sending up a smoky spray aft.

•   •   •

"Object in the water," a lookout called. "Broad on the port bow."

Miller raised his binoculars and scanned the water where the lookout had indicated. So did Morley. Something was definitely floating there, its upper surface awash. Something long, black and cylindrical.

"What do you make of it, Larry?" the captain asked. He was already fairly sure of what it was, but reserved his opinion, not wanting to influence Miller's report.

"Looks like a piling, sir," Miller said, after a moment's thought. "I suppose it could have broken loose from a dock."

"I agree. Alter course to close. It's a hazard to navigation, and recovering it should make a good exercise for the crew."

"Aye, aye, sir." Miller glanced at the gyro repeater, then at the chart, which was spread out on the compass platform, the corners weighted down to keep it from being blown away. His finger moved across the chart, tracing a course. He knew these waters well, as did most submariners, and there was deep water between *Bacalao* and the floating object—deep enough, at least.

"Come left to one-niner-six," Miller ordered.

"Come left to one-niner-six, aye," Anderson repeated. "Course is one-niner-six."

"All ahead slow," Miller ordered, speaking into the 7MC. "Control room, keep a good watch on the Fathometer, continuous soundings. Give a warning if the bottom starts to shoal."

The water should be deep enough, but he was sensibly taking no chances. Charts weren't always right.

"Good," Morley said. "Just what I would have done."

"I wouldn't want to run the boat aground on her first trip into open water, sir," Miller said. "That sort of thing can be embarrassing for everyone."

"Agreed. If we *do* look to be getting into shoal water, we'll forget about trying to recover the piling and get on the radio to the Coast Guard. They can come out in a motor lifeboat and tow it back to their station."

Ten minutes later, as *Bacalao* drew closer, it became obvious to everyone on the bridge that the object wasn't a piling, but the top fifteen feet of a telegraph pole, complete with a couple of green glass insulators. It was also obvious that there was plenty of water under the keel as they came alongside.

"One-zero degrees port rudder," Miller ordered. "All back one-third."

The boat turned slightly, the way coming off rapidly as the screws tried to pull her backward.

"All stop."

Bacalao came to a stop parallel to the pole, which floated complacently about twenty feet off the starboard beam.

"Get COB up here," Morley ordered.

In less than a minute, Gordon was on the bridge and had been apprised of the situation. "Easy enough, sir," he said. "We can handle it, no problem."

Going below, Gordon returned shortly with six men, four ten-fathom lengths of half-inch manila line, and a grapnel. One of the men was lugging a big canvas tarp.

"I'll need the starboard engines shut down while we do this, sir," Gordon said.

Miller passed the order as Gordon and his men climbed down the side of the fairwater and headed aft. With the engines stopped, the tarp was draped over the side, the ends secured to cleats, and two fenders were unstowed and dropped down over the ends of the tarp.

The grapnel was secured to the end of a line and heaved out beyond the floating pole. As the line was pulled in across the middle of the pole the grapnel snagged the pole and the men quickly hauled it in, so that the pole was nestled against the side of the boat, which was protected by the tarp.

Looking over the side of the bridge, Miller said, "You know, sir, we could just flood down, get under the thing, and come back up with it on deck."

Morley nodded. "Would you be the one volunteering to stay up here with all the hatches sealed while we maneuver under it, Mr. Miller?"

Miller laughed. "Since I was the one dumb enough to suggest the idea, probably, sir."

By this time Gordon had the pole on deck. He used a simple but effective improvised technique to get it there. Two of the manila lines were made fast to cleats on the port side of the boat, then looped under the floating pole about a quarter of the way in from each end. Three men tailed onto each line and hauled away, rolling the pole up the side and onto the deck, where it was quickly secured.

The tarp, which had protected the paint from damage, was gathered up and taken below, along with the grapnel and three of the four lengths of line. The fourth was used to secure the pole to the deck.

The whole operation took twelve minutes.

•   •   •

When the working party had gone below, Miller put the boat back on course. The sort of things that turned up floating in the ocean never failed to amaze him. In *S-42* they had once come across a nice oak dining room table drifting in the Caribbean. Since a dining room table wouldn't fit through a submarine's hatches—it was a really nice table, obviously hadn't been in the water very long, and would have looked good in the captain's dining room back in Coco Solo—and leaving it where it was presented a potential hazard to navigation, they had used it for target practice. Three shells from the four-inch deck gun had turned the table into harmless kindling.

Morley walked back to his folding seat and picked up his book. "I'll be aboard the *Lydia* if you need me," he said, smiling.

The captain was reading C.S. Forester's *Beat to Quarters*. At least, Miller thought, he *seemed* to be reading it. But he had also noticed that Morley hadn't turned the page more than three times since they left the pier, including the time they were submerged.

The novel was part of a small collection that had started to accumulate on a shelf in the wardroom, along with some others ranged along a shelf in the enlisted mess. That had been Morley's idea. He wanted to build up a ship's library and the rule was that anyone could borrow a book as long as he returned it when he was done.

Currently there were 23 books in the wardroom collection and three dozen more in the enlisted mess. Most of the books were either novels or naval history books. The novels seemed to be most popular at the moment, except with the engine room crew, who appeared to prefer studying Chief Gordon's collection of old *Popular Mechanics* or poring over technical manuals.

Miller figured that at least a third of the crew didn't really have enough spare time for pleasure reading. Any time not spent on their jobs or sleeping needed to be spent making a detailed study of every system in the boat. Submarines were different from other warships. Not only because a submarine could duck under the surface when required, but also because a sailor's rating didn't define the limits of his sphere of knowledge.

Gordon was a good example. He was a Chief Motor Machinist's Mate, which meant that he was a specialist in the care and feeding of internal combustion engines in general, and marine diesels in particular. But a few minutes before Miller had watched him handily directing a crew in getting that derelict telegraph pole aboard, which was really a job for a boatswain's mate. He could also handle diving, surfacing and trimming the boat entirely on his own—no doubt better than Morgan, who was the primary dive officer.

In subs an enlisted man's rating was just a starting point. In order to become fully qualified in submarines, and earn the right to wear embroidered dolphins on his jumper sleeve, he had to be familiar with everything in the boat, and to be able to do any job that was thrown at him. Only in a submarine did a cook have to know how to trace a hydraulic system as well as how to boil a potato.

That even applied to officers. Graduating from the arduous course of study in Submarine School wasn't enough to earn a set of gold dolphins—it took months of service in a sub, and satisfying the XO and captain that you had learned everything you could ever possibly need to know, before you got to pin them on your uniform. Sub School just got you aboard the boat.

Most of the officers had qualified in other subs before coming to *Bacalao*. Miller had earned his dolphins in S-boats, as had Morgan. Morley and Ames had got theirs in even more ancient O-class boats. The two JGs had qualified in early fleet boats. Hartman, who had handled himself so well during their first dive, was a recent Sub School graduate and was still working on his quals.

Hartman's basic job was assistant gunnery and torpedo officer. It was a good place to start a new officer. His initial service in surface ships made him familiar with various types of naval artillery. He would also have learned something about navigation and ship handling. And, since Hartman's earlier service had been in a destroyer, he had naturally learned something about torpedoes. There wasn't that much difference internally between the Mark-14 torpedo used in a fleet boat and the four foot longer Mark-15 found in a destroyer's tubes.

Most of the complexities of submarine operations would have to be learned over time. Preferably, this would be as short a time as possible. When Miller went to his first boat it normally took a year or a little more to qualify. Miller had managed to do it in eight months.

Hartman would probably manage it in six. There was a war coming before long, and everything was happening faster these days.

• • •

Miller stood quietly, keeping out of the way in the forward port corner of the control room, watching the main gyro near the auxiliary steering position. He could hear the helm and engine orders as they were passed down the 7MC, the two-way announcing system that was used when an order required a response. For general announcements the 1MC, which was a simple public address system, was used instead.

Hartman had the deck now, sending down a rapid string of orders as *Bacalao* eased herself up to the pier at the Submarine Base. Miller thought it was interesting that the captain had given the deck officer, himself on the way out, Hartman returning, the conn as the boat left the pier for the first time with this crew, and again as she was brought in. Most captains would have insisted on taking the conn themselves under the circumstances.

But Morley seemed to know what he was doing. He was on the bridge now, no doubt still looking relaxed and oblivious, but ready to take over instantly if needed. He was allowing his officers to handle the boat, getting them used to her eccentricities. After all, once the boat deployed, they would be the ones doing most of the maneuvering.

Captains decided where you were going and how to get there, but they had plenty of other things to keep them occupied, so the OOD was the one who had to keep the boat on course.

It could also be their present location, Miller thought. After a couple years as an instructor there, Morley was no doubt used to letting officers with even *less* experience than Hartman tangle with the tricky currents in the Thames River.

As for Hartman, ship handling was a basic skill for any Navy officer. It was fairly easy in open water, where there was nothing to run into. It was a lot trickier where they were now, for at the base it was not only necessary to maneuver the boat in a confined area but, being in a river, there were currents to contend with.

So far Miller hadn't heard any protests from the captain, so he presumed Hartman was managing this part of the day's test.

After securing the derelict telegraph pole to the after deck, *Bacalao* had continued with her scheduled training. Not too long after that Miller handed over the deck to Morgan, and the boat began the first of two speed runs, her powerful motors pushing her up to 21 knots for half an hour.

While that was going on, Miller had been back in the maneuvering room, keeping an eye on things. Ohara was on the main control, with all four engines on propulsion for the high-speed runs, using the full output of the generators to run the four big motors.

Forward, in the two engine rooms, Orville Hanson, the assistant engineering officer, was watching his own men. Morgan and Hanson were running the engine rooms on what was essentially a combat routine, in exactly the same way in which they were keeping the guns manned. There was always a man at the engine controls, ready to kill the diesels at a moment's notice.

In Miller's opinion, if it came to a war, being able to dive quickly was going to be a lot more useful than being able to hit a plane with a machine-gun.

Their .30-caliber machine-guns were "short range" antiaircraft weapons, as was the water-cooled .50-caliber Browning that could be set up on the forward deck. The way Miller saw it, though, the best short-range antiaircraft weapon was about 100 feet of water covering the upper deck. Shooting it out with a plane was something he thought should be reserved for when there was no other choice, such as being caught in harbor, or where it was too shallow to dive.

It was a lesson the Germans had learned the hard way. Their boats were fitted with much heavier antiaircraft weapons than any American submarine, including quad-20-millimeter and single or double mount 37-millimeter guns, but they didn't hang around on the surface to fight it out unless there was no time to submerge.

At 1600, Hartman relieved Morgan as OOD and *Bacalao* started back to the base.

Miller felt the deck quiver as the boat nudged against the pier, the heavy fenders keeping her from scraping her paint off against the pilings. After a time, while the sounds of shouted orders drifted down from the bridge as the line handlers snugged the boat against the pier, "finished with engines" was rung down from the conning tower and the big diesels rumbled into silence.

A moment later, the eight-cylinder auxiliary engine under the platform deck in the after engine room coughed to life. It's smaller 300-kilowatt generator would power the boat's systems until shore power was connected.

The captain's voice came over the 1MC. "All officers report to the wardroom."

Miller started forward. Behind him, he could hear the click of footsteps on the bridge ladder as the captain and Hartman came down into the conning tower. That was something else that would change before long, with their standard Navy oxfords replaced by soft-soled canvas deck shoes. That had been Morley's idea; he wanted every man aboard to have at least one pair. "You're less likely to slip in deck shoes," he had said. "Also, the canvas will dry faster if it gets wet, and you'll make a lot less noise when you're walking around."

When silent routine was imposed, even little things like shoes could be important, he had emphasized.

Less than a minute later they were all crowded into the wardroom. "Now," the captain said, "let's go over everything that happened today."

He may have been quiet on the bridge, Miller thought, but now it was clear they were about to find exactly what Morley had noticed while he pretended to be occupied with the exploits of Captain Hornblower.

III

Canal Zone

"ALL BACK ONE-THIRD. RUDDER AMIDSHIPS."

"All back one-third," came the reply. "Rudder amidships."

Bacalao slowed rapidly, her two big screws running reversed, trying to pull her astern. On the bridge, Ames was waiting for the proper moment as the way came off the boat.

"All stop," Ames ordered. Then, leaning over the front of the upper bridge, he called, "Let go!"

Forward, there was a brief flurry of activity as a petty officer released the brake band on the windlass, allowing the 2,200-pound anchor, which was hanging just above the water on its cable, to drop. This was instantly followed by the usual horrible din as the cable—actually a 105-fathom length of one-inch* die-lock steel chain—ran out through the fairlead.

After about five minutes, Ames seemed to be satisfied that the anchor was holding. In a surface warship he would have used a flying moor, putting out two anchors, which was more secure. But *Bacalao* had only a single anchor, a standard Navy stockless type, which was stowed on the starboard side of the boat, just forward of the bow plane.

A thousand yards off the port bow, the eastern entrance to the Panama Canal loomed, with the temptations of Colón visible astern. Miller came forward from where he had been standing near the aft TBT. With *Bacalao* now in commission and on her way to join the fleet at Pearl Harbor, Morley was running all of the officers through all watches.

---

* "One inch" was the diameter of the bar stock used to make the chain, not the length of the links. The links were six inches long.

On this particular afternoon, Miller was JOOD on the XO's watch as they came into the anchorage at Limón Bay to await their turn through the Canal.

Ames was on the phone, looking mildly irritated. "Anchored at 1708," he said, looking at Miller.

Miller had to laugh. "Couldn't drag it out for an extra five minutes, huh, sir?"

"Sometimes," Ames said, "circumstances conspire to keep you from cheating no matter how hard you try."

Ames had 1712 in the anchor pool. Just about now, back in the maneuvering room, Fireman 3rd Class Jones would be collecting $65.00 for picking the correct time of anchoring. Low man in the electrical department, Jones could generally be found with his dungarees liberally sprinkled with white acid spots from checking the electrolyte level in the huge battery cells.

Miller hadn't even come close. He had 1930.

"When are we going through?" Miller asked.

Ames shrugged. "I haven't heard yet. It could be a few hours, or a few days."

"So, no ideas about liberty, then?"

"Depends on how long we have to wait, I suppose. You've been down here before, haven't you, Larry?"

"Two years ago. *S-42* was at Coco Solo. I was with her here for six months before going to *S-35* out at Cavite."

"Not a bad place if you're single," Ames said. He was married, and still sufficiently in love with his wife after twelve years of marriage that, if he did go ashore, it would only be the Officers' Club.

Miller was single again, the divorce having been granted just before they left New London. More or less single, at least—there was still the six-month waiting period before it was final.

Miller found his current situation mildly amusing. After being stationed in Coco Solo, he knew all the worst places—including the better class of bar *cum* brothel—where a single officer could pursue the same prey as the enlisted men, though in nicer surroundings and with a somewhat smaller chance of catching anything unpleasant or being hit over the head and rolled. He didn't expect to be visiting any of them. The last time he was here, Claudia had been along, which had been enough to keep him on his best behavior, even though their marriage was already starting to fall apart.

Now he just couldn't see himself running about chasing Panamanian floozies. It was too soon, and there was still the chance of catching something you couldn't cure. A doctor regularly checked out the girls in the better places, but that didn't mean they couldn't become infected between Wassermans.

The 1MC squawked. "Executive Officer, report to the captain's stateroom."

Ames moved toward the ladder. "You have the deck, Larry," he said, heading below.

Miller moved up to the front of the bridge.

The voyage down from New London had been interesting. For most of the passage they had good weather, allowing them to run on the surface at an economical twelve knots.

Each morning they made a trim dive, with Morgan hovering over his men as water was pumped fore and aft between the trim tanks, and his careful calculations of fuel consumption were put to the test. For every gallon of diesel fuel expended from the main tanks the boat became lighter, requiring Morgan to take on extra ballast.

If fuel was drawn from the fuel ballast tanks, though, the boat *gained* weight, for the fuel consumed was lighter than the seawater that replaced it in the tanks. There was a lot of debate in the Navy about those tanks. Fuel ballast tanks added considerably to the boat's range, but they were hard to clean out and a lot more likely to start leaking at the wrong time.

Converting them back to ballast tanks after the fuel was consumed also required that someone go down into the superstructure to remove the blanking plates and reconnect the vent linkage. It was a tedious job under the best of circumstances, and Miller could only imagine what it would be like once the shooting started, bringing with it the distinct possibility that an emergency dive might become necessary while there were men working under the weather deck.

How was a captain supposed to make *that* decision? If he dived, he would almost certainly kill the men trapped under the superstructure. If he *didn't* dive, he might just kill the whole crew in an effort to save three or four men.

It wasn't something a captain needed to worry about in peacetime, but would become a very real possibility once war started. For now, though, most of their risks would come from mechanical failure and the weather.

They had run into some of that on the way south, as they approached Cape Hatteras.

• • •

As *Bacalao* steamed south, bound for her first scheduled port of call at Guantanamo Bay, Morley found himself generally quite pleased with his vessel. The crew was adapting well to a more advanced boat than most had seen before. The XO was keeping the non-quals busy with their studies, and Morley was confident he would have a fully qualified crew sometime in early 1942. He would feel better once he did.

Even the old hands, including the officers, were working on quals, as every boat was a bit different and most originally qualified in older boats. A lot of systems were different in a *Gato*, and they all had to become familiar with them. Just because the officers and experienced men had already earned their dolphins didn't mean they weren't required to stay current.

The noon sight placed them 150 miles northeast of Cape Hatteras, on a southerly course. Seas were moderate, and the boat easily maintained a steady twelve knots.

By 1500, Morley could feel something. The boat was taking the sea differently, with a slight roll starting to be felt. Going onto the bridge it was obvious that something was going to happen. The sky was darker now, and the wind was picking up.

Well ahead, but directly across their course, a literal wall of clouds spanned the horizon. At best, he thought, they were going to get very wet. At worst, they were heading into a major storm. With a wall of black clouds obliterating the horizon it was obvious they couldn't go around it.

Still, they continued to steam as before, the Pitometer log registering a steady 12 knots, and the gyro repeater just as steady on 172°. Morgan had the deck, with Hartman as JOOD. For the moment, Morley decided to stay on the bridge.

At 1620 Ames had taken over the deck and the first drops of rain were starting to fall. The sea was getting up, and Ames suggested turning a few degrees to the southwest to put the bow into the waves. The boat was well off shore, and there should be nothing along that course for them to run into, so Morley agreed.

Feeling confident that Ames could handle things on the bridge, the captain went below.

By 1800 he was back on the bridge. The rain was now coming down in solid sheets, hard enough that the foul weather gear was of little help. Everyone was soaking wet. Conditions were miserable, but Morley felt he should remain on the bridge.

It was now very clear that *Bacalao* didn't like these seas. With each new wave the bow vanished beneath a mass of green water that swept along the weather deck and broke with a hollow crash against the blunt forward face of the fairwater. The boat was pitching and rolling, and reports from below decks were now mostly of men hanging on to anything handy and trying, not always successfully, to keep from throwing up.

It was wetter on the bridge, but the violent motion was easier to take, for on the bridge a man could see what was happening. It made the motion less disturbing. Inside the hull the only visual reference was what your eyes saw as an unmoving compartment, but that your inner ear and your body declared was moving in several directions at once. This conflict between the senses is a major cause of seasickness. If a man can't get used to it—and most can, given a little time—the only cures are lying down with your eyes closed, or getting up on deck, where all of your senses perceive the same thing.

No one was getting topside without a damned good reason, so Morley just hoped there were enough buckets available.

By 2100 everyone had had enough. Morley sent everyone below and followed them down into the conning tower. During the storm the bridge hatch had been kept shut, but a lot of water had still made it below.

The Quartermaster of the Watch spun the wheel and announced that the hatch was secure. Morley went to the 1MC and keyed the microphone.

"Prepare to dive!"

A moment later Morley had descended to the control room, where Morgan was standing by to take the dive. The faces of the men around him said very clearly that getting the boat down into the relative calm of the depths would be a very good idea. He could smell the vomit in the air. There would be a lot of cleaning up to do once they submerged.

The engines were being shut down as Morley's feet touched the control room deck plates. A moment later they had a green board and pressure in the boat.

"Submerge the boat, Mr. Morgan."

"Aye, aye, sir." The engineer keyed the 1MC. "Dive! Dive!"

The klaxon sounded twice and the boat started down. By the time they had passed through 80 feet the motion had smoothed considerably. They initially leveled off at 100 feet, but there was still enough motion that Morley decided to go deeper.

Finally, at 200 feet, the boat was steaming comfortably at four knots. Down there the deck remained steady. The advantage was comfort and safety. A submarine could usually avoid foul weather by submerging, though a really bad storm—a hurricane or Pacific typhoon—could mean going as deep as 300 feet and still feeling some motion.

The disadvantage was that the boat's speed was reduced by two thirds, and they would be able to maintain even that speed for only a few hours.

Morley decided that they would have to surface sometime before sunrise, as he didn't intend to permit the batteries to be drawn down too far. The only enemy they had to face on the surface off North Carolina was the sea itself, and the boat was well able to handle those seas.

But she would handle them better if the men had been fed and managed to keep their meals down long enough to digest them. And, with any luck, the worst of the storm would have passed over by the time they surfaced.

•   •   •

When they surfaced again, after nine hours, there was only a light, steady rain to contend with. The seas had calmed, and they were able to make up some of the lost time by increasing to 15 knots for a few hours.

Once past Hatteras, the rest of the voyage was uneventful. Good weather followed them the rest of the way, and there were two very pleasant days in Guantanamo while *Bacalao* topped off her fuel tanks and took on additional food and stores.

After that, it was southwest across the Caribbean to Cristobal and the eastern entrance to the Panama Canal. In one of those little quirks geography likes to throw at people, this was located several miles to the west of the western entrance.

Looking off to starboard, Miller could see a rusty freighter getting under way, a thick cloud of black coal smoke pouring from her tall, single funnel. The pilot boat had been alongside the freighter at about the time *Bacalao* dropped anchor. Miller thought it would be interesting to know how long the freighter had been waiting. It might provide a clue as to how long their own wait might be.

Ames came back up through the hatch. "Harbor routine," he said. "We'll be here for a while."

"Any idea how long, sir?"

"The pilot is scheduled to come aboard at 0845 tomorrow."

Miller nodded. "Will anyone be getting ashore?"

"If everything on the captain's list is completed, yes." Ames let an evil grin cross his face. "So, probably, no. I'm guessing we'll finish that list about the time we're ready to take on fuel in Balboa."

The Canal transit would be a good time to work on all the projects the captain had laid out, Miller thought. In a new boat there would always be things that needed fixing, even after the extensive builder's trials leading up to commissioning. The captain naturally wanted everything to be as close to perfect as possible. In a sub, even the smallest fault had the potential to kill everyone aboard.

Going through the Panama Canal was one of those times when a minimal crew could work the boat. There was a pilot to do the navigation, and the "mules," the powerful electric locomotives running on tracks on either side of the thousand-foot long locks, would keep the boat centered. All the boat had to do was provide enough power to the screws to slowly move the boat into the lock.

"What's on the list, sir?" Miller asked.

"Oh, there's plenty for everyone, Larry. Some painting topsides, for starters—and the gyro repeater in the captain's stateroom apparently started wandering all over the place a couple hours ago."

The gyro repeaters were electrical, which made them Miller's problem. Or, more precisely, it made them Harrigan's problem, as he was the senior electrician's mate and would take care of the day to day maintenance routine. Despite having an officer in nominal charge of each department, the occupants of the goat locker were the ones who made sure the bulk of the work got done.

Officers signed requisitions, work orders and other paperwork, but the chiefs told them what to sign and, usually, why they needed the thing in the first place.

Miller figured that Harrigan would have Ohara do the actual work. From what he had seen of the man's skills so far, he was now even more certain that Ohara would probably make chief before their deployment to Hawaii was over.

•   •   •

The canal pilot arrived aboard at 0847 by *Bacalao*'s chronometer. By his own watch, he informed them, he was exactly one minute early. Climbing up onto the bridge using the steel rungs welded to the port side of the fairwater, he quickly got things organized.

At 0900 the anchor was broken out and hoisted up from the bay while a seaman played a high pressure hose over the links as they emerged from the water and disappeared up the hawse pipe. The cable was self stowing, and didn't require anyone tending to it down in the cable locker.

"Bring her around to one-eight-four," the pilot ordered. "Keep your speed down to three knots."

Morgan had the deck and passed the order to the helmsman, who immediately acknowledged. Moments later the two great screws began to turn and the boat to gather way, swinging onto the directed course for the canal entrance.

Down in the conning tower and control room a lot of canvas had blossomed during the night. The Torpedo Data Computer, SD radar console and sonar stack were all carefully shrouded, just in case the pilot had any reason to go below.

As the transit would take nine hours, it seemed likely he would need to use the head at some point. A lot of the gear he'd have to pass to get to one was classified, and even if the pilot didn't know what it was, or how it worked—and, being a retired chief boatswain's mate, according to what they'd been told, wasn't exactly likely to be a spy—he still wasn't going to get a look at it.

"I like subs," the pilot said. "No trouble at all getting them through."

"And what do you like the least?" Morley asked.

"Battleships and aircraft carriers," he said, without hesitation. "There's nothing like trying to get a ship centered in a lock when you have only a foot or so on either side to play with. You get one of those bastards through, you figure you've earned your pay."

He looked over the bow. "Come right two degrees."

Morgan passed the order and the bow shifted slightly to starboard.

"Bad engineering," the pilot continued. "When Goethals was building the locks he visited Germany and took a look at the Kiel Canal. He was told there that the minimum practical width for his locks should be the same as theirs, 36 meters, if they were going to be able to handle large warships. Except that the locks here were already being built 33 meters wide."

"That's what," Morgan asked, "about a ten foot difference?"

"About that. I'd like to *have* those extra ten feet, too."

Morley laughed. "You wouldn't get them. The Navy would just build the ships wider. The locks here are what dictate maximum beam as it is."

The pilot merely nodded, with a glum expression on his tanned face that mutely acknowledged the truth in that statement. The Navy probably *would* build wider ships if there were more room in the locks.

•   •   •

As *Bacalao* moved into the Canal, Miller left the bridge and, after collecting a writing pad from his stateroom, went into the wardroom and took a seat at the table. The captain had allowed any off-watch officers who were interested to come up to the bridge as they started the transit, but after a short time Miller figured he was more likely to get in the way than he was to learn anything. He'd been through the Canal more than a few times while he was stationed at Coco Solo.

He got a cup of coffee from a steward's mate and sat down at the wardroom table. Part of his personal routine was to write at least one letter a week to his mother. His wife—ex-wife now—didn't care what happened to him any more, but his mother did.

He picked up the cup with both hands, sipping the hot coffee and gathering his thoughts. The cup was the usual wardroom type, a china teacup, with a blue band just below the rim and a blue anchor on the side. It was one of the things that set officers apart. Most of the crew drank from thick stoneware mugs, made by the Tepco China Company. These were bigger than the usual civilian mugs, and they had no handles. The first time his mother saw one she thought it was some sort of sugar bowl.

The chiefs had similar mugs, but theirs had a handle—they called it a "padeye"—and woe betide any lesser being who was caught using a chief's mug. For a seaman, that was a particularly effective way to volunteer for a few days duty in the galley.

Miller could feel a difference in the boat's motion as they entered the Canal. It was something to write about. He tried to keep his letters home chatty, filling them with all the ordinary events of daily life. At least, the ordinary events he was allowed to talk about.

At the moment, he was writing about the commissioning ceremony. Once again, the most impressive visitor had been the captain's father, this time in uniform. By then Miller had learned more about the elder Morley's career, discovering that it had included service with Dewey at Manila Bay, and command of a destroyer squadron during the World War. He had also been a submariner at a time when the Navy's biggest sub would have just about fit into *Bacalao*'s engine room.

As the commissioning pennant was hoisted, Miller had felt an odd sense of satisfaction. He'd been with the boat from before the time her hull first started to resemble a submarine.

During the whole construction period, as well as during trials, the boat had been just plain *Bacalao*, an expensive piece of equipment that had been ordered by the Navy, but still belonged to the Electric Boat Company. With the hoisting of the commissioning pennant she had become a government warship, a fully functioning unit of the United States Navy, and prefixed "U.S.S." to her name.

Miller wrote down a few more thoughts on the significance of the change that came with commissioning. This sort of thing seemed to fascinate his mother, who still lived in the little apartment on Prospect Avenue where he had grown up.

It hadn't been a bad life for a kid, he thought. Together with three other boys, he had owned a small sailboat, which they had run all over the harbor. They rarely took the boat out past the breakwater, but he'd managed to learn how to shoot a position anyway, and the Sea Scouts had provided the usual training in basic seamanship.

In high school he played baseball, highlighting both his strengths and his weaknesses by playing right field and batting .285 his senior year—good enough to get some nibbles from professional scouts, who were suitably impressed by his batting, but not so much by his fielding. He was the first to admit that, had he been a decent fielder, he wouldn't have spent his entire high school career in right field.

The Indians moved into the newly completed Municipal Stadium the year he finished high school, so he had been able to walk to the home games that year before leaving for Annapolis. Professional football hadn't arrived in Cleveland yet, but he'd been to a few Rams games during his leaves starting in 1937.

As far as the Rams were concerned, he just wondered if they would ever settle down in one place. In their few years as a professional team, they had played their home games at Municipal Stadium, Shaw High School Field, League Park and, finally, moved back to the Stadium.

When he lived in Cleveland, he had seen the military as a way out of life in that vital, but pungent industrial city, where his future—he knew perfectly well he'd never be a good enough fielder to play pro ball—was likely to be limited to working in a shop downtown, at one of the big steel mills, or at the Standard Oil refinery that contributed so much to the distinctive smell of the city. His parents couldn't afford to send him to college, but his academic and sports record was good enough to convince their congressman to give him one of his Naval Academy appointments, and so he had entered the Class of 1935.

He had to smile at that. He had applied on a lark, with no real expectation of getting into any of the service academies. The result was almost enough to make you wonder if the Greeks were right and the Fates really *did* control everything.

•   •   •

As *Bacalao* motored across the broad expanse of Gatún Lake, Miller found himself walking slowly along the length of the forward deck, taking in the rain-filled lake that daily supplied the millions of gallons of water needed to operate the locks. With an average rainfall of over 500 inches, dry weather was mostly a matter of season. According to the pilot, it was now the wet season—in the dry season it only rained a few hours a day, instead of most of the time.

The *Santa Inez* was steaming behind them now. Locking through, the old Colombian coastal steamer had been just astern, her rails lined with passengers looking down on the brand-new American submarine. He had no doubt that there had been a few cameras up there.

There wasn't much on the upper deck that was classified, and anything that was, such as the TBTs, was kept covered during the transit. Miller didn't think that would be much consolation to the captain, who would never feel comfortable knowing that pictures were being taken and might eventually find their way into the wrong hands.

It was just that you could never be sure what a potential enemy would find useful. A good marine engineer could tell a lot about a ship just by looking at pictures. The United States wasn't at war just yet, but it was coming, and pictures could end up in the wrong hands.

Ahead, he could see the clouds building. It wouldn't be long before the brief dry interlude ended and the rain started again. Miller had seen it often enough at Coco Solo.

He started back along the deck, looking at the *Santa Inez* around the fairwater. She was a small, coastal passenger ship, only about 60 feet longer than *Bacalao*, and could probably carry no more than 200 passengers as she plied her route between Cartagena on the Colombia's Atlantic coast and Buenaventura on the Pacific coast. Her two tall funnels were pouring out a lingering cloud of black smoke from her coal fired boilers.

The submariner in Miller couldn't help evaluating her as a target. The smoke would reveal her position at a pretty good distance. With a top speed of about 14 knots, she was slow for a passenger liner, though faster than most freighters.

He decided she might make a tricky target. Her profile was similar to a much larger ship, and a quick periscope observation in poor visibility might result in an inaccurate identification. Wrongly concluding that a 370-foot ship was a 600-footer would almost guarantee a miss.

The usual method of determining range was by using the stadimeter in one of the periscopes. That used the target's masthead height and some simple trigonometry to calculate distance. If the captain overestimated the size of the target it was likely he would also overestimate the masthead height. Since all the stadimeter really did was measure the angle between the waterline and masthead as viewed from the periscope, the same angle would intersect both a 100-foot masthead and a 200-foot masthead, but the 200-foot vertical would intersect the angle at a greater distance. If a firing solution was worked out thinking you were attacking the larger ship, but it was actually the smaller ship, you would presume the target was farther away, set a greater deflection angle, and probably miss ahead.

Miller looked back at the old ship again. Not, he thought, that there was much chance she'd ever be a target. The last time Colombia had been anything close to an enemy was back when Teddy Roosevelt was busy stealing Panama from them.

The first drops started falling as he was climbing the side of the fairwater. Miller had no pressing business on the bridge, so he went directly down the ladder into the conning tower. Pausing only a moment to look around the canvas-shrouded compartment, he crossed to the port side and down the ladder into the control room.

He glanced at the big brass wheels for the diving plane controls, and at the banks of levers for the vent and flood controls, located just forward of the planes controls. Running on the surface, the diving controls were unmanned, though a motor machinist's mate was hovering nearby, keeping an eye on things and ready to start the boat down if the order was given.

That wouldn't happen here, but the watch still had to be kept. For that matter, it was also necessary to watch the controls just to keep anyone from accidentally opening a vent. No matter how well trained a crew might be, you could never be sure what would happen if someone stumbled and grabbed the wrong lever.

The planes operators were both topside, on the bridge overhead, in their alternate role of lookout. They would be the ones getting soaked in the downpour that was now falling. The OOD, and most of the rest of the bridge watch, would have moved to the covered forebridge, out of the weather. Even the Navy didn't make discomfort mandatory if there was no need for it.

Miller nodded to the petty officer and headed aft. As he left the control room he stuck his head into the galley, attracted by the smell of something cooking. "What's on the menu, Niederst?"

"Baked Virginia ham, sir," the head cook replied. "Fresh green beans, mashed potatoes and biscuits, too."

"How much longer do you expect the fresh vegetables to last?"

"Another week, maybe, sir," Niederst replied. "Unless Mr. Hartman can get more for us while we're refueling in Balboa."

In addition to his other duties, Hartman was also commissary and supply officer. It was just another of those jobs that came with being the junior officer in a submarine's wardroom. Big ships had a Supply Corps officer assigned, but Miller couldn't imagine a sub ever wasting the space on an officer whose skills were essentially those of a grocer and dry goods merchant in uniform.

"I'll make sure the captain gives him a nudge," Miller said. They would be on canned food soon enough, but there was no reason to make it happen any sooner than necessary.

The main crew berthing space, in the after battery compartment, was only dimly lit. Even in the middle of the day several of the bunks were occupied, so Miller tried to be as quiet as he could while passing through.

Continuing into the forward engine room he found Morgan, who had turned over the deck to Hartman an hour earlier, looking at his gauges and making notes on a clipboard.

"Everything still working?" Miller asked.

Morgan frowned slightly. "Despite your eternal pessimism," he said, "everything is working just fine."

"So far."

"I don't know why you distrust these engines so much. We haven't had a bit of trouble with them."

"That's what they thought with the first batch—until they all started to break down."

Morgan just shook his head. More than most, he was at heart an engineer, and he loved both the theory and the design concept behind the remarkably compact H.O.R. engines. The design was sound, he insisted. He couldn't help it if the manufacturer had needed some time and experience to get it right.

Miller continued aft, through the after engine room and into the maneuvering room. He moved aft along the narrow passageway on the port side, past the lathe and between the curved inner surface of the pressure hull and the expanded mesh cage that enclosed the main propulsion control, with its mass of high voltage wiring.

Ohara was trying to look relaxed, nestled against the after bulkhead on the red leatherette bench seat, while Fireman 3rd Class Jones, the winner of the anchor pool, operated the main board.

"How are you doing, Jones?" Miller asked.

The young man—he wouldn't even be able to vote for another two years—smiled gamely. "So far, so good, sir," he said.

"He's doing fine, Mr. Miller," Ohara said. His posture didn't exactly agree with his words. He looked as if he was ready to leap for the controls the first time Jones made a wrong move.

His look seemed to say that he had to teach the young ones everything if the Navy was going to make an electrician's mate out of them, but life would much easier if he could just keep the kids busy checking electrolyte levels and leave the controls to people who *already* knew what they were doing.

"What are your power settings, Jones?" Miller asked.

"Number one and two on propulsion, sir. Three and four are on battery charge. Minimal current draw."

"No unusual demands for the moment, sir," Ohara said. "Both batteries are fully charged, so there's just enough current going into them to maintain the charge. We could put all four engines on propulsion if you felt the need."

Miller had to smile at that. Two engines were probably more than was needed. "I don't think we'll be going that fast today," he said.

•   •   •

Miller had the advantage of being able to go below when it started to rain again, Hartman thought, feeling a bit envious. At the moment there were five of them crowded into the surface steering position, so at least they were dry.

This would last as long at it took *Bacalao* to make it across the lake. Once the boat headed into the locks for the descent to the Pacific it would be back to the upper bridge, where they would be able to see the full length of the boat.

They were about halfway across Gatún Lake when the rain started and they all ducked into the forebridge. Hartman felt a little sorry for the lookouts, who had to stay out in the rain while the rest of them could keep dry—at least, for the next dozen miles, until they entered Gaillard Cut. Then at least one officer would have to emerge into the weather.

And, he had to admit, he didn't feel *too* sorry for them. Sailors, officers included, got wet all the time. It came with the job.

• • •

The rain ended as quickly as it began. Looking through the forebridge deadlights, Morley could see a curtain of rain obscuring the southern side of the lake, so they would be running into it again.

"Typical weather," the pilot said, when Hartman commented on the sudden, intense showers.

"It rains here," Morley said. During his career he had spent a total of some six years in the Canal Zone. "And in an S-boat we never had this nice, covered bridge to hide out in. We were all out in the open and just had to take it."

The pilot laughed softly and told Anderson to alter his course four degrees to port. The helmsman was quite good at his job, but his presence had raised some odd questions for Morley. The Navy had strict rules against fraternization between officers and enlisted men, and there were good reasons for them. The rules were a little more relaxed in a submarine, but not that much.

How often, though, did it happen that the captain's crew included a boyhood friend? He'd known Calvin Anderson since grade school. When his father commanded *Holland*, Anderson's father was a chief boatswain's mate in her.

Morley had to be careful with him, but they both came from a Navy background, so it was probably easier for them. The main thing, from the captain's viewpoint, was avoiding any hint of favoritism. Anderson was long past due for promotion to Quartermaster 1st class, but he wondered if he dared promote him?

No one wanted a war, but it often seemed that without one it was nearly impossible to rise. Until the Navy started to expand, faced with the threat of German expansionism in Europe and Japanese empire building in the Far East, advancement was nearly impossible. Virtually the only way for an enlisted man to advance was to transfer to a different ship, where there was a slot in the next higher grade, or for the most senior man in his own ship to leave, allowing those below him to move up.

"Another two hours and we'll be in Gaillard Cut," the pilot said.

"You were in the Navy yourself, right?" Morley asked, mostly to pass the time.

"Thirty-three years, Captain," he responded. "Last duty assignment was as Chief Boatswain in *Texas*."

Morley noticed that he said "boatswain" and not "boatswain's mate," so it appeared he had been given some wrong information. The pilot had been a warrant officer, not a chief petty officer.

"So," Morley said, "battleship sailor, then?"

"Nothing like them," the pilot said, smiling. "A modern battleship is the most powerful weapon ever sent to sea."

Ames grinned. "Well, you know what we always say. There are only two types of ships, right, Skipper?"

"Right, XO. Submarines and targets."

"That's why they put most of the armor on the sides now," the pilot laughed. "And torpedo bulges. We need to keep you guys honest."

"So we'll just blow off your screws and leave you sitting there with nothing to shoot at," Ames said. "We don't have to sink you—we just need to keep you from being able to move around and cause trouble."

• • •

The last of the rain came down in the middle of Miraflores Lock. From that point on it was a pleasant enough trip down to Balboa.

Once there, *Bacalao* anchored out overnight, then moved over to the fueling dock to top off her tanks. There were a lot of miles between Balboa and Honolulu.

Later, submarines passing through the Canal on their way to the Pacific would spend several days off Balboa, training for what lay ahead. At this time, with the war still in the future, they simply took on fuel, got in the proper charts, and prepared for the crossing.

While Morgan was watching the fuel come aboard, Hartman was arranging for a few hundred pounds of fresh vegetables and other local supplies. They would eat well on the voyage, and Niederst would remember that Miller kept his word.

IV
Pacific Transit

THE FOUL WEATHER GEAR WASN'T DOING MUCH GOOD. Miller was soaked right through, and had already concluded that anyone who thought the Pacific Ocean was always warm and pleasant was obviously a fool who'd seen the sun sink slowly in the west as he reluctantly took his leave from Pago Pago in too many South Seas travelogues.

He pulled back his cuff far enough to get a look at his watch. The radium-painted hands informed him that it would be another hour before he could turn the deck over to the XO.

The very fact that the luminous dial was useful said nothing good about the weather, considering it was the middle of the afternoon. The rain was like a solid wall. He could dimly see the outline of the decking over the forward torpedo loading hatch, but *Bacalao*'s bow was invisible from the upper bridge.

Radar would be nice, Miller thought. The boat's SD radar was good only for detecting aircraft in the general vicinity. It was much less likely to warn them that they were about to run into a ship, though. Only the bigger warships had surface search radar. The scientists were supposed to be working on something for subs, but it wasn't there yet.

Just then, it was probably raining too hard for any kind of radar to work very well. They would have to do what every submarine did and rely on the lookouts.

Those poor guys had it even worse, he thought. At least he had something to hide behind, and he could even duck down into the covered forebridge if he wanted to. The lookouts were stuck out in the open, exposed to everything as they scanned the sea from their perches alongside the periscope shears on the bridge overhead.

At least there wasn't much wind, and the rain wasn't too cold. It was coming almost straight down, like a lukewarm shower. A very hard shower. The drops were huge.

By his feet, the conning tower hatch was closed. There was little chance they'd need to dive in a hurry, and it was raining hard enough that every time the boat rolled water would spurt up between the narrow teak planks that made up the bridge deck. There was no sense filling the conning tower with water.

If there had been a war on, they would have kept the hatch latched open and just put up with the water. In that case, the need to clear the bridge as quickly as possible would outweigh any inconvenience.

It had been raining on and off since they left Balboa. The last accurate position had been plotted as they cleared the harbor. That had been four days ago, so at an average speed of 12 knots they should have logged about a thousand miles by now.

Should have. Without being able to see anything but clouds no one could take a noon sight, or shoot the stars at night. Where they *actually* were was nothing more than an educated guess. The Pitometer log told them how fast the boat was moving through the water, and the gyrocompass dutifully reported their heading. Elapsed time gave them a rough distance sailed. Working it all together resulted in a rough position. That was the basis of dead—or, more concisely, 'ded,' contracted from 'deduced'—reckoning.

But the longer *Bacalao* went without taking a proper position the less reliable that became. After four days they could easily be a hundred miles or more from their calculated position. It was a problem that had existed ever since man first learned to use the stars to guide him from place to place. Once out of sight of land, if you couldn't actually see the stars, your position became less precise with each passing day.

Miller looked down at the gyro repeater, mounted on a platform above the closed hatch on the starboard side of the bridge. Besides supporting the compass, the platform also served to shield the open hatch from overhead, and made it less likely someone would fall through it by accident.

The current course was steady at two-seven-five, which was exactly what it was supposed to be.

A steady compass didn't mean the boat was actually on course. The downpour made it difficult to judge movement through the water. There were always currents to consider, so for all Miller could say, at that very moment they might well be making twelve knots forward and two or three sideways.

•   •   •

The lights were on full bright in the forward torpedo room. Chief Torpedoman's Mate John Collins was up to his elbows in the guts of a Mark-14 torpedo. It was an endless process. The fish were checked and lovingly maintained right up to the moment they were slid into the tubes and fired. After that, if they worked right, there would be nothing left to maintain. Just a final entry in the torpedo's log book before turning it in.

"What are you smiling about, Chief?" Marble asked. He was the senior man after Collins, a first class waiting for a chief's slot to open up, and tube captain in the forward torpedo room.

Collins shook his head. "Nothing much, Bob."

He was thinking about the torpedoes, and that he knew something about them that not even the captain was aware of. Before coming to *Bacalao* he had spent three years working at the Torpedo Station at Newport. What he knew was that, if war started, one of the first things to be done was to pull the Mark-5 exploders fitted to the warheads and replace them with the Mark-6 model. The replacements were designed to use the target's magnetic field to detonate the warhead directly under the keel, where it would do the most damage.

The new exploders were so secret that virtually no one in the submarine community even knew they existed. BuOrd had them stocked in the depots now, ready to be installed, but only a handful of men knew anything about the magnetic feature.

Collins wasn't so sure this was a good idea. Even after working on the design at Newport he still had a few doubts. They had conducted tests, naturally, firing torpedoes fitted with instrument packages under target ships and then studying the results.

But there had never been any tests using live warheads. Torpedoes were expensive, and the Navy tried to avoid actually blowing them up. And the one time it looked as if they would be able to do a live test the target came with such ridiculous conditions that it was obvious someone was just denying the request in a more subtle way. They could use the ship as a target, they were told, as long as they repaired and returned it when they were done.

Since the whole idea behind the Mark-6 exploder was to set off the warhead under the target's keel and break it in half—or, at least, break its back—causing it to quickly sink, the live-fire test was dropped. A successful test would have meant destroying the target.

What bothered Collins most, though, was that the captains who would have to use the new exploders knew nothing about them. He was sure by now that the exploders wouldn't be issued before war started. That would help keep them secret, but he thought it would make a lot more sense to let them practice with them first. It just didn't seem wise to go into battle with what was essentially still an experimental weapon.

"You look like you're having a problem with something," Marble said.

"Nah. Just thinking about how good it is to be a torpedoman's mate, with a nice, cushy job down here where it's dry and comfortable instead of being up on deck in the rain."

Marble laughed. "You should probably be glad you didn't make chief a couple months earlier then, huh? Then you'd be senior to Gordon, and that would make you COB and you'd find yourself in all sorts of uncomfortable places."

Collins had to think about that one. "Still," he said, "it might almost be worth it to be able to push Al Gordon around once in a while."

• • •

Gordon wasn't bossing anyone around at the moment, but he wasn't very happy, either. He wasn't nearly as upset as Lieutenant Morgan, though, which was something.

Sam Jenkins, *Bacalao*'s other chief motor machinist's mate, was down under the deckplates inspecting the number three main engine. Jenkins got to do most of the real work in the department. That was a negative aspect of being the most senior chief. Being Chief of the Boat meant that there was less time available to do what Gordon had always thought of as his primary job.

He loved engines—always had.

But not these damned things.

"The compression seal on cylinder six is blown, sir," Jenkins said, looking up at Morgan. It was what he'd suspected and now he'd confirmed it.

Morgan was obviously mad as hell about this, Gordon noticed. The engineering officer might like these overcomplicated, air-gobbling bastards, but *he* wasn't the one who would have to fix the thing.

The double-acting diesels were fine when they worked. The design produced considerably more power than any similar sized conventional diesel. But Gordon had to wonder just what sort of Kraut bastard engineer had thought it was a good idea to have a piston rod running through one end of a combustion chamber. It was nothing but a compression leak looking for a place to happen. And in a diesel, if you lost compression, the cylinder wouldn't fire.

"We're going to have to replace the seal," Jenkins said.

"How long?" Morgan asked.

"Ten hours, maybe, sir. We have to take the cylinder apart to fix it. The seal has to be installed from inside the cylinder."

Morgan shook his head, muttering darkly. "Okay. Get your men to work on it."

"Aye, aye, sir."

Morgan knew he was going to take some flak from Miller. He'd been on him about the engine design being prone to breakdown from the time the boat was still under construction. Now one of them had. Still, Morgan had a good engine room crew, and a pair of experienced chiefs who could be relied on to keep them running.

Jenkins got right to it. Collecting the needed men, he broke out the metric tools and set his crew to work dismantling the cylinder. In order to replace the compression seal they had to remove the piston, which was rigidly attached to the top of the piston rod.

In the H.O.R. design, the highly-polished round piston rod moved vertically in a fixed path, and did not wobble from one side to the other as in most engines. Below the cylinder, the piston rod's crosshead ran up and down a pair of guides, similar to those on a steam engine. The crosshead, in turn, was linked to another, more conventional connecting rod, which turned the crankshaft, converting the up and down motion of the piston into the rotary motion required to drive the generator.

After removing the top section of the cylinder, Jenkins and his crew disconnected the piston rod at the crosshead and hoisted the piston, with the rod attached, out of the cylinder. When that was done, one of them cleaned out the stuffing box in the bottom of the double-ended cylinder and installed a new compression seal.

The piston and rod were then lowered back into the cylinder and the rod passed through the stuffing box. It would take nearly nine hours to get everything broken down and reassembled.

"A harbinger of things to come?" Miller asked, coming back to the engine room after handing the deck over to Ames.

"An isolated problem," Morgan said. From what he'd seen so far, he was fairly sure that was the case. The engines had all performed flawlessly up to this point.

Miller just smiled. "That's probably what they said the last time—up to the point where everything started breaking down."

"All engines break down from time to time, Larry. The engine in your *car* isn't 100% reliable, either, is it?"

"If my car breaks down, it doesn't leave me stranded a couple thousand miles from the nearest help."

"Which," Morgan pointed out, "is one reason we have four main engines and an auxiliary. You don't expect them *all* to quit working at the same time, do you?"

"I'm not going to discount the possibility, Bill. Things break. And I've seen two more conventional diesels quit at the same time, which was pretty inconvenient, since two were all we had."

Morgan nodded, looking down into the empty cylinder. He was sweating. Both of the engines were shut down, but it was still over 90° in the after engine room. The air conditioning didn't help much back there.

Morgan had closed the inboard induction valve in the forward engine room and left it open in the after engine room. He had then closed the watertight door between the forward engine room and the after battery. The two forward engines then had to draw their air from the after part of the boat. Since the after induction was open, the engines drew from it, which at least kept the air circulating in the compartment.

Curiously, the engine room temperature normally rose fastest just after the engines were shut down. With the engines off, the coolant stopped circulating, so the engines radiated all of their heat into the engine room. The temperature could get as high as 130° just after submerging.

"How long do you figure before you have this thing put back together?" Miller asked.

"Two or three hours, at least."

The look that answer elicited from Jenkins suggested that he thought Morgan was being wildly optimistic.

"Well," Miller said, "I presume you'll have everything fixed by the time I take over again at midnight. Meanwhile, I'm going to get something to eat and catch some sleep."

"I'll try not to wake you."

• • •

The sky finally cleared about an hour after dawn. Noon found three officers on the bridge, sextants in hand. The captain's sight would be the official one, though he would compare his result with those Miller and Hartman worked out.

As it happened, all three results were within a one mile circle. *Bacalao* hadn't done as badly as Miller had suspected, despite the continuous rain. The noon position was 46 miles north of their dead reckoning position, but also eight miles farther west than they had expected. They were on course, and would probably arrive in Hawaii on the 29th, right on schedule.

V
Exercises

THE FIRST FEW DAYS AFTER *BACALAO*'S ARRIVAL AT PEARL HARBOR were spent taking care of the minor problems that had shown up during the crossing from Balboa. There has never been any vessel that didn't exhibit a few problems early on, from the lowliest dugout canoe to the most sophisticated warship ever built.

There was no vessel more sophisticated than a modern submarine.

To be fair to the people at Hooven-Owens-Rentschler, Miller thought, there had been no more engine problems once the compression seal on engine three was replaced. He also had to admit that it said a lot about the engine room crew that they were able to do the job at sea. On a routine crossing, no one would have said too much if they had decided to run on three engines and leave the repairs to the yard people at Pearl Harbor.

Most of the other problems were easier to deal with. The captain's gyro repeater had started acting up again, and Ohara had spent half a day tracing down the problem and getting it corrected. The problem turned out to be in the circuitry in the master gyro, which was sending an erratic signal to the captain's repeater. The fact that there had been a problem in the repeater itself, which had been fixed back in Panama, had hidden the root problem.

It was something to think about. Just because you find something broken doesn't mean there isn't something else wrong, too. At the time, Miller had no idea just how important that particular principle would be in the coming months, or how thoroughly a lot of people who should have paid it attention would ignore it.

•   •   •

With everything fixed, Morley collected all of his officers in the wardroom just after supper. "We're going to play with a couple of tin cans tomorrow," he informed them. "There will be a pair of destroyers off Lahaina in the morning. Our job is to sink them and their job is to sink us."

"Who are we supposed to be in this?" Ames asked.

"In this exercise, we will be playing the part of a Japanese submarine, defending against an invasion force."

This came as no surprise. The Germans didn't have boats with the range to operate effectively in the Pacific. And, while indications were that the Japanese didn't really want to fight the United States, they were still the most likely enemy.

The American government had imposed an oil embargo on Japan in an effort to send a message that they should stop what they were doing in China. They didn't seem to be listening. Miller's feeling was that all the embargo had accomplished was to get them mad. He presumed that was the logic behind this exercise.

To the good, they were safely in Hawaii if the Japanese ever did decide to start something. He would have been more worried if they had been assigned to the Asiatic Fleet in the Philippines. Hawaii was too far away from Japan for them to attack. They could get to the Philippines easily enough, though.

"What's the plan?" Ames asked.

"It's simple enough. We are to find and attack an 'enemy' scouting force, sometime after sunrise. The plan leaves the exact time for the attack to us, of course."

Naturally. It was hardly practical to schedule the attack portion of an exercise at an exact time—that sort of thing tended to give the defense a bit too much an advantage.

"According to the plan," Morley continued, "*Bacalao* is to attack sometime between 0800 and 1100. I imagine the destroyers will be expecting us either just after 0800, when the sun is still low, or just before 1100, when their lookouts are most likely to be getting tired.

"So we'll go in around 0945." The captain smiled. "Given the choice, mind you, I'd prefer to sneak up on them around 0630."

"Before the exercise has actually started?" Ames asked.

"You think a real enemy is going to pay attention to our schedule? Let's face it, Fred, submarines aren't designed to stand in the line of battle and slug it out, no matter what some theorists may have thought back in the 1920s. We're a bunch of sneaky bastards and we'll take every chance to cheat that we can. It's the only way you can win if the odds are all in the other guy's favor."

Nothing at all wrong with cheating if it gave you an edge, Miller thought. The captain was right about that. Submarines were just too vulnerable to play fair.

"Attack plan?" Ames inquired.

"Submerged approach, naturally. There's no real option on that. We can't sneak up on them if we're on the surface where they can see us. And one of them has radar, so even if it was dark we'd still have to go in submerged."

"Sonar or periscope?"

"We'll decide that once we get a better idea of the tactical situation as it develops."

"It would improve our chances of a hit if we use the periscope."

Morley nodded. "I agree. The question is, do we want to risk it? We'll be going in during daylight. If anyone sees the periscope and comes after us the destroyers will win."

"Do you think that's very realistic, sir?" Miller asked. "Our British friends certainly aren't killing every U-boat they detect, and they have a lot more experience than our cans."

"Well, Larry, you have to remember that the referees in the exercise are probably going to be destroyer men, not submariners. They may just be a little prejudiced."

"I agree with Larry, though," Ames said. "It's as foolish to presume that the moment a destroyer gets a sonar paint on a sub it means the sub is going to be killed as it is to presume that we'll get a hit with every single torpedo we fire."

The captain stood up and rapped on the counter at the forward end of the wardroom. A moment later Weston's face appeared in the pass through from the officers' pantry.

"Sir?"

"Coffee, please."

"Aye, aye, sir." Weston disappeared for a moment, then passed a half-filled cup of coffee through to the captain and closed the pass through. Miller figured that Weston and the other steward's mates heard everything even with it closed.

He was equally sure that they'd never tell anyone what they heard. They had it too good there. Even though the Navy only allowed black sailors to serve as steward's mates or cooks, everyone who served in a submarine had to qualify, which meant that even a steward's mate had to learn every system in the boat. Unless the Navy changed its mind about where they could serve, a sub was about as close as a black, Filipino, or Guamanian sailor was ever going to get to general service.

The captain returned to the table with his coffee. "We'll cast off at 0600, gentlemen," he announced. "I'll be staying aboard tonight."

Most nights Morley slept in his rented house in Honolulu, where his wife and children had been waiting for him when *Bacalao* arrived. They had come out by liner from San Francisco, leaving New London on the same day the boat departed. As they had crossed the country by train, and taken a fast liner for the Pacific crossing, they had been in Hawaii and getting settled into the house by the time *Bacalao* departed Balboa.

The XO's wife had come out on the same ship. Ames had no children, and the house near the Pearl Harbor Naval Base belonged to his wife, who had been born in it.

•   •   •

Bacalao cast off from where she was nested outboard *Argonaut* at 0614 the next morning, exactly one hour before sunrise, and made her way out of the submarine base. Turning to port, they steamed through Southeast Loch toward the channel. Over the starboard quarter, Ames could see the dim shapes of the big ships moored along Battleship Row. The fleet was in port, with the big battleships moored in double rows, and the boxlike shapes of the carriers beyond.

They would see no more of them that day. The two new destroyers they would be working with had departed just before midnight, and by now would be patrolling off Lahaina, their captains no doubt wondering just when the submarine would appear. They knew the limits imposed by the operation orders, that *Bacalao* could attack no earlier than 0800, nor later than 1100. Beyond that rough timetable, though, the initiative was entirely with the submarine.

During the evening, Ames had spent a couple hours in the captain's stateroom as they hashed over the advantages and hazards of using the periscope in simulated attacks. Navy policy was quite clear on the subject. Because of improvements in sound gear during the last 20 years, and the obvious risk of a periscope being spotted by a lookout—or, even more dangerously, by a bomber—the preferred method was to attack from a depth of about 100 feet, using sound bearings and ranges to set up the attack.

There were clearly some advantages. A single sonar ping gave a much more accurate range than a periscope's stadimeter, which needed both an exactly masthead height setting, and a fair amount of operator skill for an accurate range. But it was a lot harder to work out the angle on the bow with sonar and hydrophones. The same was true when it came to determining the target's course.

Ames favored the periscope. The Type 1 attack periscope installed in the conning tower had a head less than two inches in diameter. An even thinner version was being tested. He doubted that spotting one of these slender tubes was as easy as the brass seemed to think.

In the end, the captain had left it up in the air, saying that he would decide what to do when the time came. Ames wasn't too worried about that. Morley had always been one for making decisions at the last minute. It didn't mean that he hadn't considered the problem from every possible angle. It was more a matter of wanting to act only after the last bit of information was obtained, so that the final decision was based on the facts as they existed at the time and not on prior speculation.

They reached their planned diving position about an hour before Morley intended to attack. The targets would be a pair of the latest *Sims* class destroyers. And both were radar-equipped, not just one, as they had initially thought. Only a submerged approach offered any hope of success.

Ultimately, they were serving two masters, which wasn't at all unusual in these exercises. The primary task, according to the staff officers planning the exercise, was to give the destroyers some practice hunting submarines.

At the same time, Commander, Submarines, Scouting Force, Rear Admiral Thomas Withers, had made it clear that he expected his newest and most modern boat to administratively "sink" at least one of the destroyers before they managed to "kill" the sub. Just because the destroyers were supposed to win didn't mean they had to make it easy for them.

They were steaming between Molokai and Lanai. In a real combat situation this would probably be an unacceptable risk. Someone ashore might spot the boat and radio a warning. That wasn't a worry in this case, as the exercise presumed the destroyers were part of an invasion force. *Bacalao* was in "friendly" waters.

"So who *are* we supposed to be, anyway?" Ames asked, when the captain came onto the bridge for a last look around before diving.

"Our orders are a little vague. We're a Jap sub, defending some island or other."

"Do you think we'll actually end up in a war?"

The captain looked out across the port bulwark toward Molokai. "I think we're already in a war. They just haven't got around to declaring it yet."

"That's in the Atlantic with the Germans, though, Skipper. I'm more worried about the Japs just now. We're in the Pacific and the Krauts really can't get at us here. The Japs can."

"We're not going to start anything," Morley said. "I don't think the President wants to fight two wars at once and he's obviously set on helping out the British."

Ames heard a faint sound and, looking up, saw the number one periscope move slightly. Miller would be down in the conning tower, scanning well ahead with the 'scope set on high power. The extra height would let him see several miles farther than the bridge lookouts.

A moment later the 7MC squawked. "Bridge—conn. Enemy in sight."

"Bridge, aye." Morley responded, then switched to the 1MC. "Prepare to dive. Clear the bridge."

"Enemy?"

The captain smiled, watching as the lookouts tumbled down from the bridge overhead and dropped through the hatch. "May as well keep it as real as we can, huh?"

"Yes, sir."

Morley started for the hatch. "Dive the boat, XO."

As the captain dropped down the hatch, Ames and Paul were left alone on the bridge. Ames keyed the microphone. "Dive! Dive!" An instant later he sounded two blasts on the bridge diving alarm and headed below. Paul, as Quartermaster of the Watch, was the last man down, pulling the hatch shut behind him and dogging it tight.

"Stop main engines," Morgan ordered, his voice coming up through the hatch from the control room. "Ahead two-thirds."

Ames felt the usual pressure in his ears as compressed air was bled into the boat to test for watertight integrity.

"Pressure in the boat, sir. Holding."

"Open all main vents. Two-two degree dive on bow planes."

The needle on the conning tower depth gauge began to move as the deck angled down.

•   •   •

It took just over an hour for *Bacalao* to work her way into what the captain thought would be a favorable position. The two destroyers were far enough off shore that the boat was able to slip between them and

Maui. They would be able to attack from landward. The water wasn't as deep on that side—though it was still deep enough—and the captain hoped the "enemy" would take that into account and perhaps be less alert on that quarter. The land behind them might also make it a little harder to see a periscope.

Miller was at his normal position in the after port corner of the conning tower, in front of the Torpedo Data Computer. Morley was standing by the number two periscope, which it appeared he had decided to use, while the XO was at the little chart table tucked in just abaft the bridge ladder on the starboard side.

Miller's mind was working on their chances. It was odd, when you thought about it, for the likelihood of being detected and "sunk" in an exercise was probably greater than in combat. That pair of destroyers out there had a distinct advantage over a real enemy—they knew for sure there was a submarine in the area, and that it would have to attack during a specific time period on this particular day.

Assuming they were careful enough, in actual combat a real enemy wouldn't know they were even around until after the first torpedo was fired.

So it seemed logical that, even if a real enemy had a lot more to lose from being hit by a live torpedo, it was also far more likely that his lookouts wouldn't be as alert. Days on end of staring out at a monotonous expanse of ocean, looking for an enemy who had so far not appeared, would naturally dull the senses.

On the destroyers it would be easier to stress extra vigilance during the exercise. They already knew the boat was there, and they knew it had to attack before 1100. They also knew how American submarines operated.

"That's one of the things I'm counting on," Morley said, after Miller mentioned this. "They'll be expecting us to attack on sound bearings, and that means we'd need to use our active sonar to get a range. So if we use the periscope, listening for our sonar isn't going to help them very much."

"You have no idea how long I had to plead with him before he came around to that realization," Ames chimed in.

Morley laughed. "I came to that decision on my own, right after we caught the assignment. But I have to hew the Navy line, don't I? There are two things every officer needs to know about dealing with his commanding officer. The first is that part of his job is to offer his captain all the options he can think of, and to support them as fully and passionately as he can. The second is that, once the captain makes his decision, that decision is final."

"No second guessing, huh?" Ames said.

"That's for the endorsement on the after action report. And someone who spent the entire battle sitting in an office back at headquarters will write that."

Ames picked up the phone at the chart table and spoke briefly, looked at his watch, nodded quickly, and made a notation on the chart. He would have been talking to Morgan, who was down in the control room. The main chart table down there had an automatic dead reckoning plotter, which did a pretty good job of keeping track of where they were over the course of a couple hours.

"We should be getting pretty close, Captain," he said.

"Jones? What have you got?"

The sonar operator looked up. "Two targets at zero-two-five," he said. "Sound like destroyers."

"Range? Best estimate."

"About two-thousand."

"Come right to one-niner-five," Morley said.

"Come right to one-niner-five, aye," Anderson repeated.

So the captain was going to start by steaming straight at the waiting destroyers, Miller thought. It was logical. A straight-in approach would create the smallest possible amount of visible spray when the periscope was extended.

"Steadying up on one-five-niner, sir," Anderson reported.

"Mr. Morgan," the captain called down the ladder, "Make your depth six-four feet."

"Make my depth six-four feet, aye, sir."

Miller could see the needle moving up on the conning tower depth gauge. Half a minute later it steadied at 64 feet.

"Up 'scope," Morley ordered, stooping to meet it as it rose from the well and snapping down the knurled brass handles. He was looking through it as the head broke through the surface. "Stop," he snapped, still bent over, with no more than a foot of periscope exposed.

"Got them," he said. "Target bearing—mark!"

"Zero-one-two."

Morley twisted the stadimeter crank. Knowing what he would be shooting at helped. The masthead height of a *Sims* was known to the foot, and already dialed in. "Range—mark!"

"One-two-zero-zero."

"Down 'scope."

That was the first observation. They would need to make several more before firing.

"Angle on the bow is starboard three-five," Morley added. He didn't need to be looking through the periscope to report that. The angle on the bow was entirely a matter of his own judgment, and not something that was read off an azimuth ring or stadimeter dial, like bearing and range.

Miller cranked the readings into the TDC and set the complex system to work on the problem. Angle on the bow was one of those things the movies always seemed to get wrong—mostly, it seemed, they tended to confuse it with target bearing. Miller thought that made them about half right. What a submarine called angle on the bow was exactly what a lookout on the target would call target bearing if he was shooting at the sub. The British called it "reverse angle," which seemed a little clearer.

The TDC was whirring softly as the dials on the angle solver and position keeper slowly rotated. They had a full load of six practice torpedoes in the forward nest, and as the TDC worked on a solution it would automatically update the gyro angles as long as the spindles were inserted and the Gyro Setting Indicator-Regulators were on automatic.

After about five minutes, the captain cautiously raised the periscope again. As the bearing and range were reported, Miller cranked them into the TDC, replacing the original set of bearings and angles and, in the process, refining the targeting solution.

By now Jones had come up with an estimated target speed of 12 knots. He did this by counting propeller revolutions. Again, knowing exactly what they were shooting at made for an easy estimate. The propeller pitch of a *Sims* was known. That wouldn't be the case with an enemy ship.

At the conning tower chart table, Ames made a notation on the chart. He had an Is-Was hanging around his neck on a lanyard, and was working on the same solution. Like all military services, the Navy was quick to adopt modern technology, but slow to put all their faith in it. The old Is-Was, a circular slide rule used for working out firing angles, would remain as a backup for some time.

Five minutes later, Morley put up the periscope for a final observation. Three should be sufficient to put the torpedoes on target, presuming that the "enemy" cooperated and didn't make any radical course changes while they were tracking them. If they did, the sub would have to make additional observations and enter them into the TDC until they again had an accurate firing solution.

"Target bearing—mark!"

"Zero-zero-five."

"Range—mark!"

"Niner-zero-five."

"Down 'scope. Angle on the bow is starboard three-zero."

Miller cranked in the new data. After the TDC had worked on it for another couple minutes the solution light came on. "We have a firing solution," he informed the captain.

"Stand by tubes one and two," Morley ordered.

•   •   •

It had taken two hours to make the attack. Now everything had gone to hell in no more than five minutes. Putting up the periscope for a final observation, Morley gave the order to fire tubes one and two. The fish were sent on their way, exactly ten seconds apart.

These were exercise torpedoes, and were set to run at 25 feet. If they had done everything correctly, the torpedoes would pass directly under the leading destroyer. Once that happened, *Bacalao* would have "sunk" the target, after which the destroyer would miraculously come back to life and join his partner in hunting the submarine.

But as the second torpedo left the tube Morley could see the water above the bow erupt in a huge gout of foam, which would surely be visible from the nearest destroyer, less than a thousand yards away.

"Down 'scope!" Morley snapped. "Take her down to one-five-zero. Hard right, new course two-four-zero, ahead full."

The last thing Morley saw as the periscope started down into the well was the forward gun mount on the second destroyer training in their direction, and her bow wave increasing as her captain put on more power and started to turn toward them.

There was no doubt he had seen them.

"What's going on?" Ames asked.

"Somebody screwed up. It looks like the whole impulse charge blew right out the front of the tube. They saw it—no question."

Jones was working his controls, trying hard to keep the "enemy" fixed in the sonic gear.

"They're turning toward us," he said. "Both targets have increased speed and gone active."

"What's happening to our fish?"

"Still on course, but the destroyers have turned out of the way. The fish will pass them well to starboard."

"Steady on course," Anderson reported.

"Reduce to both ahead, dead slow," Morley ordered. They were making too much noise at this speed. With any luck, their course change had thrown off the destroyers. Now they had to keep them in ignorance, try to slip away and return from an unexpected direction. They still had four exercise torpedoes in their bow tubes. He wanted to fire them.

Tommy Withers is going to murder me, Morley thought. Letting the boat give away her position by blowing air out of a torpedo tube was *not* something he was likely to forget, even if he could go back and "sink" *both* tin cans.

"Sinking" them would help, though.

•   •   •

Chief Torpedoman's Mate John Collins' first thought was that the captain was going to kill him. His department had just blown it, in a very literal sense. He recognized that Lieutenant Winston was the one who would catch it from the captain, as he was gunnery and torpedo officer, but that wouldn't help Collins that much. Winston was perfectly aware that his position as department head mostly meant that he was there to sign things, and that Collins, like the other chiefs, was the one who really ran it.

In the Navy, fault worked its way up. Collins imagined the problem would eventually be traced to one of the strikers in the forward torpedo room who had turned the wrong valve or operated the wrong lever and, in the process, sent a big bubble of air out the muzzle door. Not that it would matter. He would chew the kid out, but he would also be the one who took the blame for not properly supervising him.

In turn, since Winston was gunnery and torpedo officer, he'd have to take responsibility for all this happening. He should have made sure there were no problems, and that each level of his department was properly supervising the next lower level.

And, finally, the captain would roast Winston's butt over a slow fire, which would be nothing to what Admiral Withers would do to *him*. That genial looking old man in his office at the Submarine Base was no more tolerant of failure than any other rear admiral. And the captain of a ship was *always* responsible for anything that happened in his command.

While Collins was thinking about this, he got on the growler phone to the forward torpedo room. "Bob," he asked, "what the hell just happened?"

"My fault, sir," Marble said. "I wasn't watching Morton close enough. He pressurized the impulse tank to 550 pounds. That was just too much for the poppet valve to scavenge at this depth."

The proper impulse charge for firing a torpedo at periscope depth was 300 pounds. So the young Seaman Second—who, Collins was now fairly sure, wasn't going to be making Seaman First anytime soon—had fired the torpedo with an impulse pressure appropriate for more than twice their current depth.

"I presume you'll teach him the error of his ways?"

"Count on it, Chief." His tone of voice made it obvious that he was going to make it *very* clear to Morton just how much he'd screwed up. It was the sort of thing that could get everyone aboard killed if it happened in battle.

Since Marble knew that Collins would be coming down on his own head for *allowing* Morton to screw up, and this could affect his own chances of making chief—he was mostly just waiting for a slot to open up, as it happened—his explanation was likely to be somewhat energetic.

•   •   •

Bacalao returned from the exercise in mid-afternoon, with a palpable sense of embarrassment among the crew. Despite their best efforts, the destroyers had found them a half hour after the abortive attack. They had been subjected to a prolonged depth charging—using small noisemakers, like big firecrackers, as the tin cans didn't want to actually sink them.

Finally, after they had been thoroughly "sunk," they surfaced and spent the best part of an hour recovering their practice torpedoes. Those were now tied down on the forward deck, and would shortly be offloaded and carted off to the torpedo shop for servicing.

The captain was far from happy. Both torpedoes had missed by a wide margin. The mishap with the torpedo tube had been spotted by several lookouts, which gave the destroyers plenty of time to take evasive action and then start hunting.

It did the officers no good to point out that a *real* enemy wouldn't have already known they were already around, and might even have missed the air bubble. The destroyers' lookouts knew they were there.

"Yes," Morley said, "they knew we were there. And if we get into a war and are attacking an enemy convoy you can be damned sure his escorts will also know we're around once we start shooting. I'm not so concerned that they caught us firing. What *did* upset me was that they managed to pin us down and drop all those damned firecrackers on our deck!"

Well, there wasn't much to say after that, Miller thought. Nothing to do, either, but get back to the Submarine Base at Pearl Harbor and wait for the figurative storm clouds to subside. It was obvious what was really wrong. Not only was there the embarrassment of being caught out—even if the main purpose of the exercise was to train the destroyers, which more or less suggested that they were supposed to find the sub—but the torpedo tube incident had happened at periscope depth.

Even if none of the destroyers' lookouts had spotted their periscope, the fact that they had fired at 64 feet would tell the Admiral that they had been using the 'scope during daylight.

You were supposed to keep the periscope down in daylight. Sticking it up for target practice in Long Island Sound, when you were practicing periscope shoots, was one thing. Letting your 'scope be spotted during an antisubmarine exercise was entirely different.

Sure enough, within ten minutes of tying up, Morley was summoned to headquarters, leaving the rest of them to supervise the complexities of connecting to shore power, hooking up the phone lines, and generally taking care of all the hundreds of tasks that had to be performed once the boat sidled up to her mooring outboard *Argonaut*.

That boat loomed next to them like some sort of prehistoric monster, dwarfing their own boat, which the crew tended to think of as a pretty big submarine. Still, the huge mine layer looked to be a friendly enough sort of monster, judging by the little boy who was standing on the forward gun platform, watching a gunner's mate as he worked on the recoil mechanism of the forward six-inch gun. Idly, Miller wondered who the kid might belong to, then went back to pacing the bridge.

His heart, now officially single again, was in Honolulu, happily engaged in hunting for some lovely young woman who wanted to make a newly-divorced Navy lieutenant feel good about his enforced solitude. His body, though, had the duty and was stuck on the boat.

Looking down at the forward deck, he saw Ohara, now dressed in his best white uniform, crossing the brow and passing across *Argonaut* on his way to the pier. He wouldn't be due back aboard until noon the next day, having earned some local leave for his adept handling of a simulated electrical emergency during the exercise.

He was probably going off to chase girls, Miller thought. It appeared he was in a good place for it. Honolulu had a huge Japanese population, and Ohara was a tall, good-looking guy with both an education and a good start on a career. You didn't get rich in the Navy, but it paid a man a decent living, and there wasn't all that much to spend it on while at sea. Miller figured Ohara would make a good catch for some local girl.

So would he, Miller thought, now that he was available again. Any girl who hooked up with him would never have to worry about him beating her, for one thing. After all, if he had never hit Claudia, well, anyone would be safe.

•   •   •

The next two weeks were mostly taken up by routine. Boats entered and left the Submarine Base as duty required. *Argonaut* had departed to patrol off Midway. Miller found it hard not to speculate on what would happen to that giant sub if war actually came to the Pacific.

She was the only purpose-built mine-laying submarine in the American fleet, and much larger than any other boat, with a formidable armament of two 6"/53 caliber deck guns, two mine tubes in the stern, and four torpedo tubes in the bow. But she was also slow and hard to maneuver, and couldn't safely dive below 200 feet. It was hard to get past the impression that, should she ever encounter enemy antisubmarine units, her crew might as well paint a big target on her upper deck and start the funeral service.

Bacalao had spent the last week alternately exercising and making good each small deficiency as it was discovered. There had been no more embarrassing incidents, at least, and the last time out they had managed to administratively "sink" a pair of older destroyers.

That had been that afternoon, on a Saturday. But after that success they had returned to Pearl Harbor with a drop light lashed to the sternlight stanchion. The sternlight itself refused to light.

After they tied up, getting the light fixed was added to the list of minor problems Harrigan had lined up for Ohara first thing in the morning.

VI
Sunday Morning

OHARA HAD THE STERNLIGHT TORN DOWN as the day was still dawning. If he could finish up early he would have the rest of the day to himself. Touching a circuit tester probe to a wire, he wondered if that really mattered. Last night had just been one more in a series of disasters.

On an island where a very high proportion of the population was Japanese, he was having just about zero luck with women. Hell, he thought, the white boys were doing better with them, which was *really* frustrating.

A lot of it was his own upbringing, he was sure. He *looked* Japanese, but that was as far as it went. Culturally, he was a Southerner. The local girls were much closer to their ethnic roots. One or both of their parents might well have been born in Japan, and the local community, while adamantly American in most ways, was also very stubborn about holding on to its Japanese culture and language.

His family wasn't like that. When his great-grandfather came to California in the 1860s, he wasn't thinking about making a quick fortune and then going back home. The family had been Christian—or, at least, Roman Catholic, which Ohara, a Southern Baptist, wasn't entirely sure really counted—even back in those days, so "home" hadn't been all that friendly a place. Great-grandpa came to America because he heard it was a place where he could follow his faith without being considered some sort of subversive for doing so.

When his children were born he insisted they speak only English. They were raised with the notion that their heroes should be the same men who were revered by their white neighbors. Men like George Washington, Thomas Jefferson, Ben Franklin, Robert E. Lee and Jefferson

Davis—but *not* Abe Lincoln. It had been that way for four generations now, so if they differed from their neighbors back in Atlanta it was mostly in not sharing their disdain for the coloreds in that city. There were only a couple hundred Japanese in the entire state, but that was still enough to generate some anti-Asian sentiment and make the idea of looking down on anyone else just a little distasteful.

But the local Hawaiian girls didn't seem to have any particular problem with looking down on *him*. They found the way he talked to verge on the hilarious—particularly when he mentioned his family name, which they all insisted he was butchering terribly. One thing was sure—none of them wanted to take him home to meet her parents.

His mother had her own ideas on that subject. She thought he should marry Elizabeth Yamada, his father's business partner's younger daughter. He couldn't see it. It had been some time since he'd seen Liz, but he still remembered her. Mostly, he remembered an annoying little junior high school girl. She would be older by now, but he found it hard to imagine there had been all that much improvement in the last two years.

•   •   •

Miller came up onto the bridge at 0745 to relieve Hartman. It was a little early, which Hartman mentioned with obvious gratitude. He had a girl in town and was planning to spend the day with her. An early relief would give him time to change and grab a taxi outside the gate.

"It's been a quiet watch," Hartman reported. "Ohara is back aft, working on the sternlight. Otherwise, not much to report."

Hartman went below to change. He slowly paced the length of the bridge, pausing to look down over the cigarette deck bulwark, to where Ohara had the sternlight taken to pieces.

Looking out over the anchorage, he was again impressed by the aura of solid power presented by the massive warships moored along Battleship Row. He couldn't really see the ships, but their upperworks were visible and conveyed a sense of the massive ships that lay behind the point. In the rapidly gathering light the lagoon and anchorage looked serene.

This was a time when he could really enjoy himself. The captain was ashore, now well settled into his big rented house with his wife and kids. He would be along at about 0900, so he was probably still sleeping. Ames was aboard, but still asleep in his stateroom. For the moment, Miller got to be in charge.

Miller found himself envying Hartman. He had met a girl the first day he went into Honolulu, and even seemed to be getting serious about her. She was a nurse at a local civilian hospital, and came from a good family in the cattle business. The last part had surprised Miller—he was inclined to associate cowboys with Texas, not Hawaii.

Miller wasn't having much luck in Honolulu. He knew he could change that in a minute, if all he cared about was sex. He could just go down to Hotel Street and *rent* a girl for a while. But he wasn't interested in that. Aside from being what the British called "un-officerlike," he just didn't trust a prostitute to be healthy.

Officially, there were no prostitutes in Honolulu. As usual, the official version didn't have all that much to do with reality. The local cops had the floozies nicely organized and confined to their own little section of town. There were plenty of available ladies. You just had to know where to find them.

He watched Ohara for a while as he worked on the defective light with his tester. From a few overheard comments, he had the impression that Ohara was having his own problems with the local belles. Miller had heard him complaining to Harrigan that a cute *Nisei* girl had pretty much dismissed him the moment he introduced himself in his southern accent, and with what she obviously considered his Irish way of pronouncing his family name. He evidently wasn't Japanese enough for her—or for her parents.

Miller leaned over the bulwark as Ohara finished reassembling the sternlight. "Ohara!"

"Sir?"

"What did you find?"

Ohara walked up to stand just abaft the bridge before answering. "The light and socket are fine, sir," he said. "But they're not getting any power. Looks like a bad cable."

That would mean attention from the yard people, Miller thought, or spending some time alongside a tender. It wasn't the sort of thing that required putting the boat into a dry dock, but they could figure on some workers crawling around under the superstructure deck running a new cable.

"Water damage?" Miller asked.

Ohara nodded. "Looks that way, sir."

"Okay, carry on."

Miller decided he would have to talk to Morley when he came aboard. They would need to make arrangements for repairs. Any cable that passed through the pressure hull was vulnerable to water penetration at the external fitting where it terminated, at the gland were it entered the hull, or just about anywhere along the outboard section. If water got into a cable it would short out and power would be lost. And, because the cable terminated inside the pressure hull at a switch, control panel, or other piece of equipment, any water entering a cable—which was essentially a hose with wires in it—was likely to damage whatever it was connected to.

He didn't think it was likely enough water could come through a cable to sink the boat, but it could still cause plenty of damage.

•   •   •

Electrician's Mate 1ˢᵗ Class Kenneth Ohara had just finished getting the sternlight back together, and was gathering up his tools, when a plane flew low over the boat on a course for the main anchorage. He ducked involuntarily, at the same time wondering just what that lunatic was doing flying so low inside the base. He was going to catch hell when he landed.

For the moment, it didn't occur to him that there was something fundamentally wrong with the plane's design. Then he saw it out over the harbor, a torpedo dropping from its belly. He couldn't see it enter the water—Kuahua Point was in the way—but a few seconds later the anchorage echoed to the blast as the torpedo detonated against the side of one of the moored ships.

About that time, two more planes flew over, and this time he could see the red disks on the bottom of their wings.

•   •   •

After the first torpedo bomber flew over, Miller wasn't sure just what to do next, so for a moment he did nothing. Then, about the time the next pair flew over, he shook himself out of it and yelled for the bridge messenger to sound general quarters.

Ames came onto the bridge a minute later, dressed in khaki uniform trousers and a t-shirt, with carpet slippers on his bare feet. "What the hell is going on?" he demanded. "What's with the alarm?"

Miller pointed out over the anchorage, where thick columns of smoke were now rising from the damaged ships and, beyond them, to Ford Island, where the seaplane base was also taking a pasting. Just then another plane roared over the Submarine Base, and this time both of them could see the red meatballs.

"Looks like we're under attack, sir," Miller said.

"Shit!"

That was the first time Miller had ever heard the XO express himself that way, but he couldn't disagree with his assessment.

A gunner's mate was on the forward deck now, dragging the heavy water-cooled .50-caliber Browning up through the forward hatch. It was going to take precious seconds to get the gun set up, and right now Miller wondered if they had those seconds to spare.

He ran to the back of the bridge. "Ohara! Forget the tools for now! Get down to maneuvering and be ready to answer bells if we need to get under way."

He could see Ohara's mouth moving in assent, but one of the machine-guns on the cigarette deck opened up at that moment, blotting out his words. A sleek monoplane fighter flew over, the guns flashing along the leading edges of his wings, as Ohara passed the unmanned three-inch gun. This time Miller heard him clearly as he shouted, "Kill that fucking Nip bastard!" at no one in particular.

Ohara was down the hatch and on his way to his action station in maneuvering before Miller had a chance to register just how bizarre that comment sounded coming out of Ohara's obviously Japanese face.

The bridge messenger, who had dug out the oversized helmet that allowed him to wear his phone headset while still getting a little protection, was shouting something over the cacophony of the guns as the other boats all opened up with their short range weapons.

"What is it?" Ames asked. He hadn't formally relived Miller, but it was obvious he now had the deck.

"Captain is on his way, sir," the messenger repeated. "His wife just called the guard shack."

Miller looked at the XO. "What do you figure we'll do, sir? Get to sea or stay put?"

"I'm half expecting a general sortie order at any moment," Ames said. "But I don't think it would be a very good idea just now."

"Sir?"

"Take a good look around out there, Larry. The gunners on those big ships are just as likely to start shooting at *us* right now. The safest place for a sub at the moment is either tied up right here, or down at about 300 feet and staying the hell out of the way of *both* sides."

Miller couldn't disagree with him. The Navy had always presumed that, in the unlikely event Pearl Harbor was ever attacked, subs would be involved, probably waiting outside the channel to sink anything that tried to get away. There would certainly be destroyers covering the approaches—they would be there in any case, as Admiral Kimmel had set up a security zone in that area. With an air raid in progress, it was just as likely the patrolling destroyers would shoot first and ask questions later.

"Where's Hartman?" Ames asked, looking down at the forward deck, where Gunner's Mate 2nd Class Thomas had finally managed to get the .50-caliber into action. Frustratingly, it was the most effective weapon they had for antiaircraft use.

The three-inch gun on the after deck, despite being designed to train and elevate as an antiaircraft gun, was useless for that purpose. There was no fuse setter to adjust the shells for airburst, and the only shells aboard would be useless even if they had one. *Bacalao*'s magazine contained only gray-painted common shells. There wasn't a green projectile to be found. The Navy presumed that submarines would have no reason to shoot it out with aircraft.

"Hartman said he was going ashore as soon as he was relieved," Miller said. "But he couldn't have got very far—presuming he even made it off the boat."

"Get down there and direct that .50-caliber crew until he shows up," Ames ordered. "See if you can bring down a few of those planes."

"Do you have the deck, sir?" It was a gentle reminder that he hadn't actually relieved Miller yet.

"Damn! Yes, I have the deck, Mr. Miller."

"Executive Officer has the deck," Miller repeated, making it official, and headed for the ladder to get down to the forward deck.

Where the hell *was* Hartman? he wondered. The attack had started no more than five minutes after he relieved him. He could hardly have got out of the Submarine Base in that time.

But there was no time to worry about that now. He got down onto the deck and hurried over to the gun.

Thomas was yelling and goading his crew to keep the ammo boxes coming. The water jacket covering the barrel was steaming as the water inside carried away the heat. Without the jacket, Thomas would have needed to change the barrel more than once by now.

Of the two men helping Thomas, one was part of the regular crew, but the other was a young seaman third who had come aboard just after the boat arrived at Pearl.

"Where is everyone?" Miller shouted.

"On liberty," Thomas replied, just as loudly. He might have said "sir," but if he did it was drowned out as he opened fire again, trying to get the tracers across the path of a diving torpedo bomber.

The plane seemed to fly right through the hail of bullets, but didn't appear to have suffered any serious damage. Miller realized that he couldn't identify it, or any of the other planes roaring over the anchorage. They were all aggressively modern types—nothing at all like the antiquated designs everyone knew the Japanese flew.

The makeup of the gun crew was symptomatic of the problems that day. Miller glanced up at the Administration Building, wondering if Admiral Kimmel was in his office, or still hurrying in from his home. It was obvious no one had expected a war to break out this morning or half the base wouldn't have been on liberty.

The gun opened up again. Considering the pickup crew, they seemed to be maintaining a pretty good rate of fire. The problem was that the Jap planes seemed to be ignoring all the steel and explosives they were throwing at them.

We need heavier guns, Miller thought.

Behind him, he could hear the .30-caliber machine-guns on the bridge opening up as two more planes flew across the Sub Base to get at the battleships. How much good could these light weapons really do, he wondered.

A submarine's main defense against air attack was to submerge and get out of sight, but what were you supposed to do when you couldn't submerge? He knew the Germans had heavier antiaircraft weapons. When would the U.S. Navy do the same thing?

The three-inch might have been useful, if the Navy had thought to provide a fuse-setter and the proper shells, but it still wouldn't fire fast enough to make Miller happy. And the machine-guns were really designed for shooting at soldiers climbing out of trenches, not at planes.

Thomas fired again. This time the line of tracers sparkled across the cockpit of one of the fighters. Instantly, the pilot lost control, sending the agile fighter tumbling toward the water.

"Got the bastard!" Thomas shouted.

"Well, there are plenty more of them, so keep shooting!" Miller glanced around the deck. Where the hell was Hartman? He should have been there by now.

•　　•　　•

Lieutenant Commander James Andrew Morley skidded around a corner, then had to slam on the brakes, very nearly colliding with a Jeep full of white-clad sailors. The driver was a third-class petty officer, and he didn't seem to notice as he raced toward the base. He was paying no more attention to the speed limit than Morley, and the other sailors were holding on for dear life as they urged their driver on to even greater risks.

That was all anyone could think of, Morley realized. Anyone who wasn't on base was trying desperately to get back. They all wanted to get into the fight, now that it had begun.

When all this started he was in his back yard. It was Sunday, and he wasn't due aboard until 0900, so he had gone outside to relax and read the Sunday paper. That was something he couldn't do aboard—at least, not all of it. He didn't think it presented the proper image for the crew to see their commanding officer starting out each Sunday by catching up on the latest exploits of Li'l Abner and Moon Mullins before getting around to the actual news.

His quiet contemplation of the comics was ended abruptly as a flight of Japanese torpedo bombers roared directly over his house, on a direct course for the main anchorage at Pearl Harbor.

Didn't anyone see this coming? he wondered. And where the hell was the Army? Their most important job in Hawaii was to protect the Navy Base, after all. So why were there no American fighters in the air?

By now he could see the base ahead. A dense pall of smoke hung over the area, while overhead the enemy planes went about their work of destruction.

As he reached the gate a massive explosion rolled over the base, and a huge column of smoke and flame soared hundreds of feet into the air.

•   •   •

"What the hell was that?" Miller shouted. He could actually *feel* the shockwave as the explosion shook the anchorage. The smoke and flame seemed to climb to the highest part of the sky, casting a shadow over the harbor.

But there was no time to worry about it now. There were still planes overhead, and the guns were in constant action, their barrels rising and dipping and swinging as they tracked one enemy plane after another.

Bright brass cartridge cases littered the deck, the seamen kicking them over the side to keep from slipping on them. No one was concerned with accounting for the empty brass, as they would have been a few hours earlier. If anyone should come around later and ask where the empties were, the men would no doubt tell him where the spent brass could be found and add, rather impolitely, the suggestion that he could go for a swim if he wanted to collect it.

There was time for nothing but loading and shooting. That it was mostly an exercise in futility didn't matter to them. They were under attack, and they had to do *something*.

Given time to think about it, Miller suspected that Thomas would have admitted that the fighter he'd shot down had been nothing more than the chance convergence of a lucky shot and an unlucky pilot. But while it was happening his brain would have been on automatic. There was no other way to function in this situation. If you stopped to think about what you were doing you'd just screw up.

•   •   •

Electrician's Mate 1st Class Kenneth Ohara felt pretty useless at the moment. He was at his action station, sitting at the main control board and ready to get the boat under way at a moment's notice. But he was fairly sure that notice would never come. At least half the crew was still ashore, no doubt trying to figure out what was going on even as they rushed back to the base.

No one had expected this. Ohara felt compelled to believe that, for had there been any warning at all the Army would certainly have had planes in the air to meet the bastards.

And no one would have got liberty, either. They would have kept every single man aboard, and the boat would have been ready to get under way, or even be already at sea with a full load of warshots and possibly in a position to do some good.

Looking at the board, he could see his reflection in the face of one of the meters. Was that what the enemy looked like? Were some of those bastards up there, now dropping bombs and torpedoes on his friends, actually his own relatives?

And what was it going to be like from now on? Would his friends start looking at him differently? Would they still see good ol' Ken Ohara, or would they see a potential enemy? Not everyone liked the Japanese very much, and a lot of those who didn't seemed to lack the ability to see beyond physical appearance. An American who only *looked* Japanese was no different from a real Nip to them.

Back home, they lived in a sort of middle ground, considered to be a little better than the coloreds, but by no means as good as the whites. His father's business was unusual. Most American Japanese in the South tended to be shopkeepers, running small stores, which was how his father and Mr. Yamada had started, before they managed to put together enough money to get into manufacturing.

They were quite successful now, but would that last? More than half of their business was either directly with the military, or selling components to other companies that made military equipment—radios, mostly. There were Ohara & Yamada components, condensers, resistors, rheostats and the like, in quite a few pieces of equipment in this boat.

Would the Navy, or their contractors, keep buying from a "Jap" firm? Would the fact that the company's owners were both veterans who'd fought the Germans in France be enough to prove their loyalty?

The company logo was a stylized script "O&Y," with the full name of the company beneath it. If they were smart, he thought, they would change the packaging so that only the logo was printed on it. A lot of people might not catch the Ohara part, perhaps thinking it was just an odd spelling of an Irish name. Yamada, though, was a lot more obvious.

He looked up at the overhead. Beyond the curved plating there would be more planes bringing more death and destruction. A bomb might be on its way into his lap even now.

All he could think of was that, whatever ethnic connection there might be, these men were the enemy. These were people who were trying to kill him, and might cause problems for his family for no reason other than a meaningless physical resemblance to the enemy, and an ancestral link to a country that had persecuted his forebears for their "foreign" religion.

The Nip bastards had better hope I never get my hands on them!

• • •

Lieutenant Commander James Andrew Morley ran up the brow, ducking involuntarily as a torpedo bomber roared along the length of the boat on its way to Battleship Row. Every gun was firing, the tracers streaking across the sky in a dense pattern that seemed to weave a solid fabric of death above the anchorage. Yet the planes were still darting about on their missions. It was as if the Japanese pilots had been blessed by some evil Asian god, allowed to go about their business of raining death and destruction on the American Navy with impunity.

More explosions echoed across the water as he climbed onto the bridge. A thick pall of greasy smoke from the burning ships obscured the bright morning sky.

"Readiness?"

"Ready to answer bells on batteries, Captain," Ames reported. "The ship is at general quarters. We're still missing 14 men who had overnight liberty. I suppose they were caught in the raid and haven't been able to get back yet."

"Any orders yet, Fred?"

"So far, sir, just 'stay put.'"

Entirely sensible, Morley thought. The planes obviously came from carriers. Was it possible those carriers were close enough for a submarine now sitting at Pearl to sortie and do anything about them? Not likely. They would be at least 100 miles out to sea—close enough for their planes to fly to Hawaii and back, but not so close that any ship or submarine from Pearl would be able to catch them before they could escape.

"Any orders, sir?" Ames asked.

"Just keep doing what you're doing, Fred. Shoot at any target that presents itself. It's all we can do right now."

•　　　•　　　•

So now what the hell are we supposed to do? Collins wondered. There were Jap planes all over the sky, and the big ships were under attack. And could they fight back?

Not from down here, he thought. You can't torpedo a plane!

Marble was leaning forward, standing between the tubes. Beyond him, Pappas was on his seat at the Gyro Setting Indicator-Regulator, but looking aft, and not at the GSIR. The tubes were empty and, even if they weren't, there was nothing to shoot at while they were tied up at the Submarine Base. Pappas had just automatically gone to his action station when general quarters was sounded.

Marble had already been in the forward torpedo room when it all started. Judging from his condition—he was standing there in denim dungaree trousers and nothing else—he had still been in his bunk, catching a little extra sleep on a Sunday morning. One advantage of being forward torpedo room tube captain was that he got one of the bunks there, where it was relatively peaceful.

"Now what?" Marble asked.

About all Collins could do was shrug. "Just keep your head down, I guess, Bob."

"I want to shoot back."

"Oh, we will. But probably not today." Collins smiled then, remembering his work at Newport. "And we'll have some nasty surprises for the little bastards, too."

"I just feel kind of helpless down here," Marble said. "Like I should be doing something instead of just standing around."

There wasn't much that any of them could do. This was, strictly speaking, a gun action, and that was a different department. In a normal surface gun action the torpedo department would at least be standing by, ready to get involved if a suitable target should present itself.

For the moment, they had nothing to do but stand around and worry. It was frustrating. After all those years in the Navy, constantly drilling, constantly working to hone the skills that would allow them to be most useful in the event of war, all they could do now that war had come was to wait even longer.

Just then Bill Iorio, a young Seaman Second, stuck his head through the hatch. "Captain wants you on the bridge, Chief," he said.

"Okay, let's go."

He followed Iorio back through officers' country, leaving him in the control room as he climbed up into the conning tower, then up onto the bridge.

"Good," the captain said, "you're here."

"Yes, sir."

"I've just got the word. We're not going anywhere today. Collect anyone who isn't doing anything important. We've been requested to send any spare men for working parties to assist with the rescue efforts. Get the men and report to the main gate. They'll tell you where you're needed most."

"Aye, aye, sir."

Collins hurried back down the ladder. At least now there was something to do.

•   •   •

The enemy seemed to be gone for the moment, Miller decided. Thomas had his makeshift gun crew cleaning up the deck, collecting any brass that hadn't been kicked overboard during the attack.

"Do you think they'll be back, sir?" Evans asked, using a fingertip to flip a .50-caliber casing up from where it had been trampled into the space between two of the narrow teak deck planks.

Miller looked around for a moment, taking in the thick pall of smoke hanging over the main anchorage and letting his eyes sweep over the Submarine Base and the hill beyond. The tank farm was still intact, he noticed.

"I think they will," Miller said. "If they want to put our fleet out of action, they haven't finished the job."

"What do you mean, sir?"

"So far, they haven't hit those fuel tanks above the base. We can always bring more ships from the States, but fuel is another matter. If they destroy the tank farms it would take months to rebuild them and then to fill the new tanks. We can't operate from Pearl if there's no fuel, and San Diego is too far from Japan to stage out of. They haven't really attacked the Sub Base, either. If I was the Jap admiral, I'd want to be sure I'd killed both."

Just then Collins emerged from the forward hatch, follow by 30 men. They seemed to be mostly engine room and torpedo crew, Miller noticed, along with about half of the electrical department. Men who had no vital duties aboard with the boat tied up at the pier.

Collins led them across the brow and onto the pier. There he formed them up and marched them off toward the gate. As the detail marched out of sight, Miller could hear the guns starting to fire again.

The enemy was back.

VII
Under Pressure

THIS WAS WHAT HE HAD BEEN WAITING FOR. Kirk, the duty radioman, emerged from the narrow radio shack abaft the control room and handed Morley a length of the paper tape from the coding machine. After being run through the machine, the only clear text was the addressee. The rest remained encrypted.

"Thank you, Kirk." Morley turned to Morgan, the OOD. "I'll be in my stateroom if you need me, Bill. I have to decode this one myself."

"Yes, sir."

The message was double encrypted. The initial encryption was with a onetime pad, a copy of which was locked in Morley's safe. That was then re-encrypted by machine. The machine-encrypted version was sent over the radio circuit. Kirk ran it through *Bacalao*'s machine, which revealed the original encrypted message and a header marking it as "Eyes Only: Captain."

The special codes were part of the new information given to the Pearl Harbor captains before they were sent out on their first war patrols. It seemed America had sources that could reveal where enemy ships could be found. While it was never explicitly stated, the logical conclusion was that Naval Intelligence was able to read at least some Japanese codes.

They were also told about the new Mark-6 exploders that were being installed in all of their torpedoes. The magnetic feature in those was so secret that BuOrd had waited until the war started before telling anyone about them. Collins had known, as he was part of the development team at BuOrd, but he had been unable to say anything because of security.

Until the captains were briefed, and the exploders issued, Collins had been forbidden to say anything. Now that the secret was out—at least to those who needed to know—Collins had told Morley he thought his old masters at the Torpedo Station had gone a little overboard on security, and that he, personally, thought the fleet should have been given the chance to practice with the new exploder.

No one outside Intelligence knew the spy stuff, and they were under very strict orders to keep it that way. Only the gist of the reports were to be given to the other officers. Morley could tell them where to go, and what they could expect to find, but not how he happened to know where to go. Even he didn't know the actual source, which was carefully concealed before the messages were encoded and sent out.

It took about 20 minutes to decode the signal. At the end, Morley was left with a short list of waypoints and times for a Japanese troop transport. As expected, they needed to make a course change. He consulted the chart and decided that, if they stayed on the surface for most of the night, they would be in the proper position just before dawn.

Before, finding a target was rarely more than pure chance and good guesswork. Now it would be mostly a matter of navigation, for the enemy were unknowingly telling the Americans where to find them. So long as both captains had their ships in the right place at the right time, the prize would be there for the taking. A nice, fat transport loaded with troops and supplies bound for the Philippines.

•   •   •

Morley was standing stolidly at the front of the upper bridge, his powerful binoculars sweeping the dark horizon for any sign of the enemy. Above and behind him, the bridge lookouts were quartering the sea.

The more eyes the better, Miller thought, watching the captain a moment longer. The big surface ships were now equipped with good sea search radar, but that was little more than a vague promise for submarines.

Their own SD radar—and *Bacalao* was one of only a handful of boats to even have that—was mainly good for detecting planes. At best it had a range of perhaps six or seven miles, and it couldn't provide a target bearing. It could sometimes pick up a ship, but by the time it got a solid return through the sea clutter you'd have nearly run into the target.

Just now, in the dark of a moonless night, Miller didn't think they were in much danger from the air. They were well away from any Japanese air bases, and no one in his right mind would want to land on an aircraft carrier in the dark.

Nor would any carrier captain want to turn on his deck lights to land his planes, possibly attracting the unwanted attention of a sub. Planes mostly landed at dusk and stayed on deck until dawn. It was safer all around.

Miller glanced at the bridge gyro repeater. *Bacalao* was steady on a course of three-one-five degrees—due northwest—steaming at an economical eleven knots on two engines, with the other two charging batteries.

When Morley emerged from his stateroom after decoding the latest signal he checked the chart and set a new course. If the Intelligence types had got it right, they could expect to meet up with an enemy convoy shortly after daybreak. All to the good, Miller thought. They needed to get this first patrol started off with some sort of decisive action. There was a visceral need to get back at the enemy.

It was odd, when you stopped to think about it. Back in 1915, when *U-20* torpedoed *Lusitania* without warning, it had nearly been enough to get the United States into the war. Resumption of unrestricted submarine warfare by Germany a couple years later had outraged enough Americans to bring the country into the war on the British side.

Then, between the wars, the London Conference had decided that submarines would have to abide by the Cruiser Rules when confronting any merchantman. A sub was required to surface, stop the ship, insure that the crew and passengers were placed somewhere safe—which did not include lifeboats, unless they were within sight of land—and only then was the sub allowed to sink the ship, presuming an inspection had found contraband.

The Germans had followed those rules for the first few weeks of the war, until the British started arming their freighters and running them in escorted convoys. The Cruiser Rules didn't apply to armed vessels, ships in convoy, or ships that tried to run away, making the Germans technically free to shoot without warning.

British and American newspapers uniformly ignored that little detail and roundly condemned the German submariners for returning to a policy of unrestricted submarine warfare. It was "uncivilized" and "barbaric."

That sort of condemnation evidently being a one-way street, no one in the press seemed the least bit upset that virtually the first order issued to the American Navy after Pearl Harbor was, "Exercise unrestricted air and submarine warfare against Japan."

So that was what they were doing. Somehow, Intelligence had managed to locate what was expected to be an important enemy convoy. It wasn't really any of Miller's business how they did this. All he knew was that the captain would close himself up in his stateroom when he received certain messages and emerge a while later looking a bit harried—manual decoding was never fun—and then tell them where they could find a nice, fat target.

That had happened twice to date. The first time they found nothing. There was no explanation why. Maybe Intelligence had got it wrong and they were waiting in the wrong place. Maybe the Japanese merchant captain just couldn't navigate worth a damn and wasn't where he should have been.

As for this time, they would know in a few hours.

If they found what they were looking for, Miller would be busy. His attack station remained in the conning tower, running the Torpedo Data Computer. The complex device was his baby now, and he was getting pretty good at running the thing.

Operating the TDC was a skill, bordering on an art, bordering on black magic. The operator had to take active sonar and hydrophone results, feed them into the computer, and translate everything into an accurate shooting solution.

It would be easier to stick up the periscope and take a look, but that sort of thing wasn't allowed if there was any chance there could be enemy aircraft in the area. A captain who allowed his periscope to be spotted during an exercise was going to catch all sorts of hell. And it seemed they were *always* spotted.

Miller glanced at the captain. *As he well knew, after that last time.* The minor detail that it was a mistake in the forward torpedo room that drew attention to them and *allowed* the periscope to be seen was seemingly of little importance when it was time for Morley to stand in front of Tommy Withers' desk. It *had* been seen and, besides, if *Bacalao* had been at her "proper" depth the impulse tank overpressure wouldn't have been a problem. The added sea pressure at 150 feet would have allowed the poppet valve to fully scavenge the air charge.

He raised his binoculars again and scanned the sea. As OOD he was responsible for everything that happened during the watch. He wasn't a lookout, though—procedure actually specified that the OOD should *not* concentrate on watching the sea. He looked around on a regular schedule, but the bridge lookouts standing above his head were the ones who would be responsible for really noticing any potential trouble.

His job was to make sure they did it right.

•   •   •

The captain sat at the head of the wardroom table, with most of his officers gathered around it. Weston brought coffee for all of them, then retired to his pantry, where he would no doubt hear everything and then carefully push it from his memory and carry on as if he knew nothing. It was one of the Navy's little ironies. Weston was a sharecropper's son from somewhere in Mississippi, and as a steward's mate, taking care of *Bacalao*'s officers, he got to hear all sorts of things that required a much higher security clearance than he possessed.

"Doesn't seem to be much of a convoy," Morley said. "Sonar reports only a single ship."

"Seems to be all he can hear, at least," Ames commented. "Sound conditions are only fair, though, and we're still a good way off."

The captain looked around the room. "If more turn up, good. If not, well, I suppose we'll just have to sink that lone ship, right? Hell, a target is a target."

"True enough."

"We should be up on him in about an hour," Morley continued. "We will go in at 100 feet and make our attack on sound bearings."

"A periscope attack would be easier," Ames suggested. His low opinion of that particular bit of established procedure was no secret.

"That's against doctrine. No periscope exposure during daylight hours."

"Sonar is reporting a single ship with a single screw," Ames argued. "That means some sort of freighter or a very small transport. I don't think we need to worry about aircraft this far from land."

Morley smiled. "Just because we can't hear a carrier doesn't mean there isn't one within range, Fred."

"So stick up the SD mast for a couple minutes and see if there's anything around."

The captain shook his head. "It's ironic," he said, "when you think about it. My Old Man got his Medal of Honor while he was hunting U-boats in the last war. He *loved* submarines. The only reason he was even in a destroyer, instead of some old L-boat, was that he'd been promoted a couple of times and was too senior to serve in those old boats.

"Now here we are, in a boat that's actually a little bigger than his destroyer, and is equipped with sound gear that makes the stuff he was using seem about as effective as leaning over the bow and sticking a stethoscope in the water. Our periscope has a very accurate stadimeter, and it would certainly be easier to set up the attack by using it."

"But you're not going to, are you, Captain?"

"The Navy says we don't, Fred."

"I think the Navy is being a little over cautious."

"Probably. But we'll try it their way first." He smiled. "If that doesn't work, then we'll ignore doctrine and go ahead and use the 'scope."

Collins put his head into the wardroom. "Torpedoes are all set up, sir," he reported. "We have the new exploders installed."

"Good," Morley said. "Thank you, Chief."

Collins nodded and withdrew. The new Mark-6 exploders had been brought aboard in great secrecy just before they sailed from Pearl. Collins and his crew had been busy pulling the old Mark-5 contact exploders and installing the new models, with their magnetic influence feature, in their place. This would be the only time that would happen at sea. The torpedo shop at Pearl would already have them installed in the warheads for future patrols.

The magnetic feature also provided an explanation for the mystery of why the newest warheads were being made of phosphor bronze and had a curious plug in their noses.

"Do you think the new exploders will help?" Morgan asked. He would have the dive during the approach.

"That's what Newport claims. Hell, it's hard to disagree with the idea. If you set off the warhead directly under the keel you have a sure kill."

"Still, it seems odd," Ames said. "Did you ever think you'd see the day when the Navy told you to set the torpedo to run five feet *deeper* than the target's draft?"

"Modern technology, Fred," the captain reflected. "War used to be for sailors. Now it's for engineers."

•   •   •

Miller stood by the Torpedo Data Computer in the crowded conning tower and waited to begin. Across the narrow cylinder, Morley was looking over the sound operator's shoulder. Jones-1 was listening carefully, his right hand moving up and down in a chopping motion as he counted propeller revolutions. After what seemed an eternity he spoke.

"Target one sounds like a large, single-screw vessel, reciprocating machinery, making 85 revolutions," he said.

"Target one?" Morley asked. Up to this point only a single ship had been reported.

Jones nodded. "Sound conditions aren't that good, but I just picked up a second target, still a good distance beyond the first. Two screws, turbine machinery—sounds like a destroyer."

"We could still stick up a periscope," Ames suggested, not yet ready to give up the idea. "Might tell us just what we have."

If they could identify the primary target by name they could look her up, find her screw pitch, and have a much better idea of her speed. They could also determine her masthead height, which would allow the captain to get an accurate stadimeter range.

"We're going to try to do it by the book, Fred," Morley said.

Ames just nodded. He was obviously resigned to the captain's decision not to go against doctrine at this point. After all, Ames wasn't the one who had spent an hour in Admiral Withers' office getting chewed out for being noticed off Lahaina.

Miller, still waiting for the approach to begin—which would happen for him once the first target bearing was taken and he had something to put into the TDC—was perfectly aware of the XO's thoughts on the whole 'no periscopes in daylight' doctrine, and agreed with it. It was just that the Navy believed it was suicidal to expose a periscope when there was the slightest chance a plane could spot it. From discussions in the wardroom, it was clear that Ames thought the whole doctrine to be far too cautious.

Equally, it appeared that Morley was going to follow the rules. You didn't get a command in the peacetime Navy by ignoring SOP. No matter what they said, the Navy didn't really like initiative very much. For sure, a reputation for being innovative didn't get you very far when no one was shooting at you.

And that was the problem, as far as Miller could see. The captain was still thinking like a peacetime submariner, doing everything by the book. The book said that you attacked from depth, and used your sonar to set up the attack. It was supposed to work, but who could really say? During peacetime exercises you rarely shot at anything—the scores were based on TDC solutions, not the more certain report of a lookout on the target confirming that an exercise fish, with its bright yellow practice head, had just run under his ship.

Miller had spent his first three years of service in a destroyer, and that experience had taught him that a periscope was a lot harder to spot than everyone seemed to think.

"Target bearing?" Morley asked.

"Target bearing zero-two-eight," Jones reported. During an approach and attack, most of the formalities were dropped to save time. Jones would go back to saying "sir" after the attack was concluded.

"Target bearing zero-two-eight," Miller repeated, cranking the bearing into the TDC. "Initial target bearing is zero-two-eight."

"Give me a single ping range," Morley ordered.

Jones keyed the transducer, sending a single ultrasonic "ping" toward the target. The complex electronics in the sonar stack calculated the time it took for the ping to reach the target and be reflected back, displaying the result as a trace on the center screen.

"Range is one-one-double-zero," Jones reported.

Miller cranked that into the TDC and let the computer work on the problem. *Bacalao*'s own course and speed were automatically sent to the TDC by the main gyrocompass and Pitometer log, so there was no need to manually add those. An accurate target speed and the angle on the bow would still be needed to work out a good firing solution.

As time passed, it became more and more obvious that the captain wasn't going to use the periscope. Target speed and angle on the bow were both estimated based on additional sound readings. But now, at least, Morley had elaborated a little on his plans. He was going to follow doctrine precisely in this first attack of *Bacalao*'s war. If it worked, fine, he would continue. If the first torpedoes missed, though, he would then be able to say that he had tried it their way, found that it didn't work, and that he would just have to be a little less conservative in the future.

It took about 20 minutes to work out a good solution.

"Stand by tube one," Morley ordered. "Set depth three-zero feet, high speed setting. We'll see how the magnetic feature works."

"Set depth three-zero feet, aye," Collins repeated. The targeting system in a fleet boat was a huge step up from the older boats. The TDC was linked to the GSIR, and continuously updated the gyro settings. Depth and speed were still set manually by a man adjusting the controls on the tube, but there was no need to update those on a constant basis.

The torpedoes could be fired electrically from the conning tower, or manually from the torpedo room. Electrical firing was preferred.

"Flood tube one and open outer door."

Ames looked up curiously from his position by the conning tower chart table. "Only one tube, sir?"

"One ship, one fish." Morley frowned. "Damned shortages. We can't spare another unless we're sure we need it."

"Tube one flooded from WRT, sir," Collins reported. "Outer door open."

"Final bearing, Jones?"

"Zero-one-two."

Miller looked at the dials on the position keeper. "Zero-one-two is correct," he reported. The target was at the exact bearing predicted by the TDC and the solution light was lit. Provided the fish ran true, and everything entered had been correct, the torpedo should run right under the middle of the target, where the magnetic exploder would insure the greatest possible damage.

Morley nodded. "Fire one!"

Collins flipped a switch on the torpedo control panel. The spindle light blinked out as the gyro-setting spindle was retracted from its socket in the torpedo. An instant later the ready light came on and Collins slapped the heel of his hand against the big, mushroom-shaped red firing button at the top of the panel.

"Fire one, aye!" Collins repeated.

A moment later, down in the forward torpedo room, a blast of compressed air began to push the heavy Mark-14 torpedo out of the tube.

"One fired electrically, sir," Collins reported.

After the torpedo had moved forward a bare three-quarters of an inch, the tripping latch, protruding into the tube, caught the leading edge of the torpedo's starting lever, throwing it to the "start" position as the torpedo continued out of the tube.

This caused the starting valve to release 2,800 psi air from the air flask, which spun up the gyro to 20,000 rpm in just over half a second, after which the motor disengaged and the gyro was unlocked. A reducing valve cut off the full air pressure to the gyro and began to send a sustaining flow of 125 psi air into the mechanism.

At the same time, the reducing valve dropped the pressure to the rest of the system to 450 psi and fired the black powder igniter, which sent a torch-like lance of flame into the combustion chamber. There it encountered a swirling stream of alcohol—colored pink by a noxious dye intended to keep the men from drinking the stuff—high pressure air and water. The alcohol ignited, flashing the water into high-pressure steam, which was directed into the two counter-rotating turbines through a steam gate valve mounted on the turbine housing.

By this time the torpedo was out of the tube and the two counter rotating screws were racing up to full speed. A stream of exhaust gases, mostly the unburned nitrogen from the compressed air, spewed from the hollow prop shaft as the torpedo, on the high-speed setting, rapidly accelerated to 46 knots.

After traveling a short distance from the boat, the torpedo began to turn slightly to port, following the gyro angle that had been automatically set by the by the Gyro Setting Indicator-Regulator from the TDC's firing solution, while the torpedo rose to its preset depth of 30 feet.

At the same time, its passage through the water spun a small impeller located in a groove on the underside of the heavy exploder baseplate. After the torpedo had traveled 480 yards, this would move the firing pin and primer into the booster and switch on the magnetic firing circuit. Up to that moment, if the fast moving torpedo hit anything, it would not explode. After that point it was fully armed.

After completing a run of 1,045 yards, the torpedo would pass directly under the target's keel, where the magnetic influence feature of the Mark-6 exploder would detonate the 600 pounds of TNT in the warhead.

At least, that was how it was supposed to work.

In the conning tower, everyone waited, the only sound the occasional drip of seawater leaking through number one periscope's packing gland. Collins was standing by the firing panel, holding a stopwatch and timing the run.

At the sonar stack, Jones had turned the gain way down, so that only a whisper of sound came through his earphones. He didn't want to be deafened when the torpedo went off.

Then the hull shuddered to the shockwave from the exploding torpedo. After a moment, Jones started listening again, trying to catch the sound of the target breaking up through the residual disturbance in the water.

"Nothing yet," he said. "Probably need a minute or so before sound conditions are good enough to hear anything useful."

Collins had punched the button on his stopwatch at the moment he heard the detonation. Now he was looking at the dial and frowning. "You won't hear anything," he said.

The captain looked across the conning tower. "Chief?"

Collins held up the stopwatch. "Nineteen seconds," he said. "That's only about 500 yards."

"Premature?"

"Yes, sir. No question. The fish exploded just after it armed."

"Sonar?"

"Conditions are improving." Jones listened intently for a few more seconds. "Target is still there. Revolutions have increased and it sounds like he's altered course away from us. The second target has also increased speed slightly, and I can hear long-scale pinging on his bearing."

"What the hell?" Morley said. "Did we just take a shot at one of our own ships?"

Jones shook his head. "Not one of our sets. Frequency is wrong."

"The Japs don't *have* active sonar," Morley objected. "They only have hydrophones. Everyone knows that."

"I guess someone forgot to tell the Japs," Ames commented.

"We probably should have expected something like that, though," Miller said. "They weren't supposed to have those fighters they used at Pearl Harbor, either."

"Target two is closing," Jones reported.

"Probably running down our torpedo track," Morley mused.

It was a known problem with wet-heater torpedoes. The engines burned alcohol, using compressed air to supply the needed oxygen. But air is mostly nitrogen, and nitrogen doesn't burn, so the engine consumed the 20% of the air that was oxygen and the 80% nitrogen and other noncombustible gases went out the tail pipe to bubble to the surface, creating a visible trail.

"If he's doing that," Ames suggested, "we might want to be somewhere else when he gets here."

Morley nodded. "Come right to one-six-niner," he ordered. "All ahead one-third. Make your depth two-zero-zero feet. Rig for silent running. Rig for depth charging."

As *Bacalao* began to curve onto her new course, systems were shut down throughout the boat. Fans were switched off, the air conditioning silenced, and the bulkhead flappers in the supply and exhaust lines were sealed to stop any flooding from taking that route between compartments.

In the conning tower, they could hear the thrumming of the destroyer's screws, faint but clear, as it closed the distance. A moment later there was an odd sound against the hull, like the whisking of a jazz drummers brushes on metal.

"He's found us," Jones said. "Starting his run."

Then the destroyer was crossing their course, the sound of his screws drumming against the hull, rising to a crescendo and then starting to fade, the pitch dropping as it passed over them and started to move away.

Jones turned his gain control all the way down. "Depth charges coming down," he said.

"Hang on," Morley snapped.

The boat seemed to jerk sideways as first one, and then a second depth charge detonated close by. Close, Miller thought, but not close enough to cause any significant damage. Not too bad. At least, not yet.

"Sonar?" Morley snapped, his voice sounding a little odd.

"Too much noise. Can't tell a thing yet."

"Keep listening."

"Okay," Jones said. Half a minute later he looked up. "Target is turning for another run."

"Dead slow," Morley ordered. "Nobody make a sound."

Again there was the rush of powerful screws passing overhead, followed by the sudden hush as everyone waited for the depth charges to come down.

Miller saw Morley grab one of the number two periscope hoist cables as the boat lurched drunkenly to a triple explosion. The captain was looking around with an oddly bewildered expression, his eyes moving around the conning tower, across the silent figures of his men, but seeming to focus on the thin steel plating that was all that intervened between the men and the terrible pressure of the sea. It was one of those things you knew about, but mostly put out of your mind.

"Maybe we should go deeper," Ames suggested.

"Deeper—yes, good idea."

Another pair of depth charges blasted the ocean apart, this time the shock coming from starboard. Miller found himself sitting on the deck in front of the TDC, a sharp pain radiating up from his tailbone. He had no idea how he'd wound up there.

"How deep, Captain?" Ames asked.

Morley was staring at the forward bulkhead and didn't seem to hear him.

"Andy!"

Morley looked at Ames. "What?"

Rubbing his aching tailbone, Miller got to his feet, his eyes taking in the scene by the periscope. The captain looked confused, which wasn't exactly an attitude likely to inspire confidence in the rest of them.

Ames seemed to make a decision, his attitude changing abruptly. "I have the conn, sir," he announced, rather more forcefully than usual.

Morley nodded, a look of great relief crossing his face. "Yes," he said. "Executive Officer has the conn."

Ames didn't waste any time. "Hard left," he snapped. "New course is two-one-four. All ahead full."

"New course two-one-four," Anderson repeated, spinning the wheel. "Both ahead full."

Miller wondered what the helmsman could be thinking at that moment. He had known the captain longer than any of them.

"Make your depth three-zero-zero feet," Ames ordered, as the boat gathered speed and curved around to port.

The phone talker relayed the order to the control room and the boat instantly angled down, the depth gauge starting to drop.

"Three-zero-zero feet," Paul reported.

"All ahead, dead slow," Ames ordered. "Present course?"

"All ahead, dead slow, aye," Anderson repeated. "Present course is two-one-four."

As Ames maneuvered the boat, Miller noticed that Morley never moved from his position on the port side of the number two periscope. He looked more relaxed now, though his eyes continued to scan the overhead as Japanese depth charges still dropped around them. He was out of it for the moment, Miller realized. By simply taking over the conn as he had done, Ames had effectively taken command of the boat.

Bacalao was moving at a bare two knots—just fast enough to allow the rudder and planes to bite and maintain control. But it was calmer now, and the shockwaves from the exploding depth charges now were doing little more than giving the hull a mild shaking.

They were probably exploding at about 150 feet, Miller decided, about the same distance above the keel and about 110 feet above the conning tower deckplates. Water does not compress, and most of the explosive force would be exerted in the direction of least resistance, which was up.

That didn't mean a depth charge going off above the boat couldn't kill them. Even if water was incompressible, metal was flexible and the air inside the hull *was* compressible. But they would need to get a lot closer.

At intervals, the rustling sound of the Japanese sonar brushing the hull reminded them of yet another intelligence failure. Not only did the enemy appear to have effective active sonar, but the sound of rushing screws and the tight depth charge patterns that followed immediately after made it clear that they had at least one destroyer captain who knew how to use it.

If this guy wasn't setting his charges too shallow, Miller realized, their chances of ever making it back to the surface would be virtually nil.

• • •

Motor orders were coming quickly, giving Ohara very little time to worry about the chaos outside the pressure hull. He *did* worry about the batteries. Each burst of high speed as *Bacalao* attempted to outmaneuver the enemy brought the time when the batteries were drained, and the boat would be forced to surface, that much closer.

At creeping speed they could stay down for close to two days—at full speed, hardly more than an hour. The captain was being judicious, keeping the high-speed maneuvering to a minimum, but the needles were still dropping faster than he liked.

The worst part was that there was no real warning. Up in the conning tower, the sonar operator would be able to hear the splashes and warn them. Back aft, they were just guessing. The sound of the escort's screws passing overhead was about all the warning they got.

Shortly after that happened, there would be the sharp "click" of the primer, and then the hull would quiver and shake as the ball of expanding gas from the exploding depth charge sent a shockwave thundering against it. An instant later, if they survived, there would be more noise as the sea slammed back into the void created by the detonation.

Carlisle was on the main board with Ohara. He figured the man was about ready for promotion to third class. Miller had told him that Carlisle had passed all his quals, and would get his dolphins as soon as the captain signed the papers. As for Ohara, he figured that as long as the man could do every job he threw at him, then he was probably ready to be rated as well.

When the first depth charges exploded Ohara had a moment of concern, because the younger man had looked like he was about ready to jump right out of his skin. But he pulled himself together after a second, and it wasn't as if this was something that anyone was used to. As far as Ohara knew, he was the only one aboard who had ever been depth charged before.

But that was in *Tambor*, during controlled tests. It had been frightening enough, but nothing like this. This time the intent was to *sink* them, not just to see how the boat reacted to a single charge at a fixed distance. This time there wasn't a single charge, but several at once, as the destroyer's captain tried to set them off in a ring around the boat, so that the cumulative effect would be to collapse the ballast tanks or rupture the pressure hull.

The bastards are trying to kill me! The enemy captain probably wasn't taking all this personally, but Ohara decided that *he* would.

The telegraphs clicked to ahead full, and as Ohara increased power to the motors the boat slewed around to port. After a minute the order came to reduce to dead slow.

"What was that all about?" Carlisle asked.

"Right after the depth charges go off the sonar guys on the destroyer can't hear anything for a couple minutes," Ohara explained. "That's when you try to get away. There's a brief period when you can run at full speed without being heard, so the captain is taking advantage of it."

He didn't mention the obvious danger with these tactics. They were just guessing when it came to how long the enemy sonar operators couldn't hear them. If they let it go too long before slowing down he would be on them at once.

After a couple of minutes they could hear a persistent sound against the hull, like it was being stroked by Krupa's brushes, Ohara thought, or someone was throwing sand and pebbles. A high pitched, metallic whisking sound.

"What's that?"

"That," Ohara said, "is active sonar, and nothing good can come of it."

"I thought the Nips didn't have that?"

Ohara just shook his head. There seemed to be a general feeling in the American military that all Japanese were nearsighted, bucktoothed runts who could copy western technology, but weren't smart enough to come up with any real innovations on their own. His mother was short, but he hadn't noticed any of the other traits in his own family, so why should the guys in Japan be any different? Shorter, maybe, but he doubted they were any dumber.

"I guess you thought wrong," Ohara said.

"So what's it mean, Ken?"

"I suppose it means we're going to get more stuff dropped on us."

Ohara didn't consider himself any sort of a prophet, but he was right that time. They could hear the rapid, swishing roar of the destroyer's screws as he charged down on them. The pounding beat grew in volume, and then the rustle of the sonar against the hull ceased and the roar of the screws changed in pitch, starting to drop as the can passed overhead and began to move off.

The noise from the screws was too loud for them to hear the depth charges being dropped in the destroyer's wake, but as the noise began to abate they heard a sharp double click and, an instant later, the boat bucked under the double concussion.

Ohara found himself sliding to port, falling off the bench seat at the main control and landing painfully on the platform deck in front of the tightly-dogged watertight door of the after torpedo room. Carlisle managed to hang on and keep his seat.

A breaker opened with a loud bang, and immediately the boat yawed to starboard as the motor on that side stopped turning.

Carlisle was reaching to reset the breaker when Ohara held up his hand. "Wait a minute," he said. "Do you hear something?"

Looking down through the grating in front of the seat and into the motor room beneath them, the source of the unwelcome noise was only too obvious. One of the fat copper lines that supplied coolant water for the starboard motor had snapped, and was now spraying seawater into the compartment at an astonishing rate.

At least the pump was off, Ohara thought. But the sea pressure was enough to do plenty of damage, and probably fill the compartment in no more than a few minutes. If that happened, they were all dead.

"Let's get that grating open," Ohara said. He was yelling at the top of his lungs, but at the moment it didn't seem that way to him.

Then he was down the ladder and into the motor room. The water was halfway up his calves already. It was an uncomfortable reminder that this space not only contained the motors, but lots of live power cables, with several hundred volts and enough amperage to fry a horse running through them.

Not the best place to get yourself grounded, Ohara thought.

Working his way cautiously around the broken pipe, being careful to avoid the direct stream—the pressure was probably sufficient to cause considerable injury—he somehow managed to get to the through-hull valve and close it. Submarine designers had long ago learned that you never put a hole in the hull unless you also provided a way to seal it off. Whenever possible, more than one way.

The valve was closed now, but the water continued to pour in, and Ohara realized that it had to be backing up through the discharge pipe.

So now it was back into the water to find that valve, which was now hidden under three feet of water. Presuming he survived, he decided, it was going to be murder trying to get the compartment dried out and dealing with the inevitable corrosion.

But there was nothing to do now but dive into the ever-deepening pool and work his way down the discharge line and close the outlet valve, holding his breath all the time. It seemed to take forever, but when he finally got his head back above the surface the water was no longer shooting out of the broken pipe.

Behind him, the thick port shaft was still turning, driving the boat through the depths that could as easily have claimed her.

As Ohara climbed back into the maneuvering room, Carlisle was on the phone with Lieutenant Morgan. The chief engineer, logically enough, was wondering why the boat seemed to be getting heavy by the stern.

Carlisle's voice sounded oddly distorted. That was something else they'd need to do, Ohara thought. All that water pouring in had raised the air pressure in the maneuvering room and they needed to get rid of it as soon as possible, before there was time for medical problems to develop.

•   •   •

So now what was he supposed to do? Morgan wondered. Running the trim pump didn't seem like a very good idea with a Japanese destroyer nosing about overhead. The pump was too damned noisy, and might be just enough to let the bastard get a positive fix on *Bacalao* and kill them.

But there were now several tons of extra water in the stern, and that didn't help their position, either. The only good news was that there were three watertight bulkheads between the partly-flooded motor room and the after battery. If all that seawater got to the battery cells the only option would be to surface and take their chances, or stay submerged and let half the crew die of chlorine gas poisoning.

"Blow after trim to sea," he ordered. "As near to dry as you dare."

He couldn't empty the tank completely. That would send a cloud of bubbles to the surface. But he could come close, and if too much water hadn't got into the motor room it might be enough to get the boat more or less in trim.

Then he'd have to figure out some way to get the water out of the motor room. Everything down there, including the motors, was waterproof, but that didn't mean it was okay to let the ocean in.

•   •   •

The attack continued for nearly four hours. Miller counted 22 depth charges before it stopped, and couldn't help wondering if the Jap destroyer had given up, decided he'd sunk them, or had just run out of depth charges. Whatever it was, Jones reported that he was now clearing the area.

Possibly he just needed to catch up with the transport and had no more time to waste now that *Bacalao* was too far astern to present a problem to his charge.

"Periscope depth," Ames ordered.

The captain looked at his Academy roommate curiously, but didn't say anything. It came as something of a shock to Miller as he realized that Morley hadn't said anything he could remember since turning over the deck four hours before.

"Six-four feet, sir."

"Up 'scope."

Paul worked the pickle and Ames stooped down to meet the periscope as it rose from the well. As it was slowly hoisted, he popped off the eye buffer and blinder and reversed it. The captain, like most of the officers, was right eyed. Ames, it seemed, was not.

"Enough," the XO said, still slightly hunched, with the periscope pointed roughly at the bow. "Destroyer," he continued, adjusting the focus know with his right hand. "Angle on the bow is port, one-seven-five."

Ames hadn't said anything about starting a solution, but Miller went to the TDC and cranked in the data automatically. The destroyer was heading almost directly away from them now, so the noise of her own screws should make it impossible for her sonar operators to hear them. Unless a sharp-eyed lookout noticed the extended periscope, it was unlikely the Japanese captain would be aware that his prey was trying to turn the tables.

"Target bearing—mark!"

"Zero-one-one." It was Collins now, reading the bearing off the azimuth ring.

"Down 'scope." Ames looked across at Miller. "*Asashio* class destroyer," he said. "What's the masthead height?"

Miller quickly thumbed through the recognition manual. "Niner-zero feet," he read.

"Up 'scope."

As the periscope head broke surface, Ames quickly set the masthead height on the stadimeter and worked the knob at the bottom of the periscope with his right hand. In a couple seconds he had the ghost image of the destroyer, created by the split lens in the mechanism, sitting neatly on top of the masthead of the true image. "Range—mark!"

"Eight-four-five," Collins reported, reading the range in yards off the duplicate dial on the back of the periscope.

"Target speed?"

"One-four knots," Jones reported.

"Down 'scope." He turned to Miller again. "We need to be quick with this one."

"Working on it, sir." Miller looked at the dials, watching impatiently as the complex mechanical computer hummed and chattered, digesting the inputs and transmitting the gyro angles to the torpedo tubes in both nests.

"What's the draft of an *Asashio*?" Ames asked.

Miller didn't have to look in the manual this time. He had anticipated the question. "Twelve feet," he said.

"Ready tubes two and three," Ames ordered. "Set depth at one-zero feet. We're not going to try anything fancy this time—I just want to ram a couple of fish up his ass."

"The red light flashed on. "We have a firing solution, sir," Miller reported.

"Tubes two and three are ready, sir. Outer doors are closed."

"Sonar—anything funny?"

"Target sounds like he's on a steady course away from us," Jones reported.

Ames nodded. "Up 'scope." He looked over at Miller as the periscope was rising. "Predicted bearing, Larry?"

"Zero-zero-four."

"Put me on."

Collins placed his hands over the XO's and lined up the proper line on the azimuth ring with the mark. "Zero-zero-four, sir."

"Perfect," Ames declared. "Flood tubes two and three and open outer doors."

"Tubes two and three flooded from WRT, sir," Collins reported. "Outer doors are open. Tubes are ready to fire."

"Fire two!"

"Fire two, aye! Two fired electrically, sir."

Miller could see Ames lips moving as he counted off the seconds. It was necessary to wait at least five seconds—ten would be better—after firing each torpedo before the next was sent on its way. Otherwise, they could interfere with each other.

Ames was keeping the periscope up. Miller knew he should have lowered it and gone deep, just in case the torpedoes missed and the destroyer decided to come back for another try. Equally, he could understand why he needed to see what was going to happen.

"Damn!" Ames muttered. "He's putting on speed and turning to port. Someone must have spotted the torpedo wakes."

Still he kept the 'scope up. His voice sounded detached, as it what he was watching wasn't quite real. "Target is still turning. Hell, I think we're in luck, boys—he's turning *into* our first fish. It's going to hit at a bad angle, but maybe—."

Sound travels much faster in water than in air. They could hear the detonation even as Ames shouted, "Got him!"'

"Second hit now," he added, five seconds later, sound puzzled. "Not much of an explosion. I don't think the warhead exploded. Blew up the air flask, maybe. But the destroyer is dead in the water, going down by the stern, and on fire."

Then there came another explosion, which seemed to go on for a long time, and powerful enough to shake the boat at nearly a thousand yards. "Looks like his after magazine went up," Ames said. "What's left of him is going down fast now." He shook his head. "I don't think we're going to find many survivors after that."

The XO continued to watch for another minute before ordering the periscope lowered. "The destroyer has sunk," he said. "The area appears to be clear. I think we should surface and see if we can find anything with her name on it, just in case someone questions whether we really got her."

Morley nodded, speaking again for the first time in hours. "Do that, XO." He opened the lower hatch and started down the ladder into the control room. "When you've finished your search, see me in my stateroom."

"Aye, aye, sir."

•   •   •

When they surfaced, there was nothing left of the Japanese destroyer but a spreading oil slick and a lot of floating debris. They found no survivors at all—not even any floating bodies, which struck Miller as a little odd. According to the manual, there should have been 200 men aboard when the ship blew up. It was hard to imagine that none of them would have floated to the surface.

Cruising slowly through the slick, they fished out a life ring and a seaman's cap. Both had something written on them, which they presumed was the ship's name. The characters look identical, at least. Since they had no one aboard who could read Japanese, they would have to wait until they got back to Pearl Harbor for someone to translate them and tell them who they'd sunk.

The transport was gone. They knew the general direction it had taken, but they never managed to find it again.

•   •   •

The captain sat heavily on his bunk, gesturing for Ames to take the chair. He kept glancing at the heavy green curtain drawn across the door, as if he was expecting it to open an any moment and disclose something unpleasant.

"Have you ever noticed," he said, "just how small these staterooms are?"

Oh, Christ! "No, sir, not particularly."

"My father's house in New London has *closets* that are bigger than this compartment. It's just so damned *tight* in here."

"It's also private, Captain. No one else has that kind of luxury, you know, sir."

Ames found himself being oddly formal. Normally, and particularly when they were alone, the formality went away and it became just Fred and Andy, reverting back to the camaraderie of their old selves as Naval Academy roommates.

But he didn't think this was the right time for that. His friend was captain of a submarine, an active warship, and he thought he needed to be reminded of that just now.

The captain shook his head. "I'd rather have some open space." He looked at the gyro repeater and depth gauge at the foot of his bunk. *Bacalao* was steady on a course of 274°, at a depth of 150 feet. "You know," he said, "a column of water one inch square increases in weight by 15 pounds for every 33 feet of depth, so allowing for the distance from the keel to the upper deck, that's 60 pounds of pressure on every square inch of the pressure hull." He smiled weakly. "That's doesn't seem like all that much, unless you stop to think about it. Have you ever thought of just how many square inches of surface there are over the entire pressure hull? It's not just 60 pounds, you know—over the whole hull there are *tons* of pressure."

Ames nodded, not much liking where this was going.

"You know, Fred," Morley continued, "I'm done with submarines after this patrol."

Ames remained silent. It was a rhetorical question. There was no way to answer correctly, no matter what you said. There might not even be a right answer.

He wasn't even sure his old friend was speaking to him. He could have been talking to himself.

Morley nodded slowly. "You should relieve me right now, you know, Fred. Just get Doc to put me on the sick list and assume command for the rest of the patrol."

"No, sir. You're the captain, and you will retain command until we get back to Pearl."

"Dammit, Fred, you saw what happened. We were in a critical situation and all I could do was stare at the overhead and wonder how quick it would all happen once it collapsed. I was fucking useless."

"Skipper, you can remove yourself when we get back to Pearl if you want, but right now you're the captain of this vessel and you need to act like it. As far as everyone is concerned, you were in command the whole time, and the credit for sinking that Nip destroyer is yours."

"I don't *want* to be in command any more."

"Well, you are, so you're just going to have to pull yourself together."

•   •   •

Morgan found Miller in the wardroom about an hour after they submerged again. "What do you suppose is going on in there?" he asked, gesturing across the passageway to the closed curtain across the door of the captain's stateroom.

Miller shrugged. "I suppose they're figuring out what happened." The XO had been in there with the captain for a good half hour by then.

"What *did* happen? I've never heard of an XO taking over the deck in the middle of a battle. At least, not unless the captain was dead or wounded."

"You'll have to ask them, Bill. I was too busy working out the targeting to worry about anything else."

That wasn't strictly true, of course, but Miller didn't figure it was his place to say anything at this point.

Weston came in with a coffee pot and refilled their cups.

Morgan sipped at his and put the cup down on the table. "One other thing," he said. "I want to put Ohara in for a medal."

That came as a surprise. So much had been going on in the conning tower that he hadn't had time to think about what was happening elsewhere during the attack. As long as orders were being carried out efficiently you just figured everything was okay.

"What happened? Why?"

"A seawater line broke in the motor room. Ohara was working in three feet of water getting the valves closed. I figure he's lucky he didn't electrocute himself in the process."

"It's dangerous, all right," Miller agreed. "You wouldn't get me down there under those conditions."

Morgan nodded. "I asked him about that. Hell, the man probably knows more about electricity than anyone aboard but Harrigan."

"What did he say?"

"He said, 'At the time, being electrocuted seemed less of a risk than drowning when the boat sank.' I think he was probably right. I had to do some fancy compensating with the ballast and trim to keep things more or less under control."

Miller smiled. "I never even noticed. I suppose I was preoccupied."

"Yeah, you were probably a little busy. But I was looking at some very strange angles. I don't think I'd be exaggerating if I said the man saved all of our necks. I want to recommend him for a Medal of Honor. He won't get it—there was just him and Carlisle back there at the time, and you need two witnesses—but I think the recommendation should still be made. Hell, going into a half-flooded motor room feels like 'above and beyond the call of duty' to me."

"Write it up. I'm pretty sure the captain will approve it and forward the recommendation. Then the brass back at Pearl can decide what they actually want to give him. I'm thinking either a Distinguished Service Medal or a Navy Cross, and hoping they'll go with the DSM."

Morgan nodded and sipped his coffee. "You're his division officer, so I figured you'd want to know."

Miller stood up. "Thanks. I think I'll wander back to maneuvering and see how he's doing. Have you told him about the medal yet?"

"No."

"Mind if I do?"

"Go right ahead, Larry. But don't forget, they don't have to give it to him."

"If they don't, then they're idiots. Besides, right now I think they'll probably be passing out medals for a lot less than that. This war just started and they're going to want to encourage the men to get out there and put forth their best effort. Just now, I expect you'll be able to get a medal for stuff that won't merit more than a letter of commendation in another year or two. So if someone does something that *really* deserves a medal he should damn well get it."

•   •   •

The normal patrol routine continued after the attack on the Japanese transport and the counter attack by the *Asashio*. Most of the men aboard remained unaware of what happened in the conning tower. The men who were there knew better than to talk about it.

Morley knew he had to pull himself together. He was aware of just how much appearances could affect morale. If the men lost confidence in their commander they might make fatal mistakes and, in a submarine, even minor errors could be fatal.

The hardest part came four days after the attack, when Kirk handed him another double-encrypted tape from the code machine. The contents were still gibberish, and now he had to take the tape into his stateroom, get out the code books, and decrypt the message.

Just closing the curtain was harder than he could have imagined. He had to overcome this claustrophobia if he was to function. It was only a few minutes, he thought. *I can do this.*

It took ten minutes, and despite the air conditioning his khaki shirt was sticking to his body, soaked in sweat. It was bad enough when he had to go into his stateroom to sleep, but then he could leave the curtain open. Decoding the messages meant shutting out the rest of the boat while he was doing it. What had for so long felt snug and private, an oasis amidst the constant bustle of everyday life aboard, now felt confining, as if there wasn't enough air in the tiny space.

At last he emerged, walking into the control room and signaling for Ames to join him at the chart table.

"Current position?"

Ames bent over the chart. "Here, sir."

Morley pulled a slip of paper from his shirt pocket, a little distressed to see that the paper was already sodden. It was a good thing he'd written the position in pencil, he thought. Ink would have run. Trying to appear calm, he laid the slip of paper on the chart table and found the indicated position on the chart, marking it with an 'X.' "We need to be here by 0700," he said.

"Something waiting for us there?"

"Troop transport. At least, someone thinks so."

"Okay." Ames looked at the chart. "New course should be three-one-niner."

"OOD, make your course three-one-niner," Morley ordered.

Hartman climbed partway up the conning tower ladder. "Helm!"

"Aye, sir?"

"Make your course three-one-niner."

"Make my course three-one-niner," Anderson repeated. "New course is three-one-niner."

"Periscope depth, Mr. Hartman."

"Aye, aye, sir. Five-degree rise on the bow planes. Make your depth six-four feet."

Morley looked at the chart a moment longer, then moved toward the ladder. "Conning tower, XO."

"Six-four feet," Hartman called up, as the captain and Ames entered the conning tower.

"Jones, anything on sonar?"

"Nothing, sir."

"Put up the SD mast and check the area."

After a minute, Jones reported that there were no radar returns. Morley nodded and walked to the number one periscope, ordering it raised. As it rose to its full extent he walked it around the horizon, scanning the dark sky and water for any sign of the enemy. After a careful check he ordered the periscope lowered.

"Let's run surfaced," he said. "I want the batteries fully charged before we get to the search area. It's full dark, and it doesn't look like there's anything around to give us any trouble."

Ames nodded agreement and walked to the ladder. "Prepare to surface," he called down. Then, after a nod from the captain, "Surface! Surface! Surface!"

•   •   •

Bacalao ran at 15 knots for the rest of the night, with three engines on propulsion and the fourth charging batteries. For the moment, the engines were cooperating. On the bridge, the lookouts were extra alert, within the conning tower, the radio operators were running the SD radar for three minutes at a time every ten minutes.

It might have been better to run it continuously, but there was still a fear that the enemy might be able to use the transmitter as a homing beacon. The range wasn't that great—only about six miles. But tests had shown it could be detected quite a distance beyond where it would get a reliable return. Whether the Japanese had receivers that could pick it up was unknown, but they had sprung enough surprises so far in the war that it didn't seem logical to take chances.

Around them, the sky was clear, the stars twinkling in the ebony sky. It never failed to amaze Miller just how many stars filled the sky miles out at sea, far beyond the nighttime glare of the cities. It was something that couldn't be experienced on land, even out in the country. Certainly not back home in Cleveland.

An hour before sunrise the captain had his sextant brought to the bridge for a star sight. "This should be close enough," he said, after plotting the sight. "We'll submerge and wait here. If Intelligence is right, our target should be along in about an hour and a half."

•   •   •

"Periscope depth," Hanson called up from the control room.

Morley had decided to give Ames the attack. As they prepared to begin their approach he motioned for the XO to join him at the conning tower chart table. "Fred," Morley said, "I want you to run this attack. You'll be up for a command of your own before long. This should be good practice for you. I'll handle the plot."

Normally, it was the other way around. The captain was on the periscope and the XO kept the plot. But Morley had too many doubts. How could he forget what happened the first time they encountered the enemy. It was Ames who took over then, when the captain couldn't get his body to listen to him.

He had told Ames repeatedly that this would be his last patrol. How ironic to find that after all the years spent in submarines, training constantly against the day when he would be able to command a boat in combat, he now knew he wasn't suited to it at all. *Bacalao* was huge compared to the boats he had served in before, yet now she seemed smaller even than the old O-boat that had first taken him beneath the surface of Long Island Sound on that memorable day in June 1932.

It was like being confined in a sewer pipe now. That wasn't even a bad simile, he thought, for the conning tower was eight feet in diameter and only 14 feet long. As he moved about the cramped cylinder—even more cramped now, with eight men stuffed into it—his head automatically bobbed up and down to avoid colliding with the equipment attached to the low overhead.

Everyone was now in his place. There was Ames, standing by the number two periscope, looking as calm as Morley thought he *should* be, but wasn't. Miller was waiting expectantly by the TDC. He seemed to be thinking about something, but Morley couldn't even guess what it might be.

Seven hours earlier he had been in his stateroom decoding the message that brought them to this place. It had been difficult to concentrate on the decoding, for that closed curtain seemed to him like the barred door of a prison cell, slammed shut from the outside and bolted securely by a cruel guard who did no more than laugh at his prisoner's pleas for freedom.

He could stay there no longer. Once this patrol ended there would be no more submarines for him. Perhaps, like his father, he would move on to destroyers, using the skills he learned as a submariner to hunt other subs. The best hunters, his father had always said, were those who had once been the hunted. They knew how to escape and, knowing that, were better able to bolt the door.

In the after part of the conning tower, Jones-1 was watching his dials and listening to his headphones. He seemed utterly calm, perhaps because, at the moment, he knew better than any man aboard just what was going on outside the hull. His passive sonar gave him a window on the outside world. The rest of them were deaf and blind. He, at least, could hear.

Across from him, Miller now looked bored. Morley could do that once, but no longer. All that stood between him and the Pacific was eleven sixteenths of an inch of steel plate. At their present depth, he supposed that would be enough. They were at periscope depth, only 64 feet from surface to keel. Not deep at all.

But he would still rather have been somewhere else.

Ames called for the periscope to be raised. As it came up he pressed his eye to the buffer and quickly swept the horizon, then steadied up on a bearing fractionally to starboard of their present course. "Large ship," he reported. "Two funnels, looks like a liner, but military paint and Imperial Navy ensign. Let's start a track. Bearing—mark!"

"Zero-zero-four."

In the port after corner of the conning tower, Miller cranked the first target bearing into the TDC.

"Down 'scope."

The periscope slid down into the well. The cable sheaves made only a slight whispering sound.

"Looks like a large troop transport," Ames said. "Probably an ex liner. Jones, what do you hear?"

"Three targets. One and two sound like destroyers. Number three sounds like a transport, two screws, heavy reciprocating."

Ames nodded and turned to Miller. "Let's see the manual."

Miller pulled out the recognition manual. Ames quickly flipped through the pages, slowing as he reached the section he was looking for. "This looks like her," he said. "*Hainan Maru*, 6,500 tons. Masthead height is 147 feet."

Ames moved back to the periscope. "Up 'scope. Good! Set masthead height one-four-seven feet."

"Set."

Ames quickly worked the stadimeter dial. "Range—mark!"

"Two-three-niner-zero."

"Bearing—mark!"

"Zero-zero-two."

"Down 'scope."

The slender periscope tip had been exposed for no more than ten seconds. To Morley, it seemed like more than ten minutes.

At the TDC, Miller cranked in the new target bearing and range. "Angle on the bow, sir?"

"Angle on the bow is port three-five," Ames said. "Alter course one degree to port."

"One degree to port, aye," Anderson repeated. "New course is two-five-eight."

"Jones, target speed."

Jones began the chopping motion with his right hand, which helped him get a revolution count. After about half a minute he said, "Speed is about one-three knots."

Miller added this to the TDC data inputs and then allowed the computer to chew on the data.

Morley made a mark on the acetate overlay covering the chart. Glancing aft, he could see his old Academy roommate standing calmly by the lowered periscope. He presented a picture of quiet deliberation, his features fixed in a determined frown.

The captain looked back at the chart, wondering if anyone else could tell how nervous he actually was. Keeping a manual plot of the approach, and using an Is-Was to back up the TDC didn't occupy nearly enough of his time, though it did help.

If there was even the slightest doubt before, now it was a certainty. This would be his first and last war patrol. All those years of training, all those exercises and hundreds of practice torpedoes fired, all the sweat and study and worry and strain that led up to this command had been for nothing. It had all been a waste. He should have stayed in the surface fleet, or maybe learned to fly, like his younger brother, who was now flying Wildcats off the *Enterprise.*

Ames checked his watch. It had been five minutes since the last observation. "Up 'scope."

He did three full sweeps, checking the sky as well as the sea. The boat wasn't that far from some Japanese held islands, and as the sky grew lighter the probability of enemy aircraft would continue to increase. For the moment, presumably, the sky was clear, for Ames again focused on the target.

"Escorts are still on station," the XO informed them. "Doesn't look like they've noticed anything yet. Target bearing—mark!"

"Zero-zero-three."

"Range—mark!"

"One-five-zero-zero."

"Down 'scope. Angle on the bow is still port three-five. One more look and we can probably take our shot."

Miller nodded. The position keeper on the TDC now showed a generated target bearing that almost exactly matched the range and bearing of the second observation. The new data was cranked in, which would further refine those readings and, at the same time, automatically update the gyro settings in both nests.

Ames glanced over at Morley, who was standing quietly by the chart table. What was he thinking? the captain wondered. Was he questioning how a captain could simply hand over an attack to a subordinate? Was he wondering how much of this—or if any of this—was really for training?

The minutes slowly ticked by. In the conning tower, everyone was sweating profusely by now. The air conditioning had been shut down all through the boat, both to conserve electrical power, and to eliminate a possible source of noise. The temperature was now well into the nineties, and each of the eight men crowded into the cramped space gave off about as much heat as a 100-watt bulb.

By the time this was over, their uniforms would be as wet as if they had been standing in the rain. As it was, they had already shed their shirts.

• • •

"Time," Miller said, after another five minutes had passed.

"Up 'scope," Ames ordered. "Final observation."

The periscope rose from its well with a whisper of steel cable passing over the sheaves and the soft whine of the hoist motor. The slender black tube emerged into the early morning sunlight, throwing up a soft feather of spray as *Bacalao* forged ahead at a bare two knots.

"Bearing—mark!"

"Zero-zero-three."

"Range—mark!"

"One-one-zero-zero."

"Down 'scope. Angle on the bow steady at port three-five," Ames announced.

Miller cranked the new data into the TDC as it continued to work on the data and update the torpedo settings. After three more minutes the solution light came on.

"We have a firing solution, sir," Miller reports. "Generated bearing is zero-zero-two."

Ames thought for a moment. It was a big ship. A big, converted liner, which meant a lot of small internal compartments with good watertight integrity, and not the big hold spaces of a freighter.

"Flood tubes one through four," he ordered, deciding four torpedoes should be enough. "Open outer doors."

"Tubes one through four flooded from WRT, sir. Outer doors are open."

"Up 'scope. Put me on."

As the periscope was raised, Collins, who had been reading off the bearings during the approach, placed his hands over Ames' and turned the periscope until the two-degree line on the azimuth ring was lined up with the mark. The crosshairs were centered perfectly with the aiming point on the target.

"Down 'scope. Fire one!"

"Fire one, aye!"

Collins flipped the switch for tube one and mashed the big firing button with the heel of his hand. The boat shuddered slightly, and the indicator light announced that the tube had been fired.

"One fired electrically, sir," Collins reported.

Ames silently counted to ten. "Fire two!"

"Fire two, aye! Two fired electrically, sir."

"Fire three!"

"Fire three, aye! Three fired electrically, sir."

"Fire four!"

"Fire four, aye! Four fired electrically, sir."

"Sound? What are they doing?"

"All fish running hot, straight and normal," Jones said.

"Up 'scope."

As the lens cleared, Ames swept the area for escorts, then centered the image on the target. At that moment the sea erupted in a tremendous blast about 450 yards beyond the bow.

Jones shouted and pulled off his headphones. He'd left off turning down the gain a second or two too long.

"Premature," Ames growled. He swung the periscope onto the nearest escort, which was now turning toward them, the white bow wave starting to grow as the destroyer picked up speed.

"Down 'scope. All ahead two-thirds. Take her down to three-zero-zero feet. Rig for depth charging. Come left to one-six-five."

As the boat was passing through 200 feet the hull shook to a hard detonation, followed ten seconds later by another.

"Did we hit him?" Miller wondered aloud.

"Jones?"

"Reciprocating has stopped," Jones reported, having replaced his headphones and adjusted his set. "Poor sound conditions, but I can hear clearly enough to tell that the target is slowing."

"What about the escorts?"

"Escorts are heading this way, bearing is opening."

Ames smiled at that. If the bearing was opening, then the escorts had failed to detect *Bacalao*'s course change and were still charging for where the boat had been when she fired. "Reduce to dead slow," he ordered. It would make them quieter.

A minute later everyone in the conning tower could hear the drumming of the escort's propellers as he passed astern. Jones turned the gain way down a moment later.

"Depth charges coming down," he announced.

It wasn't as bad this time, Ames thought. The escorts obviously didn't have a good fix on their position, and their depth charges exploded well astern and above them. The boat shook to the concussion, but no one was thrown off his feet and, as each compartment reported in, it appeared there had been no damage this time.

Jones turned the sound back up. "Lots of noise," he said. "Could be a ship breaking up, but I can't be sure."

"Let's hope it is," Ames said. "There should have been a couple thousand troops on that ship. If we can drown them here, they can't kill our own guys later."

"The other escort is making his run," Jones announced.

"Bearing?"

"One-seven-zero, no Doppler effect."

"He's heading for the same position as the first escort, looks like," Morley said, looking up from the chart. He smiled. "They don't know where we are."

"Let's try to keep it that way, then," Ames said, walking over to the chart table to join his friend.

• • •

Over the next five hours the escorts dropped a total of 47 depth charges. The two destroyers took turns, alternately listening and dropping, once again reminding the American submariners that prewar estimates of Japanese antisubmarine technology and skill had been far from accurate. Their sonar appeared to be at least as good as anything on a comparable American ship and, so far, the enemy commanders they had encountered all seemed to know what they were doing.

Still, none of the later attacks were even as close as the first. For all the care the Japanese captains were taking in their coordinated attack, it seemed to the Americans that they must be chasing after ghosts, or whales, or a school of fish. So far as they were concerned, it was sufficient that the depth charges weren't coming down around *them.*

Her motors barely turning, *Bacalao* had slowly moved away from the area, until the sound of the enemy depth charges was no more than a distant rumble. They stayed deep as they cleared the area. If the enemy hadn't found them yet, they would do nothing to make it easier for him to do so.

Every indication short of surfacing and taking a look suggested that they had sunk the transport. Putting down the escorts as well might have made a nice bonus, but that wasn't what they were there for. The transports, freighters and tankers were the most important targets, as were *major* combatants—battleships, aircraft carriers, cruisers and other submarines. They carried the troops, fuel and equipment that allowed the enemy to take the battle to the American troops on the Pacific islands, or provided the major firepower for sea battles. The escorts might be more dangerous to *Bacalao* on an individual basis, but killing a transport would do a lot more for the war effort.

• • •

It was well after dark when *Bacalao* at last thrust her 1,800 tons to the surface, following a long, careful look around the area with the number one periscope. Morley followed Paul onto the bridge, with Winston, the OOD, right behind them. For a moment they remained alone there, each carefully scanning his assigned sector of ocean for anything that might have been missed through the periscope. If there was going to be a surprise, the fewer topside the better.

Satisfied that they were alone, "routine" was called down and the lookouts and the rest of the bridge party scurried up the ladder and climbed to their posts. Even with the boat rigged for red it would be nearly a quarter hour before everyone's eyes had fully adjusted to the darkness, so extra caution was in order.

Morley found himself alone, surrounded by the others, yet isolated at the same time. It was going to be difficult to dive again. A *Gato* was a big vessel, as large as a World War I destroyer, yet within her cylindrical pressure hull everything was always so close that there was virtually no place a man could stand where he couldn't reach out and touch a part of the hull.

His stateroom, the one place aboard where there was an expectation of privacy lasting longer than the time it took to use the head, was hardly larger than one of the closets in his father's New London house. He could touch the curtain that covered the door from his bunk by leaning out only a little. Yet, while it had never seemed large, before the first attack it had seemed large enough.

Now it felt so small that he could hardly stand to be there. Even closing the curtain was enough to induce something close to panic, though he had to do so when they received an Ultra message. Those he had to decrypt personally.

There was simply no way around it. He would finish this patrol, because it was his job, and because fourteen years in the Navy—eighteen if you counted the Academy—had ingrained the absolute need to finish a job so deeply into his character that he was compelled to do so even in the face of death itself.

Even in the face of his own fears.

He knew that he would never be able to command another submarine after this patrol—would probably never even sail in one—and that it was going to take every bit of willpower just to finish *this* patrol.

But he would do it.

Somehow.

VIII
Change of Command

WHEN *BACALAO* ARRIVED BACK AT PEARL HARBOR at the end of January 1942, the cleanup was clearly under way. The harbor was still a mess, to be sure, and would remain that way for a long time, but it was obvious that everyone was hard at work trying to set right the damage.

The Japanese had made a lot of mistakes. They had managed to catch everyone napping, but the very nature of Pearl Harbor had worked against them. The shallow anchorage often made it tricky to work the big ships in and out. But it also made the salvage work easier. Even sitting on the bottom, the upper decks of some of the battleships were still dry. Raising them would be mostly a matter of plugging the holes and then pumping the water out and floating them into the big dry docks.

Except for *Arizona*, damaged beyond any hope of repair by a direct hit on a magazine, and the elderly target ship *Utah*, which wasn't considered to have any future combat role, the Navy had made it clear that every major combatant would be raised, rebuilt and sent off to war as soon as humanly possible.

The enemy blunder that surprised Miller the most during the attack, and continued to amaze him even now, was that they had failed to bomb the huge fuel tank farms in the hills above the Submarine Base. If they had managed to blow up those tanks they would not only have incinerated a good part of the base, but the lack of fuel would have forced any remaining fleet units back to their old bases in San Diego and San Francisco.

Destroying those fuel tanks would have done far more damage to the war fighting ability of the United States than sinking every battleship in the Pacific Fleet. It might even have left Hawaii vulnerable to the same fate as the Philippines.

He was just glad they'd screwed up.

The first submarines had been dispatched on patrol by noon on the same day the Japanese attacked. Others, already at sea, had at once gone onto a combat footing. All that fuel was still there in Hawaii, ready for them to use.

How well could they have managed, Miller wondered, if they had to start each patrol in San Diego. By the time they reached their patrol area they would have had to turn right around and go home. As it was, facilities were being arranged on Midway that would allow the boats to refuel and refit even closer to the action.

That would be good for the boats, requiring less transit time to and from their patrol areas, but the crews would probably hate it. Midway had lots of gooney birds, but no women, and the average enlisted submariner wasn't that interested in ornithology.

•   •   •

Three days after *Bacalao* tied up at the Submarine Base, Admiral Nimitz came aboard and pinned a Navy Cross on Morley and a Distinguished Service Medal on Ames. At the same time, he also pinned a Distinguished Service Medal on Ohara. His expression suggested that no one had informed him of Ohara's ancestry—if those who approved the medal were even aware of it—but the newly-promoted admiral didn't let it throw him. He even made a few remarks about America as a melting pot, and how this war would be fought and won by brave men who were loyal to America, no matter where their ancestors might have come from.

The medals had been awarded very quickly, only a few days after the recommendations were turned in. At this point in the war, recognition of almost any heroic act was of considerable importance to morale and medals were approved with astonishing speed.

On the same day, Morley received orders to take command of an old destroyer. Like his father, he was leaving submarines to go into the business of hunting them. Officially, moving up to the command of a destroyer, which brought with it promotion to commander, was a reward for a job well done, as was his Navy Cross.

In Ohara's case, there was no question that it was well earned. As Morgan had predicted, the lack of a second witness to the near disaster in the maneuvering room had scuttled any chance of a Medal of Honor, so the Navy had given him the next best thing.

As for Morley and Ames, Miller suspected that the higher ups were perfectly aware of what had happened. Ames' DSM and Morley's Navy Cross made that clear enough.[*] From the official patrol report, it was hard to tell just *what* had actually happened. Miller's feeling was that large parts of that report should have been sent off the *Argosy*, because the description of what happened in the conning tower would have made a great piece of short fiction for that men's adventure magazine.

Officially, *Bacalao* had been credited with sinking the *Asashio* in their first encounter, along with the transport and another ship of the same type two days later. Just before leaving the patrol area they added a 3,000-ton freighter to the bag. It was a good start.

And they would not have to break in a new commander. Ames was already qualified for command, so he would move into the CO's state-room once *Bacalao* was handed back following a refit at the Pearl Harbor Navy Yard. For the moment, everyone was staying at the Royal Hawaiian, and a relief crew was aboard during the refit.

Ames' step up was, Miller thought, one more indication that those who made the decisions knew what really happened.

It also meant a step up for Miller. Morgan was given a temporary promotion to lieutenant commander and made XO. He hadn't been considered qualified a few months earlier, but it appeared that those few months, and a successful war patrol, now qualified him for the job. His promotion moved Miller up to number three.

For now, they had two weeks to relax. A hotel, or rest camp, would become a regular part of the homecoming routine for each submarine crew. For two weeks the caretaker crew would come aboard to stand fire watches, handle the normal in-port routine, and keep an eye on the shipyard workers who would be busy with the dozens of minor items that always needed fixing.

There would be some who thought this sort of treatment was a bit too much, that the submariners were being pampered when compared to other sailors. But the truth was that most of the men on the big ships never experienced the sort of constant tension and danger that was the daily norm for a submariner.

---

[*] Before 7 August 1942, the Navy Distinguished Service Medal ranked immediately below the Medal of Honor in precedence, with the Navy Cross ranked third. After that date, the Navy Cross was made a combat-only award, and raised in rank to number two. As Ames received the higher ranking (at the time) medal, it suggested that the Navy believed he probably had more to do with the success of the patrol than did the captain.

They had no friends during a war patrol. Just as they hunted the enemy, so the enemy hunted them. And the enemy had the distinct advantage of being able to stay on station for days at a time if he so chose. A sub could stay down no longer than two days, and even that was stretching endurance to the absolute maximum.

Nor was it much better coming home. The Army bomber pilots who patrolled the waters around Hawaii hadn't been of any use while the islands were under attack, but they seem extraordinarily adept at finding returning submarines. Correctly identifying them as friendly, however, seemed to be beyond the pilots' capabilities. The Army pilots seemed to think they were supposed to bomb *every* submarine, no matter which side it happened to be on.

•   •   •

Miller was summoned two days after the change of command, finding Ames in his temporary quarters at the Royal Hawaiian. He was looking a bit uneasy as he sat in a straight-backed chair by a window. Miller couldn't help wondering how it must be for him, sitting there knowing that the only reason he had a command was that his best friend had just declared himself unfit for submarines.

"We've got a problem," Ames said. "With Ohara."

So it wasn't his sudden ascension to command that was troubling him. "What about him, sir? I've never noticed any problems with his performance. Far from it."

"It's not me, Larry. It's not even anything to do with the boat. Some paranoid security type on CincPac's staff wants to pull Ohara off our boat and send him back to the States."

"Did he give a reason, sir?"

"Not a very good one. He just seems to think that any Japanese sailor is automatically a security risk."

Miller shook his head. "Hell, sir, Ohara is no more Japanese than I am, regardless of what he looks like. He's also the best EM I have in my department."

"You won't get any arguments from me, Larry. If you ask me, the DSM we just gave him wasn't enough. Bill Morgan was right, he should have got a Medal of Honor. And it didn't sound like Admiral Nimitz considered him a security risk." He smiled. "Of course, I imagine you know that CincPac is an old submariner, too. *He* likes our guys."

"So what do we do, sir?"

"First thing, you get yourself into a fresh uniform and get over to headquarters and have a talk with this Commander Bataglia. I don't want to lose Ohara for the wrong reasons. It's bad enough we can expect to lose him to promotion before long. Get yourself over there and do what you can to convince this security type that we need the man."

"Aye, aye, sir."

Miller returned to the room he was sharing with Morgan and changed into a fresh set of khakis. Just what sort of stupidity was this supposed to be? Between his experience in submarines and his university training in electrical engineering—minor or not, it was still more than anyone else in the department had—Ohara was one of the best qualified electrician's mates in the fleet. Shipping him back to the States, most likely to some pointless job fixing old toasters in a depot in the middle of nowhere, would be as big a waste of resources as sending the *Enterprise* to patrol Lake Erie on the off chance that the Toronto Lion's Club would decide to launch an invasion of Cleveland.

Miller arrived at headquarters at 13:30, found Commander Bataglia's office, and settled in to wait. His yeoman said the commander was busy, but *might* find time for him eventually.

Two hours later he was admitted to the inner sanctum, where he was confronted by a short, swarthy officer with graying hair and a dark five o'clock shadow on his jowls.

"And where are you from, Lieutenant?" he asked.

"*Bacalao*, sir."

"So what are you here about?"

"According to my CO, you're trying to take away my best electrician's mate. I need him."

"What's his name?"

"Ohara, Kenneth, EM1."

Bataglia shuffled through the stack of files on his cluttered desk until he found the one he wanted. "That's the Nip, right?"

"He's from Atlanta, sir, not Tokyo."

"What makes you think you can trust him?"

"I've been working with him since the boat was under construction, sir. I think I know the men in my division."

"Your boat was here during the attack, right?"

"Yes, sir, that's right."

"Did you get a chance to see what this Ohara guy was up to while that was going on?"

"Only at the beginning of the attack, sir. He was on deck, repairing a broken sternlight, when it started. His battle station is on the main board in maneuvering, so I sent him below just after things started getting exciting."

"How did he react? Once he realized who was attacking, I mean?"

"I only heard him make one comment before he went below. As he was starting down the hatch a Zero flew over."

"What did he say, Mr. Miller?"

"I believe his exact words were, 'Kill that fucking Nip bastard,' sir." Bataglia blinked. "How did you react to that?"

"In the usual way, sir. Once the attack was over, I suggested that he might want to be a little more temperate in his language. I happened to agree with the sentiment, mind you."

Bataglia wrote something in the file. "So you don't think he's likely to be sending messages to the enemy, or possibly doing something to sabotage your boat? Japs don't really care if they die, you know, as long as it serves their emperor."

Miller just shook his head. "If he wanted to sink the boat he could have just sat on his ass and let it sink. But he didn't, so we all got back okay. As it is, a couple days ago Admiral Nimitz pinned a DSM on him for getting the situation back aft under control during a depth charge attack, and in the process saving a submarine and 77 men." He thought for a second. "Besides, I don't think Southern Baptists look very favorably on suicide under *any* circumstances."

Bataglia was still writing. "So you don't think he's a security risk, then?"

"No more so than anyone else who happened to have a great-grandfather who was born in a country we're presently at war with."

Bataglia frowned. Miller thought that he had managed to get across that he could see no more—or less—reason to trust an Italian than a Japanese where security was concerned. A man was either loyal or he wasn't, and Miller didn't think it made a damned bit of difference where his ancestors happened to come from.

"Actually," Bataglia said, "it was my father who was the first to come here, but I get your point. In any case, I'm going to let you keep your man for now."

"Thank you, sir."

"And you do know, lieutenant, that it's *your* ass on the line if anything goes wrong."

From what he knew of Ohara, Miller figured his ass was safe enough. "Yes, sir," he said. "Thank you, sir."

"There's nothing personal about this, you know, Mr. Miller," Bataglia said. "We have to sort out the good guys from the bad guys. And it's not just Jap sailors, either. We're looking at everyone with a questionable background."

"Have you found any yet?"

"No. But we still have to look, don't we?"

•   •   •

When the boat emerged from the yard and the crew returned there was an obvious, and rather jarring, change in her appearance. Miller wasn't quite sure he liked the new look.

The yard had attacked the conning tower fairwater with a vengeance. The steel bulwark plating had been completely cut away from just abaft the periscope shears, leaving the cigarette deck a naked platform. A rail of sorts had been fashioned from a few slender stanchions and some steel cable.

Above the upper bridge, the plating had been stripped off the periscope shears, leaving something that was both ugly and purely utilitarian. He had to concede that the bare shears would very likely make the boat just a little bit harder to spot against a sea horizon. It looked damned odd, though.

The differences weren't quite as obvious at the forward end of the fairwater. On the first day out of Pearl, Morley had put two men to work removing the glass from the forebridge deadlights. The yard had completed that work and removed the frames. They had also removed the surface steering station. From now on, the helmsman would have to steer from inside the conning tower, even in confined waters.

One of the yard people told Miller that they had really done only a partial job, wanting to get the boat back to sea as quickly as possible. On the next Stateside overhaul, he said, they would likely cut down the front of the fairwater as well, leaving only a platform similar to what had been done to the cigarette deck.

The .50-caliber mount had been moved from the forward deck to the cigarette deck, and pressure-proof storage had been added, so that it would no longer be necessary to bring the heavy gun up from below. It could now be stowed only a few feet from where it was mounted.

Another would probably be added to the front of the fairwater, once that was cut down. Or, if they were lucky, the Navy might decide to provide something a little bigger.

Down in the engine rooms, the lower compression seals had been replaced on all four main engines. Problems with those had become endemic, despite Morgan's certainty that the problem had been fixed after *Bacalao* first arrived in Hawaii. The fixes, if any, hadn't lasted, and they spent the last three weeks of their first war patrol dealing with engine problems.

By time they returned to Pearl, number four was completely out of service, and the other three main engines were running at no better than 70 percent. In a submarine, where it was necessary to balance the need for high surface speed with the equally compelling need to keep the batteries fully charged, the loss of an engine was always a potential disaster.

Morgan was still convinced that the basic design was a good one, but Orville Hanson, who had taken over as chief engineer when Morgan was promoted, was less ambiguous about it. He had taken up the same habit as the engineers in the first batch of boats cursed with these engines, pronouncing the initials of the manufacturer, Hooven-Owens-Rentschler, as a word.

Left up to Hanson, all the H.O.R. engines would have been ripped out and replaced with the same Winton or Fairbanks-Morse engines installed in the rest of the *Gato* class boats. Since *Bacalao* had been built by Electric Boat, probably Wintons.

Even those had their problems, Hanson admitted, but not to the same degree as the H.O.R.s, and they were a lot easier to fix. As for *Bacalao*'s current engines, Hanson thought they might make good buoy anchors.

The final operation, and perhaps the most ominous, had been removing the rescue buoys from the forward and after decks. The holes had been covered with perforated steel blanking plates. With the country at war, rescue was less a priority now. In combat, releasing a rescue buoy would only tell the enemy where they were.

The Japanese wouldn't take out the phone and ask if they could help, after all. They'd just use the buoy as an aiming point for their depth charges, so as to be sure the job was finished.

But as much as the boat had changed, the crew had changed more. A third of them were gone, their places taken by new men. About half of the replacements were non-quals, fresh from Submarine School, who would now have to combine their assigned job with completing their qualification in submarines under the watchful eyes of the chiefs and their new XO.

They didn't know it yet, but this was something else that would become part of the routine. Experienced men were needed to fill in the crews of new boats, which were now being rushed to completion, and the new men needed experience. About a third of the crew would rotate out after each patrol.

Collins had already been around to complain. The Navy had decided to promote Marble to Chief and send him off to another boat. Collins didn't begrudge the man his promotion, which was overdue in any case, but he hated to lose his forward torpedo room tube captain.

They still had both Joneses with them. With everyone else, they were now at work getting the huge pile of provisions off the dock and into the hull. It was a tedious job, for nearly everything had to be removed from the cartons it arrived in, and the individual cans, boxes and bags lowered down the ladders. Most of the cartons were too big to fit through the hatches.

Below, Niederst would be supervising the crew as they stowed the supplies in accordance with his planned menus. He had to know what would be needed, and when they would need it, before the food was even brought aboard, so that he would be able to get at it when he needed it. There was so much food packed into the storage spaces that it was impossible to get to anything stowed on the bottom until whatever was higher up in the pile was consumed.

The same rule applied to loading a submarine's pantry that applied to a junior officer getting into a boat with an admiral—first in, last out.

And it wasn't just the storage spaces, freezer and cooler, either. The big cans of food were everywhere. It was presumed that the boat could remain at sea for about 75 days before running out of fuel. The designed food storage spaces couldn't hold enough for that long, so the rest was just stuffed in anywhere there was an empty space.

The food was the last thing to come aboard. Once it was all stowed, *Bacalao* would be ready for sea. The expended torpedoes had been replaced, fuel tanks topped off, and the fresh water tanks filled. The two high-capacity Kleinschmidt fresh water stills in the forward engine room were sufficient to keep the tanks filled at sea, but it was a lot less trouble to start out with them already full.

Going below, Miller went to his stateroom, which he was still sharing with Morgan and Hartman. Morgan had the top bunk, which required a little extra effort to climb into, but had the advantage of being the only bunk where the occupant could—almost—sit erect. Miller was on the bottom. Too much time in too many rough seas had convinced him that there was some virtue in not having very far to fall.

It wasn't quite like sleeping on the deck, but it was close.

Hartman was in the middle bunk. Neither of them had much in the way of headroom. You could sleep on your side, but only if you didn't mind your shoulders rubbing against the bunk above you.

Miller rummaged around in his locker and found his writing pad. The boat was scheduled to depart on her second war patrol in the morning, so it was time to let his mother know what was up.

At least, the parts he was allowed to tell her. There was a war on, after all, and nearly everything really interesting was classified.

IX
Back to the War

IT FELT A BIT ODD TO BE GETTING UNDER WAY without Morley on the bridge, Ames thought. That was the moment when it really hit him. Before, as XO, he had shared in the responsibility, but now it was all his.

People spoke of the loneliness of command. From the outside, this seemed something of a cliché. Every commander was surrounded by his crew and advised by his subordinates. In the constant bustle of the daily routine he was rarely alone, except for those brief moments when he could shut himself up in his stateroom and grab a few precious minutes of sleep.

It was different from this angle, Ames thought. When you *became* the captain you suddenly found yourself perched on the pinnacle of a pyramid. Those below would still offer advice and would, in turn, do what they were told to do. But there it ended. At the end of the day he would be left with the entire responsibility for everything that happened.

Before the war, when that poor striker in the forward torpedo room overcharged the impulse tank and gave away their position, he wasn't the one who ending up standing in front of Tommy Withers' desk and having to take the responsibility. The responsibility had worked its way up the line. Morton had made the mistake, but was still just learning the job and the tube captain, Marble, had told Collins that *he* was at fault for not watching the new man closely enough. Collins, in turn, had assumed the fault at a higher level, since it was his department.

Then, of course, Lyle Winston, as torpedo officer, had said that *he* was responsible. Whatever the enlisted men had done wrong, he quite rightly felt that as their division officer it had been his job to ensure they did it right. And, since he was the captain, Morley had then accepted the blame for all of them. He'd take the credit for the boat's accomplishments, but he also got to take the blame when something went wrong. The captain was always and invariably responsible for everything that happened in his ship.

Now it was Ames' turn.

There was no denying they had had a good first patrol. *Bacalao* had been credited with a total of 15,300 tons, including the two transports and the *Asashio*. It was a fine start. A lot of other boats, dispatched at the same time, had come back without sinking anything.

Curiously, the same behavior that had previously been required was now being condemned. Sonar attacks were out and captains were now expected to use the periscope for submerged approaches. What had been considered an unacceptable risk only a few weeks earlier was now normal procedure. Not every commander who had taken a boat out on her first patrol was still on the bridge.

Morley was a special case, as he had removed himself. Ames found it strange that a man who had spent the better part of a decade in submarines should suddenly become claustrophobic, but he was a sailor, not a psychiatrist. He had no doubts about Morley's bravery. The simple fact that he *did* complete the patrol was evidence of that.

One or two others were gone because they were already scheduled for rotation before the war started. War or not, any command was a temporary position that would eventually be turned over to someone else while the incumbent went on with his career.

Some others were gone because someone didn't think they'd tried hard enough, which Ames personally doubted. Probably they had and it just hadn't done much good. Ames had spent a lot of time during the overhaul talking to the other COs. Some were going back out, others were not. But there had been one common thread in all of these conversations.

Everyone was wondering if the new torpedoes really worked.

It was something he had noticed during the attack on the destroyer, when the second fish smashed squarely into her stern and didn't explode. Collins had agreed with his guess, that it was the air flask that had created the weak "explosion," and not the warhead.

"You'd probably still have about 1,500 pounds in the air flask at that range," Collins had said. "The impact would probably burst the flask. Not enough to do the kind of damage the warhead could, but it would still make some noise and throw up a lot of water and pieces."

It made sense to Ames. When he was a kid, back in Illinois, he saw a welder accidentally knock over a full oxygen tank. The valve broke off and the tank took off like a rocket, going right through a cinder block wall and ending up in the front seat of a Model T on the other side of the street.

The question wasn't limited to bursting air flasks, of course. The real question was why the warhead hadn't exploded. Or, for that matter, why three more torpedoes had blown up *before* they got to the target.

Collins would have been tearing his hair out by the roots over the prematures if he still had any. As one of the men who had worked on the Mark-6 exploder at Newport he was loathe to place any fault on the design, but he couldn't explain it any other way. All three times the torpedo had blown up just about when the safety would have come off. It was a mystery. The only tangible result, in *Bacalao's* case, was that Collins had spent a couple of days in the torpedo shop before the patrol, carefully double checking the exploders in their current load.

Morgan was with Ames on the bridge as they emerged from the channel, following an old destroyer-minesweeper through the safety lane and out to sea. Morgan didn't seem any more confident than Ames that the Army pilots could tell where they were at any given moment, which led to the natural conclusion that the safety lane wasn't all that safe. Neither of them would be comfortable until they were well beyond the limits of the Hawaiian air patrols.

It was bad enough to have to worry about the enemy without having to worry about your own people. Even Morley had never trusted pilots, and his brother was one.

Ames had learned something because of that, though. One day before the war Rick Morley had taken both of them up in a rented plane and flown out over the Pacific. From 15,000 feet, they noticed, even a large ship was virtually invisible against the ruffled surface of the sea. At least, as long as it wasn't moving. But if the ship was under way, as they were now, the wake produced a clear track on the ocean's surface, with the ship located at the moving end.

It made a small vessel, like a submarine, just about as easy to find as a battleship.

Ames turned around to peer up at the lookouts on the bridge overhead, standing by the newly-denuded periscope shears. "Keep an eye out for planes," he said. "Ours, particularly. But don't neglect the ocean, either."

A Japanese sub had surfaced off California and fired a few shells from his deck gun. It hadn't done any appreciable damage, but if it they could get a sub that far, it wouldn't be that hard for them to put one close to Hawaii.

As Morley had once pointed out, submariners were sneaky bastards. That was their job. No one in the boat had any doubts that they were the good guys, yet they fought the war by adopting the same tactics as the villain in a Gene Autry movie, setting up an ambush for his unsuspecting victim.

And it worked both ways. The enemy was just as interested in ambushing them. These waters were heavily patrolled for exactly that reason. The Japanese had got a couple of midget subs into the area during the Pearl Harbor attack, presumably with the intention of sneaking them into the harbor to add to the chaos.

Those midget subs didn't have much in the way of range, from what could be determined by examining the one that washed up on shore. There was no engine, only batteries. That meant they had to be ferried from Japan, and the little sub's commander had admitted that his boat had traveled on the deck of a larger submarine. No doubt that big sub had continued to lurk nearby, on the chance that one of the big fleet units would attempt to sortie.

It was exactly what Ames would have done.

•   •   •

The early part of a patrol was usually the least exciting, Miller decided. It was a long way from Honolulu to the patrol area, and the biggest danger during that time was from "friendly" forces. The boat kept a good radar watch, though never a continuous one. Oddly, he thought, running the radar might help reduce their risk. Japanese subs didn't have any sort of radar, so if an American pilot detected radar, it was a pretty good indication that he had found an American boat.

Not that he figured it would help all that much. You just couldn't trust a pilot.

Still, other than worrying about being attacked by their own planes, or running into an unexpected Japanese warship, the first two weeks were fairly routine. Miller spent a lot of time in the maneuvering room, where Harrigan and Ohara were busy training a couple of new men.

"That's the trouble with the Navy," Harrigan complained. "As soon as you get a man trained and qualified, they take him away from you."

"I'm still here, Chief," Ohara commented.

"Yeah, but for how long?"

"I'm guessing as long as you want me. Ya'll are used to me, but I figure if they throw me into the replacement pool too many commanders are just going to see a Nip in an American uniform and throw me back."

"As much trouble as I went through to keep you here," Miller said, "you'd *better* stay around for a while."

"Yes, sir—and I appreciate it, too. I just can't imagine how awful it would have been to spend the rest of the war someplace safe and boring."

This wasn't the first time Miller had noticed that Ohara had a very well developed sense of irony. In this case, his expression suggested that he was perfectly happy with his present situation, but couldn't resist needling his division officer just a little.

Submarines were generally a lot less formal than surface ships. The sort of formality found in a battleship just wouldn't work there. Everyone lived too close together for that sort of stratification. They all depended on each other too much.

"Well," Harrigan said, "you're a Nip, but you're *our* Nip, and you damn sure know your way around this boat's electrical system, which is all I figure I need to worry about." He frowned. "Now, if you can just manage to get this new batch up to snuff, too."

"About all I can do is try, Chief."

• • •

"We'll be going after a Jap carrier sometime tomorrow morning," Ames announced, when most of the officers had gathered in the wardroom. Only Hartman was absent. Someone had to be in charge in the control room, and for the moment it was him.

"Do we know which one?" Morgan asked.

"Supposed to be the *Zuikaku.* That was one of the carriers they used to attack Pearl Harbor, according to the Intelligence boys, so we really want to get that bastard."

"Get us within range," Winston said, "and my boys will put a full salvo of Mark-14s into him."

"I'll damned sure do what I can to give you a good shot."

"This could be tricky," Morgan commented. "One of the problems with going after a carrier is that you have to expect him to have some planes in the air. Her captain would be a fool if he didn't keep a patrol up, just to keep an eye on things. Like watching out for subs."

Ames nodded. "That's something to consider. We can expect him to have at least three escorts, too."

"We're not going back to a strictly sound approach, are we, Captain?" Miller asked.

"Not a chance. The target is too important. We'll have to take our chances. It's what they pay us for."

Miller smiled. "Not enough, they don't."

"The new paint job might help," Morgan said. "With any luck the all over black will make us look like a whale from the air. It would be better if they couldn't see us at all from the air once we're submerged, but I'm not too confident of that."

"What's the weather look like?" Ames asked.

"Should be clear, not much wind," Morgan replied, glumly. "Or so the geniuses with their isobars and charts report."

"So, not good." Like any submariners, if Ames was going to have to set up an attack, he preferred heavy clouds and lots of whitecaps to hide the periscope."

"We'll just have to be careful," Winston said.

Ames lifted his coffee cup and sipped thoughtfully. "Just so those fish of yours blow up when they're suppose to, Lyle."

"They've been checked and double-checked, Skipper," Winston replied. "Collins went over every one of them personally, and he knows as much about those Mark-6 exploders as anyone in the Navy."

"Are we *sure* those things actually work?" Ames asked. "I don't remember a lot of prematures with the old exploders. There don't seem to be a lot of complaints from the S-boat skippers, either. Those old wrecks seem to be doing better with those antiquated Mark-10s than we are with modern boats and the latest torpedoes."

"They may need to fiddle with the design a bit, Captain," Winston said, "but it's a good design and a big improvement over the old ones."

Miller laughed. "Right. That's what Bill said about our damned engines."

"You mean number one through four anchors?" Hanson asked.

"Have they given you the least bit of trouble on this patrol?" Morgan asked. He would probably remain a diehard defender of double acting diesels for the rest of his career.

Hanson shook his head. "Not yet. But give them time. It's still pretty early in the patrol."

"Right," Ames said. "Let's get back on track. Torpedoes are good, as far as you can tell?"

"Yes, sir."

"Engineering—any real problems yet?"

"So far, so good, Skipper," Hanson said.

"Fine. Now, here's what I want to do. It's dark topsides by now, so we'll surface once we've finished here and run at full speed until just before dawn. That should put us in the right place to catch the carrier about 0930."

"Presuming the Nips don't get lost on the way," Morgan said.

Ames nodded. It wasn't that unusual to arrive at the proper coordinates after a high-speed run only to find that the enemy wasn't there. As often as not, they never did show up. It was popular to say that the Japanese simply couldn't navigate. More likely, though, they just changed course for some reason and Intelligence didn't find out about it quickly enough.

That was probably true for the naval units. Japanese merchant skippers no doubt shared the same predilections as those of most other countries, which did not include a Navy officer's obsession with hitting every waypoint at the exact time predicted.

"We'll just have to do what we can," Ames said.

•   •   •

Miller had the deck at first light. The night had been unremarkable, with a full moon making the lookouts' jobs a little easier. That was something of a mixed blessing, Miller thought. If it made it easier for the lookouts to spot anything in the water, it also made it easier for the enemy to see *them*. To a submarine, a surfaced submarine was just one more target.

Submerged, two subs couldn't effectively hunt each other. There was no practical way to aim. If both were at periscope depth and looking around, one of them could possibly shoot at the other's periscope, but that was about the limit of it.

With *Bacalao* on the surface, it was another matter entirely. Even after being chopped up by the workers at Pearl, the conning tower fairwater still presented a large, blocky silhouette against the night sky. Worse, at 19 knots the sound gear was just about useless. The flow noise from their passage through the water would drown out all but the loudest underwater noises.

The active gear might get a feeble return, but there was no way they'd go active if they could avoid it. Destroyers did most of their serious hunting with active sonar, but there was nothing particularly stealthy about a destroyer, so making a lot of noise was balanced by the need for a clear sound picture.

Subs used active sonar almost exclusively for range finding. The rest of the time they just listened quietly, trying not to draw any undue attention to themselves.

The captain came up onto the bridge at 0600, taking advantage of the millions of stars in the black velvet night sky to shoot several of them and get an accurate position. He had quickly gone below to plot his sights, and now he returned.

"We're right about where we should be," Ames said. "We'll dive in 25 minutes and wait for the enemy to come to us."

"Nice of the Japs to tell us where they're going to be, isn't it, Captain?"

"Let's hope they don't figure out they're doing it. I hate to admit it, Larry, but they're a lot better at this than anyone suspected before the war." He shook his head, looking off toward the east, where a faint glow was now outlining the horizon. "Hell, do you think *we* could have snuck up on their fleet at Yokosuka and pulled off the same sort of surprise?"

"We wouldn't try, Skipper. We'd have warned them we were coming. That good old American sense of fair play." Miller smiled. "And, besides, it just pisses the other guy off if you blindside him. We'd give them a little warning—not much, but a little."

"From what I heard," Ames said, "they tried. Someone told me the Jap ambassador was supposed to deliver a note breaking off diplomatic relations a half hour before they dropped the first bomb. But he was late for some reason, and they started the war without giving us that little bit of warning. Or whatever it was supposed to be."

"A half hour wouldn't have made much difference. They'd still have caught us napping."

"True enough. No one expected an attack on Hawaii even if the Nips did start something. Maybe some sabotage attempts by the local Japs, but nothing like what happened. We all assumed that the Philippines would be the logical target." Ames frowned, looking angrily along the forward deck. "Hawaii was *too far* from Japan for them to attack."

"Makes you wonder, doesn't it, Captain? What else have we missed or underestimated?"

"Like what, Larry?"

"What about radar on their carriers?"

"They're not supposed to have it."

"Are we sure?"

"Supposedly. Of course, they weren't supposed to have good sonar, either. I think it's a possibility we need to consider, but even if we were sure it wouldn't stop us from attacking." He shrugged. "Anyway, we're going in at periscope depth, so it shouldn't matter. No one has radar sensitive enough to get a return off the top couple feet of a periscope."

Miller nodded. That was probably true enough for now, though he was also sure the engineers were working on it. "When do you suppose we'll get a useful search radar of our own?" Miller asked.

"A few months, from what I've heard."

They lapsed into silence after that. The captain stayed on the bridge, mostly just looking around in the fading darkness. Miller continued to scan the sea with his binoculars every few minutes. There was nothing to see but the water and the slowly growing light.

Finally, Ames looked at his watch and started for the hatch. "It's time," he said. "Get everyone below and dive the boat, Mr. Miller."

•　　•　　•

"Three contacts," Jones reported, "bearing one-zero-five. Sound like warships. Very faint."

"Can you make out types, Jones?" Ames asked.

"Too faint."

"About the right bearing, looks like," Morgan said.

Ames nodded. "Can you make out a course yet, Jones?"

Jones listened intently, his left hand aiming the starboard projector more precisely at the target. After a minute he made another adjustment. "Target bearing now one-zero-eight," he said. "Coming this way."

"XO?"

Morgan looked at the chart. "Right where they should be."

Ames walked to the forward end of the conning tower and peered over the helmsman's shoulder. *Bacalao* was right on course, at a speed of three knots.

"Present course is three-two-zero," he said. He thought about it for a moment, making a decision. "Come right to zero-six-eight," he ordered. "Maintain present speed."

"New course zero-six-eight, aye."

The enemy was coming toward them. Putting the boat on a reciprocal course would allow Ames to close the distance more quickly. A carrier was too valuable to risk letting it get away.

•　　•　　•

Torpedoman's Mate 1st Class Curtis Hoolihan paced the length of the forward torpedo room, checking everything once again. He was new to the job of tube captain as well as to his rate. He'd been promoted when Marble picked up his chief's hat and moved on to run the torpedo department in another boat.

Marble's first hat, an old, badly stained one he'd bought from Harrigan, who wore more or less the same size, went out with the trash when they went in for refit. Marble bought a new one as soon as he got ashore. The first, used one, went the way of every other chief's first hat, retired very quickly after the rest of the goat locker finished using it for a urinal.

Hoolihan walked forward, looking again to make sure all the reloads were properly secured. You couldn't have one of those things coming loose in the middle of a depth charge attack. A Mark-14 torpedo weighed nearly 3,300 pounds. If that fell on you it would squash you like a bug.

Even worse, a loose torpedo could accidentally start. There was little chance the warhead would explode. It had to run through the water to spin the impeller and take off the safety. But that wouldn't matter all that much if you had to breathe the exhaust fumes too long. Those would kill you just as dead. And, with the screws spinning free in the air, without water resistance to slow them down, the turbines could blow apart if the overspeed governor didn't shut them down quickly enough.

Hoolihan looked forward, between the tubes. "Orrie, anything happening yet?"

Orrie Pappas—his name was actually Orrestes, but no one in the crew could pronounce it right—looked at the dials on the GSIR. They were still just now. "Don't look like him, Curt," he said. Once the TDC officer started cranking data into the computer the dials would start to move as the gyro settings were updated. Pappas was a TM3. It was his job to baby sit the GSIR.

Hoolihan nodded. He hated this part of an attack. It always seemed to take forever to close in on a target. Until they were close enough for Lieutenant Miller to start working on a firing solution there wasn't much any of them could do but wait and wonder.

He wanted something better to do.

"Any idea what we gonna shooting at?" Pappas asked. His family had immigrated from Greece in 1936, when he was 15, and his speech reflected that. Curiously, his *written* English was nearly perfect.

"No idea," Hoolihan replied. "They don't tell me that stuff. All I know it they expect to sink something today."

"Officers, huh?"

"Hell, Orrie, somebody has to run things. May as well let the officers think it's them."

• • •

"Up 'scope."

Ames let the periscope rise to its full extent, putting about four feet out of the water. They were far enough away from the target that it shouldn't matter.

He quickly checked the sky and horizon, then settled on the target. There actually *was* a carrier, so it appeared Intelligence had got it right this time.

Turning the right handgrip, Ames set the optics on full power. It brought the targets close enough to get a better idea of what they were dealing with. The carrier was a typical Japanese design, a very large flight deck with only a tiny island. The boiler uptakes were trunked down and to the side.

A single destroyer was on station ahead of the carrier, and Ames could just make out a second, still hull down, following astern.

"Bearing—mark!"

"Zero-zero-one."

Ames quickly set the masthead height into the stadimeter and worked the knob with his right hand. At a height of four feet, the periscope's horizon was no more than 4,730 yards, but the carrier's own height was added to the equation. He could see the masts, the small island structure, and about a third of the hull above the horizon.

Under the circumstances, adjusting the stadimeter involved a lot more guesswork than he liked. He had to set the bottom of the ghost image on the masthead tip of the true image, estimating just where the actual waterline might be.

"Range—mark!"

"Niner-five-zero-zero."

Ames snapped up the handles. "Down 'scope. Angle on the bow is zero." That meant the target was steaming directly toward them. For the moment they were in a perfect position, but too far away to shoot.

"He's coming right at us for now," Ames said. "But he's still a bit over four miles away, so anything can happen. Larry, get to work on a solution."

"Already started, Skipper."

"Jones, target speed?"

"Two-three knots."

"So, we shouldn't have to wait too long." Ames walked over to the chart table. "Okay, we don't want to try a down the throat shot on a carrier. It's too easy to miss, and there's an escort in the way. Anderson, left, standard rudder. Steady up on zero-five-eight."

"Left, standard rudder, steady up on zero-five-eight, aye."

Morgan glanced at the chart and nodded. "Good idea, Captain," he said. "That should give us a better angle and put the sun behind us for the approach."

"Right. With luck, that will make it harder for him to spot our periscope in the glare. It may even obscure the wakes until our fish are too close to avoid."

He looked over at Miller, who was watching the "own course" dial on the TDC moving as they changed course. All he really had to do was keep track of target bearing and other external data. The TDC would automatically keep track of what *Bacalao* did.

After five minutes had passed, Ames ordered the periscope raised and decided that he was satisfied with the results. They were closer, but the angle on the bow was now starboard 15° and would continue to open.

He quickly obtained a new target bearing and range and dropped the periscope back into the well.

Less than a minute later Jones spoke up. "Target aspect is changing," he reported.

"Up 'scope."

Ames pressed his eye to the buffer and swung the periscope onto the target. "Damn! He's made a major course change, zigging to starboard. Bearing—mark!"

"Zero-three-two."

"Range—mark!"

"Five-six-three-zero."

"Down 'scope. Angle on the bow is now port one-two-five."

What the hell could he do now? If the carrier had zigged to port they would still be in good shape. As it was, the target was now steaming away from them at nearly five times their own current speed.

Ames looked around the conning tower. Tommy Withers wanted his captains to be aggressive. Maybe this was a good time to see if he could live up to that ideal.

"Are you gentlemen up for a little excitement?"

Morgan nodded. "What do you have in mind, Captain?"

"He's going to get away. We damn sure can't chase him down here, even at full speed. There don't seem to be any planes up yet, so we'll surface and chase him on main engines.

"Sounds a little risky," Morgan said. Part of the XO's job was to be the voice of reason if the captain started taking what he felt were unreasonable risks. Another part, of course, was to nudge him if he was being *too* cautious. In either case, the captain would make the final decision.

"Up 'scope." Ames wanted another look before making a final decision. The carrier was now steaming away, beyond any hope of taking a shot.

"Prepare to surface."

•   •   •

Bacalao surged to the surface and Paul cracked the bridge hatch, hardly noticing as a couple gallons of cold water poured down over his head and shoulders. He was halfway up the ladder by the time the hatch had swung up fully on its springs and clicked into the latch, with Ames and Morgan right behind him.

The three men quickly scanned their sectors with binoculars. The carrier was clearly visible, dwindling in the distance, but there were no planes in the sky.

Ames bent over the 1MC. "Lookouts to the bridge! Start main engines. Start the low pressure blower."

A moment later the rest of the bridge party scurried up through the hatch. The lookouts climbed to their stations on the bridge overhead. The rest took up their positions on the upper bridge and cigarette desk.

Ames heard a muffled thump as the main induction was opened. Then there was the clattering of the main engines as 225-pound air was blown into the cylinders to turn them over, followed by the barely silenced roar as, one after the other, the engines caught.

"Come left to three-four-zero," Ames ordered. "All ahead flank. All main engines on propulsion. Start auxiliary and put it on charge."

Taking off after the target at full speed was going to throw up a huge bow wave, Ames thought—not to mention creating a wake that even a half-blind pilot could never miss—but it couldn't be helped. A Japanese fleet carrier was worth the risk. It was imperative that they get at least one hit on her.

That might be all it took. The British had needed a big squadron of battleships and cruisers to actually sink *Bismarck*, but the key to that victory had been a single hit from an aerial torpedo dropped by an obsolescent biplane. With her rudder jammed over, the German battlewagon could barely steer, making her relatively easy prey to Tovey's ships once they caught up with her.

Ames had to presume that, if the Japanese had no planes up yet, it was only a matter of time. They were in a race. To win, he needed to get close enough to shoot before the enemy noticed they were behind him. The odds were against them, but he had to try.

"Enemy is turning," a lookout shouted.

Ames lifted his binoculars. The big ship was turning away from her pursuer. Had he seen them?

But the escorts were turning with him. If *Bacalao* had been spotted, the carrier would turn away, but the escorts would head back to discourage pursuit.

"Has he seen us?" Morgan asked.

Now the carrier had steadied on a new course, steaming away from *Bacalao* at about a 30-degree angle. Ames looked at the sea, taking note of the waves.

"Worse," he said. "He's turning into the wind."

"Launching, then?" Morgan asked.

"Most likely."

"What do we do, then?"

Ames smiled. "We hope they go off in the wrong direction, I suppose. If they head this way, we'll have to submerge. If we do that, he'll probably get away. We're barely keeping up as it is."

"Get off a sighting report, do you think, sir?"

"Yes. Get something ready to send. Current position, one CV, two DDs, present mean course and speed. But don't send it unless we're spotted. If he isn't paying attention I don't want him alerted by our radio. Just get it coded and ready. Tell Kirk to send if he hears the diving alarm, but not before."

Morgan started below. It would take him about five minutes to write up the report and tell Kirk to run it through the code machine and have it ready for transmission.

Ames turned and looked up past the lookouts, his attention drawn by the sound of the number one periscope extending. That would be Miller, he thought, taking advantage of the extra height and superior optics to keep a closer eye on the enemy.

The boat was rapidly picking up speed. It was going to be a race, and the captain was forced to admit that the odds were against him.

He bent over the 7MC. "Conn—bridge."

"Conn, aye."

"Range to target, please, Mr. Miller."

"Range is six-three-one-niner, sir."

Ames moved to the Target Bearing Transmitter and sighted on the carrier. Even at flank speed, *Bacalao* was falling behind. The best that could be expected from a surfaced submarine was about 21 knots, and that was fresh from the yard, with an absolutely clean bottom. The Japanese carrier could probably do a little over 30 knots at full power, and would put on all available speed while engaged in flight operations.

"Bridge—conn."

"Bridge, aye."

"The carrier just launched a plane," Miller reported. "Looks like a fighter."

"What's he doing?"

"The plane seems to be flying off ahead for now. So far he's not coming back this way."

"Keep an eye on him. And any others, too."

Morgan returned to the bridge. "Kirk has the message coded and ready to transmit," he reported.

"He may get to send it, I'm afraid," Ames said. "We're losing ground and one of those planes is bound to start snooping around back here before too much longer. I don't much care for hanging around on the surface if we can't do anything useful."

"He could still change course, Captain. He's turned into the wind to launch planes, but he may come back this way once he's done."

Ames smiled. "True. But probably with his planes in front of him to home in those destroyers. I'm not giving up until I have to, but I'm afraid this one may get away."

"If we don't get him," Morgan said, "someone else will. He's been found. We can just home our boats in on him until one of them gets into the right position."

"Plane!" a lookout shouted. "Broad on the starboard bow."

Morgan and Ames both swung their binoculars up and focused on the plane. It was a fighter, and it had clearly seen them.

"Clear the bridge," Ames shouted. "Dive! Dive!"

•   •   •

As the diving klaxon sounded, Kirk flipped the transmit switch to "On" and began to send. The XO had told him that would be the signal. *If they dived, send the message.*

If they were diving, Morgan had said, it would mean that they had been seen, so sending off a brief message—made slightly less brief by adding a paragraph from the middle of *Gone With the Wind* to make it harder for the enemy to figure out what was obviously a sighting report—wouldn't make any difference. They already knew where they were.

Now it was time to make sure the rest of the American submarine force knew where to find the enemy.

•   •   •

No one was ever going to accuse Ames of lacking aggressiveness, Miller thought. It was exactly ten minutes after diving by his watch when *Bacalao* planed up to 64 feet and raised her number two periscope for a look around. Ames walked the periscope around three full circuits, his back bent uncomfortably as he clicked the left handle through the detents from full elevation to sea level.

After a few seconds he ordered the periscope lowered and looked aft at the sonar stack. "What's the sound picture like?" he asked. "There are several planes up there, but I don't dare stick the periscope up too far and the ships are out of sight."

"Three ships," Jones said. "Mean bearing two-seven-zero. Course is three-one-eight relative. Speed two-four knots."

"No one coming back this way?"

"No such indication. Targets appear to be heading out of the area as fast as they can manage."

"Makes sense," Morgan commented. "That plane sure as hell saw us, and they will have picked up our signal, so they know we're back here and they also know we're too far away to shoot at them. Their best option now is to keep their air cover up and force us to stay down while they get the hell out of the area before something happens to let us close the range."

Ames nodded. "The problem is, he *does* know we're back here, and he's got those planes up, which means we can't surface and chase him at full speed. The best we can manage submerged without running down the batteries too fast is about three knots, so he'll gain about 20 miles on us in every hour.

"At least the destroyers are staying with him and not coming back to bother us," Miller said.

"I don't think he'll let them stray, just in case there's another boat waiting for him up ahead. If he had a couple of extra cans with him I'd be less optimistic. Besides, while we're on the surface he can use his planes to attack us while he stays out of range."

Morgan was looking at the chart, walking his dividers across it as he measured distances. "You know, Captain, on his present line of advance he'll be entering the southwest corner of *Gar's* patrol area in about six hours. Maybe we should just try to encourage him in that direction and see if they can get *Gar* into position to ambush him.

"Good idea. We'll shadow as best we can. We'll also try to keep Pearl up to date on what he's doing."

"Too bad we can't be sure that *Gar* will actually be there to greet him," Miller said. Pearl would let *Gar* know that the carrier was coming, but her captain wouldn't be able to respond. If the carrier was keeping any sort of decent radio watch, her direction finding equipment would be able to detect a transmitter along his course.

And if *Gar* was on the far end of her patrol area, the carrier could still get away. But it wouldn't be safe to transmit *that* information, either. The Japanese still had most of their fleet running around the Pacific. No one wanted to give them any more information on American dispositions than necessary.

The enemy carrier's speed was her greatest asset just now. All carriers were built to be fast, with plenty of excess power. High speed was important for launching and recovering planes. You needed a good wind over the deck to help make up for the short runway, and if you couldn't turn the ship into a strong wind the next best thing was to steam as fast as possible and make your own wind.

A submerged submarine, on the other hand, was just about the slowest thing in the Navy that could move under its own power. A sub was fairly fast on the surface, but also a lot more vulnerable. Designed to disappear beneath the waves at will, a sub didn't have much reserve buoyancy. Trimmed down in preparation for an emergency dive there was even less. And there was no armor to speak of, other than a little around the bridge that wouldn't stop much more than a rifle bullet, so even small bombs presented a very real threat.

"I don't intend to let him get away," Ames said. "He probably will, of course, but if we can't catch him it's not going to be from a lack of trying."

And all because of a wrong guess. If he had turned the other way to open the angle the carrier would have come right to them. Careful tactics, strategy and the grand design often fell victim to pure chance. No doubt, he thought, Franz Ferdinand's chauffeur had expected no serious consequences when he made that wrong turn in Sarajevo, but a world war and several million deaths had proven him wrong.

How many American sailors would now be killed as a result of his own blunder? There were times, he decided, when it didn't pay to think too much.

•   •   •

Trying can only accomplish so much. With a 20-knot speed advantage, the carrier continued to move out of range for the rest of the day. Periodically, they would surface for a few minutes—rarely long enough to start the engines and try to get a little charge back into the batteries—and send off a new position report. Even if he was in no position to catch the big enemy ship, Ames was determined to make sure that her captain knew he was being chased.

The carrier's captain, who could hardly fail to notice the frequent radio transmissions coming from astern, kept his planes in the air, patrolling behind him. Each new signal quickly brought unwanted aerial attention and sent them hurrying back down to the protection of the depths.

At 1140, the carrier passed over the invisible line that marked the border of *Bacalao*'s patrol sector. They followed him right up to the line, but didn't cross it, sending off a final position report before turning back into their own area.

It was up to *Gar* now, he thought. If the messages had been received and passed along—something they weren't sure of as yet, for the need to submerge even while the signals were being sent off had made it impossible to copy any receipts—and *Gar* was close enough, there might still be one less Jap flattop before the day was over.

•   •   •

Jones-2 was sitting very intently in front of the sonar stack, his hands cupped over his headphones to block out every possible trace of ambient noise from within the conning tower. From time to time his hands would move to the metal handles on either side of the stack to adjust the alignment of the sonar heads, trying to get a more precise sound picture.

"Sound contact," he said, after what seemed like hours of very intense concentration. "Long scale echo ranging, bearing zero-one-eight. Very faint."

"More or less back where we came from," Miller said.

"That Nip carrier probably called for help," Ames said. He smiled. "If we're lucky, this new contact thinks we're still trailing the carrier and doesn't know we've turned around."

"What do you want to do, Captain?" Morgan asked.

"OOD!"

At the moment that was Miller. "Sir?"

"Dead slow. Maintain present course and depth for now." He looked over at Jones. "How much longer before he can hear us on passive?"

"I can barely hear his pinging at this range. He's hunting with his active sonar, which should make it harder for him to hear us on passive. He's still too far away to get a blade count."

"Okay. Leave the A/C and ventilating fans on for another, oh, fifteen minutes. No use making everyone miserable before we have to. After that, full silent routine. We'll let the bastard come to us and blow him out of the water before he realizes he's caught up."

Miller passed the proper orders and everyone settled down to wait. After 15 minutes silent routine was ordered. The temperature in the conning tower seemed to go up ten degrees the moment the air conditioning was shut down.

It was an illusion, Miller realized, caused by the fact that the air in the tiny compartment was no longer moving. But the increase would be real soon enough. Even with the A/C running, the average on board temperature hovered around 85°. It would be over 100° in the conning tower before they were done.

•   •   •

An hour had passed and Jones was reporting that the pinging didn't seem to be getting any closer. "No change in bearing," he said. "Either he's sitting in one place and trying to localize a contact, or the sound is bouncing off a layer and he's a lot farther away that I thought."

"Care to guess which?" Ames asked.

"I'd have to say convergence zone," Jones replied. "The water is deep enough around here, and sound conditions are good."

"So you may be listening to someone a couple hundred miles away?"

"Possible. Probably closer, though."

Ames nodded. "Well, we probably don't need to be sweating like this, then. Get the air conditioning back on. We'll take a look around and, if it seems safe, surface, ventilate the boat and start charging the batteries. OOD, make your depth six-four feet."

"Make my depth six-four feet, aye." Miller walked to the lower hatch and leaned over the rail, calling down to Hartman, who was dive officer at the moment.

It took about two minutes to come up to periscope depth. Ames ordered the number two periscope raised, doing the usual three quick circuits before making a more careful inspection of the sea. "Looks clear," he said. "OOD, surface the boat."

Miller immediately gave the order to bring *Bacalao* to the surface. Ames kept the periscope up as the boat emerged from the ruffled surface of the Pacific. Set at full power, and trained in the direction of the pinging destroyer, he saw nothing alarming and told them so.

As the boat emerged into the sun, Ames started for the ladder. He turned to Miller as he did. "Lower the number two periscope and put up number one," he said. "You stay on it. Check all around, but I mostly want you watching ahead. Whatever is out there, I want us to see him first."

"Aye, aye, sir."

With the boat trimmed down for a quick dive, Miller's actual eye level inside the conning tower was about ten feet above sea level. The periscope would raise his point of view another 40 feet. That would give him the same visual horizon as a lookout stationed 50 feet up in a destroyer's superstructure, a little over eight and quarter miles.

The advantage of keeping a surface periscope watch was that the taller, heavier superstructure of a destroyer or other surface warship should be visible to Miller long before the enemy lookouts could spot the slender tube of the periscope peeking over the horizon.

Bacalao would be able to dive with plenty of warning. Then they just had to wait for the enemy to come into their trap.

•   •   •

Cook 2nd Class Howard Niederst lifted the big pot of peeled potatoes onto the electric stove and turned the element to high. He was damned glad to be on the surface. With the main engines running there was less concern about power use. He could run the stove and ovens full blast. The generators could easily handle the load, all the while driving the boat at a good clip—it felt like about 16 knots to him—and at the same time putting a charge into the batteries.

Besides the boiled potatoes, he would be serving up fried chicken, green beans—the last of the fresh ones—and apple pie. There were no apples in the pie. The filling was made from Ritz crackers, lemon juice and some other ingredients.

Being aboard a sub, the enlisted men would have a near equal shot at the good pieces of chicken. There was plenty to go around, and only seven officers.

In a bigger ship, the officers would take all the legs and leave the rest of the crew with the backs, wings and breasts. Niederst usually saved the breasts for soup, since they always cooked up too dry and tasteless for anyone to eat. Women seemed to like chicken breasts, but the ways of women were beyond his understanding.

His wife liked chicken breasts and, mostly, he didn't understand her, either. Or so she was constantly telling him.

•   •   •

"Bridge—conn."

"Bridge, aye."

"Target in sight, bearing zero-zero-two."

"I'll come down," Ames said. He turned to Morgan. "Keep an eye on things up here, Bill. It will probably be a while before the lookouts can actually see anything."

"Aye, aye, sir."

The captain climbed down the ladder, taking the rungs one at a time. No great hurry, he thought. In an emergency you practically jumped down the hatch and, as you dropped, you'd grab the handrails to slow yourself down enough to keep from breaking an ankle.

"What have you got, Larry?"

"Looks like a tanker, sir."

"Are you sure it's the same target? I've never heard of a tanker hunting with QC. Or even having it."

"Yes, sir. Same bearing, and pinging every eight seconds."

Ames wondered if he looked as confused as the felt. "A tanker with sonar?"

"I think it might be a depth sounder," Jones offered. "There's a ping every eight seconds." The sonar operator smiled. "Doesn't seem very bright, though, unless he's actually *trying* to attract attention."

"Or maybe if you want to avoid it," Miller said, a thoughtful smile on his face.

"What are you thinking, Larry?"

"Well, Captain, we heard the pinging and figured he was a destroyer, didn't we? Subs usually try to *avoid* lone destroyers, right? Too much risk for too little return if the can isn't escorting a proper target."

Ames smiled, nodding. "That makes sense. I'd have avoided him for exactly that reason, except he was on our track back into our sector and, given the situation, I figured we had a reasonable chance of being able to ambush him."

Destroyers, at least those traveling alone, weren't generally thought of as good targets. The policy was to go after merchant bottoms and troop transports or major warships. The preferred targets were, for the most part, the ones that couldn't shoot back effectively. A battleship really didn't present much danger to a submerged submarine, since it needed to be able to see what it was shooting at. Battleships and cruisers weren't properly equipped for hunting and attacking subs.

A destroyer had both the proper equipment for finding a sub, and the right weapons for attacking it. You only took them on when the odds were heavily weighted in your favor, or when there just wasn't any other choice.

Ames walked to the periscope. "Let me have a look."

Miller stepped aside. Ames turned the eye buffer over and pressed his eyes into the soft rubber. The target was still hull down, but the bridge structure and mast were typical of a Japanese tanker. He set the masthead height at 80 feet—it was only a guess, but so was the location of the waterline, and the target was probably well beyond the accurate range of the stadimeter.

"Range is about 12,000 yards," he said. "Now, Larry, if you were running things, what would you do in this situation."

Miller had already been thinking about it. "I believe I would submerge and wait for him. He's been on a steady course for a long time and doesn't show any sign of deviating from it."

"Good plan. That's exactly what we're going to do."

Miller rubbed the back of his neck. "One thing, though," he said.

"What's that?"

"I wonder if this isn't just a little *too* easy. He's a pretty tempting target, and he's steaming a straight course. He's not a hospital ship, and he's obviously not a liner, which pretty much rules out any ship sailing under a safe conduct. He *could* be a Russian, of course, but I can't think of a good reason for a neutral to be running around this area. So it's almost like he wants us to take a shot at him."

"You're thinking of a Q-ship?"

"It's something to consider, Skipper."

"It is indeed." Ames went to the 7MC and pressed the button. "Bridge—captain."

"Bridge, aye."

"Prepare to dive."

The quiet of the conning tower was disrupted by the chaotic choreography of the bridge watch pouring down the ladder. Morgan hit the deck and immediately stepped to the right and took his place at the conning tower chart table. The lookouts crossed to the control room ladder, rushing below to take up their positions at the planes controls.

Hartman, who had been JOOD, which also made him dive officer, was right behind them. Hanson came down a moment later, followed by the quartermaster of the watch, who pulled the hatch shut behind him and dogged it tight.

The engines had rattled into silence less than a second after the first man came down the ladder. With the order to prepare to dive, the CPO of the watch, stationed in the control room, had given the order to shut down the engines and switch to batteries.

●   ●   ●

Miller felt the pressure in his ears as air was bled into the boat. As the bridge hatch was closed and dogged tight, the last red light on the hull opening panel would have turned green.

"Green board, Captain," Hartman called up the ladder. "Pressure in the boat."

Ames looked down the ladder, leaning over the rail. "Dive! Dive! Make your depth six-four feet."

The diving klaxon sounded twice. "Make my depth six-four feet, aye," Hartman responded. "All ahead two-thirds. Full dive on the bow planes. Open all main vents."

Miller was watching the conning tower depth gauge as the boat angled down. As big as *Bacalao* was, she was leveling off at periscope depth only 40 seconds after the order to dive was given.

He yawned and swallowed to clear his ears as the negative tank was vented into the boat, raising the internal air pressure in the process.

Something was always raising the internal air pressure in a submarine. The air used to blow the negative tank and the other variable tanks was vented inboard, to keep a cloud of bubbles from rising to the surface and betraying the boat's position. The worst offenders—not so much from additional pressure as from air quality—were the sanitary tanks. The excess pressure after they were blown to sea had to be vented back into the boat, and the filters didn't help all that much when it came to controlling the stench.

Ames took a quick look through the periscope and then had it lowered. It would be some time before the tanker came over the horizon, which would now have contracted to about 4,700 yards with four feet of periscope exposed.

"What next, Captain?" Morgan asked.

"We're going after a nice, fat tanker," Ames informed him.

Morgan looked a little confused. No one on the bridge had been high enough to see the oncoming ship over the horizon, so Morgan naturally still thought they were dealing with a destroyer. "What happened to the destroyer?"

"Never existed," Ames said. "Jones thinks that what initially sounded like a destroyer's QC was actually the tanker's depth sounder, pinging every eight seconds."

Morgan now looked even more puzzled. "What's the depth around here?" He looked at the chart. "We're supposed to be in 800 fathoms here. Does this guy know something we don't, or is he just stupid?"

Ames laughed. "Mr. Miller suggested he may be trying to *sound* like a destroyer, hoping the pinging will keep any subs out of visual range. Or that it really *is* sonar, and our tanker isn't really a tanker."

"Q-ship?" Morgan shook his head. "Does anyone still use those? It's not like anybody is paying attention to the Cruiser Rules these days."

"I don't think it's likely," the captain said, "but we have to accept the possibility until we can prove otherwise." He shrugged. "Or, it could be he really *is* an idiot."

Ames walked over to the chart table. "This will be a sound approach, at least for now. Jones!"

"Sir?"

"Continue tracking him. Sing out if you hear anything out of the ordinary."

"Aye, aye, sir."

"Mr. Miller, start working on a solution."

"Not much to input yet, but it's already in the TDC, Captain."

"We'll let him get fairly close, then fire a three torpedo spread. I don't want to take any chances of him getting away."

•   •   •

The hands on the conning tower clock ticked slowly around as the target steamed closer. Ames found himself wondering just when her captain would decide to make the inevitable course change and vanish, as the carrier had done. That just seemed to be what Fate was throwing at him this time. Wonderful targets would present themselves just out of reach, let him close in, and then slip away just before he could attack.

"What's he doing, Jones?"

"Bearing remains constant. He's still pinging and still coming this way. I should be able to get a blade count before long."

"Can you make out machinery yet?"

"Sounds like a pair of big diesels."

"No other contacts? Nothing trailing him?"

"Not unless he's towing something. He's all alone."

It had been ten minutes since the last observation, so Ames ordered the number two periscope raised. "Put me on the target bearing," he said.

Morgan did so. Ames rotated the right handgrip, bringing the optics to full power. "I can see the top ten feet of his mast," he said, snapping up the handles. "Down 'scope. We'll take another look in five minutes."

•   •   •

"Bearing—mark!"
"Zero-zero-five."
"Range—mark!"
"Niner-eight-six."

Ames was using the stadimeter to fix the range. Even though it now appeared certain that the pinging came from the tanker's depth sounder and not some sort of sonar, he had decided not use *Bacalao*'s own sonar to get a range. Jones couldn't assure him that an active ping wouldn't somehow register as an aberrant return on the target's depth sounder. Most likely, even if it did, a single ping would not be noticed, but he just couldn't be sure. With the way things had gone so far that day, Ames could more or less expect the Japanese captain to interpret such a false return as an indication he was about to run up onto an uncharted reef and make a sudden course change.

"Down 'scope. Angle on the bow is port four-five."

Miller quickly cranked the new data into the TDC, standing back and watching the moving dials as it worked on the calculations.

"This still doesn't feel right," Morgan commented. "Why the hell isn't this guy zigzagging? What sort of fool sails a straight course through a war zone?"

"An unlucky one, I hope," Ames said. He turned to Miller. "How are we coming on a solution?"

"Shouldn't be long, sir. This guy is making it pretty easy."

"Right," Morgan said. "Too easy."

Ames turned to Collins, who was standing by the firing panel. "Make ready tubes one, two and three, Chief. Don't flood the tubes, but make them otherwise ready to fire."

"Aye, aye, sir."

Collins crossed the conning tower to the phone talker to relay the orders to the forward torpedo room.

The red light on the TDC clicked on.

"We have a firing solution, Captain," Miller announced.

•   •   •

Seaman 1st Class Nick Bryant spoke a brief acknowledgement into the phone and looked across the compartment to where Hoolihan was talking quietly to Pappas. "The captain says to make ready tubes one, two and three, but do not flood tubes yet."

Hoolihan straightened up. Finally, they were going to do something. Now they would earn their pay, and maybe get a little excitement in their lives. The recruiters never mentioned how boring the job could get when you weren't doing anything.

Not that they didn't try to keep you busy.

"Clark, Austin, Helstrom—get your butts moving. Check that tubes one, two and three are drained and the pressure equalized. Orrie, set gyro angles to zero and withdraw spindles."

The three men quickly checked the sight glasses and pressure gauges on each tube and reported them normal. There was no good reason they shouldn't be, but you always checked. As a final check they opened the drain cocks, which were just as dry as they were expected to be.

"Okay," Hoolihan said, "get them breeches opened up. And watch yourselves with them doors. I don't want nobody breaking an arm or something."

Each man in turn attached the handle to the square extension on his tube's locking ring pinion gear and rotated the locking ring to the unlocked position. The heavy bronze breech doors were then swung open, number one and three to starboard, number two to port. The doors were hinged on the outboard side of the tubes.

As Hoolihan had warned them, each man was careful to control his door until it had clicked into its latch.

The torpedoes were already loaded into the tubes.

"Okay. Now, charge impulse tanks to 300 pounds. Keep an eye out for leaks."

Each reported in turn when the impulse tank for his tube was properly charged, and that there were no air leaks.

"Make sure the tail stops are backed out full," Hoolihan said. "Okay, close the breech doors."

The heavy doors thumped shut against the rubber gaskets, and then, one at a time, the locking rings were cranked back to the locked position, sealing the tubes. There were six tubes in the forward nest, but only one handle.

"Okay, screw them tail stops in tight. Good. Now, back them out a quarter turn." The tail stop, which was attached to a rounded handle in the center of the breech door, pushed against the hollow propeller hub, pressing the guide stud that rode in the groove at the top of the tube against the stop bolt and holding it securely in place. *Bacalao* had the older, hard metal stops, which had to be backed out slightly. Newer tubes had thin rubber pads on the tail stop faces, and those were just snugged up tight.

"Spindles in," Hoolihan ordered. "Okay, Orrie, get 'em programmed."

The gyros on the torpedoes in the forward tubes were always set to zero angle when the fish were loaded. In the after torpedo room they were kept set at 180°. Now the spindles were inserted into the sockets and Pappas moved a lever, linking the gyro setting spindles to the GSIR, which was set against the forward bulkhead between the two banks of tubes.

"Okay, now check them poppet valves."

•   •   •

"Tubes one, two and three are ready," the conning tower phone talker reported. "Tubes are dry, outer door closed."

"Set depth two-zero feet all tubes," Ames ordered. "High speed setting."

"Depth set two-zero feet, sir," the talker reported. "High speed setting selected."

"Flood tubes one, two and three. Open outer doors."

"Tubes one, two and three flooded from WRT, sir. Outer doors are open."

"Final observation. Up 'scope."

The slender tube rose from the well and Ames snapped down the handles, centering the crosshairs on the planned impact point at the center of the target. "Bearing—mark!"

"Three-five-eight."

"Range—mark!"

"Niner-zero-five."

"Down 'scope. Angle on the bow port five-zero."

He glanced at Miller, who was looking at the dials on the angle solver. "Perfect, sir," he said. The target was exactly where the TDC had predicted it would be.

"Fire one!"

"Fire one, aye!"

Collins flipped the switch for the number one tube to ready. At the instant the ready light came on he slammed the heel of his hand against the firing button. The boat shook slightly as the torpedo was ejected from the tube.

"One fired electrically, sir."

"Fire two!"

"Fire two, aye! Two fired electrically, sir."

"Fire three!"

"Fire three, aye!" Collins hit the firing button again, but this time nothing happened. "Fire three," he called to the phone talker.

A moment later the last fish was off. "Three fired manually, sir," the phone talker reported.

"I'll get someone to look at the firing circuit on that tube once we secure from battle stations, sir," Collins said.

•   •   •

The first torpedo sped along its course, curving slightly to port under the direction of the rapidly-spinning gyro. Within a few seconds of leaving the tube the torpedo had accelerated to 46 knots and was streaking along a precise intercept course to the oblivious target.

As the torpedo raced through the Pacific waters, a small impeller set in a groove in the heavy baseplate of the Mark 6 exploder was spun by the water.

After the torpedo had traveled 463 yards—the calculated distance was 480 yards, but there were always slight variations—the impeller driven mechanism had lifted the primer out of the safety chamber and into the booster cavity. The same shaft also turned a delay wheel that initially grounded the generator output, then, after the fish had traveled a safe distance from the boat, routed the power to the exploder. This device was calibrated to sense the horizontal component of the target's magnetic field, which would induce a voltage in the sensing coil and pickup rod, discharging the condenser into a solenoid. The solenoid, in turn, moved a lever that released the firing pin mechanism in the contact exploder and triggered the detonation cycle.

What no one had realized yet was that the earth's magnetic field wasn't constant from one place to another. The magnetic signature off Newport, Rhode Island, where the Torpedo Station was located, was somewhat weaker than it was in this particular sector of the Pacific.

The exploder, incorrectly interpreting the stronger magnetic flux as the hull of a ship, closed the firing circuit and detonated the warhead. A few seconds later the second torpedo, the "brain" in its exploder suffering a similar delusion, also blew up as its safety came off.

In *Bacalao*'s conning tower the captain was looking through the periscope and demonstrating an astonishing mastery of what the Navy would no doubt have termed "un-officerlike language." It took nearly a minute of cursing before he started to repeat himself.

The third torpedo, which had a defective detonator, kept going. It was calibrated incorrectly, but the "wrong" setting—actually a defective sensing coil—was just about right for local conditions, so the torpedo continued on toward the target.

•   •   •

Captain Asahiro Hasegawa ran out onto the bridge wing as the ocean leaped skyward from two heavy explosions about 500 meters off his port bow. Now one of the lookouts was shouting excitedly that there was a torpedo track coming from the same direction. He took his best option in the circumstances and ordered the helm put over, turning onto a reciprocal course. With any luck, the torpedo might miss down one side or the other.

As the ship swung onto the new course, the alarm bells were sounding throughout the hull, sending the crew to their action stations. Having resigned himself for the moment that his next move would have to await the will of the gods, he sent a signalman to haul down the flag and hoist their proper ensign.

•   •   •

"Oh, Christ," Ames muttered. "This doesn't look good. The bastard has turned into our last fish." He looked nearly as frustrated as he had when the first two torpedoes blew up long before reaching the target. "He also just hauled down his meatball flag and hoisted the rising sun in its place."

No one commented on that. There was no need, as they all knew what it meant. The Japanese national flag, which was also used as their merchant ensign, was a plain white flag with a red ball in the center. The rising sun flag, the *Asahi*, which added a set of red rays extending from the ball to the edges of the flag, was the naval ensign, flown only by commissioned warships. That meant that the innocent looking tanker would be carrying hidden guns, with gunners who knew how to shoot and, probably, a good supply of depth charges.

"Short scale pinging," Jones reported.

"Well, Larry," Ames said, "it looks like you were right." Short scale pinging meant that what they had been hearing *was* sonar and not a depth sounder. It also meant that the operator was now trying to zero in on a target.

"I didn't need to be right, you know, sir," Miller said.

Ames still had his eye pressed into the buffer. The third fish was still running, which meant there was still hope.

•   •   •

The Japanese captain's quick maneuver was nearly enough. Had he managed to straighten out no more than 20 feet to port the torpedo would have passed along his side. It might have exploded, but it would not have been under, or in contact with the hull. Instead, his course turned out to be exactly reciprocal to the torpedo.

This time, the magnetic feature almost worked. Instead of exploding directly under the target's keel, 660 pounds of TNT exploded just before the warhead passed under her port bow, ripping a big hole in her stem. Had the tanker actually been a tanker, this could have spilled thousands of gallons of oil or gasoline into the ocean, and very likely started a fire. If it had been gas, it might even have blown up the ship.

But nothing at all happened, other than his sonar going silent, the heads wiped off by the blast. After a few seconds some metal barrels bobbed to the surface. It was a classic Q-ship trick. The tanks were filled with sealed, empty barrels to provide extra buoyancy. Even with a big piece blown out of her bow, the barrels would probably hold her up. As it was, only the forward-most compartment was open to the sea.

Still, Ames thought, unless he was foolish enough to surface and expose the boat to the powerful guns that were no doubt concealed on the Q-ship, they were relatively safe. Without his sonar, the Japanese captain wouldn't be able to find them.

"She's damaged," Ames said. "But it doesn't look like she's sinking. I saw some barrels popping up near where our torpedo hit, so the tanks are probably full of them. I have a feeling the only way to sink her would be to literally blow her to pieces.

"Are we going to try?" Morgan asked.

"No. She's stopped now, so we'll maneuver around and try to put a torpedo into her engine room. After that, well, we can always hope for a storm. And we'll report her position. Maybe someone can get some bombers out here, if there's a carrier within range. But we've still got 20 torpedoes left, and I want to save most of them for more valuable targets.

"So we're settling for damage, Captain?" Miller asked.

Ames nodded. "Normally I wouldn't, Larry. But I'm not going to waste half our remaining fish putting down a ship that's already mission killed. We hit him on the bow, and if he's stopped pinging that means we probably destroyed his sonar heads. Hell, if we can put a shot into his engine room it may even let in enough water to sink him even with all that extra buoyancy. Even if we can't sink him, he can't do much damage dead in the water.

He looked around the conning tower, wondering if his decision was making any sense to the others. They all knew why they were there, and that their primary job was to sink merchant ships and transports. That still wouldn't make leaving an enemy warship—particularly one that could obviously be converted back into a tanker—any more palatable.

"Chief Collins."

"Captain?"

"Two of those torpedoes blew up prematurely. From what I could see through the periscope, probably just after the safeties came off. If the third fish hadn't worked right, we'd probably be trying to get away from that bastard right now instead of deciding what to do with him. I want the magnetic feature deactivated on the rest of our torpedoes. We'll do it the old-fashioned way from here on."

"They're not going to like that back at Pearl, sir."

"They'll like it even less if we get sunk because our fish give away our position instead of sinking enemy ships. I know you worked on those things, but even if they worked in Newport, they obviously don't work here."

"I'll take care of it, sir."

"Good. Look, Chief, you know more about those things than anyone else out here. If they're not working for you, then there's either something wrong with the basic design, or there's some other factor at work here that no one anticipated. All I know is that they're not doing what they're supposed to. Until we know why, then I think we'll be better off relying on the contact exploders.

Collins nodded, looking resigned. "As much work as we put into those exploders, I suppose I have to agree with you, sir. They should detonate when they're close to a large mass of iron or steel, not in the open ocean. We'll get them deactivated. It's easy enough to do—we just have to remove the pickup rod. If you can spare me here, I'll go below and get the men started.

"Go ahead, Chief. We're going to work into a good firing position. Take care of a reload for tube one first, then load it and report when the tube is ready to fire."

"Aye, aye, sir."

•   •   •

Collins climbed down the ladder into the control room and started forward through officers' country to the forward torpedo room. He had a feeling there would be hell to pay for deactivating the magnetic feature. He'd spent enough time at BuOrd to know how they thought. If anything went wrong, it could never be the design that was at fault. The operators were always the problem—that was a basic tenet at Newport.

But *he* wouldn't be the one to catch it. The captain had ordered the feature deactivated, so it was all on his shoulders now. Collins was just following orders.

"Hoolihan," he called, stepping through the hatch.

"Chief?"

"Let's get a reload ready for tube one. The captain wants the magnetic feature deactivated on all torpedoes, so we'll do that one first. Get the plug out and pull the pickup rod while your men get the tube ready for reloading.

•   •   •

"Up 'scope."

The upper sheaves on the number two periscope were squeaking again, which annoyed Ames more than it should have. He decided it had to be the stress of the approach, coupled with the frustration of the two prematures and the probability that the Q-ship would manage to survive no matter what they did to her.

"Have someone oil those damned sheaves," he said. "Mr. Miller, start your solution. Target bearing—mark!"

"Three-five-niner."

"Range—mark!"

"One-two-zero-five."

"Down 'scope. Angle on the bow is starboard niner-zero. Target is dead in the water."

Bacalao was closing the disabled Q-ship at less than two knots, after working around for a straight run in on her starboard side. It would be like shooting at an anchored target."

"Tube one is reloaded and ready to fire, sir," the telephone talker reported.

"Final observation," Ames said, signaling for the periscope to be raised. "Target bearing—mark!"

"Three-five-niner."

"Range—mark!"

"One-zero-five-four."

"Angle on the bow, starboard niner-zero. Target speed zero."

Miller added the new readings to the TDC, which took less than a minute to digest the unchanged bearing before the red solution light clicked on.

"We have a firing solution, Captain."

Ames glanced over his shoulder. "Gyro angle one degree starboard, right?"

Miller nodded. "Yes, sir."

"Not much of a surprise. Set depth to eight feet, high speed setting. Flood tube one and open outer door."

"Tube one flooded from WRT, outer door open, depth set at eight feet, high speed set, sir."

"Fire one!"

"Fire one, aye! Tube one fired electrically, sir."

Ames pressed his eye into the buffer. The torpedo's wake was arrowing straight at the after section of the disabled ship. With the periscope at full power he could clearly see the ship's crew on the upper deck. So far, no one seemed to be paying any attention to the torpedo. That would probably change before long. A Mark-14 left a pretty clear wake, and it was even more pronounced when it was running shallow in a moderate sea.

The seconds ticked by, the wake drawing swiftly and inevitably closer to the enemy ship. "We got him," Ames said. "Should hit him right in the engine room."

Miller looked across the control at Morgan, who was smiling as he stood by the chart table. Even if they couldn't sink this target, they would at least put him out of the war.

"What the fuck?" Ames snarled. "Down 'scope, dammit!"

"What is it, Captain?" Morgan asked.

"The goddamn thing missed!"

"How?"

Ames walked over to the control room hatch and leaned against the guardrail. "It went under him. The wake ran straight up to the side of the target, but the fish never hit him. I could see the crew jumping up and down and pointing." He turned aft. "Is that fish still running, Jones?"

Jones listened for a moment and nodded. "Still running, Captain."

"What's the draft on one of those things, anyway?"

Miller got out the book and flipped to the proper page. "Fully laden, 35 feet. With her tanks full of air, still at least 25 feet."

"And the torpedo was set to run at eight feet," Ames said. "How the hell does a torpedo running at eight feet go *under* a ship with a 25-foot draft? Shit!"

There was a sudden explosion well to starboard.

"Sounds like he's shooting at us," Jones reported.

"Okay, make your depth two-zero-zero feet," Ames ordered. "Come left to two-six-five, all ahead one-third."

"Getting out of it, Captain?" Morgan asked.

"For the moment." He smiled suddenly. "Somebody must really like that bastard. I'd love to have one of those deck guns off *Narwhal* or *Nautilus* just about now. Something with enough range to stand off where he can't hit us. There wouldn't be any point in even trying to shoot at him with our little popgun.

He walked across the conning tower to the chart table. "We'll maintain this course and speed for the next ten minutes. Then we can surface and get off a report."

•   •   •

Ames was still fuming when *Bacalao* surfaced about an hour after dark to charge batteries. They had gone back for another try at the Q-ship two hours after the second attack. This time the torpedo had hit right at the point of aim, but the Japanese captain's lucky streak continued. The torpedo clearly hit the tanker, but didn't explode despite being what looked like a perfect shot.

That had been the final straw. "The hell with him," Ames had said. "Let's go find something else to sink. This bastard is just too damned lucky."

His mood was only slightly tempered by the knowledge that it had certainly been time to clear out. After firing the final torpedo they had withdrawn out of gun range and surfaced, with the main deck awash, for a few minutes while Kirk got off a contact report. As he reported that Pearl had receipted the message, he mentioned that the Q-ship was filling the air with a lot of very fast Morse.

He had no idea what the Japanese captain was saying in the coded messages, but it wasn't hard to guess. *Help, I'm being mugged. Get here quick and kill these guys.*

When the SD radar started picking up contacts, he decided that the message had been received and prudently pulled the plug. The idea of having to slip away without doing more damage didn't sit all that well with him, but there seemed to be no alternative. They had fired five precious torpedoes at the same ship, with only one of them doing any damage. With the Q-ship's extra flotation even that damage, which might have been fatal to a real tanker, looked to be nothing more than an annoyance to the enemy captain.

But there would be other targets.

X

Interlude

STANDING IN COMSUBPAC'S OFFICE after submitting his patrol report, Ames found himself wondering if he even wanted to continue. It was hard not to think of the entire patrol as a waste of time and materiel.

It turned out that he wasn't alone. Enough complaints had come in about bad torpedo performance that the expenditure of 22 of the precious tin fish with only a small coastal freighter sunk and damage to a Q-ship didn't bring the chewing out he'd expected.

He thought that attaching Collins' report on the erratic behavior of the Mark-6 exploders probably didn't hurt. It was one thing to blame problems on a captain who, just possibly, couldn't shoot as straight as he should. It was something else entirely when you had a report from an expert stating in no uncertain terms that there was something wrong.

The report had been accepted, and would work its way up through channels until it ultimately ended up in a classified file cabinet. Collins' report would no doubt make its way to Newport, where his former colleagues would find it mildly amusing, decide the Chief was losing his touch, and continue to deny that there was anything wrong with the exploders or the torpedoes.

Two more torpedoes had run under a target when they should have hit it. That was also in the reports.

"We're looking into this," had been the response. "You're not the only commander who's been complaining. BuOrd says there's nothing wrong, but I want to know for sure."

"My chief torpedoman's mate worked on the Mark-6 when he was at Newport, sir. If he thinks something's wrong, I have to go along with his judgment."

"Nothing wrong with that, Fred. But you can't deactivate them any more, either. That has come down from, well, higher than me. You'll just have to be more careful, right?"

"Yes, sir."

"Anyway, good patrol report. *Bacalao* gets a second battle star." He smiled. "You get to keep your job. But you might want to think about doing some editing on the next one. You could probably say the same thing in about half as many words."

•   •   •

It felt good to be home, Ames decided. Velma was waiting for him on the front porch when the Jeep dropped him off. Navy wives always seemed to know.

Just after the war started there was talk of shipping all the dependents back home. The disaster in the Philippines did a lot to push that idea. No one wanted to think of their wives and children spending the war in a Japanese prison, which was exactly what had happened when those ill-fated islands fell.

Ames wasn't sure they'd have been able to get Velma out of there even if they'd tried. She had been born in the base hospital at Pearl Harbor, and her father was an admiral now. He didn't think his wife had ever been really happy outside these islands. She merely tolerated Groton, and absolutely hated Washington.

Not that he could blame her. He didn't really care for the place himself, even knowing that getting past captain was going to require spending a lot of time behind a desk at the Navy Department.

"How was your patrol?" Velma asked, after a perfunctory hug and kiss on the front porch."

"Could have been worse. Could have been a lot better, too."

Despite the very proper greeting on the front porch, no doubt duly noted by his driver and the neighbors, they were far from passionless people. It was just that both had been raised in very strict Methodist homes, and what a person did in public had to meet certain standards. Neither smoked, and Ames had never found the "dry" ships in the American Navy to be a problem.

What happened behind closed doors was another matter. They still didn't smoke or drink when they were alone. They didn't talk much for the next three hours, either.

But there was quite a bit of noise.

•   •   •

As far as Orrie Pappas was concerned, it had been a good patrol. He thought of a patrol as being like an airplane. With a plane, you went up, you came back down. With a patrol, you went out, you came back. With either one, if you got back alive it was good.

Nellie, he thought, was also good. Okay, she wasn't a girl he'd write home to his mother about. He wasn't going to say, "Hello, Mamma, I have met a girl called Nellie. I am in love, and we are going to be married." Nellie was good, but not someone you married.

Pappas wasn't interested in getting married just yet. He just wanted to get laid. So he gave Nellie some money, she flopped back onto the bed, and he was a very happy sailor for a few minutes. He thought he might have been happier if he didn't have to wait in line for two hours first, or go the pro station after, but at least he could get laid and, so far, the movies were wrong and he hadn't caught anything.

His pal Sammy was in the next room with a little Japanese girl who called herself Kumi. Sammy seemed to like Japanese girls, when he could find one. He said that, with the war on, it was America's duty to fuck the Nips, and this way was a lot more fun. Sammy, in Pappas' opinion, was some sort of wise ass.

As for Pappas, he figured he'd have fun for the two weeks he was in port. After the war, maybe he'd find a nice Greek girl, settle down, and make his mother happy with a lot of grandkids. For the moment, Nellie would satisfy his needs.

•　•　•

The first day ashore, about all Miller cared about was that he had a soft bed and no one to roust him out of it every four hours. He was out like a light and didn't get up from noon, when they checked in, until a little after four the next afternoon. He figured he'd probably sleepwalked to the head once or twice, but he didn't remember doing it.

When he finally got up he stood under a hot shower for a good ten minutes, mostly because he could. There was no such luxury afloat, where Navy showers were the rule. Half a minute to get wet, shut off the water, lather up, and then turn the water back on for another half minute to rinse off. There was no water rationing at the Royal Hawaiian.

Feeling refreshed, he carefully shaved and dressed in a nicely pressed khaki dress uniform. He was going to be prowling the bars in Honolulu with Morgan, looking for unattached females. He found himself wishing he had more to put over his left breast pocket than a couple of service ribbons, which everyone out there had, and a set of gold dolphins. The dolphins were nicely polished, at least.

Once they hit the bars he knew they were doomed. One of the things you learned in the Navy was that, despite the old stories about a girl in every port, most of the girls in those ports were already staked out by the guys who were stationed ashore. You also learned that, when it came to getting the girls, a set of wings trumped a set of dolphins. The pilots were doing a lot better than they were, and the Army pilots were doing better than the Navy pilots.

The Army guys were all stationed around Honolulu, which gave them a big advantage. The Navy pilots, like the submariners, spent a lot of their time at sea. Their main advantage was the notion that fliers were somehow more dashing and romantic than submariners.

Well, Miller thought, if you were a girl, what image would most appeal to you, a dashing pilot, smiling into the wind with a long, white silk scarf trailing jauntily in the slipstream, or a submariner with a scraggly beard, wearing sweaty, rumpled khakis, and smelling more than a little like bus exhaust.

The movies had a lot to answer for.

As they looked around the bar, the worst part of it was that all the women seemed to be with Army pilots and most of them—the women, that is—were Navy nurses.

"Absolutely treasonous," Morgan commented. "Consorting with the enemy."

True enough, Miller thought. For a submariner, the Army pilots often *were* the enemy. Not only were they taking their women, but the idiots never paid any attention to their recognition manuals and were as likely to bomb them as the enemy. More likely, probably, since the enemy wasn't hanging around Hawaiian waters so far as anyone could tell, so if they tried to bomb a sub in that area, it was probably friendly.

"There are quite a few women here, at least," Miller said.

Morgan looked around the bar. There wasn't a lot of light, most of it coming from candles stuck in red glass jars. It gave the place a reddish glow that felt all too familiar right after a patrol.

"Yes," Morgan said, "there are. Hardly any of them seem to be alone, though. I think we may need to look in a few other places. Maybe we can find one where the Air Corps hasn't already invaded."

"Okay. There's bound to be some place an honest sailor can find some comfort."

Miller wasn't too confident, though. He'd never been very good at picking up girls. Morgan was a lot better at it, since he hadn't spent the last several years tied to one woman—and the wrong one, at that. Miller decided he would just continue to hang around with him. Maybe he'd find the right woman in the process.

•   •   •

The relief crew system had a lot of advantages, Ames thought, but there were also times when he could see some faults. Handing over command to a relief captain for two weeks was supposed to allow him to relax and recover from the last patrol. For two weeks, he didn't have to think about the day-to-day details. Someone else would supervise the yard people, see that fire watches were stood, and take care of everything else in the way of routine.

The problem was, once he was safely ashore and supposedly resting in his own home, he really couldn't stop thinking about the boat. He doubted he could entirely forget her, or stop worrying about her, even when the time came to hand her over to someone else.

But it wasn't just thinking about the boat. That wouldn't be so bad. Even when he was ashore, a captain needed to plan for his next patrol, decide what he might do differently next time. He looked back, reviewed his tactics, saw what worked and what didn't. The idea was to get better each time, so that he could become more effective against the enemy and, at the same time, reduce his own risks.

The problem was, he also wound up thinking about what he did in human terms. If he stopped to think about it at all, he could see where the perception and the reality diverged.

"We lie to ourselves, you know, Vel," he told his wife.

She looked up from her knitting. At the moment she was making a heavy black pullover for him. "Lie about what, Fred?"

"What we do. They way we look at things. We shoot at ships. We sink ships. That's what we say, and that's what we report. We sank a 4,800-ton AK at 0912 on such and such a date."

His wife looked at him curiously. "Isn't that what you did?"

"Sure it is. But what we don't think about, what we lie to ourselves about, is that besides a good-sized general cargo ship we also just killed maybe 30 or so sailors. You don't just kill the ship—likely as not, you kill the men on her, too."

"Do you think they take it personally, Fred? They have to know you're shooting at the ship, not at them, right? You don't try to shoot them when they're swimming around afterwards, do you?"

"No, we don't. But it's hard to be philosophical about this sort of thing. When someone is shooting at *my* ship, or dropping depth charges on us, I'm afraid I *do* take it personally. It's pretty hard not to."

"Is there something you want to do about it?"

Ames shook his head. "Complain, mostly. That's the biggest problem with being captain, Vel. There's no one you can really talk to about this stuff. Not in the boat, anyway."

"What about your XO? Didn't Andy unload on you sometimes?"

"That was Andy. We could talk about nearly anything, but we've also known each other since 1923. Hell, I've known him longer than I've known you. The first time I met Bill was when I reported aboard *Bacalao* just before she was launched. He's a good man, and a good XO, but I just don't know him well enough to talk about anything *too* personal."

Velma leaned against him, resting her head on his shoulder. "So talk to me, then."

"It's duty and humanity. When a war starts duty becomes everything and humanity become subordinate. And that's the problem, Vel. There are things you just have to do because it's your duty. When I first entered the Academy they mentioned that. Normal people don't enjoy killing other people. It's a lot easier to say you're just killing ships, destroying big lumps of floating metal. Ships aren't people. Most of the time it isn't all that hard. The target is far enough away that you can hold on to that illusion. You see the ship, but you don't always see the people."

"But you know they're there, don't you?"

"Sure."

"Should you really care, Fred? They're Japs. They'd be happy enough to kill you."

"Maybe that's the difference. We *do* care. We didn't start this war. I should hate them for what they did to us. I know plenty of men who do."

"I sense a 'but,' Fred."

"Yes. But we're not out there killing the politicians and senior officers who started it. We're killing the ordinary sailors who are stuck with fighting the war their bosses started. Hell, considering our job, most of the men we kill are probably civilians—merchant seamen. Guys who are just trying to earn a living."

"Somebody started it."

"I don't think it was them. Okay, from a practical viewpoint, I know what we're doing makes the most sense. If you can cut off the enemy's supply lines he'll eventually lose the ability to fight, so you attack cargo ships, tankers and transports. You can go after a warship if you run across one, but most of the time they're not the primary target. A battleship can't do much if you've already cut off his supply of fuel and ammunition.

"But that still doesn't make it feel any better when you blow up the transport. You can even say that drowning a couple thousand enemy troops is a good thing, that you've probably saved three or four times as many of your own troops in the process. I've said it myself, and intellectually I can even believe it. It's just that you have to deal with emotions, too."

"Well, what can you really do, Fred? It's your job."

That was it, wasn't it? It was his job. Just as a millwright's job was fixing a blast furnace, or a cobbler's job was fixing shoes, his job was sinking ships. It was the profession he had chosen, nearly 20 years before.

Or was it? Did anyone back then really think they were going to have to fight another war? They'd called the last one the war to end all wars. Everyone had believed that World War I was so terrible, so costly in lives, that no one would ever think of starting another.

But someone had. And, whether Ames liked it or not, he would have to go back and do it all again once the refit was completed.

Quitting wasn't an option.

•   •   •

"Shouldn't you be resting up right now, Chief?" Lieutenant Plaut asked.

"I suppose so, sir."

"So why are you hanging around here? It's not that I don't appreciate your input. It's just that I'm not really sure just why you're here."

"I spent a lot of time at Newport working on these fish, sir," Collins said. "It bothers me when they don't work the way we designed them."

Which was why he was dissecting a Mark-6 exploder instead of finding a nice bar and getting drunk like a proper sailor. There had to be something they were missing that would explain why the torpedoes were blowing up too soon, or not blowing up at all.

It was hard to express just how disappointed he was. Before coming to *Bacalao* he spent more than two years working on the exploder design. Particularly, he had worked on the magnetic feature. It should work, but he had to agree with the captain that, at least in their boat, it didn't.

As complex as the exploder was, the concept itself was so simple that it was hard to imagine any real problems cropping up. The earth was a huge magnet, with lines of magnetic force running from pole to pole. If you passed a big piece of ferrous metal through those lines of force, it created a disturbance. The metal concentrated the magnetic

force, making it temporarily stronger. All the magnetic influence feature did was detect the disturbance, recognize that it meant the sensor
was under a ship, and set off the warhead.

The same principle had been used in mines for years, though the
torpedo exploder was somewhat more sophisticated, as it was used in a
rapidly-moving torpedo and not an immobile mine. A mine didn't need
much more than a simple compass connected to the firing circuit.

With all the prematures, it was hard not to suspect that the magnetic feature was the culprit. The last three prematures had come at 26,
28 and 30 seconds into the run. The torpedoes armed, officially, at 481
yards. Collins figured this meant anywhere between 450 and 500 yards
in the field. A Mark-14 torpedo on the high-speed setting traveled a
little over 17 yards in a second, so those run times put all the prematures
right in that range.

Unless the fish hit something in the middle of its run and tripped
the impact exploder, it seemed obvious that the magnetic feature had
somehow been tricked into thinking it was under a ship.

That was the most frustrating part. If the exploder worked as it was
designed, a kill was virtually assured. Setting off 660 pounds of TNT
directly under a ship's keel would almost certainly break her back. If the
ship didn't break in half at once, it was only a matter of time.

Lieutenant Plaut was looking over his shoulder. "Finding anything,
Chief?"

"Nothing that helps, sir. Nothing that helps."

"I heard your CO had you deactivate the magnetic feature on your
last patrol. Is that right?"

"Yes, sir."

"Well, it's come down that you can't do that any more. I have orders
to paint the screw heads on the sensor rod plug and the exploder baseplate, so we'll be able to tell if they've been removed."

"That should work, sir," Collins said.

He decided that he would have to find out what paint they were
using and make sure he had some aboard.

XI
Surprises

BACALAO WAS RUSHING THROUGH THE DARK PACIFIC AT 20 KNOTS, on a roughly parallel course with a Japanese convoy. "We should be well ahead of the enemy and in a good position to attack about two hours before sunrise," Ames said.

The captain lifted his binoculars and scanned the empty ocean. The night was cloudy, the horizon obscured.

They had sighted the convoy just before dark, at extreme range, just where Intelligence said it would be. They were expecting three ships and three escorts. From what they could tell, Intelligence had been right this time. That made it a fairly typical Japanese convoy.

In the Atlantic, the British were assembling up to a couple hundred ships and pushing them across the ocean in convoys covering many square miles. This allowed them to concentrate the escorts. It also made the odds of any single ship getting through far better.

It seemed logical that the big convoys would just provide more targets for the U-boats, but it didn't work out that way. The German system of central control from shore meant that the U-boats were on the radio a lot. It wasn't too difficult to triangulate their position and steer the convoy around the hunters.

Even more important, the British escorts had radar, which allowed them to find any surfaced U-boats with relative ease. If they could find them, they could attack them, forcing them to go deep as they tried to escape. Even if the escorts couldn't manage to sink the U-boat, they could still keep him down where he couldn't do any damage as the convoy sailed on out of reach.

But it wasn't like that in the Pacific. The Japanese ran smaller convoys, and their escorts lacked radar. It gave the American subs a considerable advantage compared to the Germans.

Once *Bacalao* found the convoy, Ames decided to do an end around. It was likely they would need to submerge to attack, and to do that they needed to be ahead of the convoy. These were new ships, modern freighters, making an average 13 knots. He had to either get ahead of them or give up and let them go.

And he couldn't let them go.

•   •   •

Right on schedule, two hours before sunrise, Ames came about and started his approach. He had decided to take a page from the German play book. They would attack on the surface. The clouds still obscured the sky, and there was no moon.

Miller agreed with the idea. It would be hard to see anything through the periscopes. The Target Bearing Transmitter on the bridge had larger optics, and would work better in the poor light.

Looking down onto the forward deck, he could make out the unfamiliar shape of the new deck gun. The old three-inch on the after deck had been removed during the refit. An even older gun, removed from an S-boat, had been installed on the forward deck. So now they had a 4"/50, along with a new 20-millimeter on the cigarette deck, replacing the old water-cooled .50. Neither would be of much use against even a small warship. Either could be quite useful against smaller ships or barges—vessels too small to warrant the expenditure of a torpedo.

At the moment, the 20-millimeter was manned. The deck gun was not. When it came time to dive, no one wanted to have men on the main deck. It would take too long to get them below, as the only hatch ever opened at sea was on the bridge.

Ammunition for the deck gun was passed up through a special scuttle, essentially a large pipe with a pressure-proof hatch on each end, that came up through the pressure hull. It was big enough for a shell to be passed up in its storage tube, but that was all.

Ames was at the front of the bridge, bent over the TBT as he lined up a shot on the first freighter. "Too bad we can't do a Sergeant York," he said. "He used this old turkey hunting trick. He'd shoot the guy at the back of the line first, so that the guys in front didn't notice what was going on.

"A torpedo is probably a little too noisy for that," Miller said.

"Right. So we'll shoot the guy in front first."

The lookouts were extra alert now. *Bacalao* was moving slowly on the surface, barely a thousand yards from a column of enemy ships. So far, no one had noticed them, but how long could that last?

Jones had reported active sonar on the convoy's far flank. For the moment, that wasn't a worry. The enemy's sonar was only a threat if they were submerged, though someone listening with hydrophones might pick them up. But if the Japs were using their active gear, Miller thought, hydrophones would be less effective. The noise from the sonar would tend to interfere.

"Target bearing," Ames said, clicking the button on the left TBT handle. The transmitter in the pelorus base would send the bearing down to the conning tower.

Miller lifted his binoculars and looked over at the target. The ship was a large freighter, and not as new as they had expected, given the convoy's speed. "Looks like an old banana boat," he said.

Ames continued to sight on her. "I agree."

It made sense. Even with refrigerated storage, bananas would spoil fairly quickly. Joking aside, the ships built to transport them were normally faster than general cargo ships.

"We'll fire single shots," Ames said. "A spread would be surer, but if we're lucky firing a single shot may just gain us the time to go after a second ship. I don't think anyone knows we're here, and if none of their lookouts spots the wake, they may think they've hit a mine. Not very likely, but it's happened before."

"You're not getting too tricky for your own good are you, Captain?" Miller felt he had to ask. It was Ames' decision, but it was a question Morgan would certainly have asked.

Morgan was down in the conning tower at the moment. He couldn't ask, so Miller did.

"Maybe," Ames conceded. "But so far the enemy hasn't figured out we're here. I'm relying on pure luck in this, of course. Sometimes you just do that."

"Firing solution, sir," the bridge talker reported.

"Flood tube one and open outer door."

"Flood tube one and open outer door," the talker relayed. "Tube one flooded from WRT, sir. Outer door open."

"Fire one!"

The water seethed along the starboard bow. On the surface, the poppet valve couldn't scavenge the full impulse charge. It made less difference, though. The boat was obviously visible if anyone happened to look in the right direction, and a few bubbles weren't going to give much away.

•   •   •

The old banana boat went down with reasonable speed as Ames watched through the TBT. Still, there was a certain dignity in the old ship's passing, as though she was reluctant to admit that her end had finally come. For several minutes the old-fashioned counter stern projected above the dark sea, before finally sliding down into the deep.

It looked like their luck was holding. The whole convoy, escorts and all, had changed course away from the submarine. Ames wondered if they really *had* mistaken the torpedo for a mine.

"Move in close," Ames ordered. "We'll see if we can find a life ring or something to take back with us. No more than a couple of minutes to look, though. We need to get after the others."

Miller was OOD and gave the order. Turning briskly, *Bacalao* pointed her bullnose at the spot where the ship had gone down.

As they drew closer, Ames could see a number of men in the water. A single lifeboat was pulling through the swimming survivors. He saw the lifeboat stop twice to pull a man from the water, but for the most part the boat seemed to ignore the swimming men.

"Don't they care?" Miller wondered aloud.

"Maybe they're only picking up the officers," Ames said.

There was a sudden commotion by the lifeboat as several men made a concerted effort to get aboard. After a moment of struggle there was a sudden flash of light, followed a few seconds later by the sharp "bang" of a pistol shot.

"What the hell was that?" Ames muttered.

"Did that Jap just shoot one of his own men?" Miller asked.

Ames scanned the water with his binoculars. "Does that crew seem a little big for a ship that size, Larry?"

"What?"

"Move in close to those swimmers. There's something screwy going on here and I want to see what it is."

"Aye, aye, sir."

As they drew closer, Ames could hear the survivors shouting. At first, it was just an indistinct murmur, hard to hear over the noise of the diesels and the sound of the night sea sluicing along the hull. Then the noise resolved itself into words, and Ames felt cold despite the warmth of the tropical night.

The swimmers were yelling in English.

Ames bent over the 1MC and pressed the talk button. "Rescue party to the bridge. Prepare to pick up survivors."

He looked back at the bridge gunners. "Keep an eye on that lifeboat. If he tries anything funny, shoot the bastard."

He suddenly remembered what he'd told his wife. If there was ever a time when he felt like breaking his own rules and deliberately shooting someone, this was it. The voices of the swimmers were clearly American. That would mean prisoners, and it would also mean that whoever was in charge in the lifeboat planned to leave them to drown.

The rescue party came up through the hatch and climbed down the side of the fairwater. By now everyone could hear the swimmers, and it was obvious that most of them were American.

"Prisoners, do you think, sir?" Miller asked.

"They just about have to be," Ames replied. "We'll know in a couple of minutes."

Bacalao moved gingerly into a knot of survivors, who were quickly hauled aboard by the rescue party and hustled up the side of the fairwater. Everyone moved quickly, which suggested that these men hadn't been held captive for very long. The Japanese were noted for neither the quality, nor the quantity, of their prisoner rations. It didn't take long for their captives to suffer all sorts of physical problems.

Ames grabbed a man who was dressed in khaki trousers and a torn T-shirt. "Who are you?" he asked. "How did you end up on that ship?"

The man smiled weakly. "Johnson, sir," he said. "Hal Johnson, chief machinist's mate. We were in *Unicorn*, stalking this same convoy, when a Nip plane came in on the deck and managed to drop a bomb right into the maneuvering room. Thirty of us got out before she went down and a Jap can picked us up. That was eight days ago. He was detached from the convoy two days back and transferred us to that damned freighter before he left."

Johnson paused, looking around as more and more survivors were brought up onto the bridge before being sent below.

"It wasn't that bad on the destroyer," he went on. "No one was mistreated, which, honestly, surprised the hell out of all of us. That AK was a different story. Her skipper was a pure bastard who obviously didn't much like American submariners."

"Probably likes us even less now," Miller commented.

"We were just lucky, sir," Johnson said. "The bastard had us all penned up on deck. I'm pretty sure his idea was that we'd be exposed to the weather and be just as miserable as possible as a result. But when you put a torpedo into him it meant we were on deck and not locked up in a hold, so we were able to get off the ship and into the water."

Ames nodded. "I'm not even sure we'd have taken the shot if we'd known you were aboard. You don't happen to know where they were taking you, do you?"

"No, sir. The destroyer's captain spoke English, but when he put us aboard the freighter he just apologized and said that he'd been ordered elsewhere and we were staying with the convoy."

"Apologized?"

"Sir, to be honest, I'd have to say that Commander Ishii—that was his name—was one Jap you could even call a gentleman. Said he regretted that circumstances had made us enemies, and that it grieved him that our two countries should be at war, as he actually liked Americans quite a lot. He really talked like that, very fluent English, and not that much of an accent. Other than the usual questions, which no one answered, the only thing he wanted to know was how the Yankees' prospects looked this season. Seems he went to school at Columbia and spent a lot of time at Yankee Stadium during the summer breaks."

"Probably explains the humane treatment," Miller said.

"But the freighter's captain wasn't like that, I take it?" Ames said.

"No, sir. You'll notice there are no officers in our group. That little bastard Ishikawa had the skipper and the other two officers who survived tossed overboard once the can was out of sight." He looked over to starboard, where the lifeboat was just in sight. "You aren't planning to just let him sail away, are you, sir?"

Ames nodded. "Yes. *We* don't shoot up lifeboats. At least, not if they don't start shooting first."

"He shot one of my guys a few minutes ago. Does that count?"

"Unfortunately, no. If it makes you feel any better, there's a pretty good chance he won't make land. There's a front moving in behind us, and the convoy escorts obviously aren't coming back for him. With any luck his boat will swamp and drown him."

Gordon came up onto the bridge. "That looks like everyone, sir," he said. "We picked up 26 men."

Johnson nodded slowly. "That's all of us, then," he said. "Ishikawa dropped the three officers into the drink, and killed one more man after he was sunk, so that's the lot."

"Going to be a little crowded for a while," Gordon commented.

"If I could make a suggestion, sir," Johnson said.

"Sure."

"You might want to consider putting us all to work. Every one of the men you picked up is fully qualified in this class boat. Should make it easier all around if you just integrate us into your watch, quarter and station bill."

"Good idea, Chief." Ames turned to Gordon. "COB, get everyone's rate and qualification and then use them to augment our own men. And see if you can stuff Chief Johnson here into the goat locker and find him a decent uniform."

"Aye, aye, sir."

Ames watched as the last of the survivors were taken below. As Gordon had said, it was going to be a little crowded with 26 extra men aboard. The good news was that, if there enough of them, and in the proper rates, he could probably add an extra watch for the rest of the patrol. That would let everyone get some extra sleep. A tired man was more likely to make mistakes, and submariners were *always* tired.

•   •   •

Radioman 2nd Class Elmer Bloch leaned across the searchlight at the rear of the periscope shears. He was finding it difficult to concentrate on his sector. Not enough time, he thought. It had been only two weeks since he was pulled from the sea, and only eight days before that he had been standing in virtually the place same above *Unicorn*'s bridge when the plane had caught them. The plane hadn't come from his sector, and there was no way he could have seen it approach, but he still couldn't forget it.

Now he was spending too much time looking at the sky and not enough looking at the sea, he thought. The threat had come from the sky the last time. It might not the next time. He needed to concentrate. It had happened before and it could happen again and he couldn't help fearing that, the next time, he might be the one at fault.

Not surprisingly, when *Unicorn* went down, the men on the bridge and in the conning tower and control room had made up the majority of the survivors. It had been a race between the water pouring into the hull, dragging the boat down, and the men trying desperately to get out through the only open hatch. Those who were closest, or who were already on deck, had the clear advantage. In 600 fathoms you couldn't wait for the boat to settle on the bottom and swim up. You either escaped before the boat went under or you died.

Had he been in his bunk at the time, he would have been dead. No one who had been forward or aft of the control room had got out. Bloch was fairly sure that not everyone had even made it out of the control room.

Standing on the bridge overhead now, looking toward the east, where the horizon was starting to grow indistinct as the sun fell ever lower in the western sky, Bloch thought he saw something. At first, he wasn't sure what it was. Just some imperfection in the fading horizon.

Concerned, he lifted his binoculars to take a closer look. Even with the heavy 7x50 binoculars it was still indistinct, but now it was just clear enough to recognize.

"Smoke, bearing one-three-five, sir," he called out. "Source is below the horizon."

Miller was OOD and immediately moved to the starboard side of the bridge and trained his binoculars on the indicated bearing. "Good work, Bloch," he said. "I believe you're right."

Bloch went back to scanning his full sector. Just because there had been something off the port quarter didn't mean there wasn't something else sneaking up on them.

Miller moved back to the front of the bridge and bent over the 7MC. "Conn—bridge!"

"Conn, aye"

"Raise number one periscope and put someone on it. We have smoke below the horizon, bearing one-three-five. Report the results as quick as you can. And point the sonar along the same bearing, see if you can hear anything."

"Aye, aye, sir."

Behind and above him the forward periscope rose out of the shears, the head turning at once toward the smoke. The high power setting on the periscope was no stronger than his binoculars, and the binoculars had better light gathering ability, but the periscope's head was 30 feet higher, which meant that someone in the conning tower might just be able to see what was making the smoke.

Ames appeared on the bridge a minute later. "Looks like you found something, Larry," he said. "Whatever is making the smoke is still below the horizon, but sonar reports faint machinery and screw noises on the same bearing. Sound conditions don't seem to be particularly good at the moment, and being on the surface isn't helping any, but Jones is fairly sure there are several ships."

"Bloch spotted the smoke, sir," Miller said.

"*Unicorn* man?"

"Yes, sir. Aft lookout now."

Ames looked up at the men on the bridge overhead. "Bloch!"

"Sir?"

The man turned his attention to the captain, but kept his eyes where they belonged. Ames smiled—not everyone could manage to do that, even when he knew he should.

"You just got a commendation letter in your file. Good job."

"Thank you, sir."

"What will we do, sir?" Miller asked.

"Check it out, naturally. We still have 23 torpedoes aboard. Maybe we can use up some of them. Get us headed over that way. I want to get close enough not to lose them once it gets dark.

"Aye, aye, sir." Miller moved to the 7MC. "Conn—bridge!"

"Conn, aye."

"Come right to," he glanced at the gyro repeater, "zero-seven-one. All ahead two-thirds."

"All ahead two-thirds, aye, sir."

Miller looked at the captain. "Fast enough, do you think?"

"Yes. I want to get just within visual range before we lose the light, but not so close that they can see us. We'll close in after dark and attack surfaced."

Ames lifted his binoculars and studied the smudge on the horizon as the boat came around onto her new course. "That's right on the route between Truk and Japan," he said. "It could just be something worthwhile."

"I hope so, Skipper. A few more ships would make for a good patrol."

"Well, Larry, until we're sure what we're dealing with here, I want an extra lookout. We'll put on sky lookouts, too. Until we can rule out a carrier we need to keep an eye out for planes."

"Aye, aye, sir."

"If there's no carrier, we should be in good shape. We're far enough from any islands with airfields that carrier planes are the only likely problem. Anyway, I'll be below. Keep me informed, and as soon as you can identify what's out there let me know."

"Aye, aye, sir."

The captain went below. Miller called up a fourth lookout, so that Bloch now had to cover only the starboard aft lookout's sector, from 080° to 190°, and not the full aft sector of 120° to 240°. He also brought up three more lookouts, who would be specifically told to watch for aircraft while the others mainly concentrated on the sea.

Studying the smoky smudge through his binoculars, Miller decided that the smoke might be slightly heavier to the northwest. He couldn't be certain, as the wind could affect the distribution, but it was a good bet that whatever was out there was bound from Truk back to Japan, or to one of the islands in between. If that was the case it might mean less damage to the enemy in the form of lost cargo—ships returning to Japan would likely be in ballast—but the ships themselves were just as important as the cargo.

· · ·

Bacalao caught up sufficiently to get a good idea of what they were chasing just as the sun was sinking. The confused sound picture had improved enough that Jones was able to report eight separate sound sources.

By midnight, they knew for sure, and were closing in and maneuvering for an attack position. The convoy was made up of three columns of two ships each. The most distant column was leading, with the middle column 100 yards back and the same distance abeam, and the third column another 100 yards closer to the submarine, but only about 25 yards back from the lead ship in the far column. Both ships in the two outer columns were freighters, all about 3,000 tons and similar enough that they probably came from the same yard. The lead ship in the middle column was another freighter of the same type, but the second ship was a large, modern tanker of about 10,000 tons.

"The tanker is riding fairly low in the water," Ames commented, as *Bacalao* began her approach. "But he's headed for Japan, so it's about an even chance there's nothing in his tanks but seawater."

"Big convoy, though," Miller said. Hartman was down in the conning tower, working the TDC. Miller had the deck again, after four hours off duty.

"True. For the Japs, anyway."

"And only two escorts."

A destroyer was trailing the convoy. There was only a large patrol boat guarding ahead, similar to the old wooden sub chasers of World War I, with a single unshielded gun on the forward deck and some depth charges at the stern.

Ames confirmed his plan to stay on the surface by removing the lens covers from the forward TBT. "We'll fire a four torpedo spread," he said. "If we target the closest freighter there's a good chance we can get the lead ship in both other columns at the same time. I want to target tubes one and four on the closest ship, and go for the farthest with tube two and the middle column leader with number three."

If Ames managed to set up the spread correctly, the torpedo from tube two would pass ahead of the ship at the front of the near column and hit the lead ship in the far column. Number four would be aimed to hit the near ship, as would tube one, while number three would pass behind the lead ship and, it was hoped, hit the leading ship in the middle column under her bridge.

It was a bit more complicated than a simple deflection shot, but if done properly could take out half the convoy with the first salvo.

"Once we start shooting it may get a little exciting," Miller said. "The sub chaser looks like the most immediate threat. He can get to us faster than the can."

Ames nodded. "I agree. That's why I'm keeping tubes five and six in reserve. If he comes after us we can take a shot. I don't know if we'll hit him, but we may at least keep him too busy ducking to do anything."

"Pretty shallow draft, I'd think," Miller said.

"No doubt. We'll have the fish in those last two tubes set to run at five feet. And we'll use contact shots on all of them." The captain smiled. "Chief Collins brought some pink paint with him, so he can repaint the screw heads on the exploders if we have to take any of them back with us."

"He's already deactivated the magnetic feature, I presume, sir?"

"The day we reached the patrol area."

Ames bent over the forward TBT and sighted on the lead ship in the closest column. It was time to begin.

The first torpedo left the tube at exactly 0105, aimed to strike the closest ship near the center of the target. Ames had tube two fired immediately. The second torpedo was aimed for the lead ship in the far column, angled away from the first, so there was no danger of interference.

Since all even numbered tubes were located on the port side of the boat and all odd numbered tubes on the starboard side, they could be fired in sequence, one after the other, as long as they were aimed on divergent tracks.

"Fire three!" Ames yelled.

"Three fired electrically."

The third torpedo went off on a starboard track that should take it astern the first target and into the lead ship in the middle column.

"Fire four!"

"Four fired electrically," the bridge talker repeated.

"Now we wait," Ames said. He looked up at the lookouts. "Keep your eyes open, men. It's likely to get a little exciting here in another minute or so."

Miller looked at him curiously. He thought the captain was understating the likely outcome just a bit. Once the first torpedo hit they could expect very quick attention from the sub chaser, and the destroyer probably wouldn't be far behind.

Ames was leaning over the TBT again, watching the first target, mentally counting the seconds as the Mark-14 torpedo rushed toward the freighter at 46 knots.

The first torpedo hit just abaft the superstructure. It must have struck right at the turn of the bilge, for the ship seemed to lift out of the water, then drop back with a sickening crash that left the hull sagging above the impact point.

Number three was equally well aimed, passing right aft the first ship and smashing into the engine room of the lead ship in the second column. That ship stopped at once and began to go down by the stern while the tanker, following a quarter mile astern, altered course to keep from smashing into her.

Number two, aimed to pass ahead of the first target and hit the leading ship in the far column, missed when the captain of its intended target put his engine full astern. The torpedo passed ahead by no more than a foot.

The last torpedo fired also hit the first target. This time the only result was another ruptured air flask. The warhead broke away and plunged to the sea bottom without exploding. It no longer mattered, though, except as a way of irritating Ames, for the ship was already doomed.

"PC is turning toward us, sir," a lookout called. "Bearing three-five-zero."

Ames swung the TBT onto the sub chaser, lining up the illuminated crosshairs on its bow. "Bearing—mark!" His thumb pressed the designator button. "Snap shot, down the throat. Fire five!"

"Fire five, aye! Five fired electrically, sir."

"Fire six!"

"Fire six, aye! Six fired electrically, sir."

As the last torpedo left its tube, the sub chaser opened fire with its deck gun.

"Hard right!" Ames ordered. "Ahead full! Steady up on one-three-five."

Miller found himself ducking involuntarily as a shell tore past the bridge.

"The sub chaser is turning," a lookout called.

"Must have seen the wakes," Ames commented.

Miller had his binoculars on the sub chaser. "I think he's screwed up, Captain," he said. "He should have stayed on his original course."

A moment later the first torpedo hit the sub chaser amidships, just as the deck gun fired for the final time. The little ship virtually disintegrated, vanishing completely in a cloud of debris ten seconds later as the last torpedo struck the bow.

"Duck!" someone shouted.

Miller ducked back under the bridge overhead without thinking. Moments later the boat was bombarded with dozens of small fragments from the shattered sub chaser. A heavy bronze cleat clanged against the bulkhead, landing at his feet. A moment later there was a heavy thud and something soft hit the back of his leg.

He turned around and found the captain on the deck, blood flowing from his scalp. He wasn't moving, but Miller could see his chest rising and falling, so he was at least still alive.

"You and you," he yelled, pointing at two of the extra lookouts, "get the captain below, then get back up here."

Miller decided that he didn't have time to do a lot of thinking just now. For the moment he was literally in charge of the boat. At least until the captain came to, or Morgan relieved him.

"Come around to one-seven-zero," he ordered. "Reduce to ahead one-third."

They were kicking up too much phosphorescent plankton at full speed, he thought. Reducing speed might make their wake a little less obvious. The sub chaser was gone, possibly taking Ames with her even after she was destroyed, but the destroyer was still coming up from behind the convoy.

The turn would bring the four stern tubes, which were still loaded, to bear on the convoy.

"Keep a sharp eye out for that destroyer," Miller shouted, moving to the aft TBT and removing the lens covers. The two ships they had hit with their first spread were nearly gone now, and he sighted on the three remaining freighters. The tanker was beyond the freighters, probably out of danger for the moment.

"First bearing—mark!"

"Destroyer is steaming up the near column," a lookout called. "He's not changing course. Looks more like he's trying to sort them out, sir."

We're in luck, then, Miller thought. Probably the destroyer had lost sight of them in the pitch darkness.

A moment later, he spotted the destroyer in the TBT and realized that he was purposefully steaming toward the spot from which *Bacalao* had fired.

"Bridge—sonar."

"Bridge—aye."

"Short scale pinging, bearing one-six-three."

The poor, dumb bastard thinks we're submerged, Miller thought. He's looking in the wrong place. By staying on the surface they had been able to use the submarine's speed to advantage. If they had attacked from submergence they would almost certainly be on the receiving end of a rain of depth charges in another minute.

As it was, there was a very good chance they could turn the tables on the destroyer. Standard procedure was to go after the merchant bottoms and more or less ignore the escorts, but now there was a chance to get rid of the only real defense available to the convoy. Get rid of the destroyer, he thought, and we can pick off the ships at leisure.

Miller had his final bearing in three minutes. Over the next forty seconds he fired all four stern tubes, with a 20° spread. Three of them hit, but only number nine, which hit the destroyer right under the forward gun mount, exploded. The fourth, fired from tube eight, passed ten feet astern the destroyer, then managed to miss both the second ship in the near column and the tanker beyond it by less than 20 feet, passing ahead of both.

The destroyer broke in half, the after section driving itself under in seconds. Half a minute later the Pacific glowed bright yellow, rising up in a huge, domelike fountain as the ready-use depth charges exploded.

The ships in the close column had both been hit by duds. The first, pretty much undamaged except for a dent in her bow, continued on course. The second ship had slowed to about three knots and was falling behind. Miller focused his binocular on her and realized he could see light from below her waterline, just abaft her single tall funnel. The warhead hadn't detonated, but it had evidently hit smack between two frames and punched a hole in her hull. So water was probably pouring into her engine room. The freighter's chances now hinged on the skill of her crew, and merchant crews usually were lacking in both the number of men and the constant damage control drills that could often keep a warship afloat.

Morgan came up onto the bridge, walking aft to where Miller was still standing by the TBT. Since they would want to withdraw a little distance while the tubes were reloaded, Miller hadn't ordered a course change since firing.

"How's the captain?" Miller asked.

"Still out. Doc says he'll be okay. There was a big gash in his scalp, which is why he was bleeding so much, and he's got a good knock on the head. What happened, anyway?"

"When the PC blew up some of the pieces made it this far. I think he probably got hit by that cleat over there." Miller pointed at the offending chunk of Japanese bronze.

"Well, I think we're on our own for now," Morgan said. "The captain should be okay, but he's not going to be in any condition to do much for a while."

"You taking command?"

"As of three minutes ago."

"Well, we're in good shape right now. We've fired ten fish and got five hits with detonations. Two more missed and three were duds, but one of the duds looks like it still stove in the hull plating on that freighter over there at two-two-five. He's slowed down and falling behind."

"The last salvo got the remaining destroyer, so the convoy is unde-fended except for the guns on the *marus*. We should be able to stay out of range of those. I can think of no good reason why we shouldn't end this night with five freighters, a tanker, a sub chaser and a destroyer." He grinned. "Medals all around, probably."

"Could be. They're working like crazy people down there getting the tubes reloaded.

•   •   •

With ten more torpedoes loaded in the tubes, *Bacalao* again reversed course and headed back for the convoy. Morgan had decided to stay well beyond gun range while they reloaded, and now he put on full speed to get ahead of the four remaining ships, which were now sailing in a single column, with the tanker sailing between two freighters. The damaged freighter was continuing to fall behind as the others put on all available speed to get out of the area before their enemy could return for them.

The bridge phone talker looked up. "Captain is awake, sir," he said. "Doc says he's talking, but can't get up yet. Captain says that the XO is in command for now, and he's putting himself on the sick list for the time being."

Morgan frowned. "He must still be pretty much out of it," he said. "Otherwise he'd be back up here, even if it meant he had to have someone hold him up."

"He got hit in the head with a ten pound bronze cleat," Miller said. "That would take a lot out of just about anyone."

"I suppose it would. Anyway, it looks like it's up to us to finish off this convoy for him."

"Up to you, from the sound of it," Miller said.

Morgan laughed, looking out over the starboard bulwark at the distant convoy. With *Bacalao* running at full speed they were rapidly overhauling the enemy merchantmen. It would soon be time to come about and attack.

"If I'm in temporary command," Morgan said, "then the third officer must be the temporary XO. So it's us against the bad guy."

"Sounds like back to Bancroft Hall."

Morgan nodded. "It does, doesn't it?" He looked at the convoy again. "Take a bearing on that lead ship with the aft TBT. I think we're about ready."

"Aye, aye, sir."

Miller walked aft and centered the bow of the lead freighter in the illuminated crosshairs. "Bearing on lead ship is one-six-three," he reported. "Range about two-five-double-zero."

Morgan looked at the gyro repeater. "Present course is three-two-zero." He turned to the phone talker. "Come right to new course one-two-three. Reduce to all ahead one-third."

As the instructions were relayed and confirmed, the boat began to slow and swing around onto a reciprocal course. If he had judged it right, Morgan thought, they would be approaching the convoy from the front, with the convoy 500 yards to port of their course.

He moved to the TBT. "We'll do a five shot spread," Morgan said. "Let's engage the leading target with tubes two and four, and go after the tanker with one, three and five."

The appropriate bearings were quickly sent down and in only five minutes a solution was ready. The targets tried to maneuver, but they really had no chance. All of the merchant ships carried an old gun on the fantail, but with *Bacalao* attacking from ahead the Navy gun crews couldn't shoot.

"First bearing," Morgan said. "Three-four-zero."

•   •   •

"Fire five!"

"Fire five, aye! Five fired electrically, sir."

One and two, fired twenty seconds apart at different ships, hit almost simultaneously. Both exploded. Number two hit directly under the leading freighter's bridge, ripping a massive hole in her side. Number one hit the tanker close to the bow.

"No secondary explosion," Miller observed.

"Salt water doesn't burn," Morgan said. "They're on their way back to Japan, probably."

"Too bad we couldn't have got him going the other way."

"True. I'd like to destroy the oil, too, but at least we can make sure he's delivered his last load."

Number three hit the tanker amidships. Once again there was no explosion. "This is getting very annoying," Morgan groaned. "What he hell is the matter with these damned things?"

"That one worked," Miller said, as number four detonated against the first ship in the middle of the after hold. "He's going down.

"But where the hell did five go?" Morgan asked. The last torpedo's track ran right up to the tanker's stern, but there was no explosion and no sign of a burst air flask. "Went under him. It had to. What was the depth setting on those fish?"

"One, three and five were set at 20 feet. Even in ballast that tanker should draw at least 35."

"Dammit. How hard can it be to get the depth setting right?" Morgan shook his head. "The hell with it. Let's get those last three bow reloads into the tubes. I want that tanker." He smiled grimly. "I want those two freighters, too, but the tanker is more important."

"Aye, aye, sir."

●   ●   ●

Hoolihan watched as the last reload slid into tube three. It was hard to believe how quickly everything was happening. Less than three hours ago there had been 23 torpedoes remaining. Now there were only eight, four in each nest.

The last three bow torpedoes had gone into tubes one, two and three. This had been done for entirely practical reasons. Tubes one through four were located above the deck plates and were the easiest to get at. Tubes five and six were below the platform deck, requiring the deck plates to be lifted for reloading.

"That's it," Hoolihan said. "Once these last fish are gone we should be on our way home pretty quick."

"He's good by me," Pappas said. "We shoots these damn fish and get on back by Pearl, huh? You guys, you okay, but I'm rather hang out with girls."

"Yeah," Hoolihan said. "Some girls. Why don't you find a nice girl and settle down instead of blowing your whole pay on whores the first night you're back in port?"

"What, nice girl like you wife? I don't notice you being in any hurry to get back to San Diego."

"Leave my wife out of it, Orrie."

Pappas was watching the dials on the GSIR, which were moving as the gyro angles were updated from the TDC. "Hey, don't worry, I seen you wife. I gonna get married some day, it's gonna be a nice Greek girl, with a little meat onna bones." He laughed. "But not *that* much, I gotta tell you."

•   •   •

"Okay," Morgan decided. "We're going to use all four remaining bow torpedoes on that tanker. The one hit we got hardly seems to have slowed him down."

Miller studied the tanker, which was now on a course that would cross *Bacalao*'s bow at just over 1,000 yards. She was bigger than he had initially thought, at least 15,000 tons. A ship that size could carry enough fuel to keep a carrier battle group at sea for a couple of months. If it needed four more torpedoes to finish the job, then it would be worth it.

"Still two more freighters left, though," Miller commented.

"We'll finish them off with the stern tubes. One of them's already damaged, so two fish for each should do the job."

Morgan clicked the button, sending the final bearing down to the conning tower.

"Ready to fire, sir," the phone talker reported.

"Here we go, then," Morgan said. "Fire one!"

•   •   •

Gunner's Mate 1ˢᵗ Class Albert Thomas opened the breech of the big deck gun and sighted down the bore. There were no obstructions, and he stepped back and signaled to his first loader, Gibson. "Load one round, common," he said.

Hanson was up on the bridge, ready to watch the fall of shot and call down any needed corrections. He felt responsible for what had happened so far that night. Or, more correctly, for what had *not* happened.

Of the last four bow torpedoes, three had hit the tanker and blown up nicely. The fourth had been another dud. The three hits, combined with the previous hit had been enough.

Then only two of the four stern shots had exploded. They had fired a total of 23 Mark-14 torpedoes, resulting in only 13 hits with proper explosions. Three more had missed, and the other 7 had been duds.

The torpedoes were his responsibility, after all. He took it personally when they didn't work the way they were supposed to. And now he was going to have to use the deck gun to finish off the last ship.

"Open fire."

The four-inch gun went off with a sharp bang, the barrel recoiling as it spewed a brilliant streak of flame that was going to play hell with everyone's night vision. Hanson watched for a splash. It was right in line with the ship's bridge, but short.

"Up one-five-zero," he ordered. "Fire!"

The gun barked again, and this time the shell penetrated the thin hull plating, exploding inside the target's forward hold.

"On target," Hanson shouted. "Fire for effect!"

The gun crew was working like madmen. The bigger gun was far more effective than the old 3"/50, but it was also a lot more work. The shells were heavier, and the antiquated 4"/50 was one of the last single action deck guns in the modern Navy. After each shot, the breech had to be manually opened, the shell casing ejected, and another shoved into the breech. The loader then had to swing the interrupted screw breech closed and manually lock it before the gun could be fired again.

The three-incher had been semiautomatic, using the recoil to open the breech and eject the empty casing. Shoving another shell into the breech automatically closed the breech and readied the gun for firing.

Someone on the enemy freighter was trying to shoot back, but the shells were going wide. Hanson noted with interest that the Japanese gun wasn't spitting a huge tongue of flame with each shot, the way his own gun was doing. He wondered when American armament engineers would come up with a good flashless powder. The big burst of flame from the standard powder not only gave away their position, but made it a lot harder to continue hitting the target as their eyes were assaulted by the bright light.

Morgan tapped Hanson on the shoulder after they had fired 19 rounds from the deck gun. "He's going down," he said.

Hanson nodded. "Cease fire! Secure the gun."

"Good job," the XO said.

"The gun crew deserves most of the credit, Bill. I'll tell them."

"Thanks."

"Now what?"

Morgan lifted his binoculars and watched as the last freighter slid beneath the waves. "I talked to the CO while you were shooting up that last AK," he said. "We'll set a course back to Pearl. Not much sense hanging around out here now that we don't have anything left to shoot at the enemy."

"I don't suppose anyone can complain about that. We've only been out here 34 days. Nice bag, too. Seven freighters, a tanker, and two escorts."

"Looks to be about 35,000 tons," Morgan said. "I don't know that anyone has ever done that well in a single patrol. Should be a commendation for the boat out of this."

"Helluva night," Hanson said.

"It was at that," Morgan agreed. "Now I have to plot a new course. If the enemy cooperates and we can avoid having to dive to avoid aircraft we should be home in about a week and a half."

•   •   •

"I don't like this," Ames said. "It just feels wrong."

"Neither do I, sir," Morgan said. "But I can't see where we can do anything about it."

Bacalao had submerged an hour earlier, after sighting a two ship convoy. There was a big, new destroyer with the heavily laden freighters. With all her torpedoes expended, there was nothing the sub could do. She could only go deep and sneak away. A gun action was out of the question. The boat's locally controlled deck gun wouldn't stand a chance against the destroyer's five director-controlled 125-millimeter guns.

Still, they were on their way home after what could only be termed a spectacularly successful patrol. *Bacalao* had fired 24 torpedoes and 19 rounds of four-inch common, in the process sinking a total of six freighters, a tanker, a sub chaser and a destroyer. The captain's official estimate was 32,300 tons.

"We did okay on this patrol, Captain," Morgan said. "No one can complain about the totals."

"I can. Too many duds. If everything we fired had blown up the way it was supposed to we'd still have some fish left to go after this convoy."

Morgan shrugged. "We'll be back here in a few weeks. I don't suppose all the targets will have vanished."

"No, I suppose not. I just find it frustrating. The Navy spent a lot of money and time developing those torpedoes. You'd think the damned things would work better."

"Well, sir, for now I think we're well out of it. There's no sign the enemy knows we're here, so we continue to slip away, give them time to get out of range, and then we can surface and resume course for Pearl." He smiled. "Nothing wrong with going home early if it's to rearm."

Ames picked up his coffee and sipped at it. "I guess not, Bill." He was looking at the cup distractedly. "Odd," he said.

"What is?"

"Huh?"

"You said something was odd, Captain."

"I did?"

Morgan studied the captain. The man looked confused, as if he was in an unfamiliar place. Certainly he knew the wardroom of his own boat? "Are you okay, sir?"

Ames shrugged. "Yeah. I've just had a miserable headache for the last couple of days. I guess things are a little foggy."

As if in a dream, Ames pushed his cup out of the way and put his head down on his arms on the wardroom table.

Morgan shook him, but there was no reaction. He quickly walked to the communications panel. "Doc," he yelled, "get to the wardroom right now!"

Just over a minute later, Doc—Pharmacist's Mate 1st Class Gene Rosenzweig—trotted into the wardroom. It took him only a few seconds to figure out what was wrong.

"He's nonresponsive, and his pupils are uneven, sir," he reported. "Considering he was hit on the head and knocked out two days ago, I'd have to say there's something leaking into his skull. A damaged blood vessel, causing a hematoma. After enough time the pressure builds up and you lose consciousness. After some more time you die."

"What can you do about it?"

Rosenzweig looked nervous. "This is really a job for a neurosurgeon, sir. You have to relieve the pressure and fix the bleeder, and the only way to do that is to open up his skull."

"Can you do it?"

"I don't have the proper instruments, sir. I may be able to improvise something to relieve the pressure, but there's no way I can go in and fix the leak. You'd need X-rays to find it, and even if I knew exactly where it was I'd be more likely to kill him than to help him."

"You said you could probably relieve the pressure, though?"

"I'd just need to make a hole in his skull to do that, sir. If you can get me a hand drill and, say, a half-inch drill bit. The bit is really bigger than

I'd need, but a thicker bit would be easier to keep from going all the way through."

"Well, I can get the drill and bit from the engine room tools."

"Okay, sir. You've got a gas welding set back there, too, right? Hold the tip of the bit in the flame for maybe ten seconds. Let it cool a bit, then stick it into a bottle of isopropyl alcohol. That should be enough to sterilize it. I'll get the other things I need. We can use the wardroom table." He paused. "This is strictly emergency, stopgap surgery, sir," he said. "I can't make any guarantees, and we'll still need to get the captain to a competent doctor as quick as we can."

"It's okay, Doc. I know you'll do your best. No one is expecting miracles."

Rosenzweig frowned. "No miracles, sir. But if we're lucky he may survive."

•   •   •

With the wardroom table draped in a clean sheet, Rosenzweig had the captain laid on his back, his head resting on a folded towel. He used a scalpel to make a v-shaped one-inch incision on the back of his head, laying back the flap to expose the bone.

"Shouldn't you be using some sort of anesthetic?" Hartman asked, observing from the passageway.

"He's already unconscious, sir," Rosenzweig said. "I wouldn't be able to tell how much to give him."

The drill bit was still warm as Rosenzweig chucked it in the drill. Placing the tip against the exposed skull he started to turn the crank. He worked slowly, applying minimal pressure as the sharp bit began to cut away at the bone. He didn't want to push too hard and accidentally push the bit right through.

After five minutes of careful drilling, blood began to flow around the tip of the drill bit. Rosenzweig stopped at once and removed the bit. "Hold onto him," he said. "He'll probably wake up pretty fast."

"Oh, Christ. . ."

"See?"

"What am I doing here?"

"It's a long story, sir," Morgan began.

XII

Hunter's Point

THE RETURN TRIP TO PEARL HARBOR TOOK THREE WEEKS. Four days after the emergency surgery on Ames, *Bacalao* had rendezvoused with a King-fisher float plane from a heavy cruiser. The captain, conscious and complaining, had been ferried over to the plane in an inflatable boat. There were proper doctors on the cruiser, which was also headed for Pearl. Rosenzweig had been more than happy to turn his patient over to the doctors. Once the pressure had been relieved, the pharmacist's mate had been in constant dread that an infection would set in.

With Morgan again in temporary command, *Bacalao* continued on her course. Progress was slowed considerably when first the number four engine, followed three days later by number one, went down with broken timing gears. This time there would be no fixes en route—they would just have to make do with the two remaining engines.

One day out from Pearl, they were down to a single engine. Not one, but three lower compression seals blew out in the number three engine. By this time even Morgan was ready to concede that there were problems with the design.

Three hours after tying up at the Pearl Harbor Submarine Base, *Bacalao* was towed over to the yard. Morgan reported to ComSubPac's office in the Administration Building, taking along the addendum to the patrol report he had written after Ames took off in the float plane. Ames had taken the original report with him, at least partly as insurance against the boat being lost.

"Welcome back, Commander," ComSubPac said, gesturing for Morgan to take a seat. "I've read the report submitted by Commander Ames, as well as your annex. An outstanding patrol in all respects, I must say.

With some confirmation from Intelligence, *Bacalao* is being credited with nine ships sunk and 35,800 tons. How do you like that?"

"I like it just fine, sir."

"So do I. Now, when he got back here Commander Ames made some recommendations. You and Mr. Miller were both commended for continuing the convoy attack after the captain was knocked out. He recommended you both receive a Navy Cross, and that has been approved. He also recommended that you get your own boat, and that he would like Mr. Miller promoted into your current job if you did."

"Quite an honor, sir," Morgan said.

"Yes. Well, here's what's going to happen. Ames has been promoted to full commander. The doctors want to keep him ashore for at least the next six months. They say your pharmacist's mate did a damn good job of saving him—he's getting a Commendation Medal, by the way—but they want to keep him close to medical attention until they're sure there won't be more problems.

"So you're getting *Bacalao*, and effective immediately your rank is permanent. We're also following Commander Ames' suggestion about Miller, promoting him to lieutenant commander and, provided you concur, making him *your* XO."

"I'd be glad to have him, sir. I've known him since the Academy, and I think we make a pretty good team."

"Good. That's settled, then." He flipped through the patrol report. "Now, I see you've had more trouble with the engines?"

"Yes, sir. Three went out on our way back. The yard has the boat now, of course, so I presume they'll fix them."

"They'll do a quick, temporary fix, is what they'll do. Once that's done, you're on your way to San Francisco. *Bacalao* is due for a major overhaul in any case. While you're there, they'll modernize anything that can be updated, and all four engines and the auxiliary will be replaced."

Morgan nodded. "I had great hopes for those engines, sir," he admitted, "but I guess I'm ready to admit they're not working out. Do you happen to know what we're getting?"

"She's an EB boat, so I'd guess the same Wintons that *should* have been installed in the first place."

"Will Commander Ames be getting a new command, sir? He's a very good sub commander."

"Once the doctors sign off on his health, I should think so. I agree, he's too good at his job to keep on the beach." ComSubPac rose. "Now, my yeoman has your new orders, and everything else you'll be needing. Good luck, Morgan. I think I'm putting *Bacalao* into competent hands. Prove me right."

"Yes, sir. Thank you, sir."

• • •

It was shortly after dawn when *Bacalao* picked up the pilot and steamed under the Golden Gate Bridge into San Francisco Bay. The water was covered by a thin mist—it wasn't heavy enough to be called fog—as they passed the grim outline of Alcatraz, heading for the docks at Hunter's Point.

Morgan and Miller stood together at the front of the bridge. The changes in the wardroom had been handled easily enough. At the moment they were one officer short, with a new ensign promised sometime during the overhaul. Morgan had moved into the captain's stateroom for the voyage from Pearl, and Miller had stayed where he was, though now he was only sharing the three-man stateroom with Hartman.

Hanson would join them once the new officer arrived.

"We'll be tying up at the pier for now," Morgan said. "The schedule calls for the boat to be moved into a dock in three days."

"We're already assigned quarters for the men," Miller said. "The enlisted men will be quartered on a barge inside the yard. I have a list made up for local and home leave. Since we're the only bachelors in the wardroom, we'll be at the BOQ. Hartman lives here, so he'll bunk at home. Some of the others have made arrangements to bring their families out for the six weeks we'll be here."

Morgan smiled. "That's your job now, XO," he said. "You get to take care of all that administrative stuff and I get to be the brilliant tactician and take all the credit."

"Well, there's no way anyone can live aboard while the yard has the boat. You've seen the plans. It'll be almost like being back at Electric Boat, when we were under construction."

The overhaul plans amounted to nearly a complete rebuild. The four main and one auxiliary H.O.R. engines were to be ripped out. The main engines would be replaced by V-16 Wintons—really General Motors products, since the larger company had bought out Winton years ago, but still made at the old Winton plant in Cleveland—and the auxiliary by an in-line 8-cylinder GM diesel.

All 252 battery cells would be replaced, along with every foot of wiring in the boat. The conning tower fairwater was expected to come in for a more drastic cutdown. Since *Bacalao* already had a four-inch deck gun, that would remain, but they would gain another 20-millimeter once the old forebridge was cut away. There was still no intention of shooting at airplanes, but the guns could also be used for shooting up sampans and other Japanese small craft, which didn't rate a torpedo.

"You have any particular plans while we're here, Larry?"

"Chase women, I suppose. What else is there to do?"

"Well, I would personally like us to see if we can start a new tradition for this boat."

"Such as?"

Morgan looked around the harbor. "As you know," he said, "I am now *Bacalao*'s fourth captain. Except for Karl, we all got the job because somebody died, got hurt or had other problems. It was thinking it might be nice if I could arrange that the next guy gets the job because I'm done with it and ready to move on."

"I'll try to watch your back," Miller said. "But we can still hunt for single women, right?"

"Larry, we are now both lieutenant commanders, holding positions of great responsibility in the United States Navy. We should be happily married with kids by now."

"I was," Miller said. "Except for the kids part—and the happily part. Anyway, if we don't chase women, how are we going to find those wives you think we should have?"

The harbor pilot crossed from where he was standing by the compass platform. "We should be at the pier in five minutes, Captain," he said.

"Thank you. XO, set the maneuvering watch. Prepare to come alongside. All line handlers topside."

•　　•　　•

"We're here," Ohara said. "We'll be tied up in a minute or two." If they were opening up the main deck hatches, they had to be nearly at the pier. They were never opened at sea.

"About time," Harrigan said, grinning. "I've got a wife in San Francisco."

"I thought your wife lived in Illinois, Chief."

Harrigan just smiled. "What are you going to be doing, Ken?"

"Staying out of sight, I suppose. I think being Japanese is still illegal in California."

"We'll be here long enough, and I'm sure you've got some leave coming. You could always go home."

Ohara shook his head. "If I did, my mother would just be trying to match me up with somebody."

"What's wrong with that?"

"Different tastes, Chief. I just never really liked anyone she picked for me. And it's not that easy telling her 'no,' either."

"My mother more or less picked out my wife for me. Worked out okay."

"The one here, or the one in Illinois?"

"The real one, wise guy."

"Well, my mother is a little—well, you ever read *Terry and the Pirates?*"

"Sure."

"Picture the dragon lady, only just barely five feet tall and in a polka dot house dress and you've got my Mom."

"Dad's not the boss?"

"At work. At home, well, I guess she lets him *think* he's in charge."

• • •

Morgan and Miller stood quietly on the edge of the dock, looking down into the dried-out basin. *Bacalao* was a mess. The after superstructure had been removed, and the big hard patches over the engines cut away, leaving gaping holes in the pressure hull.

The original engines were still on the dockside, waiting to be hauled away. One of the new Wintons had already been installed. The others were waiting to be hoisted into place. Once that was done, the hard patches would have to be welded back into place. It would be a critical operation.

"I hate to see her like this," Miller said.

Morgan nodded, jumping at a sudden clatter beneath the hull. It was one of the Kingston valves, dropping to the concrete floor of the dock after being cut free. The main ballast tanks would now be left open at the bottom, with only the closed vents to keep the water out. Flood valves would only be retained for the fuel ballast tanks.

"What was the point in removing the Kingstons?" Morgan asked. "We never close them, except in harbor, but why cut them out?"

"One of the yard guys told me there's a lot of tin in them. The scrap use is more important than keeping them. That's what he said, anyway."

Morgan began to pace along the edge of the dock. It was like seeing your child strapped down on an operating table and cut open. *Bacalao* was his boat now, and he knew he needed to keep up with her progress.

It didn't make it any more comfortable, though.

Forward, men were attacking the fairwater with cutting torches. The entire forward section had been cut away as far back as the periscope shears, leaving a gaping hole above the lower bridge deck. Now they were cutting two big chunks out of each side of the remaining bulwark plating below the lookout platform. From now on the elevated upper bridge would be gone, and everything from the newly-created gun platform at the front of the fairwater to the cigarette deck would be on one level.

Sometime in the next weeks a new open bridge would be put together, with a venturi shield that was supposed to keep down spray. Another 20-millimeter gun would be added at the front of the fairwater.

The effect would be to lower the bridge, making *Bacalao* harder to see against the horizon.

The extra gun would be welcome, but the most welcome addition of all would be fitted to the top of a new mast the yard had added at the front of the periscope shears. For the first time they would have useful surface-search radar.

Now, Morgan thought, if I can just get through the next few weeks and get back to sea!

XIII
Heading South

SOMEHOW EVERYTHING WAS PUT BACK TOGETHER, and *Bacalao* once again set out across the Pacific, tying up at the Pearl Harbor Submarine Base on the first day of September 1942. It would be a short stay. After taking on a full load of torpedoes, ammunition, food and water, they were under way again on the 9th.

This time they would not be coming back. New orders directed *Bacalao* to patrol southward from Hawaii to Australia, with the patrol ending in Fremantle. They would come under Admiral Christie's Southwest Pacific command upon arrival. Fremantle would be their new base.

Collins was somewhat less than optimistic about what that meant. "I knew him at Newport," he told Morgan. "He practically invented that magnetic feature on the Mark-6. From what I hear, he won't even consider deactivating it."

"You've got lots of paint, don't you, Chief?"

"Naturally."

"I won't tell him if you don't."

As they followed their escort through the transit lane out of Pearl, Miller was on the cigarette deck, looking aft at the broad wake spreading out behind them. The gun crew, standing by the 20-millimeter, were quietly going about their business. At the moment that was mostly keeping their eyes open, just in case.

Miller was forced to admit that he had changed since coming aboard this boat. The peacetime officer was now completely gone, and he wasn't sure he really liked the man who had replaced him. He didn't trust people as much now, and he was also XO, which meant he was required to be something of a bastard.

In particular, he didn't trust pilots. Safe transit lanes had been established in and out of all Pacific Navy bases. The same had been done in the Atlantic. Submarines were supposed to be able to operate freely on the surface in these lanes, which the pilots were instructed to stay away from.

But they didn't always do that. He suspected that pilots in general, and Army types even more so than naval aviators, just couldn't be bothered with keeping track of their actual position, or with verifying what they were shooting at. *A submarine is a submarine, and all submarines are the enemy,* seemed to be the airman's motto.

The situation certainly wasn't unique to Americans. Miller had heard a story of a British boat sending a message that they would be arriving back at their base at a specific time "...friendly aircraft permitting."

He looked down at the deck, idly wondering how Morgan's latest engineering project was faring. Just before they started back from Hunter's Point Morgan and Gordon had spent most of one day taking apart a 1936 Indian "Chief." The various pieces of the big motorcycle were lowered down the forward hatch and stowed away anywhere space could be found.

The frame, which was too big to fit down the hatch, had been lavishly coated in cosmoline, wrapped in oiled paper, coated with more cosmoline, and secured inside the after section of the conning tower fairwater, under the cigarette deck.

The captain had planned to bring the pieces out and put it all back together in Honolulu, but the transfer to Fremantle meant that it was all still stowed away. Miller wondered how the frame was handling the daily immersion in salt water, even with its rust-resistant coating, but that was Morgan's worry, not his.

Miller had been OOD when they arrived at Pearl. When they returned from a patrol there was usually a band and a good crowd turned out to greet them. That hadn't been the case this time. Just making it back from the States was routine. He supposed they might have got the band if they'd run into a Japanese convoy between San Francisco and Pearl.

He looked around again. The sky was still clear. In another hour the escort would turn back. After that they would head south.

• • •

Morgan came onto the bridge just before noon, carrying his sextant. Miller watched as he shot the sun, then quickly worked out the sight.

"So, where are we?"

Morgan tapped the chart. "Right here."

"So, tonight, you think, Captain?"

"Three degrees north," Morgan replied. "Looks like it. We'll have to keep an eye out for anything unusual in the water."

"Well, I've got the list."

"I'm just glad I'm not on it."

"So am I," Miller said. "Once is enough—at least as a participant."

"Don't mind being a spectator, though, is that it?"

"Watching is fun."

•   •   •

Shortly after midnight there was a commotion forward, as if the boat had bumped into something. Or, Morgan thought, smiling at Miller, someone had fired a water slug from a forward tube. Half a minute later there was shouting from forward, and the 7MC popped to life.

"Captain—forward torpedo room!"

Morgan grabbed the microphone. "Captain, aye."

"Captain, there is a disgruntled and horribly disreputable looking character up here waving around a trident and demanding to know what we're doing trespassing in his realm." It was Harold Cushing, one of the two new ensigns they'd picked up in San Francisco. He sounded more than a little nervous, which Morgan thought was appropriate, considering what was about to happen to him.

Miller was smiling and looked at his watch. Like Morgan, he had been expecting this to happen about now.

"Be this the captain of this here vessel?" a voice inquired. Morgan recognized Harrigan, doing his best to imitate Wallace Beery doing Long John Silver.

"This be—uh, this is the captain. And who might you be, to be invading my ship and intimidating my junior officers?"

"Why, Captain, I be Neptunus Rex, sovereign of these here seas, and I be here with my court to determine how this swarm of insignificant pollywogs happen to be aboard this fine vessel."

"Playing it to the hilt, isn't he?" Miller said.

"That he is, Larry." Into the 7MC he said, "Let me check our position, and I'll see if you have a case, your disreputable majesty."

Miller looked at the main chart table, with its automatic position tracker. "Seven minutes south, Captain," he said. "He's got us, sir. The poor pollywogs have had it."

"So it would appear. You're safe though, aren't you, Larry?"

"Very. I've been south several times. You, too, right, sir?"

"Once, back in '38."

"So we just get to watch, then," Miller said. "And a damn good thing, too, if you ask me. You have to know that they've brought the Royal Barbers with them, and I'd just as soon not arrive in Fremantle looking like I have mange."

"Actually," Morgan said, "I get to watch. They'll be needing the captain to introduce them to the victi—er, crew. Including our young friend Ensign Gould, who I believe is currently on the bridge. Go up and relieve him and send him down here for his punishment."

"Aye, aye, sir."

•   •   •

The whole boat was rigged for red. It was something Morgan had insisted on when he met with the conspirators to set up the ceremony. The crew could have their fun, but he wasn't taking any chances of impairing anyone's night vision. The ancient—if not particularly solemn—ritual of crossing the line would have to take second place if the enemy decided to put in an appearance.

Morgan walked forward through officers' country and into the forward torpedo room. There was Harrigan, wearing a gleaming crown, which seemed to be constructed of tinfoil wrapped around cardboard. He was dressed in a dirty sheet, draped around him like a toga, and he had suddenly grown a long, white beard, which bore an astonishing resemblance to a yarn-mop swab.

He was accompanied by Her Highness, Queen Amphitrite, only coincidentally looking a lot like Pharmacist's Mate 3rd Class Hiram Ingersoll, who had come aboard at Hunter's Point. Ingersoll was also dressed in a sheet, and was wearing another swab head for a wig. Her majesty's lopsided bosoms sloshed as she moved.

The third part of the Royal Trio was the Royal Baby, who could only be Seaman 1st Class Jacobsen. Despite his lowly rate, Jacobsen had been in the Navy for nearly 20 years, which explained why he was the only member of the crew not rated as a petty officer who had already crossed the line. He had made it as far as Boatswain's Mate 1st Class at one time. Jacobsen was a good sailor, but only when he was at sea. Ashore, he was a fight waiting to happen, which it nearly always did, followed by the inevitable mast and demotion.

Just now, his ample belly was hanging over a makeshift diaper, and he was sucking on a huge cigar, with a pink ribbon attached to it, like a malodorous pacifier. His gut was gleaming from a coating of cooking lard and heaven only knew what else.

Oh, God, Morgan thought, *I'm glad I've already done this!*

The rest of the Royal Court, Davie Jones, the Royal Prosecutor, the Royal Scribe, the Royal Undertaker with his coffin, and the two Royal Barbers, were as motley a crew as ever terrified the seven seas.

There were 34 men in the crew who had never before been south of the equator. These victims were gathered by the Shellbacks in the crew—the men who had crossed the line before—and herded, in small groups, into the forward torpedo room, where they were consigned to the tender mercies of His Majesty and his court.

There, one by one, each man was condemned for the crime of being a Pollywog—an insignificant creature who had never once, in his entire worthless lifetime, crossed the equator—and, as punishment, was forced to kiss the Royal Baby's belly, tossed into an inflatable children's wading pool filled with sea water, and sent on to the royal barbers. One of them lathered the victim's face with a mixture of soap, lard and used engine oil, then "shaved" him with a dull, wooden razor. Another gave him a haircut of such intricate complexity that the only reasonable way for the recipient to set foot in public would be to shave his head and start over.

When it was all over, and the newly initiated men were slinking back to their quarters or duties stations, their butts aching from the final indignity of passing through a gantlet of shillelagh wielding Shellbacks, they were declared to now be members of that ancient order, and given elaborate certificates signed by Neptunus Rex himself.

Nor was the Royal Court any gentler with the officers. It turned out that only Morgan, Miller and Lieutenant Carl Norton, who had become engineer officer after the Hunter's Point overhaul, had previously crossed the line. Hartman, along with the two new ensigns, Gould and Cushing, were run through exactly the same procedure as the lowliest seaman.

All of them knew better than to try to exact any sort of revenge on their tormentors. Morgan had been quite explicit about that.

•   •   •

"Bridge—radar!"

"Bridge—aye."

"Surface contact, bearing three-zero-two, range one-two-thousand."

"Keep me informed." Hartman had the deck. Around him, the sky was pitch black, low clouds obscuring the stars. Their current position was about 300 miles north of Mindanao. Anything in the area could be presumed to be hostile.

Morgan emerged from the hatch and leaned against the bridge coaming. "I think I like this radar," he said. "The best lookout who ever lived couldn't spot a target at nearly six miles on a night like this."

Hartman nodded. "I have no idea how those operators do it, though. Have you seen that screen? Just looks like a lot of jagged lines to me."

"I suppose that's why the Navy decided they needed a radarman rating. This new stuff is so complicated that you need a specialist to take care of it."

The Navy had created several new ratings during 1943. Jones, who had formerly been Jones-1 until the other Albert Jones was rotated out, was now a Sonarman 1st Class. The only radiomen in *Bacalao* were now the men who actually worked and repaired the radios.

"What do you suppose we've found, Skipper?" Hartman asked.

"Too far to tell yet. Whatever it is, we'll probably have to sink it. There won't be anything friendly hanging around here."

"Presuming the torpedoes work," Hartman commented.

"We're not under Admiral Christie's control yet," Morgan said. "Until we are, we follow Admiral Lockwood's directive and keep the magnetic feature deactivated."

"You think our new boss is taking this whole problem a little too personally?"

"He's got a valid point, Tom. If the magnetic exploder works right it makes the torpedo a lot more effective than the contact exploder. Where we'll be patrolling there's going to be a lot of tanker traffic, and those things are hard to sink."

"Sure, but the magnetic feature doesn't work. Seems like the only one who doesn't realize that is our new boss."

Morgan shrugged. There was no reasoning with admirals. Once they made up their minds that was the end of it. About the only way anyone was going to get Christie to change his mind was for a more senior flag officer to overrule him.

"Contact bearing now three-one-zero, range one-one-five-zero-zero."

"Okay," Hartman said. "He's moving to starboard." He bent over the 7MC. "Have you got a speed estimate on target?"

"Estimated speed is one-eight knots, sir."

"Fast," Morgan said. "Whatever he is, he's not a freighter or tanker. Could be a warship."

"Do we have a sound contact yet?" Hartman asked.

"Negative on sound."

Morgan moved over to the gyro repeater. "OOD, I'll take over up here. Get below and give me the best course to intercept."

"Aye, aye, sir."

Hartman dropped down the ladder. He was gone for less than three minutes. "Best course should be one-five-two, sir," he said.

"Bring her around. All ahead full."

"Aye, aye, sir."

•   •   •

It was astonishingly easy, Morgan thought. Using the radar for guidance, they had worked their way into a good attack position in less than two hours. Now *Bacalao* was waiting silently, just where he judged the best shot could be fired.

Not only had the radar allowed them to keep track of the target, which had by now been identified as a big troop transport, but figuring out her zigzag pattern had been greatly simplified. If he had got it right, the transport should be turning toward them in about three minutes.

Steaming right across his sights.

Once *Bacalao* slowed to await her target, Jones was able to get a good sound picture. There were two ships, the big transport, and a fleet destroyer. The transport was fast, steaming at 18 knots and, quite possibly, still with a few knots in reserve. It would require a destroyer to handle escort duties—a sub chaser or destroyer escort wouldn't be fast enough.

"Target is turning onto starboard leg," Gould reported, from the conning tower.

Soon, then, Morgan thought. He bent over the TBT and focused on the transport. "First bearing," he said, thumbing the button.

The TBT reading appeared in the conning tower. "Three-two-seven," Miller read.

"Bearing three-two-seven," Gould repeated, dialing it into the TDC.

It still felt odd to Miller. He had operated the TDC for so long that he was having a hard time getting used to someone else having the job. But he was Executive Officer now, which meant his job was to keep the plot during the attack.

He only hoped Gould was good at his new job. Just because he had turned over the responsibility to someone else didn't mean he was ready to trust his replacement. Drills were one thing, but a real combat approach was something else.

Putting his concern aside, Miller traced a line on the acetate sheet covering the chart. He knew where *Bacalao* was. The target was somewhere along that line.

The captain called down for a radar range. Seated at the after end of the conning tower, Radarman 2nd Class Herman Carson quickly keyed the transmitter. The radar was less likely to be noticed than a sonar range, but now that they were in visual range there was no sense in taking chances by running it continuously.

"Range is one-two-five-zero," Carson reported.

"Okay," Morgan said. "This is going to have to be fast. Ready tubes one, three and five."

"Starboard tubes only?" Miller asked.

"He's going to be crossing our course in about two minutes, Larry. I think if we fire just as he does it should give us our best chance. I'd estimate about an eight-degree starboard deflection."

"Doing it in your head, sir?"

"I always did. Hell, maybe I'm using a left over brain from an old World War I skipper, huh?"

"Could be." Miller lifted his binoculars and peered out over the ruffled waters. *Bacalao* was moving at eight knots, her bow wave creating considerable turbulence that seemed to glow from phosphorescent plankton disturbed by the boat's passage. "Second bearing, you think, Skipper?"

"Yes." Morgan bent over the TBT, lined up the glowing crosshairs and pressed the button. "Three-four-six," he said. "So far, so good."

Miller looked out over the bow and decided he didn't particularly care for tropical waters. Was it really possible no one aboard the enemy ships could see all that phosphorescence? Cold water wasn't as pleasant, but it also didn't glow in the dark.

"TDC officer has a firing solution, sir," the phone talker reported.

"Generated bearing?"

"Three-five-eight, sir."

Morgan bent over the TBT and lined up the crosshairs. The bearing matched.

"Flood tubes one, three and five and open outer doors."

"Tubes one, three and five flooded from WRT, sir. Outer doors open."

"Fire one!"

The boat jerked slightly, and a patch of white foam erupted on the starboard bow. On the surface, there was little in the way of sea pressure exerted on the tubes, so there were always some escaping bubbles. It didn't matter that much there. The boat's position was obvious to anyone who happened to be looking in the right direction.

"One fired electrically, sir."

Morgan counted slowly to ten. "Fire three!"

"Three fired electrically, sir."

Again the slow count. With all three fish coming from the same side of the boat, and using the same aiming point on the target, the separation was important.

"Fire five!"

"Fire five, aye! Five fired electrically, sir."

"Lights on the destroyer, sir," a lookout called. "He's turning this way."

Morgan nodded. "Hard left. Steady up on one-seven-seven. Ahead full."

"Staying on the surface?" Miller asked.

"For now."

"That destroyer reacted awful fast."

"I suppose he heard the torpedoes being fired."

"What do you suppose those lights were? Warning the transport?"

"Probably." Morgan bent over the 7MC. "Maintain course and speed for two minutes, then reduce to ahead one-third." He looked over at Miller. "There's a good chance he's presuming we're submerged, so once we put a little distance between us I don't want to leave a big bow wave and wake for his lookouts to notice."

"Hit, sir!" a lookout cried. A moment later the sound of the explosion rolled over the water. This was followed by a second flash and its slightly delayed bang.

After that, there was silence. Two out of three, Miller thought. A third hit would have been better, but two fish should have been enough to put the transport down.

A minute later *Bacalao* reduced speed, her phosphorescent bow wave dropping as she slowed.

"Sonar reports the destroyer is pinging short scale," the talker said.

Morgan grinned. "Good. That means he *does* think it was a submerged attack." He looked over the bulwark with his binoculars. "Yes. It looks like he's searching the area we fired from."

"What are we going to do, Captain?" Miller asked.

"We are going to sneak away like the dirty, ambushing scoundrels we are, of course." He was silent for a moment. "You know, Larry, that third torpedo should have hit. If it did, and it didn't explode, then we've still got a dud problem. I don't think I want to test that on something that can shoot back effectively. We got what looked like a 7,500-ton transport. I think I can be satisfied with that."

"So, on to Australia?"

"On to Australia."

XIV
Chance Encounter

MILLER LAY ON HIS BACK, looking up at the bottom of Hartman's bunk, thinking about the curious turns life could sometimes take. When he went into Fremantle that morning, about the only thing on his mind had been delivering a packet of documents to a liaison officer at Australian headquarters. That had turned out to be a simple enough job, once he managed to actually find the man.

All in all, it took about an hour. That left him with some free time, as he wouldn't be on duty until 1800, so he decided to wander around the business district.

Eventually, growing hungry, he went into a small restaurant to get some lunch. The place was crowded, mostly with Allied officers. There were no enlisted men, and only a few civilians, most of them older men well past military age.

He found himself standing next to a WRANS officer as they waited in line—on queue, he supposed the locals would say. After a few minutes, the young officer looked up at him and smiled. "You're alone, are you, Commander?"

Miller nodded. "Yes." He found himself a bit tongue-tied. The Aussie officer was a genuine beauty, with flaming red hair, neatly gathered at the back of her head and tucked up under her uniform cap. At some point in every man's life he encounters a woman so strikingly beautiful that his brains are instantly scrambled and he was lucky if he could remember his own name. Now it was Miller's turn.

"We might get a table faster if we shared," she suggested.

"Good idea," he said. "I'm Larry, uh, Miller."

"You're sure?" Her smile seemed to light up the room. "Sarah King."

"No relation to the admiral, I suppose." *What sort of stupid question was that?* he wondered.

"Great-grand-daughter," she replied. Miller looked more than a little puzzled at this answer to what he had presumed was a lame joke, so she added. "Ours, not yours. He served in the RN back in the '80s."

"Oh."

They had reached the front of the line by then. After a further short wait a table for two did become available, so they followed the proprietor to a table in a bay window at the front of the restaurant.

After they had ordered, Sarah said, "Gold oak leaves is a *lieutenant* commander, right?"

"Right. Gold is a lieutenant commander, silver a full commander."

She smiled. "I'm afraid I still find your rank insignia a bit confusing at times. The collar rank, that is—the shoulder boards and sleeve lace look normal enough."

Miller looked at the single stripe circling her sleeve, with a diamond shaped loop at the top. "And you would be, what? A sub-lieutenant?"

"Third officer. Same thing, really. WRANS have different names for the same ranks."

They talked generalities for some time before the food arrived, and then both went to work on a hearty mutton stew. Sarah seemed to have a good appetite, despite her slim build.

As they were finishing, Miller found himself smiling at his accidental lunch companion. He had never considered himself very lucky with women. Sailors had a reputation of having a woman in every port. He had exactly one, Claudia, and *she* had found him, back in the days before she decided she really didn't want to be a Navy wife and set off for Reno and the bucolic life on a little bitty ranch with Ernie the cowboy.

Ernie's 'little bitty ranch' had turned out to be a piece of Texas the size of Connecticut. Claudia was doing quite well without him, it seemed.

For that matter, he guessed he was following the same pattern here. Sarah had spoken to him first, hadn't she? Now, he supposed, it was his turn, and he was having trouble thinking of something witty and seductive. Where was a good line when you needed one? He knew he'd think of a dozen perfect things to say as soon as he got back to the boat.

Finally, he settled for the mundane. "I don't suppose you'd like to go out some evening?" he asked, rather lamely, adding, "We'll be here for—well, for a while, anyway."

"Can't say how long?"

"It's the Navy. Security."

She smiled. "Always the same, eh? In any case, I'd love to see you."

"You would?"

"Of course. Why do you think I suggested we eat together? I wanted to get a better idea of you."

"You did?"

She touched his hand. "Yes, I did. And I did—get a better idea of you, that is."

"So you'll go out with me?"

"You said you'd be here for a while, right?"

He nodded. "More or less. You never know for sure, do you?"

"So, will you be coming back here?"

"To this restaurant?"

"To Fremantle, silly. I presume you'll be going back to sea. Do you think you'll come back here when you do?"

He just shrugged. "I really don't know. But I think I hope so."

Sarah looked at her watch, frowning. "Time for me to be getting back." She took a small notebook from her bag, scribbled a number on a page, and tore it out. "You can call me here," she said. "It's my office number, so I'll generally be there during the day. And I shall be free any evening this week."

When he mentioned that he had the rest of the afternoon free, and really nothing to do and nowhere to go, Sarah seemed happy enough to have him walk her back to her office. By the time they reached it, they had made arrangements to meet for supper the next evening.

· · ·

They decided to take in a movie after supper and wound up in a small theater—Sarah called it a cinema—where they could sit in the dark and escape from the war for a couple of hours. Naturally, the main feature turned out to be a war movie.

Set aboard a submarine.

Miller found it to be both inspiring and unintentionally hilarious at the same time. It was clearly intended to inform the folks back home that their submariners were brave, resourceful types who would no doubt go on to win the war for them.

He didn't for a moment think that the enemy was as incompetent as the Hollywood types wanted to imply. And the submarine was so primitive that Miller couldn't help wondering how their marksmanship could possibly be so good. There were no duds in *their* torpedo racks.

As depth charges rained down on the fictional sub, Miller could feel Sarah gripping his arm. "It is really that bad, Larry?" she whispered.

"Nothing like that," he replied.

It was a lot worse, he thought. He didn't think he needed to tell her that, though. He could hardly forget that his first depth charge attack had nearly been his last. Would have been, but for Ames taking over in the conning tower and Ohara's quick action back aft.

"We try to make sure they miss us," he added, putting his arm around the girl, who obligingly snuggled up to him.

"Good. You're an interesting fellow. I want you coming back."

Despite the lovely young woman sitting beside him, her head resting on his shoulder, Miller still felt unsure of himself. She seemed to like him, but he had to wonder why. Was he really that attractive? Or was it just the chronic man shortage in Australia that had proven such an advantage to American sailors?

Maybe, he thought, it was one of those things you didn't question.

•   •   •

They went out three more times that week. By then both had learned a fair bit about the other. He'd discovered that Sarah was a widow, and she now knew that Miller was divorced. She seemed willing to accept that, though she thought her father might have some reservations.

Miller wasn't looking forward to meeting that man. Sarah's father was an Anglican priest. Just to make him more intimidating, he was also a retired RAN captain, and the son of a full admiral.

"I think I'd rather be hiding a couple hundred feet under a Jap destroyer with a good sonar fix on us than confronting your father," he commented.

"Oh, he's a darling, really. Just an old softy, once you get past the crusty exterior. He's a vicar, after all. He's *required* to be compassionate and understanding."

"Sure. But you're his daughter. He may tend to be a bit more protective."

"Ah, well—he is, I suppose. But he put up with Wally, didn't he? And he was very much the typical Australian man. Loud, a bit crude, and loved his beer."

She frowned. "But Wally is gone, and you're here. And I think I may just be falling in love with you."

"You know, Sarah, that's something I never quite understood. Your family name is King, and so was your first husband's family name. You didn't marry a cousin or something, did you?"

"No. No relation at all. His family came here from Germany about the turn of the century. I believe their name was originally Koenig and they translated it."

"Oh, well, I guess that explains it, then."

"He was a good man, but he's been dead since May 1942, and we never had any children. I expect I'm ready for a new romance."

Miller smiled. "And yet you're here with me."

"I like you. You're quite handsome, you know."

"Sarah, I know you've seen me in a good light, so I have to wonder if you've got glasses hidden away somewhere that you should be wearing."

"Twenty-twenty, chum," she laughed. "And *I* happen to think you look pretty good."

"Well, no accounting for taste, I suppose. Not that I have any reason to complain. As long as you continue in that delusion, maybe I can keep you around."

"You've got me, Larry."

He still found that hard to believe. Sarah King was surely one of the world's great beauties, and she thought *him* handsome. It just wasn't a word he would use to describe himself. He was sure he was quite ordinary.

But he was willing to take the relationship for what it was. Someone up there was being kind to him. If this girl cared for him, then that was enough for him. He'd been madly in love with her from the moment she first appeared in that restaurant.

"Can you come with me tomorrow, Larry?" she asked. "I really do think it's time you met my parents. Don't worry, you'll do fine."

He shook his head. "I can't. Not tomorrow, anyway."

"The next day, then."

"Uh, no. Not for, well, a while."

She frowned. "Back to sea, then? Is that it?"

"Can't say." Which was as good as saying it, he knew. They both did. It was the usual security issue. Even when the sailing date was known, and there would be the usual locals wandering about on shore watching the boat depart, you weren't supposed to say anything.

"You're coming back to Fremantle, though, aren't you?"

"I hope so. As far as I know."

"How long?"

"I can't tell you." He smiled. "I really don't know, anyway. We could be gone eight to ten weeks, or we could use up all our torpedoes in a couple of weeks and turn right around before we even run out of fresh vegetables."

"I'm hoping you don't get to the tinned food," Sarah said.

"So am I."

She looked at him curiously. "Just now," she said, "I rather wish I lived alone. I'd like to take you home and be with you until the very last possible moment."

Miller nodded, looking at his watch.

"Which, I'm afraid, is in about ten minutes. But I'll be back, just wait and see." He grinned. "I'll even risk meeting your father."

"Just hurry back, Larry. That's all I ask."

●   ●   ●

Bacalao departed the following morning. For the next 62 days, Miller tried to concentrate on his job. Mostly, he managed. But Sarah was always in the back of his mind.

Sometimes he managed to push her well back, knowing that thinking about her would be dangerous. With a Japanese freighter on the way to the bottom, and a pair of destroyers nosing about overhead, no outside thoughts could be allowed to intrude.

At other times, particularly when he was off watch during the day, resting in his bunk, it was sometimes hard to get to sleep for thinking of her. He found it odd, for nothing had ever managed to keep him awake before. Even back when he was courting Claudia, sleep had always come the moment his head touched the pillow.

"You're in love, kid," he told himself.

"That's nice," Hartman said. "Now shut up and go to sleep."

●   ●   ●

For some reason, Miller found himself thinking of the story of Isaac and Rachel as *Bacalao* edged up to the pier in Fremantle. Isaac, who had worked for seven years in order to get her hand, and so important to his life was she that it had seemed only a brief interval.

It was the same, he thought, with Sarah. They had been at sea for two months, yet when he saw her standing on the pier—arrivals rated a reception committee, complete with a brass band and an admiral or two ready to come aboard the moment the brow was in place—it was as if they had never been apart.

He wanted to jump down off the bridge and run to her. A futile wish, he thought. There was the normal arrival routine first. So all he could do was wave and hope the admiral didn't take up too much of their time and he could get ashore quickly.

And the admiral had specific news for him. Miller wasn't quite sure how to take it. He'd have to talk it over with Sarah once he got ashore, though he knew there was only one possible answer and it was the one he gave. He just wondered how it would affect the rest of his life.

•   •   •

And now it would come to the test. Sarah had found a way for them to be alone, and they had taken advantage of it. But he hadn't told her his news yet. He had been so lost in the moment that it didn't seem important.

Now it loomed over everything.

"There's something I need to tell you," he said.

"That doesn't sound like good news."

He shrugged. "I suppose it depends on your point of view. I'm getting my own boat."

"Well, Larry, that's wonderful. I do come from a naval family, after all. I know how important a command is to any officer."

Miller leaned back in his chair. "It's something I've been looking forward to ever since I graduated from the Academy." He sighed. "But the boat's in San Francisco. And she's an old S-boat, which means there isn't much chance of being sent out here. They'll keep her on the other side of the Pacific. Up north, maybe, where it's a little quieter."

"Oh." She frowned. "Well," she said, "you can write, can't you? I'll expect a letter every day when you're in port, and really long letters when you're at sea."

"I'm just afraid you'll find someone else."

"I don't want someone else, Larry, I want you."

"I'll get back here somehow," he said. "Or find a way to get you to where I am. I mean, if you'll wait—if you'll have me, that is."

"Are you trying to propose?"

Miller nodded, smiling weakly. "I'm not very good at it, am I?"

"You're good enough." She kissed him. It might not have been the longest, or the most passionate kiss in human history, but it seemed so to him.

"Was that a yes?"

"I think you should actually ask the question first, my love."

"Oh. Then, will you marry me?"

"Yes." She smiled, looking more beautiful than ever. "I think I knew I would from the first moment I saw you. Some things are just meant to be."

"For me, the first moment I saw you is a little vague," Miller admitted. "You're so beautiful I'm afraid my brain short circuited that afternoon."

"You're silly." She frowned suddenly. "So, just when do you leave?"

"Another week."

"Can you get leave?"

He nodded. "The relief crew has already taken over. I'll officially hand over my duties to the new XO tomorrow. After that, I'm just waiting for transport back to the States. Leave shouldn't be a problem. Why?"

"Well, if we are now engaged, I think you *have* to meet my parents. If you can arrange a car, it's about an hour and a half by road."

"Your father is a priest?"

"Vicar, we'd say, but yes."

"And a retired captain?"

"Yes."

"I'll manage a car. Just don't be too surprised if I seem a little nervous. I almost think I'd rather face the enemy than your father."

"Bloody coward."

"You'd better believe it."

•   •   •

I was right, Miller thought. Depth charges *were* less frightening than the man standing on his front walk waiting to meet him.

Sarah's father was tall and lean, with that weathered look you often saw in Australian men. There was something about him that suggested he hadn't always been a clergyman. Certainly not a man you'd want to get on the wrong side of.

Well, he was also a retired captain, wasn't he.

He realized that Sarah was nudging him along. What sort of impression was that going to make?

He was out of his element, that was the problem. These people spoke the same language—more or less—but they weren't American, and their ways were different when it came to so many things. Or, perhaps, it was that Australians were so often like the Americans of the Old West—the Hollywood West, where everyone drank too much and got into a lot of fights, but without Randolph Scott arriving in the nick of time.

He knew damned well that a lot of Australian men resented the way "their" women were going about with American servicemen. He wasn't sure that the resentment extended to the girl's fathers, but he was about to find out.

"So this is him, is it, Sarah?" her father asked. He didn't sound particularly friendly.

"This is Larry, Dad. Lieutenant Commander Miller."

Reverend King looked him up and down. Miller had worn khaki dress for this encounter, complete with medal ribbons and his shiniest set of gold dolphins.

"Well," her father said, after considering it all, "at least he isn't English."

XV
S-56

MILLER ARRIVED AT MARE ISLAND ON TUESDAY. As efficiently as the Navy operated at sea, there were times when he truly despaired of its ability to get anything accomplished on dry land. It took four hours to work his way through the bureaucracy, and another twenty minutes—no one could spare a Jeep or driver—to walk to the dock were *S-56* was resting on blocks, her hull festooned with cables, bare metal gleaming where the paint had been stripped from her hull and the workers had finished dealing with the rust. A new coat of paint would soon follow.

The upper deck work was coming along well. The typical S-boat chariot bridge now sported a low forebridge extension, with a 20-millimeter mount installed. The gun itself was still absent. At the rear of the bridge a mast had been installed, and a group of workers were in the process of installing an SD air-warning radar antenna. An SJ antenna was mounted at the front of the periscope standards.

It took a few more minutes to find Commander Jonas, who seemed absolutely delighted to see Miller. It was hard to blame him. With his promotion to commander, Jonas was moving on to better things.

Specifically, he was moving a few hundred feet away, to a building slip where a new boat was starting to take shape on the stocks.

"She's a good boat," he told Miller. "Even more so now, what with the modernization she's getting. They've added a good search radar, updated the sound gear, even added air conditioning."

"Good," Miller said. "I spent more than enough time sweating in these old boats before the war."

"Where?"

"Coco Solo and Cavite."

Jonas grinned. "At least from Cavite you could move to Shanghai in the summer. Coco Solo is just too damned hot *all* the time."

Miller nodded agreement. "I don't suppose I'll have to worry as much about being too hot if they've added air conditioning."

"Don't let that fool you. If you end up back where we've spent most of our time, air conditioning will be a pretty minor consideration. What you'll really be needing is heat."

"Aleutians?"

"You'll love Dutch Harbor."

"I've been there. I didn't love it. *Fremantle* I loved—or, at least, someone who lives there."

Jonas laughed. "Have a bit of a fling there, did you?"

"We're getting married. This command sort of complicates matters, of course. If I'd stayed with *Bacalao* I'd still be coming back to Fremantle between patrols."

"Sure. But you'd miss the opportunity of your own command and a chance to freeze your kiester off in the process."

"I'll be looking forward to that, I assure you, sir."

They were in the engine room now. After the big V-16 GM diesels in *Bacalao*, and the slightly smaller and far less reliable H.O.R.s they had replaced, it was remarkable how primitive these old monsters looked. The M.A.N. diesels in *S-56* were copies of a German design that dated back to World War I.

"I always liked to give the impression of being extremely solicitous of the condition of these old engines," Jonas said, "but I don't think I ever really fooled anyone. Mostly, I was just trying to stay warm, and I'm fairly sure the crew knew it."

"Any particular quirks?"

"Just the usual things. Too old, too slow and, as you'll be getting her just after docking, with a nice clean hull, she'll probably leak like a sieve."

S-boat hulls were riveted, so seepage was always a problem. This became particularly acute whenever the boat was cleaned up, for it was the accumulated crud and corrosion that helped seal the leaks.

Jonas spent the next couple of hours taking Miller through the boat, pointing out some of the nonstandard equipment that had been added in previous modernizations. A modern Kleinschmidt fresh water still had been installed in the engine room, which Miller found welcome after memories of how miserly they had always been forced to act in prewar boats of the same type. The major fresh water hogs in any submarine were the batteries, which required constant topping up with distilled water. According to Jonas, the yard had promised that the new still would produce enough fresh water to handle cooking, drinking, keeping the batteries serviced, and have enough left over to allow the crew a reasonable standard of cleanliness.

Being the last S-boat built, *S-56* was also the most modern of the lot. Her design was somewhat different than earlier boats, including a separate maneuvering room abaft the engine room and a single stern tube.

The one thing that remained lacking was a TDC. There simply wasn't enough room and, in any case, the older Mark-10 torpedoes that were used in S-boats hadn't been designed to be linked to the automatic setting mechanism of a TDC and GSIR. The more modern Mark-14s, which would, were too long to fit an S-boat's tubes and reload racks.

So it was back to using the old Is-Was and Banjo. The two older devices had been used as a backup in *Bacalao*, just to confirm the TDC bearings, so he had at least maintained his proficiency. Using the two—the Is-Was was a circular slide rule, the banjo a simple angle solver—it was possible to set up a torpedo attack. Firing a spread was generally a good idea, as neither of these devices was really accurate enough for precision targeting.

The automatic position keeper in an S-boat's targeting system was between the captain's ears.

•   •   •

Miller was bored. He had expected more of his first command, but *S-56* was exciting only because he expected something new to break at any moment. The last of the S-boats constructed and, he presumed, the most modern in consequence, she was still very primitive compared to a fleet boat. He didn't even have a private stateroom, but had to share a two-man room with Lieutenant John Miglietti, his executive officer. The other three officers slept in the fold-down bunks in the wardroom.

He glanced down at his thickly-gloved hands, wondering just how long it would take before his fingers were frozen solid. Above his head, the SJ radar kept up its vigil, and the bridge lookouts clung precariously to their perches, searching the black waters for any sign of the enemy.

Miller didn't expect much. It was 1520, on the shortest day of the year, and the sun wouldn't peek over the eastern horizon for another hour and sixteen minutes. At 2216 it would complete its transit and drop into the sea to the west. The entire daylight period would pass in less than six hours.

If they found anything, it would probably be a radar contact. Presuming there were even Japanese ships foolish enough to be sailing in these waters at this time of year. In three previous patrols they had seen nothing. The last Japanese troops had slipped away in July, so there wasn't much in the Aleutians for *S-56* to guard.

It was Miller's considered opinion that the enemy had no plans to return. He wasn't even sure there was much reason, beyond the fact that the Aleutians were part of an American territory, for the *Americans* to be there.

The boat was a wet, uncomfortable torture chamber much of the time. The weather was relatively good at the moment, which meant that it wasn't raining or snowing and the seas were only running about five feet. It was still cold as hell.

It wouldn't be all that much better below decks. Jonas had been right about the air conditioning. It was run only to dry out the air and keep down the condensation. What they really needed were better heaters. Except for the engine room crew, who were half cooked with the big diesels running at full power, everyone else was cold most of the time.

He thought back to his old boat, wondering what she was doing these days. The last he'd heard, Morgan still had *Bacalao*, and continued to run up an enviable record. Ames was back at Annapolis, a captain now, teaching another crop of midshipmen, and probably inspiring at least a few of them to consider volunteering for submarines.

The contrast between the three officers Miller had served under in *Bacalao* was something to distract himself from his boredom. It was really hard to categorize Morley. He'd been one of the best officers Miller had ever served under—right up until the attack on that freighter.

But that was the test, wasn't it? No matter how well you performed in the day to day routine of running a ship, or even in the expected turmoil of a storm or breakdown, it wasn't until you were confronted by the enemy that you really knew how you were going to perform.

Still, if Morley was unfit for submarines, he had done just fine in general service. He'd gone on to command destroyers, winning a Navy Cross—clearly deserved this time—in a two-day running battle with a U-boat in the Atlantic. The last Miller had heard, he'd been promoted to rear admiral and was now commanding a division.

Ames, as far as Miller could tell, was one of those men who simply lacked the ability to feel fear. Morgan fell somewhere between the two. He wasn't fearless, but his aggressiveness made up for any doubts he might entertain.

And what about me? Miller asked himself. He certainly had his doubts. He had participated in a lot of attacks, spent his share of time sweating out enemy depth charges, and he was still here. Maybe that was all there really was to it.

He suddenly thought back to that first day out in *Bacalao*, with Morley quietly pretending to read *Beat to Quarters* while unobtrusively keeping an eye on his as-yet-untried OOD. He had a copy of the same book in his quarters. Could it be that Forester was right? That courage in battle wasn't a matter of being brave so much as it was of just holding back the crippling effects of fear long enough to get the job done?

How much of that would he need in this job? Was courage more important in *S-56*, on her lonely Aleutian patrols, or was it just a matter of endurance?

Still, he had a good crew, though at least one crew member served as a clear reminder of just how quickly the Navy was expanding. Bob Marble, who had served as a Torpedoman's Mate 1st Class in *Bacalao*, was aboard as COB. The fact that a chief with slightly less than two years in rate was senior was clear proof that men were moving up very fast. It also pointed out that S-boats were mostly getting a lot of very junior chief petty officers, with the more senior men going to the fleet boats.

Miglietti stuck his head through the hatch. "Permission to come up?"

"Granted."

The XO climbed through the hatch and moved to the front of the bridge. "I thought you might want to get out of the cold for a few minutes, Captain."

Miller nodded. "You thought correctly, John. It's cold as hell up here. But nothing that a few minutes in the engine room and some hot coffee won't fix."

The bridge speaker popped as someone keyed the circuit.

"Bridge—radar. Contact, bearing three-six-zero, range niner-three-double-zero. Evaluate as single vessel."

Miller laughed. "So much for a break." He bent over the microphone. "Radar—bridge. Keep us informed."

"Target?" Miglietti asked.

"Shouldn't be anything friendly up this way. Maybe the Japs are trying to slip a few troops ashore to set up a weather station or something."

"Could be raiders, maybe? Some sort of hit and run attack on a village—try to draw us away from something else, like they did before."

Miller thought about that for a moment. The Japs had invaded the Aleutians in the first place to draw American forces well north, hoping to have the fleet too far out of position to interfere when they attacked at Midway.

"I don't think so," he said. "They could pull off the raid, but I don't think they have the big fleet units they'd need to fight a major engagement any more." He shook his head. "Keep an eye on things up here, John. We'll be going to general quarters before too long—presuming the target's course lets us close on him—and I think I might be able to function a little better if I'm not shivering so much that I can't line up an attack."

"Torpedoes?"

"Gun, probably. Most likely some sort of small cargo vessel. We'll have a better idea once we're close enough to get a sound picture. A cargo vessel is likely to be single screw unless it's really big, but any warship should have at least two shafts."

Miglietti smiled. "Go get your coffee, sir. I have the deck."

•   •   •

"Range?"

"Four-five-double-zero," August reported.

Miller glanced down at the compass. *S-56* was now steaming directly toward the spot on the horizon where the sun would rise at 16:36 on this cold, dreary winter afternoon.

"Target evaluation?"

"Weak return. Still looks like a small coastal freighter on radar."

"Sound? Do you have him yet?"

"Single screw, slow diesel machinery. Sounds like some sort of small freighter, or maybe a large fishing boat."

"Going with a gun action, then, sir?" Miglietti asked.

Miller nodded. "Yes. We'll save the torpedoes for something bigger."

"Why? Do you think we'll ever *see* anything bigger out this way?"

"Why, hell, John—at least we have something to shoot at. Most of the time, the only things these patrols accomplish is to give everyone some sea time."

"I can think of better places to do that," Miglietti said. "Someplace warm, for instance."

"It was warm in the South Pacific, John, but every time you turned around someone was trying to kill you. Here it's mostly just the ocean that's out to get you."

"Ship, sir," Laurence called, from his perch on the periscope shears. "Dead ahead."

Miller lifted his binoculars, but couldn't see anything. "What can yo make out, Laurence?"

"Just his masthead so far, sir."

"Keep an eye on him, but don't neglect the rest of your sector."

"Aye, aye, sir."

Ten minutes later, the top of the target's mast was visible from the bridge. "We've got him," Miller said. "Bearing hasn't changed in the last ten minutes. Unless he zigs away, we'll nail him."

The course had been chosen entirely by chance, but this time it appeared that chance would favor *S-56*. The sun was coming up directly behind the target, silhouetting it against the lightening horizon, while *S-56* remained concealed against the dark of the western sky. They could see the enemy, but Miller didn't think the enemy could see them yet. If he had, he would have taken some action to escape.

"Something doesn't look right, sir," Laurence called down.

"What is it?"

"I don't think that's a freighter, sir."

Miller climbed up beside Laurence and focused his binoculars on the proper bearing. More of the enemy's mast was visible from there, and he could make out the upper part of the bridge structure. Several antennae were strung from the mast, and he could just make out some men perched on a narrow platform just above the bridge.

"John!"

Miglietti looked up. "Sir?"

"Target is some kind of warship. Sub chaser, maybe."

Miller dropped back down to the bridge.

"Cancel the gun action, then?" Miglietti asked.

"Damned right. We'll see if we can close to within torpedo range before he sees us. With luck we can put a couple of fish into him."

"Those little ships are pretty shallow draft. We'll have to set the torpedoes to run at minimum depth. If his lookouts are any good he's likely to spot the wakes and come after us."

Miller shrugged. "We'll have to take that chance. It doesn't look like he's seen us yet. At least, I hope not."

He clipped his binoculars into the TBT and bent over to take a bearing. An S-boat TBT was more primitive than the one on a fleet boat, but it worked well enough. The target was still centered on the submarine's jackstaff, just as nice as anyone could want.

What he had to consider was the possibility that the enemy ship *had* seen them, and was deliberately sailing a converging course, waiting for them to come within point-blank range before opening fire. The hunter often became the hunted in this business.

"Radar—bridge. Range to target?"

"One-four-one-zero."

Miller looked up from the TBT. "This is too damned easy," he said. "I think the bastard may be waiting for us to get so close that his gunners can't miss."

"How close do you want to get, Skipper?"

"We'll try to close to within 1,000 yards and then fire three fish." He keyed the bridge microphone. "Torpedoes—bridge. Make ready tubes one through three. Set depth at five feet."

Miglietti frowned. "I hope none of those broach on the way in."

"Something we'll just have to risk. If I've got him identified correctly, he only draws about ten feet. We don't want our fish going under him."

He bent over the TBT again. "Bearing—mark!"

"Triple-zero."

"Range?"

"One-one-double-zero."

"Angle on the bow is starboard four-five. Estimate speed at nine knots."

Miglietti was spinning the celluloid disks of the Is-Was. The boat was making a steady nine knots, but the torpedoes would be running at 35 knots, which meant they would miss ahead if they were fired with a zero gyro angle.

"Recommend first torpedo angle three-five-one, second three-five-zero, and third three-four-eight, Captain," Miglietti said.

Miller called down the settings and ordered the outer doors opened on the three tubes. They were committed now.

"Clear the bridge," he ordered. "I want to dive the second that third fish is away."

He took a final look as the last man dropped down the hatch into the red-lit world below.

"Fire one!"

The boat jerked slightly as the torpedo was thrust from the tube. In the subdued light he could clearly see the wake as the old Mark-10 started on its way.

"Fire two!" He waited the proper interval, then, "Fire three!" The instant the last torpedo was away he gave the order to dive, and within seconds the sea was roaring into the ballast tanks.

Ahead, there was a flash from the target's bow. The shell whined overhead, falling into the sea a hundred yard astern. But the enemy captain had left it too late, Miller thought, dropping down through the hatch into the tiny conning tower and pulling the wire lanyard to close the hatch. He kept tension on the lanyard, and as the quartermaster of the watch climbed up two rungs and spun the handwheel he could hear the sea rising around the fairwater. A few years earlier he would have been able to see it as well, but the conning tower deadlights had been plated over in the first overhaul after the war began.

"Two hundred feet," he shouted.

Miller dropped down the ladder into the control room, joining Miglietti by the helm position. "Come right to two-eight-zero," he ordered. Normal practice after firing was to make a radical course change, but the enemy would know that as well, and Miller was hoping the less radical ten-degree course change might throw him off.

"Time!"

Marble showed his stopwatch. "Ten seconds to go for the first fish, sir," he said.

"What's he doing?"

Kiley looked up from his sound gear for a moment. "Target is turning. I heard a second engine and screw start up a few seconds ago."

That Japanese captain was a sneaky little bastard, Miller thought. Running on a single screw, sounding like a merchantman or fishing boat, would be just the thing for luring an American submarine into gun range. It would have worked, too, but for Laurence noticing the telltale design of a warship's upperworks over the horizon.

A second later everyone in the boat could hear the shatter blast as the first torpedo smashed into the sub chaser.

Ten minutes later they surfaced. The little warship was gone, leaving only an oil slick and some floating debris. There was enough to provide confirmation, including a life ring with the ship's name stenciled on the face.

There would be no prisoners. They saw several floating bodies, but by the time they reached them the men were dead, frozen stiff in the frigid water.

XVI
Back to Bacalao

It felt odd to be walking up *Bacalao*'s brow again, after nearly a year of separation. It was like coming home to a semi-familiar family, for most of the original crew had been rotated out over time, with new faces filling in all the blanks.

Gordon was still there, and still Chief of the Boat. Harrigan, who had been Miller's right hand in the electrical department, had been promoted to warrant officer and gone on to a job aboard an aircraft carrier. But Ohara was still there. He'd got his chief's hat when Harrigan left and moved into the goat locker.

And Hartman had taken the step up to lieutenant commander. He would be Miller's executive officer, now that he had returned to take command.

The rest of the wardroom was new since his departure for *S-56*, and he discovered, with something of a shock, that he and Hartman were now the only regular officers aboard. All of the new officers were reservists.

With the crew assembled on deck, Miller read the orders assigning him as captain. Morgan, looking suitably impressive in khaki dress, with the new fourth stripe still shiny on the shoulder boards, handed over the boat and retired to his—now Miller's—quarters.

Morgan had everything packed into a single bag. You didn't need that much in a submarine, even considering the constraints of water rationing and the consequent limitations on laundry.

"Anything new I need to know about?" Miller asked, when they were alone.

"Port shaft is leaking pretty steady if you get below 200 feet. COB thinks it needs the packing replaced and I agree with him. We've got the gland tightened down about as hard as we can, but it hasn't been enough. There also seems to be something adrift in the forward super-structure. It gets fairly noisy if you need to put on much speed while you're submerged."

"What is it?"

"We haven't been able to figure that out." He shrugged. "Maybe they can find it at Hunter's Point."

Miller wouldn't be taking *Bacalao* on patrol right away. She was tired, so the first order of business would be to sail her back to San Francisco for overhaul. If there was something loose, the yard people should be able to find and repair it.

"What about the crew?" Miller asked. "I see a lot of new faces."

"Young but good, for the most part," Morgan said. "A lot of reserv-ists now, wardroom included."

"I noticed that."

"Even with accelerated classes, the Academy just can't turn out enough new ensigns to meet current needs. So, instead of men with four years of training in naval leadership, tradition and practices, along with a solid engineering degree, we're getting a lot of guys with a degree in American history and a 90-day crash course in how to be an officer." He smiled. "Surprisingly enough, most of them seem to be managing pretty well."

"It's all through the fleet," Miller said. "I was the only regular in *S-56*, and we managed well enough. Besides, I've always got Hartman."

"You'll do fine, Larry. Hell, you've got a nice, quiet trip back to the States to get used to her again."

Miller nodded. "Where are you off to, by the way? Now that you've got your fourth stripe?"

"New London. Staff job at the base, and probably some instructing at the Submarine School." Morgan shook his head. "I think I'm ready for it, too. I've been at this too long. Six war patrols are more than enough for any commander."

"You were good at it, though."

"True. That may be the problem, you know. If you're *too* good at what you do they may not let you stop."

A messenger—one of the new men—brought in the mail. There were two personal letters for Morgan, with the rest 'Attention: Com-manding Officer.' Those would go to Miller now. His personal mail hadn't caught up with him yet. With any luck it might find him in San Fran-cisco.

Morgan opened one of his letters and quickly glanced at it, smiling. "From Fred Ames," he said.

"How is he? The last I heard he was teaching at the Academy."

"He's a rear admiral now, and back with Morley, as a matter of fact."

"He is?"

"They're both in Washington now. We all know Morley turned out not to be a very good combat sub commander, but he was a *lot* better at hunting them. These days he's running a desk at the Navy Department."

"You know," Miller said, "I really did like Morley. He was a good commander—at least up to the point where he cracked up. Looks like he's done a good job since, too."

"Must have," Morgan agreed. "You don't get to be a vice admiral if you keep screwing up."

There was a polite knock on the stateroom door frame, and a young seaman 2nd class brought in Miller's kit bag.

"Another new face," Miller commented, after the seaman left.

"Kirk," Morgan said. "Bow planesman. Our old radioman's kid brother, as a matter of fact."

"It's going to be a chore learning them all," Miller said. "Seems like everyone I knew was reassigned while I was gone."

"Ah, you'll learn everyone's name quickly enough, Larry. And you've got good chiefs, of course."

Miller laughed. "At least there some familiar faces in that group."

"Right. I don't think they'll ever get Gordon and Collins out of here. They just don't want to leave, and the Navy is indulging them so far. With Ohara, I think it's more a case of morons who just see another Jap and figure that as long as we want to keep him they'll leave him here. Considering how good he is at his job I just kept hoping the morons would prevail."

Miller rummaged through his bag and pulled out a framed picture, which he place on the fold-down desk.

Morgan looked curiously at the picture. "You still involved with her, are you?"

"Sarah? Absolutely. She's in San Francisco now, at the Australian Consulate. Once the boat is safely turned over to the yard I'll be taking a few days off for a honeymoon."

"Still engaged, are you?" Morgan shook his head. "I have to admit I figured that would sort of fizzle out once you were several thousand miles apart."

Miller smiled. "It didn't. Some of us never learn, I guess."

"My friend, if you keep making the same mistake, I have to say you've always had damned good taste in who you pick to make it with."

•   •   •

They cast off at 0630 on a Tuesday morning. As they would be able to make the entire voyage on the surface, only submerging for the daily trim dive, it was expected they would arrive in San Francisco Bay sometime on Monday. There was supposed to be a dock waiting for them at Hunter's Point when they arrived.

Personally, Miller expected they would get to the yard, find their dock already in use and then have to wait around until the yard found an available dock to get them out of the water.

He decided, if that happened, he wouldn't really mind. Sarah was there, and it appeared they would have a month or two to get married and act like a couple of silly newlyweds. If it took longer for the overhaul, they'd just have more time together before he had to get back into the war.

After clearing the channel, they set their course for the first leg of the voyage. On a chart, the projected course would appear wildly out of the way, seeming to go far north, traveling to their destination in a deep arc. In fact, it was roughly a straight line when you laid it out on a globe. Flattening out the earth's surface for a chart played hell with directions over a long distance.

They would have air cover for the first 500 miles out of Pearl. This was a mixed blessing. Enemy aircraft were deadly, and the air cover would insure that none got too close. But at this point in the war, Miller wasn't too concerned with Jap planes close to Hawaii. What *did* concern him was the knowledge that a number of subs had been sunk by aircraft, and that not all of the planes had belonged to the enemy.

The best guess as to what happened when *Dorado* went missing en route to the Canal from New London was that *she* was the "U-boat" reported sunk by a bomber out of Guantanamo. There were supposed to be security zones around submarines, where friendly aircraft didn't operate. Submariners universally doubted that pilots paid any attention to those notices and, moreover, couldn't tell one nation's submarines from another.

Hartman came up onto the bridge as they steadied on their initial course. He'd come a long way from the green ensign filling out his qualification notebook as the boat took shape in Groton. When Morgan left, his XO, Sam Cutts, also departed, going to Portsmouth, where he would commission a new boat. That gave Hartman his step up. If the war lasted long enough, he would no doubt get his own command.

"Nice to be going home," he commented.

"You're *really* going home, aren't you?" Miller asked.

"San Francisco. Born and raised there. Should be a nice surprise for Mom. I wrote her, but we'll probably get there before the letter—and I couldn't say just when we'd arrive."

"Have to maintain security, Tom."

Hartman laughed. "And then some. Chief Ohara was thinking of asking his parents to come out, but he was afraid they wouldn't let them into California. Seems odd, doesn't it?"

"How?"

"Look, there's Ohara, a chief petty officer in the United States Navy, and the son of a defense contractor, and he's afraid the government won't let his parents into California because they happen to *look* Japanese. Hell, right after the war started they just rounded up every Jap in California—no one bothered to ask whether they were loyal or not—and stuck them in camps out in the middle of nowhere.

"Meanwhile, out in Hawaii, they rounded up a couple hundred that were actually suspected of being enemy agents or sympathizers, and the rest were just left to go about their business. The closer they were to where the local Japs could actually do any real damage, the less anyone seemed to worry about it."

He was right, of course, Miller thought. "What's your take on it?"

"Hawaii couldn't function if they locked up all the local Japanese. The whole place would just grind to a halt. That wasn't a danger in California, but the Japanese there owned an awful lot of really good farmland and lots of small, very profitable businesses. The locals didn't much like Asians in general, and tossing out the Japs was a great chance to snap up their land and businesses for a fraction of their value."

"You're a cynic, Tom."

"I'm a Californian. We're just as rotten as anyone else, when you come right down to it."

•   •   •

Miller stood on the raised chancel at the front of the chapel's sanctuary, looking expectantly down the aisle. He shifted slightly, adjusting the unaccustomed weight of his sword. It was the first time he'd worn one since his days as a midshipman, and he hoped he could get through the ceremony and out of the chapel without tripping over it.

The chaplain, who had donned a black robe and clerical stole for the ceremony, stood quietly in front of the altar, holding a leather-bound Bible in his folded hands. At Miller's side, Hartman, who had been pressed into service as best man, checked his pocket for the ring for what Miller thought might have been the hundredth time.

The pews were filled by a combination of familiar faces and complete strangers. Miller's mother had taken the train out from Cleveland with his Aunt Isobel. The two sisters were in the front row, his mother's expression combining joy with the clear hope that her son wasn't making another mistake.

Behind them were seated as many of *Bacalao*'s crew as had been able to get free and hadn't already gone on leave. They were seated in order of rank and seniority, the officers at the front, with the chiefs behind them, and the rest of the men completing the groom's side of the aisle.

The bride's side was more sparsely filled. Sarah's parents hadn't been able to come out from Australia. Everyone had agreed it would be too risky to make the long voyage just to attend the wedding, though they would have had no hesitation about doing so had it not involved sailing through a war zone. It might have been an acceptable risk if they could have sailed directly from Australia to San Francisco, but the only route they could take would involve going around the Cape of Good Hope to England, and then across the Atlantic to New York.

The Japanese had never seemed to learn to use their submarines properly, wasting them hauling supplies, and often ignoring the valuable transports and freighters even as they threw away torpedoes trying to sink the escorts. Some odd notion of honor, Miller had heard—a warship was a "worthy" opponent and a freighter or transport wasn't.

But the Kings' ship would have to cross the Atlantic, and the Germans were under no illusions about which ships were most valuable to the Allied war effort. To a U-boat captain, an escort was just an obstacle between his boat and his target.

So the bride's side of the chapel was mostly filled with people from the Australian Consulate, along with a handful of Australian officers who happened to be in San Francisco and took advantage of the open invitation.

At the rear of the chapel, an Army captain, with the plain silver cross of a Christian chaplain on his lapels, kept his own vigil. In their rush to put the wedding together, the happy couple had encountered one major roadblock—every Navy chapel in the San Francisco Bay area had already been booked on their selected date. After a bit of finagling, they had managed to get the use of the lovely old Army chapel at the Presidio.

A Navy chaplain would conduct the service, but Chaplain McNeill would also be there to keep an eye on things.

The organist started the processional. Miller smiled to himself. Columbia University couldn't play it's own Alma Mater at football games because it was sung to a Hadyn melody that the Germans also used as their National Anthem, but he could still get married to the music of Hitler's favorite composer.

Then Sarah appeared at the back of the chapel, on the arm of a Royal Australian Navy captain, who was standing in for her father. He was in dress uniform, complete with medals and sword. Sarah was in a simple white satin gown that complemented her slim figure. Her red hair had obviously received a lot of attention.

This is it, Miller thought.

•   •   •

Ohara woke to the sound of chattering birds outside the window. It still seemed odd to him, the light through the window, the birds in the trees outside, and the soft mattress, percale sheets and thick comforter.

Things had seemed more normal during the three days it took the train to get him from San Francisco to Atlanta. The Pullman berth wasn't that different from his bunk in *Bacalao*'s goat locker. But now he was back in his old bedroom in his parents' house, and everything just seemed too soft.

The pajamas felt wrong, too. Home was the only place he ever wore them now. Aboard the boat he slept in his underwear, like any normal person.

Stretching, he got out of bed and started to dress. His shirts were now hung in the closet, freshly washed and neatly ironed. His mother had done that as soon as he started to unpack. She had also pressed his blue trousers and jacket.

He didn't bother with a tie for the moment. He'd put one on if he left the house, but didn't feel it was important at home. His shoes were perfectly spit shined. That was one task he took care of himself, for he didn't feel it was something that could be trusted to any civilian—not even a parent.

His mother was in the kitchen when he came down. "What do you want for breakfast?" she asked.

"Cereal will be fine," he said.

She looked at him severely. "Nonsense. I think some nice bacon, a couple of eggs, and some grits ought to be about right."

Ohara sat down at the kitchen table. He was just over six feet tall, a chief petty officer in the United States Navy with a chest full of ribbons on the blue jacket hanging in his closet, and he was still unable to stand up to this middle-aged, four-foot-ten woman. When it came to getting what she wanted, Scarlet O'Hara had nothing on his mother.

"What are you planning to do today, Kenny?" she asked, having settled the question of his breakfast to her satisfaction.

"Probably just hang around the house," he said. "Where's Dad?"

"He had to go in to the office this morning."

"On a Saturday?"

"It's the war. They're running three shifts now, just to keep up with the demand. Your dad figures that if the workers need to be there that much, the owners should be putting in some extra effort as well."

His mother turned back to the stove. "Oh," she said, "and you'll be home for supper tonight, won't you?"

"Sure."

"Good. The Yamadas are coming over."

"Ma! Just what are you up to?"

"Me? Not a thing."

"Why do I have the feeling you are?"

"I have no idea. Now, here's your bacon and eggs all ready. Be a few more minutes on the grits."

•   •   •

Chief Torpedoman's Mate John Collins stood at the edge of the dock, watching as a crane lowered a new deck gun onto *Bacalao*'s forward deck. It was a recently rebuilt 4"/50-caliber wet mount, just like the one it replaced.

As the war progressed, there were fewer targets for his torpedoes and more and more that could be better dealt with by the guns. The barrel of the old gun was worn out. The *Gatos* had been designed to mount a five-inch gun, though they had originally been fitted with a much lighter three-inch gun.

The Navy was working on a much better gun, a version of the 5"/25, specially modified for submarines. But that one would be going to the new boats first. The older boats would have to wait.

He glanced at his watch. The captain should be leaving the chapel and heading off on his honeymoon about now, he thought. He wondered how long that would last. He couldn't see Miller staying away very long with his boat being subjected to the tender mercies of the Hunter's Point workers.

They were busy now, too. Down in the pump room the clattering old trim pump was being replaced by a brand-new Gould centrifugal pump. The new unit would be slightly more efficient than the old model. Even more important, it would be far quieter.

That was the new catch phrase in submarines. Quiet is good. Compared to a surface warship, a submarine was already very quiet. But a sub still put out plenty of noise. The screws driving her through the water were the main source. And tests had shown that just about anything you could hear inside the boat could also be heard by an alert sonar operator on an escort.

It might not have mattered that much to the German engineers who had designed the old pump for their U-boats in the years leading up to World War I. Hydrophones weren't very sensitive back then, and active sonar had yet to be invented.

Now it was different. Modern hydrophones were highly effective at isolating even insignificant noise from deep in the sea, and the old trim pumps could be heard for miles. The new design cut the noise significantly.

If they can't hear you, Collins thought, they can't find you. And if they can't find you, they can't kill you.

•　　　•　　　•

At his mother's suggestion, Ohara had put on his dress uniform while they waited for their guests to arrive. His mother had just sewn the new gold bullion stripes and hashmarks on his left sleeve. He had completed his twelfth year of service the previous month, and with good conduct ratings for all those years had qualified for the gold rate badges at that time. He just hadn't had the time to sew on the new ones before going on leave.

His father had been home for about half an hour, looking more tired than his son thought healthy. "You should take a day off, Dad," Ohara had protested. "It wouldn't hurt you to rest."

His father had just shaken his head. "Wouldn't be right. I've got all those people working overtime—seems to me that if they're doing that, Jim and I should be there, too. It's important work, you know. I expect you've got some of our products on your boat."

Ohara and Yamada—the markings on the packages had been changed to just the O&Y monogram since the beginning of the war, though the original name remained chiseled into the granite slab over the main entrance to the factory—manufactured a wide assortment of MilSpec electronics parts. Most of the parts would have been hard to spot once they were removed from the packages and soldered onto the chassis of a radio or radar set, but Ohara had no doubt that his father was right.

The doorbell rang and Ohara's mother went to answer it. The Yamadas were kitchen door guests. Close family friends as well as business associates, they would have considered it more than a little snobbish to use the front door for anything short of a formal occasion.

Jim Yamada was a short, dynamic man who seemed to thrive on extra work. He didn't look nearly as worn out as his father, Ohara thought.

"Why, Kenny, you look real good," Mrs. Yamada said, following her husband through the door. "All dressed up in your uniform and just as handsome as ever."

"Thank you, ma'am." Both Yamadas had been trying to get him to call them by their first names for several years, but it just wasn't something he could do.

"Hi, Kenny."

"Liz?"

"Well, who else would it be?"

For the first time since he'd been home it occurred to Ohara that his mother might *not* be the annoying, meddlesome little southern dragon lady matchmaker he'd been thinking she was. She was clearly a wise, doting parent with his best interests at heart.

And this wasn't the same scrawny, annoying kid he remembered from a couple years ago. This was what Miss America would look like if she happened to be Japanese.

"You, uh, grew."

•   •   •

Miller pulled the car to the curb and got out to remove all the tin cans and old shoes someone had tied to the rear bumper. He found that he also had to pop off the Ford coupe's hubcaps, which one of his friends had thoughtfully filled with gravel.

There wasn't much he could do about the big "Just Married" signs they had daubed on the doors and trunk lid in white paint. It would take a hose and scrub brush to get rid of those.

He got back into the car and continued south, out of the city. They had reservations at a small coastal hotel about 30 miles south of San Francisco.

Miller was still in his dress uniform, the sword tossed onto the shelf behind the seat. Sarah had changed into a cream-colored traveling suit, with a pillbox hat. To Miller's way of thinking, she had never looked lovelier.

She could wear anything, really, and make it look glamorous and terribly sexy. Miller always saw her that way and had from the first moment. He was quite sure that, eventually, she would become the world's sexiest and most glamorous great-grandmother, and everyone would be wondering just what this vision saw in the decrepit old geezer she was with. He could see himself getting old, but not her.

•   •   •

The dockside was cluttered with coils of old wiring. Every foot of cabling had been ripped out early in the overhaul, and now a team of electricians was pulling new cable through the boat. A submarine ran on electricity—good wiring was as important as a sound pressure hull.

In the forward engine room, both fresh water distillers had been removed. The old Kleinschmidt units would be replaced by new Badgers in a few days.

More men were at work in both engine rooms, as all four of the huge GM 16-278A V-16 diesels underwent a complete overhaul.

The auxiliary engine, hidden beneath the after engine room platform deck, was being left alone. The 8-cylinder in-line engine was run far less than the main engines, showing only a third of the hours on its log. It would wait for the next overhaul.

•   •   •

The room, Miller thought, was perfect. His bride thought so, too, delighted with the private balcony and the view of the Pacific stretching out to the western horizon.

Miller's idea of perfection hadn't really included the view—he was a typical male and felt that, for a honeymoon, the big bed was all that would be needed—but he had to concede that the view didn't hurt.

Still, considering that he spent most of his time on, or under, the same ocean he could see through the French doors, the view seemed different mostly in being seen from higher up.

That, and there was very little chance there was anyone out there off the California coast who wanted to kill him.

•   •   •

Ohara pulled up to the curb and rolled down the window, smiling benignly at the car hop's momentary confusion as she tried to reconcile a Japanese face with an American Navy uniform. Once she managed that, she wrote down their orders and scurried back inside.

"When I was a kid," Ohara said, "they used to jump on the running board and start taking your order as you pulled in."

"They didn't do that for us," Elizabeth commented.

"No running boards on a '41 Ford."

It was his father's car. There were no new cars to be had, so this one would be like his current enlistment. It would have to last for the duration. With 87,000 miles on the clock he wondered if it would.

The car hop was back a minute later. "Okay," she said. "Three mustard dogs, a Coke and a beer."

"Thanks."

The car hop was looking at the windshield. "How does a sailor get an X-Card?"

"It's my Dad's car. He has to drive a lot, I guess. Government contractor."

"Oh. Just wondered. All we have is an A-Card."

"Shortages," Elizabeth said, when they were alone again. "I never really understood why they couldn't produce enough gas to keep the military supplied and still have enough for the rest of us, too."

Ohara grinned. "They can and they do. There's never been any real gas shortage. It's rubber that's in short supply. They ration gas so that people don't drive too much and wear out their tires."

"Not a problem for us, though," she said.

"No, not really. But I still feel funny driving too much. Dad got that unlimited ration card because of his job, not so that his kid could go joy riding."

"You're not a kid, Kenny."

"You're not a kid any more, either."

She laughed. "I'm glad you finally noticed."

"Well, the last time I saw you, you still were."

"And now?"

He shrugged. "And now I wish I had a longer leave."

•   •   •

Collins smoothed the sheet on his bunk and tucked it in. "So how was your leave, Ken?" he asked.

Ohara was putting away his gear. "Too damned short. But I did manage to get married."

"Oh, you poor sap. How the hell did that happen?"

"You know, I really think it was all my mother's idea. I've known Liz since she was a kid, but hadn't seen her lately. She grew up. . . really nice." He smiled. "The hardest part was tracking down the captain to get permission. Everything else just sort of happened."

Collins shook his head. "Well, son, the honeymoon is over. It's back to the war for us."

"Do we know where we're going?"

"Hell if I know. Back to Australia would be my guess."

Ohara chuckled softly. "The captain would love that, wouldn't he? He marries an Australian girl, then gets shipped off to Fremantle and his wife stays in San Francisco."

"That's the Navy for you." Collins paused, partway into the passageway. "Anyway, I'm only guessing. You know how it is—we'll know where we're going when we get there.

XVII
Unexpected Bag

"UP 'SCOPE."

Miller stooped to meet the periscope as it rose from the well, snapping down the handles and pressing his eyes into the buffer, waiting impatiently for the lens to clear.

"Enough," he said, the moment the thick head of the number one periscope was clear of the waves. Acting from habit and conditioning, he quickly made the standard three full circuits of the horizon, starting at full elevation and clicking the left handle down one click of the detent with each circuit.

Then he had the target centered in the crosshairs, feeling momentarily confused by the odd silhouette. "Down 'scope."

He looked at Hartman, who was waiting expectantly by the tiny conning tower chart table. "Submarine," Miller said. "I think it's a Kraut."

"Here?"

It was an understandable question. They were a few hundred miles from Java—a long way from the north Atlantic.

"Get the German recognition book," Miller said.

The book was produced, still pristine, as there had never been any reason to open it before this night. Miller quickly flipped through the pages of German warships until he found what he was looking for.

"Here it is," he said. "German Type IX/D2, long-range U-boat." He turned to Cushing at the TDC. "Start your setup. We're going to get him before he figures out we're here and decides to dive."

"What do you think he's doing here?" Hartman asked.

"I understand the Krauts have been sending some of their long-range boats to Penang. I suppose this is one of them. The Japs are always short of strategic materials, and the Germans can supply some of it if they can find a way to get it through. Their ships don't have much of a chance as blockade runners any more, but a sub might make it."

He signaled for the periscope to be raised again, lining it up on the low conning tower fairwater that was almost, but not quite, lost in the waves. *Can't be a very good sea boat,* he thought. *Wouldn't take much of a wave to wash right over that bridge.*

"Target bearing—mark!"

"Zero-one-one," Hartman said.

"Masthead height?"

"Three-oh feet, more or less." It was difficult to give an exact masthead height for any submarine, for it would vary with the trim, or whether the periscopes, which stood in for the nonexistent mast in the equation, were extended or retracted.

Miller set the stadimeter and worked the dial, adjusting the split lenses in the range-finder. "Range—mark!"

"Two-one-double-zero," Hartman said, reading the range off the second dial on the rear of the periscope.

"Angle on the bow is starboard four-five," Miller estimated. "Speed?"

Jones was still counting. After a moment he said, "Speed one-two knots."

Cushing cranked the data into the TDC as they settled down to wait until it was time for the next observation. This was usually the hardest part, creeping slowly closer, wondering if the target would still be where you expected it the next time you put up the periscope. It took at least three observations, about five minutes apart, to be sure of a good setup.

There were times when those 15 minutes seemed more like 15 hours.

•   •   •

The final observation matched the TDC's generated bearing, and at a range of only 800 yards Miller figured they were in good shape for a hit.

"Flood tubes one and two," he ordered.

"Tubes one and two flooded from WRT, sir."

"Open outer doors."

"Outer doors are open, sir."

"Fire one!"

"Fire one, aye! One fired electrically, sir."

Miller could feel the boat shudder as the torpedo was thrust from the tube. Slowly, he counted to ten.

"Fire two!"

"Fire two, aye! Two fired electrically, sir."

"Both fish are running normally," Jones reported, listening to the fast-turning screws through his headphones.

"Up 'scope."

Just as the periscope's head came clear of the water the first torpedo hit the U-boat just abaft the wicked-looking Vierling gun on the bandstand at the rear of the conning tower fairwater. The second torpedo missed just astern—not that it mattered.

Miller had seen more than a few ships torpedoed, but nothing had prepared him for this. The torpedo hit low, only a foot above the deepest part of the keel. As it exploded, the U-boat started to lift bodily from the water.

A moment later, the hull split in half, the center rising up like an inverted "V," throwing the men on the bridge into the water. A pyramidal column of explosive gases and water soared high at the apex before subsiding. As it did so, the shattered U-boat sagged and started to sink in two sections, the bow and stern rising from the sea as the air trapped in the forward and aft compartments held the ends of the boat up for a moment before it disappeared beneath the waves.

A couple more heads bobbed to the surface and then it was over.

"Put up the radar and take a good look around," Miller ordered. "We surprised him—I don't want anyone returning the favor."

"Nothing in the vicinity, sir," the radar operator reported. By this time the German submarine had gone completely. Here and there it was possible to make out the image of a man treading water. Common sense dictated wearing a life jacket while on a submarine's bridge, but the difficulty of getting through the hatch in a hurry in a bulky life jacket meant they were often left below in good weather.

"Surface," Miller ordered. "Lookouts and rescue party to the conning tower."

"Picking up survivors, are we?" Hartman wondered aloud.

Miller nodded. "Doesn't look as if there will be very many. But, unlike the Japs, I think *these* guys will be quite happy to let us collect them.

Bacalao surged to the moonlit surface and Miller followed the quartermaster through the hatch and onto the dripping bridge. Within seconds, he had given the all clear and the lookouts were scrambling up behind him, climbing to their positions on the periscope shears, while the rescue party climbed down the side of the fairwater to the main deck.

His guess about the Germans was correct. *Bacalao*'s crew naturally manned the guns, but there was no fight left in the dripping seamen and, being Europeans, there was also none of the Japanese *bushido* victory or death attitude.

They collected eight of them, two officers and six enlisted men of, for the moment, indeterminate rate. One of the officers had two rings around his sleeve, with a gold cogwheel device above it. The other wore three rings under a five-pointed star, though with the point up, instead of down, as it would have been on an American uniform.

The three-ringer had also managed to hang on to his white-covered cap, which was now settled soggily on his head as he was brought up onto the bridge. He looked at the silver oak leaves on Miller's collar and saluted—the traditional military salute, and not the stiff-armed Nazi version Miller had expected.

In his haste to get to the bridge, Miller had left his cap below. He returned the salute anyway.

"You are the commanding officer?" the German asked, in good, though strongly-accented English.

"Lieutenant Commander Lawrence Miller," he said. "Welcome aboard *Bacalao*, sir."

An odd smile crossed the captured officer's face. "Interesting," he said. "I am *Korvettenkapitän* Kurt Müller—the same name, you see?"

He looked around at the remnants of his crew. "So few," he said. "How deep is the water here, if I may ask? We have not taken a sounding recently."

Miller bent over the 7MC. "Control room—bridge. Give me a sounding."

"One-niner-double-zero fathoms, sir."

"One thousand nine-hundred fathoms," Miller repeated.

Müller frowned. "Then I do not expect there will be any more. Even if the bulkheads did not rupture, it is much too deep to escape."

"You were the captain?" Miller asked.

He smiled weakly, pointing at his dripping cap. "White cap, you see?" he said. "Only the captain wears one in a German submarine."

Miller found it interesting that he said "submarine" and not "U-boat." It wouldn't be until later that it would sink into what he thought of as his sometimes thick head that "*Unterseeboot*" was simply the German word for "submarine," so Müller naturally translated it when he was speaking English.

"Your English is quite good," Miller said.

"It is a requirement for command," Müller said. He shivered suddenly. "It is a warm night," he said, "but my men and I are a bit damp just now."

Miller leaned over the side of the bridge. "Get the prisoners below," he ordered. "And get them some dry clothing." He looked back at Müller. "If you'll come below, we'll see if we can find something dry for you as well."

Miller started down the bridge ladder into the conning tower. "You have the deck, Mr. Hartman."

"XO has the deck, aye, sir."

"Commander Müller? This way, please."

They went straight down through the conning tower and into the control room, where the crew's initial fascination with their prisoners seemed even more intensified by the appearance of the German commander.

"COB? Where did you put your prisoners?" Miller asked.

"Crew's mess for the moment, sir," Gordon said. "We've borrowed some dungarees from some of the men, and I've got Krause showing them how to use the shower. He speaks passable German. Anyway, I figured it would be a good idea to get the salt water off of them."

Müller looked at him curiously. "You have fresh water showers in a submarine?"

Gordon just smiled.

"We can't waste fresh water," Miller said, "but the stills produce enough for the batteries, keeping the drinking water tanks full, and still let us take Navy showers. You turn on the water long enough to get wet, shut it off, lather up, then quickly rinse off. You can manage a shower with no more than two or three gallons of water."

Müller nodded. "Very different," he said. "We have not had a fresh water shower since we left, er, our base some four months ago. There is only saltwater soap, and a saltwater shower is not very satisfactory. We can make fresh water, but only enough for the batteries and to drink. There is none to spare for hygiene."

"We'll get you into a shower, then, Commander Müller."

"That is not quite correct," he said.

"What?"

"My rank. I am a *Korvettenkapitän*—in your Navy that would be the same as yourself, a lieutenant commander."

Miller smiled. "Ah. I'm not that familiar with your rank insignia. In our Navy, three stripes are a full commander."

"In the *Kriegsmarine*, he would wear four stripes, with the second from the top narrow."

"Well, for now you probably won't be wearing any rank insignia, but we'll get you an officer's uniform, in any case. We will take your medals and badges for safekeeping." Miller looked apologetic. "I suppose you'll get them back at some point." *If someone doesn't steal them first.*

Müller removed the Nazi eagle and swastika insignia from the right breast of his uniform jacket. "This," he said, with a remarkable amount of contempt, "you can keep."

Miller led him forward. As he was about Miller's size, he gave him one of his uniforms and showed him the officer's shower. The German didn't seem to mind that Miller watched him strip. He no doubt understood that they couldn't trust him all that much, even if he appeared to be cooperating at the moment.

Miller explained the shower and let his prisoner get on with it. After he had dressed, he was taken to the wardroom, where Miller showed him one of the fold-down bunks.

"You'll sleep in here," Miller said. "There will be a man watching you, of course."

"Of course."

"Are you hungry, by any chance?"

The German nodded. "Always."

Miller rapped on the pantry pass-through and asked Washington to bring in some food. At about the same time, Lieutenant Gould brought the other officer into the wardroom, also dressed in a khaki uniform. The other officer started talking excitedly in German.

Müller smiled. "*Leutnant* Hessler seems to have fallen in love with your engines, Commander. Engines are his life, of course. He is—was— my leading engineer. He tells me that you have four, and that they are all running astonishingly smoothly for such an arrangement."

"They're good engines," Gould commented. He was *Bacalao*'s chief engineer.

"He also says that my men are being fed, with fresh bread and quite excellent food. So, you have just left harbor, true?"

Miller shook his head. "We've been out for 34 days now."

"And you still have fresh bread?"

"Of course. We bake it every night."

Müller looked astonished. "Amazing," he said. "With us, it is always a race. Will we eat the fresh bread and vegetables, or will the mold destroy them first?"

"Well, we have refrigeration and a freezer," Miller said.

"And a lot of stuff in cans," Gordon added, still standing in the door.

"Powdered eggs," Gould contributed.

"Yes," Miller said. "The menu runs the gamut from quite good to it's-the-best-we-can-do."

Washington came in with fresh coffee and some sandwiches, then returned to his pantry. Hessler said something in German. Müller shrugged, sipped his coffee, and started to work on a baloney sandwich.

"What was that?" Miller asked.

"*Leutnant* Hessler was curious about your servant."

"Washington? He's not a servant, he's a steward's mate."

"There is a difference?"

"Well, a Navy steward's mate is also a sailor. Washington is a fully qualified submariner. He's rated as a steward's mate, but he can do just about anything in the boat if he needs to."

"We were told that you have no Negro sailors—that they are only allowed to wait on officers."

"Not any more," Johnson said. "It used to be that way, but not now."

Hessler nodded. Evidently he understood English, even if he didn't appear inclined to speak it.

"Do you understand what we're saying?" Miller asked, his gaze locked on Hessler.

"Yes. Not good speak, but understand."

"Officers who wish to command a submarine must speak English," Müller said. "Engineers do not have this requirement."

Miller nodded. "In our Navy, submarine officers are *all* engineers. We don't have a separate engineering branch."

"We are more sensible, then. What makes a good engineer does not always make a good seaman or commanding officer, no? Your British allies would no doubt agree—their system is the same as ours."

"*Ja*," Hessler agreed. "To make engine good run art is. *Aber*, for you, is I think easier with those engines. Much more power than in German boat."

"We had German engines when this boat was first built," Miller said. "They kept breaking down."

Hessler seemed curious. "How?"

"Bad timing gears, problems with piston-rod seals on the lower combustion chambers. The company that built them is called Hooven-Owens-
Rentschler, and usually we just call them by their initials, H.O.R.. Mostly,
we said it as a word and called them H.O.R.s."

Müller laughed. Hessler just looked confused. "H.O.R.," Müller explained, "sounds like the English word for *Hure*."'

"What kind of engine was this?" Hessler asked. "If you can say."

"Nothing classified about it," Miller said. "We got rid of them a long
time ago. They were based on a M.A.N. design, a nine-cylinder, double
acting type. I believe you used a larger version of the same engine in a
light cruiser."

"*Leipzig?*"

"Might be."

"That is very good engine," Hessler protested. "To build them is
very difficult—very much hand fitting all the parts, must be extreme
precise—but good engine. How can you make enough for many *Unter-
seeboote?* For reliable, long time to build each engine is taking."

Miller nodded. He seriously doubted that H.O.R. did a lot of hand
fitting on their engines. They would have mass produced them, just as
GM and Fairbanks-Morse mass-produced theirs.

He remembered a lot of stories suggesting that M.A.N. had sold the
Navy plans with deliberate errors in them, so that the engines would fail
under stress. Could it have been something as simple as a design requiring much closer tolerances than the American factory could achieve?

It was an interesting subject for speculation, but Miller was still just
as glad that the engines were gone.

•   •   •

The prisoners settled into their new life as captives with surprisingly
little disruption to the boat's routine. With bunks for 66 enlisted men,
and only 72 in the crew, the dozen who had to hot bunk were joined by
six more who would now have to share their bunks with prisoners. The
Germans didn't feel in the least inconvenienced by this. In their own
boat *everyone* had to share a bunk, and the American submarine at least
had laundry facilities, so the sheets were changed more than once every
six months.

Of *Bacalao*'s crew, Torpedoman's Mate 3rd Class Irving Krause was
most inconvenienced. He was the only German speaker aboard, which
meant that he now had to spend nearly all his time with the prisoners.
None of the German enlisted men spoke any English.

During their first night aboard, once they had been plucked out of the sea, given showers, and provided with Navy dungarees to replace their own sodden uniforms, Müller had given his surviving crew members a stern lecture.

Bacalao's captain had naturally been curious about what was said. He didn't understand a word of it, and for all he knew Müller was setting out his plan to capture the sub and continue their mission. But Krause summed up the long, harsh-sounding lecture in only a few words. "Keep out of the way, don't touch anything, and do what they tell you."

The men took their captain at his word. It helped that they were all trained submariners. They knew better than to risk their own lives by fooling with the unfamiliar controls. Submarines all worked more or less the same way, but the controls were in different places and worked in different ways.

So the prisoners slept when they had the chance, and were content with the good food, showers and air conditioning. Compared to the Type IX/D2 U-boat they had been aboard for the last four months, *Bacalao* was like a deluxe hotel.

Miller found the contrast with his own crew amusing. His men were all volunteers, but there wasn't one of them who wouldn't admit that there were more comfortable places to be. Most of them, given any choice, would really prefer to be ashore, between patrols, and busy chasing women. The Germans were absolutely delighted to be right where they were. They were alive, and they were comfortable, and that was enough for the moment.

The Germans were certainly far less trouble than the handful of Japanese prisoners they had hosted during the course of ten previous war patrols. One Japanese prisoner—a civilian fisherman and not an Imperial Navy sailor—had spent most of his time aboard being as helpful as possible, and had turned out to be a fairly useful assistant for the steward's mates. The other eight Japanese prisoners had resisted being picked up, and wound up spending most of their time aboard locked up in the storeroom under the galley with the food.

The two German officers were even less trouble. Both slept in the spare bunks in the wardroom, which meant no one had to share a bunk with them. It was a little inconvenient for *Bacalao*'s officers, who had to be a bit quieter, but nothing they couldn't live with. The German officers were already on the same day-for-night schedule as the Americans, so sleeping all day and being awake all night wasn't a problem. It also helped that they both spoke English—Müller fluently and Hessler at least adequately—so there was no need to tie someone up translating for them.

Müller spent most of his time in the wardroom, sitting at the table, writing on a yellow legal pad he'd scrounged from the ship's clerk. As time passed, he filled page after page, on both sides, with his tiny, neat script.

"It's a novel," Krause informed Miller, who had asked him to look at what the prisoner was writing. "Mostly it's the flying Dutchman story, but set on a submarine. A little convoluted for my own tastes, to be honest, sir, but German stories tend to be that way."

"Flying Dutchman, huh?"

"You remember the story, sir. A Dutch captain is trying to round the Cape of Good Hope in a storm and vows he'll accomplish it if he has to sail forever, so he's cursed to do just that. In Captain Müller's story, it's the captain of a U-boat, and he's cursed to sail on forever not because he's vowed to round the Cape, but because he deliberately sank a neutral ship and then killed the crew trying to hide what he'd done. When he tries to kill himself by jumping overboard after the guilt gets to him, instead of dying he finds himself in an ancient U-boat, with ghosts for a crew."

While Müller continued his adventure in German literature, Hessler spent most of his time with Gould. At first he had marveled at the smooth power of the four main engines, presuming that they were coupled together and attached to the propeller shafts. Once he learned that the engines drove generators, and there was no physical connection to the shafts, he became even more enthusiastic. It seemed such an obvious idea, and infinitely better than contending with a U-boat's cantankerous clutches and the inevitable vibration at certain speeds.

Miller recognized that the two German officers were going to end up knowing a lot more about American submarine designs than they should. There was no avoiding it, though, and he knew he couldn't have left them to drown. He decided it wouldn't matter too much. The Allies had been ashore in France and advancing toward Germany for months. The war in Europe might be over before the two officers even reached a POW camp back in the States.

• • •

Ingles, the duty radioman, tapped on the doorframe of Miller's stateroom. "Just decoded, sir." He handed over the paper tape. As was frequently the case, the message was still gibberish and would require manual decoding.

"Thank you, Ingles."

Miller drew the green curtain and unlocked his safe. As quiet as the patrol had been so far he actually welcomed the chore of decoding the message. Except for the chance encounter with the German submarine, the patrol had been uneventful.

The Germans had been aboard for a week now. None of them had caused any problems, beyond the obvious one. Someone had to watch them, and the extra mouths meant that they might have to cut the patrol short by a few days.

It required about fifteen minutes to decode the message, though by the time he was halfway through Miller knew it wasn't likely to make the patrol any more exciting.

"Lifeguard duty," Miller informed his officers.

"Where are we going?" Hartman asked.

"The Army B-29 boys on Saipan will be doing some raids against Jap installations on Formosa. They want us about 100 miles southeast of the island. Far enough out to avoid likely Jap air patrols, but on the bomber route, just in case anyone has to ditch or bail out."

"Off the shipping routes, though," Gould observed.

"We're not hunting for ships this time," Miller said. "They want us deliberately off the shipping routes, where we can stay on the surface. If someone needs help it won't do him any good if we're stuck at 300 feet dodging depth charges."

"Well," Hartman said, "it's not like there've been all that many ships even *on* the shipping routes. We've been out 42 days and only fired two torpedoes."

"Which got us that Kraut sub and our guests," Lewis noted.

Müller had been quite cooperative in most ways, Miller thought, but not to the extent of telling them what they'd sunk. All he had to put in the patrol was 'one U-boat, Type IX/D2,' which they had known before the torpedoes were fired. Beyond that, the boat was just U-? as far as they knew.

He figured Intelligence would fill in the blanks. Since they knew Müller's name, it wouldn't be that difficult to find out what he had commanded. There were only so many of the big, long-range boats.

Hartman's remark pointed up a reality of war. On her eleventh war patrol, *Bacalao* would probably not have that much to shoot at. The Japanese merchant fleet was shrinking fast by mid-1944, and a lot of supplies were now moving by smaller vessels. Sampans, coastal steamers and sea trucks were the most common targets now.

During the last overhaul the 20-millimeter guns on the forebridge and cigarette deck had disappeared, replaced by 40-millimeter wet mount guns. No one expected to shoot at aircraft with them. Depth was a submarine's main antiaircraft weapon. The heavy automatic weapons were there for shooting up vessels too small to be worth the expenditure of a torpedo.

Miller didn't expect to find any where they were going.

"Let's hope for a really boring stretch," Miller said. "If we get busy it means someone got shot down."

• • •

Lifeguard duty wasn't as boring as Miller had hoped. On the second day of the raids *Bacalao* picked up a distress call, followed shortly by a low-flying B-29 trailing smoke from two engines. Vectored in by radio, the big bomber ditched less than a quarter mile from the surfaced submarine.

Designed to fly through the air, the bomber didn't make a very good boat. It sank in less than two minutes, leaving three rubber rafts on the surface. Out of a crew of ten, only four men made it out before the plane sank.

"Come right to one-zero-eight," Miller ordered. "Ahead slow."

In a submarine, it was a lot less trouble to bring the boat to the men than to inflate and launch the rubber boats. They were up on the survivors in five minutes and the rescue party was hauling them aboard.

"It's going to get a little crowded if this keeps up," Hartman said.

Miller nodded. "All in all, I think just a little *more* crowded would be better. Seven men went down with that plane, and these guys are on *our* side."

"We'll find a place for them, Skipper."

Miller leaned over the venturi shield and looked at the rescued men. Three officers and a sergeant technician. The lieutenant—no, these guys were Army, the *captain*—was probably the plane commander. The other two officers were first lieutenants.

"Get those men up here and resume surface routine," he ordered. "Sink the rafts, then get the rescue party below."

"Aye, aye, sir," Gordon shouted, from where he was standing beside the deck gun and supervising the rescue.

The four men were brought up the side of the fairwater and sent below. Gordon had one man slash the rubberized fabric of the inflated rafts in several places, so that the weight of the air bottles was enough to drag them under in a few minutes.

"I was sure glad to see you guys when we were coming in to ditch," the captain said. "I'd hate to have to spend too much time floating around out here in one of those rafts."

"Glad we could help."

"Well, I'm Lionel Jeffries. Tom Hill was our navigator, and Bill Hamilton was my copilot. Al Riley there was one of our gunners."

"I just wish we could have got the rest of you out, Captain."

Jeffries shook his head. "No one else to get out, I'm afraid. Jap fighters got the rest of the crew before we ditched. We're all that's left."

"Okay. Well, Mr. Cushing there will get you all below and find places for you. I'm afraid officers' country is getting a little crowded. We've got two German officers stuck away in the wardroom already."

"German?"

"We sank their U-boat a while back. Picked up two officers and six enlisted. None of them are any trouble. I think they're just glad to be out of the war."

"What the hell are Krauts doing in the Pacific?"

Miller shrugged. "They won't say."

"Don't have to, I guess. They tell us not to say anything, don't they?"

"This way, gentlemen," Cushing said, gesturing toward the hatch.

•   •   •

Gus Schultz watched the circular cathode ray tube as he trained the radar antenna through a full circuit of the horizon. The new unit was a big improvement over the original. The plan position indicator, added at the last overhaul, made interpreting the return a lot easier.

There was nothing remarkable on the screen. All Schultz could see was the usual electronic noise caused by a moderate sea and, off to port, the sort of solid return caused by the top of a mountain. The PPI chart, overlaid on the screen, indicated exactly that.

In the overheated conning tower he was dressed in dungaree trousers and a sweat-stained T-shirt. His dungaree shirt was below. As hot as it was, Schultz would have been quite content to just go around naked, but even in the decidedly informal confines of a submarine there were limits.

Schultz momentarily looked away from the screen. You couldn't stare at it continuously or you tended to fall into something like a trance and the next thing you know you were missing things. He rolled his head around in a circle, stretching his neck muscles, and glanced at his watch. Only another hour, he thought.

As he looked back a spot of light appeared on the screen. Schultz studied the return, directing the antenna across the bearing. It was moving only slowly, so that meant a ship and not a plane. He flipped the switch on the 7MC.

"Bridge—radar. Ship, bearing one-seven-five, range four-five-zero-zero."

●   ●   ●

"Bearing—mark!"
"Zero-two-five."
"Range—mark!"
"Niner-eight-eight."

Miller snapped up the knurled brass handles. "Down 'scope. Angle on the bow is port one-three-five."

Cushing worked the TDC dials. "Almost there, Captain," he said.

Miller nodded. "Make ready tubes one through four."

"Make ready tubes one through four, aye, sir."

They had been stalking a big tanker for three hours now. It would be soon, Miller thought. This was the eighth observation during the approach, which had proven more complicated than usual. The Japanese captain was unusually diligent in zigzagging, and Miller was having trouble figuring out exactly what he was doing.

Zigzag patterns were usually predictable after a relatively short observation. This captain was harder to figure out. The only pattern Miller could see was that he zigged on some multiple of two minutes, but never the same multiple, and not in any recurring pattern. He was changing course at seemingly random intervals. His base course was easy enough to determine, but setting up a shot was a lot harder than usual, since they couldn't determine when he was likely to change course right out of the setup.

"Solution, sir," Cushing said. "Generated bearing is zero-one-eight."

"Up 'scope. Put me on."

"Zero-one-eight, sir."

Miller smiled. "Right under his bridge. Flood tubes one through four and open outer doors."

"Tubes one through four flooded from WRT. Outer doors are open."

"Fire one!"

"Fire one, aye! One fired electrically, sir."

●   ●   ●

The tanker must have been loaded with gasoline, for it went up in a single, massive detonation that felt like it would toss the submarine right out of the water. One moment four torpedoes were streaking toward the target, and the next there was a flash and the ship was gone. One of the two destroyers escorting the tanker, which had been moving up her side when the torpedo hit, was thrown onto her beam ends by the force of the blast.

"Two for one," Miller reported. "Jones! What do you hear?"

The sonar operator shook his head. "Nothing. The shock must have demagnetized the bar."

The receiver for the JP hydrophone, along with the training wheel, was located in the forward torpedo room. Jones had a repeater in the conning tower. He called down and had the JP operator plug the head— a long, flat bar located on the upper deck—into the power supply on his panel to remagnetize the core. Usually, this only happened with a close depth charge explosion, but the tanker had gone up with sufficient force to do the job.

Miller shifted the periscope astern of where the tanker had been, and where the luckless escort was now floating on her side. The second escort had escaped damage, and was now putting on speed and turning toward *Bacalao*.

Miller decided that it was now time to hide.

"Down 'scope. Come left to three-four-zero. All ahead full. Make your depth three-five-zero feet."

•   •   •

Müller looked across the wardroom table at Hessler and nodded. Both had been mildly amused at the reaction of the fliers when the target exploded. The two U-boat men had recognized the familiar sound of the torpedoes being fired, so the explosion had hardly been unexpected. Only the tremendous force came as a surprise.

Jeffries, though, looked like he expected the boat to fill with water at any moment.

"Relax, Captain," Müller said. "That was just the target blowing up."

"*Benzintankschiff?*" Hessler said.

"*Ja.*" Müller looked at the pilot. "Gasoline tanker. A hit on one can be, uhm, spectacular."

"I thought someone got *us* for a minute there," Jeffries said.

"Not yet."

"What?"

"Can you feel what the boat is doing now, Captain? We are turning, increasing speed, and diving. You do this when someone is coming after you." He smiled grimly. "In a few minutes, you can expect it to get very noisy."

The pilot shook his head. "How do you get used to this?"

"What makes you think that you do? It's just part of the job. Do you get used to flak?"

"No. But you can at least see it coming. It makes me nervous to be down here where you can't see where you're going."

The boat began to slow to creeping speed. "Now," Müller whispered, "it is time to be very quiet."

• • •

WHAM! WHAM! WHAM!

Miller hauled himself back to his feet and glanced around the conning tower. "That was way too close," he commented.

Hartman made a mark on the chart. Beside him, the quartermaster of the watch ticked off the three depth charges on his tally. The destroyer had dropped nine so far, in sets of three. Hartman decided that they were probably rolling one charge off the stern and firing the other pair abeam.

"This guy seems to know what he's doing. I don't much like that."

"He's getting the depth right, too," Miller said. "When this is over, remind me to send five pounds of fresh manure to that bastard congressman who blabbed about them setting them too shallow."

"Coming in again," Jones reported.

• • •

Jeffries felt as if he was about to go out of his mind. He had noticed that Müller and Hessler always seemed to know when more depth charges were about to explode. It was a momentary change of attitude. A flick of the eye toward the overhead, and a conscious effort to relax their bodies to ride out the shock.

He had no idea how they could tell. Jeffries hadn't noticed the sharp click of the primer as it initiated the detonation sequence. It was something any experienced submariner would know—particularly one who had spent several years in the crucible of the north Atlantic, where the number of German U-boat men who returned from their war patrols made up only a small portion of those who rode the boats out from their bases—but it wasn't a part of Army Air Force training.

"I really hate this," Jeffries whispered.

"All you can do is wait," Müller responded, his voice barely audible even in the hush of the silenced boat. "Captain Miller is doing everything correctly, so far as I can tell." He shrugged. "The water is still where it belongs, on the outside of the boat. As long as it is, we are safe."

"I think I prefer the flak and fighters."

"Too dangerous," Hessler remarked. "Airplanes much too dangerous are. Why they stay in the air at all, this I cannot understand. In *Unterseeboot*, at least everything makes sense. What can happen you can know, you can feel safe, familiar."

"You can, maybe."

The boat began to accelerate, turning to port.

"More *Wasserbomben*," Hessler said.

"Moving fast makes noise," Müller explained. "If the captain is doing this, then there are *Wasserbomben*—depth charges—on their way down to us and, for the moment, making noise is less important than getting out of the way."

Jeffries felt his head pulling into his shoulders despite his best efforts to look nonchalant. "I still hate this," he said.

•　　•　　•

"Depth charge coming down," Jones said. "Only one this time."

"That will be number 16," the quartermaster said.

"We just need this one to miss, then," Miller sighed.

Cushing looked at him curiously.

"If he's only dropped one," Miller said, "that probably means it's the last one he has. This guy is good, but he would have been working with another can if we hadn't got lucky when the tanker blew up. Twice as many depth charges available, and one of them could have tried to pin us down while the other attacked."

Jones turned down the volume on his headphones.

Again there was the sharp click of the depth charge's primer, followed by a single, punishing blast. The boat lurched violently to starboard and Miller heard a sharp "snap!" as one of the hoist wires slapped against the number two periscope.

Off to port, there was another bang as the sea rushed back into the void created by the depth charge explosion. Slowly, the boat came back onto an even keel, her motors still turning slowly, pushing her through the depths at just over two knots.

Miller glanced at the conning tower depth gauge. It was steady at 375 feet. Had the last depth charge actually pushed them deeper?

"What's he doing, Jones?"

"Destroyer is moving off. Bearing three-two-niner. Sounds like he's putting on some speed."

"He really *is* out of depth charges, then," Hartman said.

The tables were turning. If the destroyer was out of depth charges, then their relative positions were suddenly changed. His guns were useless against *Bacalao* unless she surfaced, which Miller had no intention of doing. The submarine's torpedoes, though, would be quite effective against *him.*

"All compartments report no serious damage, sir," the phone talker reported.

"Good," Miller replied. "Open the control room hatch."

"Aye, aye, sir."

"Mr. Sandelin!"

"The young lieutenant looked up the ladder from the control room. "Sir?"

"Make your depth six-four feet."

"Make my depth six-four feet, aye, sir."

"Going after the Jap, Captain?" Hartman asked.

"I'm pretty sure he doesn't think he's sunk us. That's probably what he'll report, but I doubt if he believes it. He wouldn't be in that big a hurry to get out of here if he thought we couldn't shoot back. Jones? Speed estimate on target?"

"About 23 knots and still speeding up."

The depth gauge had moved up to 330 feet. "Ahead two-thirds. We need to get up to periscope depth faster or he'll get away."

XVIII
McCall's Murderers

BY THE TIME *BACALAO* REACHED PERISCOPE DEPTH they had learned two things. The first was that the Japanese destroyer had put on flank speed and was moving off at 31 knots, making the two torpedoes fired at her retreating form little more than a gesture.

The second was that one of the depth charges had knocked something loose. At anything beyond bare steerage way something was banging in the superstructure. If they couldn't fix it at sea it would be necessary to cut short the patrol.

After ten hours, Miller was forced to concede defeat. They had found where the noise was coming from, but it would require docking to fix. He sent a message to Fremantle informing them of the problem.

When the reply arrived, it gave an indication of something else that had changed. They wouldn't be returning to Fremantle. The new orders were for Apra, on Guam. A floating dock would be waiting for them, along with new operational orders. The prisoners and airmen would be turned over to the proper people at the base.

• • •

Bacalao stood out of Apra fourth in line, following directly astern *Angelfish. Angelfish*, in turn, was following *Dugong*, which was taking her cues from U.S.S. *Gorton*, an old flush-deck destroyer that had been converted into a destroyer-minesweeper before the war.

Gorton was an odd-looking creature. Two of her four stacks had been removed during the conversion, along with the boilers they had served, leaving a strange gap between the remaining pair. You didn't need a lot of speed to sweep mines. Or to get a group of submarines through the security lane, which was what she was doing at the moment.

Captain Carl McCall was riding in *Angelfish*, no doubt already annoying her captain, who would have to share his stateroom with the commodore. McCall had spent the first six months of the war commanding the old *Tambor* class fleet boat, and Miller wondered if it was some sense of nostalgia that made him pick *Angelfish* over the much more modern *Dugong*—a *Balao* class boat—as his flagship.

Miller never even considered the possibility that McCall would pick *Bacalao*. The two of them just didn't get along all that well. You could work with someone you didn't like, he thought, and even respect him for his abilities, but that didn't mean you wanted to share a stateroom with him.

In any case, McCall had come home—a sentimental connection Miller found that he *could* empathize with. Miller didn't consider himself to be overly sentimental, except where Sarah was concerned, but he'd been forced to admit that the day he returned to *Bacalao* had been the happiest he could remember.

Not that he was ever going to say that to his wife. It had been all the extra stress involved in the whole wedding experience that had pushed it back to number two. By comparison, taking command of a warship was easy.

"It's going to be a little different this time," Hartman observed.

"Yeah. 'McCall's Murderers.' Our commodore isn't exactly given to subtlety, is he?"

Hartman shrugged. "That's about all war is, isn't it, Captain? A lot of people running around slaughtering a lot of other people, but you can get away with it because the government says it's okay."

Hartman, Miller thought, would make a lousy diplomat. He had too strong a tendency to say exactly what he thought. Diplomacy was largely the art of lying in a soothing manner while you picked the other guy's pocket with one hand and fondled his wife with the other.

Hartman would never have been a good pickpocket. He'd just figure it was easier to hit him over the head with a club and get it over with.

They passed a channel marker, and Miller called down the minor course change. The helmsman was new, a quartermaster 1st class called Quist, who had broken his wrist in an accident aboard *Gar* some months before. When he got out of the hospital and was certified fit to return to duty his own boat had long since returned to sea, so he was assigned to *Sperry*.

The tender passed him on to *Bacalao* when the usual crew rotations found the sub needing a good quartermaster.

Another new face, Miller thought. There was hardly anyone left of the boat's original crew. Hardly any men left who had still been aboard when Miller left for *S-56*, come to that. Of the original crew, only Hartman, Collins, Gordon and Ohara remained.

This would probably be Hartman's last patrol, too. He was ready for his own command. Miller had made the formal recommendation the day before they departed. When *Bacalao* returned, he expected Hartman to be detached and sent on a PCO cruise, then given one of the older fleet boats when her commander was rotated home for a rest and, probably, new construction.

The chiefs would likely remain, mostly because they knew how to work the system and could exert whatever influence they needed to stay aboard. It was odd, when you thought about it. The longer you stayed in the same boat, the more likely it was you'd be aboard on that last patrol, when the enemy got lucky, or someone in your own boat got careless, and no one came back.

Everyone knew this, yet it always seemed that anyone senior enough, or with sufficient drag, would try to stay. The odds would catch up with someone else. They didn't apply to you.

•   •   •

Chief Electrician's Mate Kenneth Ohara tried to be unobtrusive as he watched one of the new men checking the bank of battery chargers the tender's crew had installed at the aft end of the forward torpedo room. The chargers came with the load of new Mark-18 electric torpedoes.

Collins had seemed only slightly enthusiastic about the new fish. Battery powered, they were essentially wakeless. Everyone recognized this as a valuable advance. There was always a worry that someone on a target would see the torpedo's wake in time to change course and get out of the way. Ohara could remember a few times when complaints from the attack party indicated that this had happened.

But the new torpedoes were slower, only 29 knots against a Mark-14's 46-knot top speed. They also had a smaller warhead. And Collins, still an old Gun Club man even if he'd vehemently disagreed with their stubborn refusal to recognize the problems with the Mark-14 and it's Mark-6 exploder, was subject to a touch of not-invented-here syndrome. The Mark-18 was an American adaptation—produced by Westinghouse, not Newport— of the German Navy's G7e torpedo.

As usual, there had been problems. The batteries had to be serviced and charged, making the new fish more labor intensive than the older, faster models. There had also been a problem with corroding rudder shafts that sometime caused the rudder to jam and make the torpedo run in a circle. That had involved replacing all of the shafts with stainless steel.

Ohara had noticed Collins sitting on his bunk in the goat locker, carefully checking the log book for each of the Mark-18s, to be sure the modifications had been made. The old chief torpedoman's mate had always tended toward being overcautious. It was a quality Ohara liked in the man. You just couldn't be too careful in a submarine.

Ohara looked at his watch. The new man seemed to know what he was doing, and Ohara would be taking over as Chief of the Watch in another 20 minutes. Time to get something to eat. Four hours in the control room would go better with a full stomach.

· · ·

It was the largest Japanese convoy Miller had ever seen. Ten big freighters and two transports, escorted by six destroyers. Someone had figured out that Okinawa would be invaded soon and the Japs were rushing whatever reinforcements they could manage.

It was McCall's Murderers' job to make sure none of the troops and supplies made it to their destination.

The three-sub wolfpack was in position to intercept, with *Bacalao* at the northern end of the patrol line across the convoy's route. This came as no surprise to Miller, who had expected McCall to place his own boat in the middle of the line. They would be using low-powered voice radio to communicate once the action started. It would be easier if the commodore, who would exercise control, was in the middle and could keep the radio power dialed down as much as possible.

"So, do you really think the Nips can't receive these radio frequencies?" Hartman asked.

Miller slowly shook his head. "No. Our own radio guys say that they can't, but I really don't believe it." He smiled crookedly. "Hell, up until now, it seems like just about every time we've been confidently informed that the Japs couldn't do something, or didn't have some technology, it turns out they could and did."

"But we still have to use the radio, don't we?"

"True. I suppose the best we can hope is that even if they can receive on these frequencies they won't have anyone listening who can understand what we're saying."

Hartman laughed. "Be nice to have one of those Navajos the Marines are using in each boat, wouldn't it, Skipper? Have someone doing the talking who can pass orders and information in a language we *know* the Nips can't understand."

"Yeah. But I guess we'll have to settle for English."

Miller leaned over the port bulwark. *Angelfish* was somewhere over there in the darkness. Two miles at 270°, according to the radar. Too far for anyone to see on a moonless night, even with their passage through the warm ocean water creating a glowing wake of phosphorescence.

The phosphorescence wasn't as easy to see as someone might think, Miller knew. At least, not from another ship. The normal waves kept the phytoplankton sufficiently riled that the wake was usually lost amid hundreds of patches of dim light. The wake was probably very obvious from a plane, but there was no carrier with the convoy. Aerial escort was just one of the lessons the Japanese had failed to learn in this war.

Miller had never believed the cliché that the Japanese couldn't adapt and improvise when the tactical situation required. They could, and they often did. What they never seemed to grasp, though, was the real nature of modern war. Old notions of individual bravery, honor and single combat were, if not exactly outmoded, certainly lost under the weight of modern industrial progress. Industry, raw materials and supply sources, as much as manpower, now determined who would win. In the same time it took the Japanese to build a single new aircraft carrier the United States could build twenty of them.

In the end, Miller thought, it was a question of one side refusing to cooperate with the other side's game plan. Yamamoto had never wanted to start a full-scale war with the United States. He had lived in the U.S., serving as naval attaché and studying at Harvard, and knew first hand the industrial might and manpower that would be arrayed against his country in a full-scale war. His goal had been to deliver a quick, hard blow that would do enough damage to make the United States negotiate a settlement and allow Japan to continue unmolested in Asia. Yamamoto was a poker player and he had been bluffing, but his opponent had called instead of folding.

If war could be likened to a game, it seemed to Miller that the Japanese had been playing baseball and the Americans playing football. Both were team sports, but how they were played was vastly different. Baseball was, by far, the more elegant and individualized of the two. At any given moment in a game, baseball was really a duel between only two men. Just who those two men might be would change constantly—pitcher *vs.*

batter, hitter *vs.* fielder, runner *vs.* second baseman, pitcher *vs.* a running trying to steal, and so on. But it always came down to that single combat model.

It was the way the Japanese had always fought. The baseball player reflected a lot of the Samurai mentality. Of a team, but really fighting on his own. A single champion against another.

In football, of course, the entire opposing team simply tried to trample the ball carrier into the ground. His teammates would try to block, try to defend the man with the ball, but it was ultimately eleven men against one.

That was precisely what they were doing to the Japanese. The full industrial might of the United States had been directed into building the ships, planes, weapons and equipment that were being used to grind down the enemy on both fronts.

"Maybe," Miller said, "we should be speaking German on the radio. This whole wolfpack idea was theirs to begin with."

There were differences, but they weren't that great. American wolf-packs used low powered voice radio for local control, while the Germans used high powered radio for central control from shore. In the scheme of things, the Germans talked too much, allowing the Allies to use direction finding equipment to locate the U-boats and either go around them or attack them. The efforts of the code breakers also kept the Allies mostly informed of where the enemy was, though neither Miller nor the Germans had any idea to what degree.

The low-powered American radio was harder to pinpoint with direction finding equipment, and only used during the actual attack.

The most obvious similarity was that both German and American wolfpack tactics emphasized night surface attacks. The Germans had more or less abandoned that after 1943, when Allied radar advances made it too risky. But even in late 1944 Japanese radar deployment was hardly up to what the British were doing in 1940. A few of their newest destroyers had it, and there was certainly the possibility that some of those radar equipped ships would be with this convoy, but in general all of the radar advantage was with the submariners.

Miller bent over the 7MC. "Radar—captain!"

"Radar, aye."

"Any indication the Nips are using radar?"

"Nothing, sir. Picking up returns on SJ frequencies at two-seven-zero. That should be *Angelfish*, sir. Nothing from ahead."

"What's the range to the closest target now?"

"One-five-five-double-zero, sir."

Still out of sight from the bridge, Miller thought. Out of range, too. Maximum range on a torpedo had nothing to do with how far you could really shoot. You could shoot reliably up to about 1,800 yards, though some captains seemed to have a knack for getting hits beyond that.

Miller liked to get in close. Getting the range down under 1,000 yards made the setups easier. It also gave the target less time to spot the torpedo and maneuver to get out of the way.

The only way they could get a hit at the present range would be to use the deck gun. Common sense ruled that out. Trying to lob four-inch shells into the convoy at this range would only make them change course. The chances of a hit with a locally-controlled gun trying to rely on radar-based target information were pretty slim.

•   •   •

Things were getting exciting now. *Bacalao* had fired four torpedoes at this point, with one hit. That fish had struck the engine room of a big troop transport. The ship looked like a converted passenger liner, and probably carried most of a division.

Now the big ship was dead in the water, angle on the bow port 45°, bearing 020°. It was the sort of shot you dreamed about. Miller could have maneuvered around for a straight shot, but with the target not moving he could have calculated the deflection in his head.

The ship was down by the stern now. One more, aimed right at the middle of the target, should do it, Miller decided. There were a lot more ships to be attacked. He'd save the other fish for targets that could still get away.

"Flood tube five and open outer door," he ordered.

•   •   •

The log book for torpedo number 25037 was securely lodged in Collins' files. The pages of the slender volume were filled with the usual maintenance notes. One of these indicated that, on 6 July 1944, TM2c Albert Firth had replaced the original steel rudder pins with the new stainless steel version.

The entry was wrong. It had been near the end of a long work day, and Firth had been anxious to return to his quarters and change for an evening of drinking and chasing women in Honolulu. He had replaced the rudder pins, but in his rush had unintentionally put in another set of ordinary steel pins. For all practical purposes, the torpedo hadn't been modified at all.

Since that time, the batteries had been charged at regular intervals. Torpedo number 25037 had also been involved in one aborted attack, its tube flooded and opened to the sea, but never fired. The torpedo crew cleaned it up after the tube was drained and did all the usual maintenance. But the salt water had done its work. The non-stainless steel rudder pins had started to rust inside the bearing sleeves.

Now the torpedo was again in a flooded tube, waiting to be fired.

• • •

"Fire five!"

"Fire five, aye! Five fired electrically, sir."

Looking out over the bow, Miller could see the torpedo as it left the tube and began to curve around onto its preset course. The phosphorescent plankton made a clearer wake than the wet-heater engine of a Mark-14.

Until a torpedo was fired, the gyro was still, and could be turned onto the proper deflection angle with ease. Once the torpedo was fired and the gyro was spinning at full speed, it would continue to rotate in the same horizontal plane until the torpedo hit or it ran out of power. The rudder was linked to the gyro. Once the torpedo and gyro were moving in the same direction, the rudder centered and the torpedo continued on a straight course from that point.

Unless the rudder pins were rusted and frozen in the bearings.

One of the lookouts shouted, "That fish is circling, Captain!"

Miller trained his binoculars toward the point the lookout was indicating. The phosphorescent wake, which should have described a 23° turn to starboard before straightening out and speeding for the target was describing a wide circle. It didn't take a lot in the way of geometric skills to see that, on it's present course, the torpedo was going to come back to its source.

"All ahead emergency!" Miller shouted. "Sound the collision alarm."

• • •

Ohara was hardly conscious of the transition from routine to disaster. He was standing by the after torpedo room hatch, watching Phipps as the young fireman 1st class operated the main board. He was ready, Ohara thought. He would recommend that the Old Man promote him to EM3c.

The motor telegraphs rang sharply as the annunciators both snapped to the "ahead—emergency" marks. Phipps didn't wait for Ohara to confirm anything. He just reset the control levers, sending full emergency power to all four motors, and reaching up to move the dials to the proper position, indicating to the conn that he had complied with the order.

As this was happening, the collision alarm started sounding. Phipps looked curious at Ohara. "What the hell?"

Ohara opened his mouth to answer, but the reply came in a more forceful manner. Without any noticeable transition from his orderly world he felt the deck plates rising beneath his feet and the maneuvering room suddenly seemed to heat up like a furnace.

Then there was a falling sensation, and he was plunged into salt water. He was outside the boat, he realized, and floating in the sea.

It was disorienting, to say the least.

•　　•　　•

Collins clung tightly to the ladder as the world went crazy. The boat seemed to be tumbling wildly, and the forward torpedo room was plunged into complete darkness. Without the ladder to orient himself, he would have had no idea which way was up or down.

There was a horrible metallic crash, followed by a scream that was cut off like the slamming of a door. Even without being able to see, Collins knew what had happened. One of the reload torpedoes had wrenched itself free of its restraints and rolled off its rack, crushing some-one beneath its 3,300-pound bulk.

Collins had no way of knowing if there was anything left aft of the bulkhead. All he knew was that the boat was wildly out of control, and the popping in his ears told him that the air pressure was rising fast. That could only mean one thing. There was water coming in—a lot of it.

And then the bow section of the boat slammed into the bottom, dropping Collins painfully to his knees. Somehow, he kept his grip on the ladder.

"Is everyone okay?" he shouted.

There was no answer, and it occurred to him that anyone who hadn't had a good grip on something had probably been tossed about like a rag doll and, if he was lucky, only knocked unconscious and not killed.

The hull shifted slightly, and he could hear the loose torpedo roll-ing. At that moment he heard a sharp, metallic "click," immediately followed by more mechanical sounds and the hissing of compressed air. Then there was a hard "bang," and a loud, high-pitched whine filled the room.

It was one of the old Mark-14s, and somehow the starting lever had been activated. It shouldn't have been possible—there was a safety device to secure the lever, and there should have been a propeller lock installed. Both must have broken when it fell off the rack, he decided.

However it had started, once it had, Collins realized he had very little time to act if he wanted to stay alive.

He scrambled up the ladder in the darkness, coughing as the room began to fill with the noxious exhaust fumes. He knew the torpedo was unlikely to explode, but that would hardly matter once the room was filled with the exhaust. You were just as dead whether you blew up or suffocated.

Climbing into the escape trunk, Collins slammed the lower hatch and spun the dogging wheel.

How deep are we? he wondered.

His escape gear was somewhere in the shattered hull. The theoretical limit for a free ascent without it was claimed to be around 300 feet, but Collins had his doubts. And without any light, or a depth gauge, there was no way to know just how deep he was.

Nothing to do but try, he decided. He'd spent more than enough time in submarines to learn that once you hit bottom you got out as quickly as possible. The high air pressure at depth once you flooded the escape trunk could lead to the bends if you stayed there too long.

He worked the controls by feel, hardly able to tell up from down in the pitch darkness. It was hard to keep calm as the cold water rose in the trunk. The air pressure increased rapidly. The water level was above the upper edge of the door by the time the pressure equalized and it stopped coming in. Collins opened the door, ducking back into the escape chamber twice to take a breath while he rigged and deployed the ascent buoy and line. Then he closed the door, more from training than any real hope that anyone in the forward torpedo room was still alive.

Resigned, he started swimming up toward the distant surface, remembering to exhale continuously as he ascended, and to swim up at the same rate as the air bubbles. If you tried to hold your breath, he remembered, your lungs would explode.

Then his head burst up through the surface. He'd never tasted anything as sweet as the warm night air.

After a moment, treading water, he started shouting in an effort to find out who else had managed to get out.

●　　　●　　　●

As the boat was lifted out of the water and flung to one side by the exploding warhead, Miller felt himself flying through the air before splashing feet first into the sea. He struck out strongly for the dark surface, coming up a few feet from another swimmer.

It was Wilson, the lookout who had first noticed the circling torpedo. He was struggling, trying to keep his head out of the water. As Miller swam up next to him he realized that the man was barely conscious. He must have been injured when the blast threw everyone off the bridge.

Then Morton, who had been quartermaster of the watch, was swimming beside him. Together, they supported Wilson. The lookout seemed to be slowly coming out of it.

•　　•　　•

Gordon was standing by the trim manifold when the collision alarm sounded. He hardly had time to react before the boat leaped under his feet, throwing him painfully to the deck.

As the boat slammed back into the water the deck immediately tilted down toward the stern. Gordon could hear water roaring into the hull beyond the after bulkhead.

"Everybody out!" Gordon bellowed. "Up through the conning tower—out now!"

But even as the first man started up the metal ladder the sea began to pour down through the hatch, knocking him off the metal rungs and sending him sliding down the tilting deck.

Gordon now found himself almost standing on the after bulkhead as the deck tilted up at nearly a 70° angle. The torrent coming through the conning tower hatch could only mean that everything from the bridge hatch aft was under water.

It also meant that everyone on the bridge was either dead or thrown overboard. Otherwise someone would have closed the hatch.

At first, the water coming down through the hatch had been draining into the pump room, but now that was full, and the control room itself was starting to fill.

Gordon started trying to climb toward the bridge ladder, holding on to pipes and fittings as he climbed along the port side.

Then the boat slammed into the bottom, leveling out as it did, and momentarily dropping the water level in the control room. It did nothing to stop the torrent coming down through the hatch. The water was thigh high and rising rapidly.

So far, the lights were still on, and the bulkheads seemed to be holding. If they could just get that conning tower hatch shut they might still have a chance, Gordon thought. If they could stop the water coming in they might be able to get to the forward torpedo room and use the escape trunk located there.

He had reached the ladder by now, and could see the depth gauge over the planesmen's station, its needle steady at 215 feet. That would mean the upper deck was about 190 feet from the surface.

He grabbed a seaman and pulled him through the fast rising water. "Come on," he shouted, his voice oddly high pitched from the increased air pressure. "Help me get that damned hatch shut if you want to survive!"

But even with a sturdy young sailor pushing from below, the force of the water pouring through the open hatch was too great for him to get up the ladder, and by now the water in the control room was neck deep and rising fast.

"The only thing we can do now is let the control room fill up and try to find an air pocket to breathe in until it does. Once the pressure equalizes the water will stop coming in and we can try to swim out." Gordon smiled, knowing the men in the control room would be looking to him for leadership in this situation. Ensign Lewis, who had been dive officer, was dead, his head crushed when he was thrown against the barrel-shaped main gyro housing.

"Just stay calm," Gordon said. "We can still make it."

Then the lights went out, leaving only a dim glow in the water from several lit battle lanterns.

Gordon floated up, his face pressed against the overhead. There was no air pocket there, and as he tried to hold his breath he felt a strange sense of resigned contentment. Everything seemed to be slowing down, and he could hear the blood flowing through his veins—an odd, soothing sound, like the surf on a beach.

His senses were muted now, and nothing seemed to matter. He was coughing, and water was entering his lungs as his air-starved body began to breathe reflexively. Somehow there was no pain. It was as if it was all happening in a dream, and the dream was painlessly fading into oblivion.

•   •   •

Several men had collected around Miller by now. Ohara and another electrician's mate, a first-class named Dalton, had the most fantastic story. As near as they could figure out, the boat had broken in half just forward of the after torpedo room bulkhead, spilling the men on duty in the maneuvering room into the sea.

Neither of them could explain why they seemed to be unhurt, for the torpedo had obviously detonated almost directly under their feet.

Nor could they say what had happened to young Phipps, who had been no more than a few feet from them. They had found themselves swimming close to each other. Phipps was nowhere to be seen.

A few other heads were popping up now, most of them with the mouthpiece of a Momsen Lung gripped between their teeth. Miller continued calling to his men. They would have a better chance if they could stay together.

Angelfish and *Dugong* were both close by—might even have seen the explosion. Miller had tried to radio McCall just before the torpedo hit. He couldn't remember if he had just reported a circular run, or if he had mentioned that it would unquestionably hit.

If they were lucky, one of the other boats would find them before the Japanese.

He wasn't too confident of their chances if the enemy got to them first. They might not even bother to pick them up.

"Over here!" he shouted.

•　　•　　•

Collins found himself in the middle of a small group of survivors, wondering if anyone else had managed to get out. He would have expected several survivors from the bridge party, but there was only Seaman Jernigan, one of the lookouts, and Torpedoman's Mate 3rd Class Paulson, who had somehow managed to make it up from his station in the conning tower just before the sea reached the lip of the hatch.

Paulson said that Lieutenant Sandelin had been right behind him, but the sea had washed over the bridge and swept him away before he could see if the officer had made it out.

Their group also included Ensign Simpson, who had come up from the after torpedo room using a Momsen Lung, along with Torpedoman's Mate 3rd Class Cummings, who had escaped at the same time.

The last in their group was Norton, who had been sitting in the pointer's seat on the after 40-millimeter when the torpedo hit.

•　　•　　•

Dugong found them just before sunrise, still clinging together for mutual support. A party of seamen scrambled down from the bridge, throwing lines over the side to help the exhausted survivors climb over the bulge of the ballast tanks.

"Hey!" one of *Dugong*'s seamen shouted. "This one looks like a Jap!"

"Yeah," Ohara said. "And ya'll sound like a goddamn Yankee and I just stole this chief's uniform while I swimming around out here. Now just get me out of the fucking water, will you?"

A chief torpedoman's mate, supervising the rescue party, looked over the side and smiled. "That you, Ken?"

"Hey, Tim. I sure am glad to see you."

The big chief reached down and helped Ohara up onto the deck. "What the hell happened, Ken?" he asked.

Ohara shook his head. "I guess they finally got us," he said.

Miller was coming up over the side and caught their conversation. "Actually," he said, "we got ourself. The last fish we fired decided to come back."

"Circular run, sir?"

"That's right, Chief."

"Mark-18 electric?"

"Yes."

"Damn. I thought they fixed that problem"

"I guess not." Miller looked around. "Did you find anyone else?"

The chief shook his head. "I'm afraid not, sir. An even dozen of you. We didn't find anyone else."

•   •   •

Collins continued to tread water as the ship slowed. There was a cargo net hanging over the port side, with several seamen standing by to help them up.

There were also several others, dressed like seamen, but wearing gaiters and holding rifles at the ready, towering over the others. Japanese Imperial Marines, Collins thought.

An officer looked down at them, frowning. "Up! Climb up!" he snapped.

Collins decided compliance would be the best policy. The officer looked impatient, as if he really didn't care about enemy survivors. Collins suspected he'd order the Marines to start shooting if they didn't get up the net quickly enough.

XIX
Reunion

THE WIND WAS OFF THE LAKE, bringing some comfort on a hot July day. Miller was with his wife, standing by a display torpedo, when he saw Ohara coming through the gate. The former chief electrician's mate still stood very erect, but now his black hair was pure white under the navy blue ballcap with silver dolphins and "U.S.S. *Bacalao*" embroidered on the front.

"He looks old," Miller commented.

Sarah looked up at him and smiled. "Whereas you merely look like any other 85-year-old junior high school student, right?"

"Being around you keeps me young."

"I'll remember that the next time you need someone to pull you up out of your chair."

Ohara walked up the concrete path, his wife beside him. Miller thought that Sarah was very well-preserved for a woman of 80, but Liz Ohara was still absolutely stunning. Like many Asian women, she never seemed to age. He knew she was in her early 70s. She looked about 45.

"Looks like a good day for it, Admiral," Ohara said, sticking out his hand.

"It does at that, Professor." Ohara had done his twenty, then retired, picking up a doctorate in military history, and spending the next 25 years teaching it at Georgia State.

Ohara grinned. "So, where are the rest of the geezers?"

"Plenty of us wandering around here by now. And Ted Collins is here, too. He's going through the boat with his grand-kids."

"That's John Collins' oldest son, right?"

Miller nodded. "He's here for his father, he told me. Said that his dad would have been here if he was still around and he wanted to make sure the family was represented." He smiled. "Of course, Ted spent most of his career in the boats, too. He started in these old smoke boats, then went nuc."

"It was a shame about John," Ohara said. "He died way too young."

Collins had lived only another ten years after being freed at the end of the war. When he was released the poor nutrition and grueling labor in the Ashio copper mines had cut him down to 108 pounds. The big chief torpedoman's mate had never really recovered, but his son had followed him into the Navy, even striking for the same rating. Now the son was retired as well. He'd finished his career as a master chief torpedoman's mate.

"Anyone else?" Ohara asked.

"Jones, our old sonarman. He's aboard as well. I think he managed to talk one of the people here into letting him up into the conning tower so he could pay his respects to the sonar stack."

"The fat one or the skinny one?"

"The skinny one, though you wouldn't know it now."

"I lost track of him. What did he do after the war?"

"Got out and went to school. Moved to Seattle and wound up as a judge."

"Seems like everyone did pretty well," Ohara commented.

"Well, we ran a lot of men through *Bacalao* in 12 war patrols. Stands to reason a lot of them would have done well."

"You know, Admiral," Ohara said, "that's really not how you're supposed to pronounce that."

"I know." Miller looked toward the lake, just in time to see Morgan hauling himself up out of the after torpedo room hatch. Another one of us gone to pot in his old age, he thought. The old Annapolis athlete had somehow been replaced by a bald, rotund man wearing a blue Sub Vets of World War II vest over his white shirt.

Miller hadn't gained more than ten pounds since the end of the war.

"Anyway, no one ever pronounced *Gato* right, either, did they?"

"Not that I ever noticed, no." Ohara put his arm around his wife, who smiled up at her husband.

We've both been lucky, Miller thought. We're alive. Somehow we've both managed to find the one woman who would continue to adore us as we deteriorated.

"So, how many of us are here this year, Admiral?"

"Thirty-five said they'd be here for the reunion. As of the last count, there are still 58 men who served with us hanging on to life. Lots of old men. A lot more who are gone, including the 40 who went down with the boat. We lost eight in the past year, including Tom Hartman."

Fate, Miller thought, would always win. He thought of all the men who had served with him in the war. *Bacalao*'s original crew, and the men who had come aboard as those original men were rotated out. How many had gone on to other boats? How many of those had then died in the new boat?

How many others had stayed, yet still died? How many had left and lived? Or stayed and lived? For those who had escaped at the end of that final patrol, had staying in *Bacalao* made any difference in their fates? Had they left, would they still have survived?

Or, for that matter, how many of the original and replacement crews who went on to die in other boats might have lived if they'd stayed? All of them? None of them? Who was right, the ones who said that the span of your life was predetermined, and only the way you would die on that appointed day was left to chance? Or the ones who said that chance alone determined the span of your years?

Miller wasn't sure. He wasn't philosopher enough. He was just an old submariner who had been very lucky in surviving the war, and in his career after the fighting ended. He had a wife he still loved as much as when they were first married. And, remarkably, she still seemed to love him just as much.

He looked north again. *Bacalao* had looked very much like the preserved fleet boat where they were having their reunion. The same covered wagon bridge cutdown, nearly the same vintage, both products of Electric Boat. Except for the painted up victory flags and number on the fairwater, and the newer deck gun, the two boats could have been twins.

He looked back at Ohara. "Well," he said, "why don't we go aboard? I think it's time to bring back some memories."

Glossary

1MC: The general announcing system in an American warship.

3"/50: A submarine deck gun, firing a three-inch diameter shell, with a barrel length of 50 times three-inches (150").

4"/50: A submarine deck gun, firing a four-inch diameter shell, with a barrel length of 50 times four-inches (200").

7MC: The intercom system in an American warship.

AK: The Navy designator for a general cargo vessel.

AO: The Navy designator for an Oiler. Used in patrol reports to indicate a tanker.

AP: The Navy designator for a transport ship.

CincPac: Commander-in-Chief, Pacific. During all but the first two weeks of World War II, this was Fleet Admiral Chester W. Nimitz.

ComSubPac: Commander, Submarine Force, Pacific.

CV: The Navy designator for an Aircraft Carrier.

DD: The Navy designator for a Destroyer.

DE: The Navy designator for a Destroyer Escort.

GSIR: Gyro Setting Indicator-Regulator. This device receives the gyro angle from the TDC and sets it in the torpedoes in each nest. Located between the banks of tubes, it can also be manually operated should the need arise.

JP: A type of passive hydrophone, located on the upper deck and usable only when submerged.

JOOD: Junior Officer of the Deck.

Maru: A Japanese merchant ship. From the suffix *maru* appended to the names of non-military ships in Japanese practice, as in *Hainan Maru*.

May, Andrew Jackson: A Kentucky congressman and chairman of the House Military Affairs Committee, May revealed to the press that the Japanese were setting their depth charges too shallow. This was printed and the Japanese started setting their depth charges deeper. Vice Admiral Charles Lockwood estimated that this indiscretion was probably responsible for the loss of 10 submarines and 800 men.

Negative Tank: An internal variable ballast tank, flooded to create negative buoyancy and speed diving. This tank is blown "to the mark" after the boat is submerged, to achieve neutral buoyancy.

OOD: Officer of the Deck.

Poppet Valve: Part of a torpedo tube, the poppet valve collects as much of the impulse air as possible and vents it into the boat before it can escape from the muzzle of the tube and send a cloud of bubbles to the surface.

QC: The active sonar part of a fleet submarine's listening gear. Also used as a generic term for any active sonar.

Safety Tank: An internal ballast tank with the same water capacity as the conning tower, and normally kept flood while submerged. If the conning tower floods, Safety can be blown to compensate.

S-Boat: American submarines, designed during World War I and mostly completed during the 1920s. These were modern enough to be used on active service in World War II, mostly in quieter areas. The real S-boats were named S-1 through S-51.

SD Radar: A simple, omni directional air search radar, with a range of about six miles. This unit could indicate the presence of aircraft in the area, but could not provide a bearing.

SJ Radar: Surface search radar used on American submarines starting in late 1942. This type later incorporated a Planned Position Indicator

(PPI), which electronically superimposed a local chart over the radar screen for clarity.

TBT: Target Bearing Transmitter. A set of waterproof binoculars mounted on a pelorus (bearing indicator), used for aiming torpedoes while surfaced. The bearing was electrically transmitted to the conning tower when the operator pressed a button on a handgrip.

TDC: Torpedo Data Computer. An electro-mechanical analog computer used to determine torpedo gyro angles before firing. Angles are automatically transmitted to the torpedo rooms.

WCA Stack: The main sonar console, located in the conning tower.

WRT: Water Round Tube tank. An internal tank in each torpedo room normally used for flooding the tubes before firing. If necessary, the tubes can also be flooded from the sea. Flooding from the WRT simplifies trim control.

LaVergne, TN USA
24 November 2010
206213LV00001B/31/A